To Sandy,

for those first, second, and third reads,
you have my gratitude

Summer
by the River

DEBBIE
BURNS

sourcebooks
casablanca

Published by Sourcebooks Casablanca, an imprint of Sourcebooks
P.O. Box 4410, Naperville, Illinois 60567-4410
(630) 961-3900
sourcebooks.com

Printed and bound in the United States of America.
VP 10 9 8 7 6 5 4 3 2 1

"Eventually, all things merge into one, and a river runs through it."

—Norman Maclean

Chapter 1

THE OVEN TIMER WAS buzzing when Josie pushed through the swinging door into the kitchen. It was hard to believe two hours had sped by since she'd placed the six trays of blueberries into the commercial ovens to dry them out. With the tea garden hosting their first wedding, there'd been no doubt it would be a whirlwind of a weekend, but Josie hadn't expected this craziness. She'd been going nonstop since dawn, and her empty stomach was grumbling in protest.

She was loading the last of the trays onto the baker's sheet pan rack when the doorbell rang, its melodic chimes resounding through the old mansion.

Leaving the oven mitt on the kitchen counter, she headed down the hall toward the front. She was almost to the door when the back screen door thwacked open.

"Mooooommm! Mommy?" Zoe called, her tone brimming with the demanding urgency of a six-year-old.

"Up front, babe. Someone's here."

Josie checked out the side window before unlocking the door, proving old habits never die. She ran through a mental list of the expected guests. She'd thought everyone who was coming had arrived. The crowded back terrace certainly made it seem so.

This guest was alone, and just the kind of guy whose presence instinctively stirred up female hormones. He was taller than Josie by half a foot and, judging by the fit of his jeans and black T-shirt, in good shape. He was older, too, but not by much, early- to mid-thirties maybe. His eyes, bright blue-green, warred for attention with a broad smile accented by the short, brown stubble on his cheeks and chin.

Zoe zoomed down the hall and smacked into Josie, plastering her petite body into the back of Josie's leg. Half-hidden, she peered around Josie's hip at the visitor while muttering something about the two boys she'd been building sandcastles with.

"Hang on a second, Zo." Before returning her attention to the man, she ran her hand over Zoe's long chestnut hair, her fingers raising a few of the baby-fine ends by her forehead like little exclamation points. "Hi. You're here for the wedding?"

The stranger's easy smile widened at her question. "Well, that depends. If you're the bride and you're still taking offers, I could be tempted to throw my name into the hat."

Josie worked to keep her jaw from falling open. Did guys really say things like that anymore? She was a bit out of touch—by design—but she was pretty sure they weren't supposed to.

Zoe tapped Josie's arm, demanding her attention. "Did you hear me, Mommy? Those boys aren't sharing."

Josie scooped Zoe up at the same time the man offered his hand.

"My bad, sorry." Clearly, he'd picked up on her lack of enthusiasm for his compliment. "I'm looking for Myra Moore. I believe she's expecting me. I'm a freelance journalist working on an article for the *New York Post.*"

A rush of lightheadedness flooded her. *A journalist?* She attempted to readjust Zoe, who was too big to be held any longer, on her hip. "Why?" she managed to get out, forgetting about his white teeth and blue-green eyes.

"I'm in town researching a missing person and what might be an unresolved murder. I'm hoping she can help me find the answers I'm looking for."

Josie's muscles went rigid. *No, no, no. Not like this. I'm not ready.* Her mouth gaped, but nothing came out, and her vision went from spotty to almost completely gray. Her arm locked around Zoe's slim torso as she struggled to remain standing and alert.

Swaying, swaying. Was it the room swaying or her?

She smelled the stranger closing in around her before her spotty vision could process it. The woody, sweet scent of sandalwood filled her nostrils, the one concrete thing she could process.

She might as well have been a doll in *The Nutcracker*. She could feel Zoe sliding off her body and onto the floor and the man stepping closer, and she could hear their muffled talking but couldn't process the words. She struggled to stay conscious—to tell him to back off—but words wouldn't come. Then she was in his arms and he was carrying her, and her vision was clearing from gray to spotty again.

The next thing she knew, Josie startled to find herself lying on the couch in the front parlor when she hadn't even realized he'd set her down. She startled even more to find the stranger hovering over her, staring. Had she passed out? It hadn't seemed that way, but the last couple seconds—or minutes—were disjointed.

Movement in the entryway caught her attention. Zoe was pulling Myra, the tea garden's eighty-year-old owner, into the parlor and tugging on her skirt. Myra's faithful Corgi-Pomeranian mix, Tidbit, trailed in at her side.

"You won't believe it, Myra!" Zoe chirped. "Mommy's eyes were fluttering like butterflies and I thought we were going to fall and this man catched her and carried her all the way over here."

Caught. The word rose to Josie's lips reflexively, even though she couldn't voice it. The irony didn't escape her that she was worried about Zoe's grammar at a time like this. Somehow, she forced herself to sit up using limbs that reacted like boiled noodles.

The stranger cleared his throat and directed his words to Myra.

"Sorry, ma'am. I let myself in. Your, uh, this woman fainted—sort of."

"Heavens." Myra leaned over and pressed her palm across Josie's forehead. "She's been running herself ragged the last few days. Zoe, be a dear and get your mom a glass of water, will you?"

Zoe gave Josie a questioning glance. "You're all better now, Mom, right?"

"I'm fine, baby." Her words come out squeaky, barely audible.

If Zoe had been distraught to see her collapse like that, she seemed to be processing it fine now. "Make sure nothing happens till I get back." Then she dashed out of the room and down the hall.

"You all right, Miss?" the man asked.

Josie dropped her gaze to the floor and repeated that she was fine.

Standing beside him, Myra offered him her hand. "I'm Myra, and this is my house. Bob phoned just now and said you'd be coming. I'm afraid I've forgotten your name."

"Carter." The man took Myra's arthritic hand with care. "Carter O'Brien."

"It's nice to meet you, Carter. Once I see to Josie, I'm happy to answer your questions." Myra sank onto the sofa next to her. Tidbit scooted back to make a running jump to clear the couch with his short legs, then nestled down between them. "You all right, dear?"

"I'm fine." Josie kept her hands folded across her lap as Tidbit sniffed her arm. *How could Myra know he was coming and not tell me?*

Like a rabbit frozen in the grass, she waited for him to proceed with whatever devilry brought him to her doorstep. She couldn't imagine how he knew. All she could think was it had to have been the shady man in Chicago who'd forged her and Zoe's papers. The process had been complicated, to say the least. But Josie and Zoe Waterhill were legitimate people now. Falsified, maybe, but legitimate. They had social security numbers and birth certificates. Josie hadn't been comfortable using the man's services, but she would never have been able to register Zoe for school otherwise.

But what might it have cost her?

Carter squatted in front of her, balancing on the balls of his feet, resting his forearms against his thighs as he eyed her in concern. "When I was growing up, I had a cousin with low blood sugar. My aunt kept orange juice on hand. It helped when she crashed. If you have any, I'd be happy to get you a glass."

"Do be a dear and try, will you?" Myra answered for her. "If Linda, the kitchen manager, isn't in the kitchen, Zoe will show you where the glasses are kept. It's down the hall and to the right."

He nodded and headed down the hall toward the back of the house. Josie finally noticed the gaping-open front door. His bag—most likely a laptop case—was still abandoned on the stoop. A ridiculous urge flooded her to grab it and run for the river where she could toss it into the gray-black water in hopes it might carry its secrets into the abyss.

But even if her spent legs would obey, there'd be no point. Whatever information he had in there was surely backed up some-where else. No, whatever Armageddon he was bringing was already rushing her way.

Beside her, Myra swept aside a lock of her hair and brushed her thumb over Josie's cheek. "I know what you're thinking, Josie. I was coming inside to tell you about the call and heard him as I walked in. I'm sorry for the scare it has caused you, but you've got it wrong. The wind that blew him here has nothing to do with you."

Josie searched Myra's gentle eyes for the truth since, for the first time in over five years, she found herself doubting her words.

Chapter 2

THE KID WAS CUTE. And precocious. A smile tugged at Carter's lips as she shimmied up the counter and rose onto her knees for a juice glass. She clunked it down and slid off with both feet smacking the hardwood floor at once.

"My mom doesn't like orange juice much," she said, grabbing a gallon jug of it from inside a massive commercial fridge that was impeccably organized. She held it up for him. "I like it lots, but I can't pour it without spilling."

Carter relieved her of the jug, poured it, and returned it to the spot on a wide shelf in front of two more gallons. The librarian had told him this place operated as a tea garden, which explained the baker's rack filled with scones, cakes, and dried berries, the massive fridge, the abundance of juice, and five or six pounds of unsalted organic butter, among other things. "If I were to guess, I'd say you're pretty self-sufficient, huh?"

"Pretty what?"

Has it been that long since you've been around a kid? He wracked his brain for a simpler explanation as he took in the rest of the kitchen. Aside from the telltale high ceilings, transom windows, and thick crown molding, the room, with its oversized stainless-steel appliances and quartz counters, stood apart from the rest of the ancient house. Glancing out the kitchen window, he was surprised to see thirty or so people gathered around metal dining tables with pots of tea, fancy cups on saucers, and tiers in the centers piled with slices of cake and other goodies.

"It means you can do a lot of things for yourself," he answered.

"I start first grade on Monday," she said, grabbing the glass of water she poured before he came in. A little sloshed over the rim and splashed on the counter. "So, I guess so."

That librarian hadn't been kidding about this place being the real thing. Carter wouldn't have been surprised to find the servers dressed in *Downton Abbey* attire instead of khakis and black T-shirts. When he'd carried Zoe's mom, he'd noticed her shirt had a cartoonish outline of a tea bag with the words "Tea Shirt" inscribed inside.

With his next question, he attempted to be quiet enough that his voice didn't travel down the hall. The way the redhead had fainted at his words like that had sparked more than his concern. "So, your mom, has she fainted like this before?" Taking the juice, he followed her out of the kitchen.

"Nuh-uh. Never."

Carter replayed the last few seconds before she fainted. He couldn't help but feel he'd missed something. That some unusual truth was glaring him head-on and all he needed was a few more minutes to rehash it.

But the sight of her as they reentered the parlor was enough to derail his concentration. She met his gaze from her spot on the couch, and her eyelids narrowed the same way pupils did when a light flicked on.

Guarded or not, she was damn good-looking. There was something about her, an ageless elegance, that might be traced to generations of good breeding or simply luck of the draw. In addition to that red-gold hair, she had eyes as blue as the summer sky, and his nose still tingled with the scent of something lemony like dish soap coupled with the soft trace of perfume.

But she wasn't why he'd come here. He cleared his throat in hopes of clearing his thoughts.

He offered her the juice, but when she uncrossed her arms to reach for it, it was obvious she was too shaky to hold it. Myra, who reminded him of an aged willow tree—tall but bent and weathered with the grace of a life well lived—took it instead. Her dog raised up on both legs to give it a sniff, then lost interest quickly.

Myra suggested the kid head back outside to play. Her voice was kind but commanding enough that the girl took note and, after giving them a long look, reluctantly shuffled down the hall. Soon after, the back door banged shut.

"Ms. Moore," he began when both women directed their attention his way, "my timing may not be great, but I believe Bob told you I'm in town researching a story. I make a living as a freelance writer, but the story that brought me to Galena is a personal one."

"Is it? Well, I'm pleased to make your acquaintance. Mr. O'Brien, was it?" Myra didn't wait for his confirmation. "Writers amaze me. I love to read, and I appreciate the gift of eloquence when I come across it."

"Thank you, ma'am, but that isn't a gift I claim." He hooked his thumbs into the pockets of his jeans. "I'm a journalist by trade. The truth tends to be easily written and typically without great expression."

"If you mean that, then I daresay you've not come across any great truths, have you?"

A laugh bubbled up his throat. "No, no great truths."

"Well, when you do, I suspect the gift of eloquence will find you."

"One can hope, Ms. Moore."

The redhead, seated beside Myra, had been listening quietly. She shot an exasperated look at the woman as if she wasn't sold on the small talk. Myra offered a gentle shrug in reply and handed her the glass of juice. Seeming steadier, she took it and sipped tentatively.

Myra pointed a bent finger his way. "Moore was my maiden name, though there are people in town, Bob included, who've never stopped calling me that." She sat up straighter and slid her hands over her knees. "Why don't you pull up a chair and tell me this story that brought you here in search of your great truth?"

Carter followed her gaze to a desk and headed over for a wooden chair with a narrow seat that he suspected was as old as the mansion.

He set it down a few feet in front of the couch and took a seat, feeling a bit like he was auditioning for a part. And, as if asserting he had a role in the decision-making, Myra's dog, who was eyeing him curiously, let out a determined bark.

"Ah, well, for starters, I'm here on a bit of a whim, researching family history. Back in the early 1900s, my family owned one of the country's biggest tool manufacturers in the Northeast. My grandfather took over its operations after his father's death in the late twenties. By the mid- to late thirties, the company was bankrupt, and my family's fortune was nonexistent."

A wave of apprehension washed over Carter regarding what he was about to tell Myra. "My grandfather stuck around long enough to witness the birth of my father. Then he took off and was never heard from again, leaving a destitute wife to fend for herself and her son at a time when people needed all the help they could get. No one knows what became of him.

"My father had me later in life, and he's getting up there in age," he continued. "This last year or so, he's become set on learning the truth behind his father's disappearance. Recently, he uprooted a lead pointing to Galena. I've no idea what I can uncover for him after all this time, but I owe it to him to find out what I can."

"That's *it*?" the redhead interrupted, her voice little more than a whisper.

Carter eyed her in surprise. "Sorry to disappoint. That's about as dramatic as I get."

Myra pursed her thin lips. "Tell me your grandfather's name, son."

"Myron. Myron O'Brien."

Myra pulled in a slow breath and closed her eyes, reminding him again of a willow tree just before a late fall storm. "And fate has sent you my way after all these years."

Carter shifted uncomfortably in the straight-backed chair. Knowing there was a possibility his words could cause this gentle woman pain, he chose them as cautiously as he could. "After what I showed him, your librarian believes there's reason to think it might be my grandfather's body that was dumped in the Galena River in 1940. The body was recovered fifty or so miles downriver from here but was in bad enough shape it was never identified. Their descriptions are a match. The man had been shot twice in the chest."

"That murder was the talk of the town for years; at least that's how I remember it from my childhood. I was an infant at the time of the shooting, born that very year," Myra said. "And why is Bob directing you to my doorstep?"

"The, uh, victim was linked to your family—to this house. It was believed he'd been contracted to do some work here. I was hoping you may have some information about him."

"On a carpenter who worked here eighty years ago?"

Carter swallowed. He'd come all this way but was close to abandoning further inquiry. Then he caught something in the old woman's gaze, a strength—more than a strength, a challenge—and pressed forward. "I found a series of editorials published around then too. Some of them were filled with gossip about a controversial friendship between a married woman and an out-of-towner. Not just an out-of-towner. Her carpenter. The same person one of the later editorials alluded to having found his way to a watery grave. When you connect the dots, it seems as if a few people in town suspected that the woman might have been a Moore. Your mother, Bob was guessing."

"Oh, that's enough!" the redhead blurted out, setting her juice noisily on the side table. Grabbing the arm of the couch, she pushed to her feet and steadied herself. "Myra doesn't need this. *Especially not today*. Her friends are getting married here tomorrow, and she's under enough stress as it is."

"Josie," Myra said before he could reply. "Sit, dear. If this young man wants to ask questions and make inferences about my mother, it doesn't hurt me."

When she kept standing and set balled-up fists against her hips, Myra pushed up from the couch with similar effort, only her struggle wasn't temporary. The dog stood up on his short legs but didn't jump down. "Sit down before you fall again, Josie. You're shaky still. I can see it. And you," she said, turning to him with a bright intensity in her eyes. "I'd like to see your face better, young man. Come over to the light by the window. The more I look at you, you seem familiar to me. Hauntingly so."

Surprised but agreeable, Carter allowed Myra to lead him toward the side window of the parlor, guiding him to step into the light pouring inside.

She regarded him in silence for what felt like an eternity. Her eyes were a light, faded blue, and he wasn't entirely sure if they were watery from age or if there were a few tears brewing on her lids.

Finally, she gave a slight nod and patted his cheek. "Those eyes of yours are remarkable. Startling even. I've never seen them in color before."

Before? "I'm afraid I don't understand."

"I knew they were light. In my youth I spent many hours wondering about their color—blue or green—but I never would have guessed such a perfect mixture of both." She slid her hand down his arm, closing her soft, bony fingers over his wrist. "How silly any of us is to think the past is swept away. It surrounds us, just waiting for the opportunity to be let in."

"Are you saying you think his accusations are true?" the redhead—Josie—said, joining them by the side window.

"Forgive me for being cryptic, Josie, but I spent many hours of my youth looking at this man's picture—or an uncanny likeness of him anyway. I used to dream I'd marry someone so handsome."

Using Josie as a brace, Myra returned to the couch and smoothed her hand over her dog's back. "When the time came, I married for sense, as was my duty. I had all but forgotten that face by then. And now that you've come knocking on our door, it's as clear as if I looked at it yesterday."

"Ms. Moore, do you mind explaining?"

"You have your grandfather's eyes, of that I'm certain. For so long, I hoped to learn that man's identity. Over the years, it became no more than a shadow of a hope. But now that shadow has come knocking. Life is funny that way, isn't it?" She smiled. "Please, have a seat again, Mr. O'Brien."

Josie settled back on the couch, looking as pleased by the turn of events as she might over the arrival of a swarm of termites.

Silence fell over the room a second time, and Carter noticed that the front door was still wide open, and his laptop case was abandoned on the stoop. He headed over and grabbed it, then shut the door.

From the way Myra was running her fingers over the stitching on her skirt, he sensed she needed a moment to collect herself.

"This house is remarkable." He glanced up toward the high, molded ceilings as he sat down. "I took a couple architecture classes. I'm a fan of old Victorian mansions like this one. I'm guessing it's mid-nineteenth century, correct?"

Myra's face lightened at his words. "You're right on the mark. It was finished just after the Civil War. Ulysses Grant is rumored to have dined here on occasion. It's been in my family for three genera-tions. My husband and I ran it as a B and B for over thirty years. I shut it down after he died." Myra paused and pursed her lips. "The gardens are still as spectacular as ever, though most of the thanks for that goes to our neighbor. He's a retired horticulturist who doesn't seem to know where his yard ends and ours begins, though I've had no mind to complain. He's unofficially taken on the role of master gardener. When Josie has her legs under her, she can give you a tour."

"I'd like that."

Even though Josie had pulled a pillow onto her lap and was fidgeting with the silky frays along the side, she seemed to freeze under his direct gaze, reigniting his curiosity.

"Do you like weddings, Mr. O'Brien?" Myra asked.

"Ah, not particularly. Though I've no objection to them so long as they aren't mine."

"How about tea, then?"

"Tea? It's tolerable when the coffee's gone."

A short-lived smile lit Myra's face. "Will you be in town tomorrow?"

"Ah, yeah. I planned a day or two break here. I'm driving across the country."

"Wonderful. As Josie mentioned, two of my dearest friends are getting married here tomorrow. It's all but consumed us these last few weeks. When it's over, I'm certain I'll have more to share with you than I do today. Everything's a jumble now."

Carter tried not to show his disappointment as impatience bristled under the surface of his skin. His dad's quest had rubbed off on him. Especially now that he was so close to an answer. "I'd be happy to come back once it's over and you've had time for this to settle in."

"Wonderful. And where is it you're staying?"

"A hotel outside of town."

"Not a chain? With you being a fan of architecture?"

"Actually, it is. I'm not big on B and Bs, with the exception of the architecture. That was all I could find in town."

"You'll find Galena's strongest boast is its history. Most of our original homes and buildings are still intact. And your stay won't be the same if you aren't in town. I suspect, if you want to understand your grandfather best, you'll need to embrace this world, not simply pass through it."

Josie stopped pulling at the frayed pillow and looked at Myra abruptly.

Carter held up his hands, a polite smile returning to his face. "As I said, this is a favor for my father. I'll settle with simple facts this trip."

In reply, Myra pressed her eyes shut and kept them closed as she spoke again. "I suspect he was very much like you. Defiant, boyishly charming, and quite the chip on his shoulder. Except he carried a weight you know nothing about. And I daresay, maybe never will."

Carter kept quiet, hoping she'd offer more. To his disappointment, she didn't. Instead, she exhaled and reached for Josie's hand.

Josie didn't bother hiding her dislike of Myra's idea. She shook her head abruptly. "No, Myra." It came out as a whisper, drawing his attention even more.

"It turns out we've readied a bedroom just for you, Mr. O'Brien. Nolan's son cancelled yesterday. Josie, you'll show him to it, won't you, if you've gotten your legs back? I'd like to sit here and collect my thoughts. So much is coming back in a rush. I wasn't quite prepared for it."

Josie's cheeks flamed bright red. "Myra, we don't even *know* him."

"And now we have an opportunity to do so. Carter O'Brien is welcome to stay as my particular guest. Something tells me you could use the reprieve, couldn't you, young man?" She directed her last words his way. "I can promise you the best quiche and scones in a hundred miles, by far. And we have tea blends strong enough to suit even the most steadfast of coffee drinkers."

Beside her, Josie drummed one bare heel in rapid succession on the hardwood floor. Carter met her gaze with one that he suspected revealed a hint of his amusement over her discomfort. He had no idea what her story was, but he certainly wasn't opposed to finding out while he was here.

"I'll gladly stay with your permission, ma'am. I know an opportunity when I come across it."

Chapter 3

MOST DAYS, MYRA COULDN'T remember what she'd had for dinner the night before. Thanks to Carter O'Brien, memories that had been undisturbed for decades were sweeping in with a startling clarity. Myra could practically feel the floor digging into her sitz bones as she hid in her mother's closet at age eight, a photograph clutched in her hands that wasn't meant for her.

Pressing in on the edges of this memory were others: of a father and mother who were decades apart in age but seemingly amicable toward one another; of whispers alluded to in town by the older generations but never directly addressed.

Alone in the parlor with her dog curled into a ball and snoring softly beside her, Myra closed her hands over the top of her head. It wasn't that she wanted to stop the memories from coming. They were like a tangled mess of rope. She wanted to separate them out, take her time examining them.

She overheard Josie stepping out of the kitchen as Carter hauled his luggage inside and down the hall. The dear girl asked for his driver's license the same as she would if he were checking into an operating B and B, and Carter didn't object.

Myra didn't blame Josie for being cautious. With a past like hers, having faith in strangers would most likely remain her biggest challenge. Myra wanted to tell her not to worry, at least not to worry about the things she was worrying about this afternoon.

Carter O'Brien meant no harm. Myra was certain of that much.

But she was transfixed with the memories sweeping over her just the same as if she were riding a magic carpet and peering down at a panorama of the past. All she could do was sit still and let herself be taken away.

Her eight-year-old self had found a photograph tucked inside the back seam of her mother's prayer book, and she'd wanted a private place to examine it. It was a black and white image of a grown man, and a distinctively handsome one at that. Even as a child she'd known it. Her pulse had raced wildly as she imagined her mother, whose beauty had been the talk of the town before she'd married, with this man instead of her father. Her father's hair had grayed at the temples, his shoulders were narrow and, in his older years, his mouth had turned down in a frown, even when he was pleased.

How guilty she'd felt by the traitorous thought. She'd loved her father wildly. Born of a family from Sussex, he'd given her a lifelong appreciation for a good cup of tea just as he had a love of books. He'd not wanted anything more than living out his life quietly in this house, and he had.

What secrets had been in her mother's heart? Now, at the eve of Myra's life, a stranger had come knocking, and the truth, if she wanted it, was most certainly hers to know.

Chapter 4

A SUAVE AND POLISHED journalist showing up unannounced to dig up long-buried secrets wasn't a good thing. Josie was certain of that.

By the time she got the temperamental printer working and copied Carter's driver's license, Zoe had abandoned the sandbox and had tugged Carter outside for a tour of the two-acre grounds. As she stepped out to join them, Josie noticed most of the weekend's guests had finished their tea, cake, and scones and were dispersing.

Zoe and Carter were halfway down the hillside, and the hair on the back of Josie's neck prickled at the sight of Zoe being so carefree with a stranger. Her feet itched to join them, but she checked herself. Certainly, there was no better place than here to give Zoe a bit of trust and see what she did with it.

Josie busied herself with cleaning off the empty tables on the expansive brick patio. She smiled as she overheard Zoe. The toad abodes, butterfly boxes, and bird feeders were among Zoe's most animated stops along the flower beds as they wound their way back up the gently sloping hillside.

Out of the corner of her eye, Josie caught Zoe wrapping a small hand around Carter's as she pointed out the spot where she was certain she caught a glimpse of a garden fairy this spring. Perhaps sensing the impropriety in the touch, Carter dropped her hand to ruffle her hair. Unabashed, Zoe found it again as soon as he was finished.

Breath catching in her throat, Josie let one of the delicate cups clank against the spout of a kettle nearly hard enough to break it. Zoe had the most trusting nature of anyone she knew. *She's just like Sam.*

As they rounded the top of the yard, Carter nodded toward Josie. "Myra's right. These gardens are spectacular."

"Thanks." She set the packed-full busser tub on the closest table and headed over. She slipped his license out of her back pocket and offered it his way.

"Would you like my card?" he asked as he tucked his license back into his wallet. "As I mentioned, I'm freelance, but you can Google me. Plenty of my work is online."

"Thanks."

It was a simple, gray-scale business card with his contact information and an image of an old-fashioned typewriter. She'd never known anyone who made their way on this earth exclusively by stringing words together, and was impressed. She was a numbers person. With numbers, she could always find her way. Words were different, complicated. Sometimes they told the truth; other times they were wickedly deceitful.

"So, tell me," he said with a lopsided grin, "was your asking for my license a formality in case I steal a few towels while I'm here, or in case I follow in my grandfather's footsteps?"

Josie fought back a laugh as his words sank in. "Around here, you never know."

Carter was boyishly charming—she'd grant him that. She bet that smile could grab attention a hundred feet away. And then there was that dimple on his right cheek. But the stubble on his face and the visible strength in his shoulders and arms belied those boyish parts, leaving her in no doubt he was a man in his prime.

"Do you, uh, want to see your room?"

"Sure, that would be great."

"Wait, Mom! I want to show him my castle first." Zoe dragged him toward the back of the yard. Josie trailed after them, making mental notes of all the things she needed Zoe to understand before the start of school on Monday.

"Which one is yours?" Carter asked.

Still barefoot, Zoe hopped inside, sinking to her knees in front of the three separate mounds of sand. "Mine is the best one." Zoe's challenge was evident in her tone. "I'm really good at making sand-castles. I do it all the time. And those boys are new."

"Zoe," Josie corrected her, "honestly."

Carter seemed unfazed. He knelt, sinking onto the backs of his heels. He clicked his tongue as he inspected the three distinct mounds with the rapt attention of a county fair judge. One was clearly out of the running, hardly any better than a misshapen hill. The other two were close in detail and scope. She knew Zoe's right off by the trademark curve of the bridge and the tiny sticks she placed atop the spires.

After seeming to notice the direction of Zoe's hopeful gaze, Carter pointed to it. "This one, right?"

Zoe beamed. "See, Mom? Mine is better. Those mean boys don't know anything."

"They aren't mean, Zoe. They're just young, like you."

Zoe rolled her bright hazel eyes and offered a small huff. "They are *too* mean. You just weren't there to see it."

Carter stood up and cleared his throat, probably a bit more amused than he wanted to show.

They headed inside, with Zoe pausing to point out all her favorite places on the lower floor, such as the window seat in the breakfast room at the side of the kitchen that had a clear view of a robin's nest.

"This house is truly phenomenal," Carter said as they ascended the massive staircase to the second floor. The stairs were wide enough for Zoe to easily walk along next to him. Josie could have, too, but she chose to take up the rear. She forced her gaze away from his fingers as they brushed the top of the mahogany banister.

"How many rooms does the place have?" Carter tapped the rounded newel as he took in the second-floor split hallway.

"Six with private bathrooms," she answered, "plus two on the third floor that share a bathroom. There's a family from Ohio up there this weekend, but we usually stick to the second-floor rooms. It's too expensive to heat and cool the third floor. Your room's down the hall. It's a great room—a lot of space and one of the best bathrooms in the house. And a wonderful view of the gardens out back."

"Spoken like someone who knows it well."

"You could say that." Josie opted not to add that, when it was just her, Myra, and Zoe here, she often went into that room for a soak in the oversized bathtub after Zoe was out for the night.

"Nice," he said as she swung open the door. He paused to take it in and nodded appreciatively. "They don't make houses like this anymore, do they? Great bone structure."

"If it wasn't for the Victorian wallpaper covering it all up, you mean?"

He grinned, his teeth gleaming. "Looks like I'm in a lady's retreat after all. Is that what happened to the guy who pulled out? He didn't have a tolerance for lace and doilies?"

"He's mad at his father for getting married again," Zoe piped up.

"Zoe, honestly. Sometimes I think you hear through walls." Josie shrugged. "It's one of those weddings that's not without a bit of controversy. They were childhood sweethearts who ended up marrying other people. Their spouses have passed away, and now they've found one another again."

"But Linda says they're hurting everybody's feelings," Zoe added. "Acting so in *looove*." She drew out the word like it was replete with cooties.

Carter laughed. "Kid, you're wise beyond your years."

Josie ran her fingers down Zoe's hair. "So… Make yourself at home. You're Myra's guest. The key is on the dresser. It's bulky to carry around. If you don't want to take it with you into town, you can drop it with Myra."

He strolled over to the dresser and inspected the brass skeleton key. "No plastic cards here, huh?"

"We're all about authenticity. Oh, I almost forgot. The room was already set up before the guy and his wife canceled. In honor of the wedding, everyone's being treated with the getaway package from back when this place ran as a B and B. That means you get home-made cookies and wine delivered each night around nine. There's a menu on your bed for tomorrow's breakfast. And there's champagne in the mini fridge and some extras on the tub as well." Her cheeks warmed involuntarily at the last bit.

He cocked an eyebrow. "Is that so? Too bad I'm traveling alone. So, you asked for a license but not a credit card. What are you charging for this? Something tells me it isn't enough."

"You can take that up with Myra. You're her *particular* guest, after all." She took Zoe by the hand to leave.

"And you'll just be down the hall if I have any questions about how to work the tub or anything, right?" Carter asked, the playful grin returning to his face.

After that introduction of his, it didn't surprise her that he was a flirt. "You strike me as being technologically advanced. But if you have trouble, ask your questions early. I'm off duty tonight after I deliver cookies."

He tsked. "What a shame."

Josie pulled Zoe out of the room and closed the door before the smile that was tugging at her lips broke through to the surface.

Chapter 5

MYRA WOKE THE NEXT morning with a lightness in her stride she'd not felt in years. She didn't mind that she was a dinosaur who'd lived her life in a relic. People hardly ever lived out their lives under one roof these days. Gone, too, in all but a fraction of society, were servants at the ready and houses designed with rooms for a specific activity. The old place had a morning room, a sitting room, a parlor and a library, a dining room, a drawing room, a nursery, a butler's pantry, a kitchen and, of course, enough bedrooms to house a large family and host a constant flow of guests.

Her great-grandfather had made a fortune in mining galena out of the river after emigrating from Sussex, but like Carter's grandfather's company, the company went bankrupt during the Depression. By the time it had come for her to marry, even scrupulous as her parents had been, there'd been little chance of their being able to afford the taxes, maintenance, and repair that came hand in hand with ownership of this home. Had it not been for her own fierce determination, the house would've passed into another family's care back then.

When she was in her late twenties, she accepted marriage to a man with both kindness in his soul and a respectable depth to his pockets. They'd put their heads together and come up with the idea for turning it into a B and B. The house had thrived while all that bustle had filled its walls every Wednesday through Sunday.

Now, nearly a lifetime later, a comparable dilemma was weighing her down, and she'd been craving someone to put her head together with the way she'd done with her husband. She needed someone other than Josie, who was too close to see the path forward objectively, to help her figure out the next best step. Only, at Myra's age—and with her diagnosis—her options had seemed considerably more limited. At least until Carter O'Brien found his way to her.

Myra had been so startled yesterday at the news Carter brought that it had taken her awhile to realize he was exactly the one to help her. A few sleepless hours in the middle of the night had gotten her thinking of new possibilities, and thanks to a long round of prayers, she'd woken up with a certainty she'd not experienced in years.

Life had taught her that, whenever she stepped out from all the things that weighed her down and *really* prayed, her prayers had always been answered. And this time, the answer was Carter O'Brien.

Now, all she needed was for him to see this.

By the time Myra made it downstairs, most of her guests were eating breakfast. She was eager to talk to Carter, but she first made the rounds with her friends and their families as they savored the breakfast of quiche, roasted sweet potatoes, and fruit salad. Tidbit trailed along with her, lingering at the tables when he thought a handout might be coming.

Myra checked in briefly with Josie, who'd gathered an armful of loose gladioli and was tying them on the trellis. "It's a remarkable day for a wedding."

"It is. You holding up okay?" Josie asked. "I thought you might have a hard time sleeping considering all this commotion." Her gaze shot over to Carter, who was eating alone and working on a laptop.

"And I thought your tension had to do with all the work I've left you for this wedding."

Josie paused mid-tie on one of the gladiolas. "These are your best friends; I'm happy to do it. Happy enough," she added with a half smile after catching Myra's pointed look. "I just don't like the pressure Carter's creating for you."

"There are many ships in the ocean, dear. You needn't be angry because his path has carried him alongside ours a short time."

"As long as it's what you want."

"It is what I want. Now, so long as you're fine, Linda's managing in the kitchen, and my friends are enjoying breakfast, I'll sit with him awhile. Call if you need me."

"Yeah. Sure." Josie turned back to her flowers as Myra headed off.

Carter's back was to her, and he didn't notice Myra's approach until she was nearly upon him. "Would you mind some company, young man?"

"I'd love it." Moving his laptop aside, he rose to pull out the chair next to him at the wrought-iron table. "But don't feel you have to. I'm sure you're busy."

"My house is a bustle of activity, but I've surrounded myself with a few of the finest and hardest-working individuals you'll ever meet. Which is a good thing, because these old bones can't take much exertion." Myra raised hands that were a touch misshapen from age and arthritis. "Though I did my fair share for many years."

Carter glanced over toward Josie. "I offered to help but was refused."

"And refuse you she will." Myra chuckled. "I'd advise you to leave Josie alone to be Josie. Today, anyway. Tomorrow, when everyone leaves, she'll be more relaxed." Having determined she was staying put for a while, Tidbit took off on a stray cat hunt in the gardens.

"What's her story, anyway?"

Myra shook a finger at him. "As a writer, you of all people should know that every character's story is entirely dependent upon the narrator."

"Myra, you're a trip."

"However, even though Josie's story isn't mine to tell, I'm quite tempted to share it with you. Some of it. As long as you keep in mind the limitations of the narrator."

Carter nodded for her to continue. "I'm all ears."

Myra faltered a second or two. "I should tell you I hold that young woman dearest to my heart of all my acquaintances, blood and water combined."

A bit of the levity left Carter's expression at her words. "Okay."

"And," Myra continued, "while she'd be quite furious with me for speaking even a whisper of this to you, I can't help but feel with zero doubt you are *supposed* to learn it."

"I, uh… Are the two of you related? Do you think she's any relation to my grandfather?" Carter sat forward in his chair, watching her expression.

Myra's hand came to rest on Carter's arm. "That's putting the cart before the horse, I'd say."

"It just seems to make sense." He leaned back in his chair and shrugged.

"Before your hopes rise any further, there's a great improbability of her being your long-lost cousin. But in the same breath, I'll agree you have reason to hope for a relative in Galena. Though, as I said, I can't summon the energy to share that story with you until this wedding is well and done. Your grandfather's fate is far too personal to me. With your blessing, we'll save what I know of his story for later."

Carter made a clear attempt to swallow his disappointment. "Sure. Take whatever time you need, Myra."

"Thank you. Then, this morning we'll talk of Josie, who most likely has no connection to you aside from the fact that we're all born of the same cosmic dust. You may want to know why I'm willing to break her confidence to tell you her story, but that, too, I hope to make clear."

Carter twisted to face her. "I'm all ears."

"Where to begin? Isn't that always a challenge?" She brushed the tip of one finger over a crust of pollen, grinding it into the wrought iron. "When I first laid eyes on her, I suppose. That was five years ago in May. Most of the time it feels like it's been just a fraction of that." A shadow slipped over her heart the same as if clouds had covered the sun.

"It was a dark few years for me. My husband had been gone nearly a decade, and my kids were grown and far away. One of them chased a love across the country, the other two, careers. My debts were mounting, and I was feeling tremendous pressure from both my accountant and my oldest son to sell this place. I was foolish to close the B and B down when I did. I thought the money my husband left would last forever. But there were taxes, and I shared what was left with my children, and before I knew it, I was in a pinch."

Carter glanced behind them at the massive house. "I can only imagine the cost of keeping this place up."

"It's a pretty penny, for certain. That day Josie and I met, I remember it well. It was cold, and the wind was whipping. I felt a chill in my bones, telling me I was too old to think of opening this place up again. My car wouldn't start that morning. So, naively, I walked down the famous steps that span the bluffs of the river into town. You walked them last night, didn't you?"

"Yeah, it was quite the haul back up." Carter chuckled.

"It is. There are upward of two hundred if you take them all the way from the bottom. In my youth, I walked them every day just for the challenge of it. But I'd forgotten how old I was and how heavy a mere half-gallon of milk, a loaf of bread, a few apples, and some cheese could be on the ascent."

Carter glanced toward the swollen ankles beneath her skirt but did nothing more than nod.

"When I first laid eyes on Josie, she was sitting on a bench on Main

Street out of the wind. She was feeding Zoe pieces of a banana. I smiled at her as I passed, but I'd be a liar not to admit it was a bit of a reproachful smile. She looked too young to have a baby." Myra clasped a hand over her chest, trying to soften the rush of guilt sweeping through her for sharing this with a stranger. *He's not just any stranger*, she reminded herself. "My first thoughts toward that young lady weren't kind, I'm afraid; they were judgmental and self-serving. What is it in us that feels satisfied to know other people's mistakes aren't ours to claim?"

Carter's gaze traveled to the sand pit where Zoe was embarking upon another castle-making contest with the two young boys.

"I walked on from her and started home, where a hot cup of tea would lessen my worries. I wouldn't have given her any more thought, but my wrists started hurting less than two flights up. I set the bags down, frustrated and alone and feeling quite sorry for myself." She paused and held up a finger. "Let me backtrack a minute. You see, I'd spent the morning praying harder than I had in years. Certainly since my husband was on his deathbed. I make no excuses for being the selfish Christian that I am. My prayers are always more fervent when I'm passionate about the subject."

"You aren't alone there, Myra."

"So, there I was with a weighty decision on my shoulders and a prayer once again on my lips. And what do you know, that girl—Josie—had come up behind me, baby in tow. She told me she'd carry my bags, and she did. All the way to the top. I was too winded to speak, and she was too burdened with a whimpering baby and my bags. I took notice of her though. She was underdressed for the weather. And the baby wasn't any better, I'm afraid to say. When we finally reached the top, I noticed that all she carried for herself was a single plastic bag. What mother walks around without a diaper bag? So, I judged her again and waited for her to ask me for money. I decided I'd give her a few bills and hand out a bit of judgment along with it. But do you want to know what, young man?"

"What?" Carter asked, clearing his throat.

"She didn't ask. She put her hand on my shoulder and asked if I could make it home from there. I told her I could and watched her look around at the view. It was clear she'd never seen the view from the top of the steps before. She looked down on my town below and told me she'd never seen anything more beautiful. Then she started back down without giving me or my money a second thought."

"Then how'd you hook up again?"

"I didn't let her leave. I called down to ask where she was headed, and she yelled up that she didn't know. So, I waved her up and told her I'd make her a cup of tea. And, as I'm sure you've guessed, she's never left. Even then I was no stranger to the fact that God works in mysterious ways, but I still had no idea that girl and her baby were the answer to my prayers. Dear God, were they ever!"

Myra wrapped her hand around Carter's forearm again and gave it a gentle squeeze. "My children, as you might imagine, weren't pleased. But they'd gone away. Josie and Zoe were my decision, and the best one I've ever made. Josie's saved my life a dozen times in a dozen different ways. Now, it's my time to do what I can for her. And that, young man, is where you come in."

Carter's brows furrowed as if she'd just spoken French. "I don't understand. What is it you think I can do?"

"That's the easy part. Whether it's age or circumstance, I can better see when my prayers are answered nowadays. And just yesterday I spent the better part of the morning praying. And you—a man with the gift of eloquence—and with your connection to me! God's been good to me."

Carter shook his head. "I'm sorry; I don't understand."

"This confidence I'm about to offer isn't yours to share with anyone in my acquaintance." Myra's pale eyes grew bright with intensity. "Most especially Josie."

He took a few seconds to answer. "All right."

She swallowed back the fear of speaking her next words aloud. She glanced at the sandbox and Zoe and found strength. "A few weeks ago, I discovered a tender lump in my abdomen. I've not yet told Josie. I didn't want to worry her until I knew it was nothing. Turns out it wasn't nothing."

Carter swallowed and shook his head.

"And I have some weighty decisions to make. To prolong my life, I've the option of a cumbersome and risky surgery. With it, I'll likely have five more years of sunsets and summer nights. First winter snows. School plays. All those small little miracles I can never seem to get enough of." Knowing she needed to, she added, "Without it, I'll hardly last one."

Seeing the look on his face, she paused to lift a finger in protest. "You can stop there, young man. I won't accept sympathy from a practical stranger. Besides, I've a great need of you."

Carter dragged the palm of his hand over his chin. Myra could see the blood draining from his face. Of course, he'd not been prepared for this. He came here wanting to unearth some family history, and here she was entrenching him in the present. "Sure. Anything, Myra."

"I suggest you be careful with your promises, young man. What if I'm a kook and ask you to marry that girl and give Zoe the father she's been longing for?"

Carter's eyes widened in alarm until Myra chuckled.

"I said *what if…*"

He huffed at her humor. "Anything within reason, then."

"Would it be within reason if I told you I intend to leave everything I have to those two girls of mine? My own children have already been given their share of their father's money. And while I love them dearly, I gave them life, and now they're living it. They don't love this house any longer. Not the way Josie does. I want this house to be hers when I pass from this earth."

Carter shook his head. "Myra, I'm no lawyer. Whatever it is you're thinking, I probably can't be any real help to you."

"I have a lawyer. What I need is a writer. I have things left to say. Only, when I think of saying them, the words get lost. I want my children to know I love them. I don't want them to begrudge Josie and Zoe. I want them to bring my grandchildren to Galena to vacation in summer, and I want it to be under this roof. And I want them never to question Josie's authority to run the tea garden or to own this place." Myra stopped short, finding herself impossibly close to tears.

"You want me to write for you? Your stories?"

"Yes. I want you to write what's in my heart, even when it won't rise to my lips."

"I'm a journalist, Myra. I know a few people back home who'd be better suited for that. You could offer them the room you've given me, and I bet they'd be happy to spend a week or two here."

Averting his gaze, Myra smoothed out the front of her blouse. "Young man, you have no idea how perfectly suited you are."

Chapter 6

THE CLOCK ON THE windowsill ticked persistently in the darkness. Josie swayed her head to the rhythm, struggling to stay awake. She scooted closer to her brother and counted out the seconds, losing track as they ticked into minutes. From outside their locked door, the muffled ranting of her mother reached her ears.

After a countless string of minutes, the ranting ceased, and silence filled their small apartment. Feeling a swell of bravery, ten-year-old Josie shook her brother awake.

"Sam, wake up. I think she's asleep."

Their shared bed was nothing more than a mattress on the floor. Josie's year-younger brother moaned in protest and curled deeper into the blanket. A mass of wavy brown hair was the only thing that stuck out.

"We can't stay here tonight. Wake up. We need to leave."

When their mother got like this, there was no telling how bad things would get. Josie brushed the tips of her fingers over her brother's cheek. It was still warm where her mom had slapped him, and her long nails had gouged two short scratches in his flesh.

Just yesterday Josie and Sam and their mom had spent the whole afternoon in the living room, turning it into a castle of blankets and sheets held up by chairs and locked into place by windows and tied onto doorknobs. They'd eaten leftover Taco Bell and taken turns creating stories and making wishes. It had been the best day in forever.

And today, this.

Even though her mom had promised it would never happen again, Josie had known it would. Whatever drug it was that Skye Pictures craved had a stronger hold than any promise she'd ever made. And Sam—he didn't know how to pull back when the fights started. He didn't know when enough was enough.

But this time, Josie had a plan. She and Sam had somewhere to go. In the six weeks since they moved here—to the public housing complex in East LA that was supposed to help their mom get back on her feet again—they'd only met one person Josie could trust, a foreign-speaking older woman she and Sam met the day the elevator was broken.

What if she doesn't answer the door?

The only other person in the apartment complex Josie knew was a man with big muscles and colorful tattoos up and down his arms. Her mother had been to see him so many times Josie had lost count. But he had calloused hands and even harder eyes. The thought of running there for help made her lungs clamp tight.

Josie tried hard to remember the apartment number of the woman. She'd given them a plate full of something sweet and puffy, like a crispy long john doughnut, after she and Sam helped her carry a bunch of stuff up two flights of stairs. She didn't know the woman's name, but she had kind brown eyes and gentle hands.

Sam finally stirred after she shook him a third time. "Can't we stay?" His voice was thick and groggy. "The door's locked."

"If she gets in and something else happens, they'll take us away again. Only this time for longer, I bet. We weren't together last time. What makes you think we'll get luckier next time?"

Her words must have sunken in. Sam sat up and threw off his covers. "I *hate* her."

"Just follow me and don't make a sound."

She unlocked their door and peered into the hall. The TV was on but muted, radiating soft light across the floor. Their mother was in the kitchen huddled in the corner, her legs pulled in against her chest.

Josie paused in the shadows, a wave of longing washing over her before her gaze strayed to her brother's cheek. *No.* They were doing the right thing.

She waved Sam toward the door and was unbolting it when their mom spotted them. Her incoherent ranting resumed, full volume. A glass smashed against the wall between the window and the door, shattering. Shards sprayed against Josie's arm as the deadbolt gave, and she jerked open the door.

The older woman lived one floor above and down a long corridor. Josie recognized the apartment by a dark wooden cross visible behind a gap in the curtain.

Making a wish that snaked all the way down to her toes, she raised her hand and knocked, softly at first, then louder. After what seemed like an eternity, a teenage girl answered. She had long, dark hair with purple and pink tips and brown eyes. She was dressed in a spaghetti-strap tee and bikini underwear. She placed her hands on her hips and frowned down at them. "It's too late to be knocking on somebody's door."

"Is your mom home?" Josie and Sam asked in unison.

The teenager spat out something angry and unintelligible, then called over her shoulder. To them, she added, "She's my grandmother, not my mom. If you don't even know that, you shouldn't be here."

After an agonizing wait, the woman appeared behind her, tying a robe closed. The two of them exchanged rapid-fire words in a language Josie didn't understand.

She held her breath, crossing her fingers behind her back. She could pick up on the tension in the air like it was another person in the room.

Finally, the woman waved the teenager out of the way, eyeing

Josie and Sam like she'd found something unexpected in her soup. "What are you doing outdoors in the middle of the night?"

"We didn't have anywhere else to go."

"So many of us don't," the woman said after a pause. "Who hurt you, *piccolo*?"

Josie froze as the woman traced her fingertip under the spot along Sam's cheek.

"We were playing," Sam interjected.

After giving them both a knowing look, she turned to Josie and said, "Then you must have the nails of a woman."

Josie balled her hands into fists, hoping to hide her bitten-to-the-quick nails. "We can't go back tonight."

"Where is your father? Can you call him?"

"There isn't anybody we can call."

"Send those kids on their way, Nonna," the teenager spat from wherever she'd disappeared to. "They're only going to cause you trouble, and my dad gave you enough of that."

"Hush your mouth, Sofia. And put clothes on or go back to bed." She opened the door fully and ushered them in. "You two need to rest your heads until morning? Come in. You can sleep on my couch. It's big enough to fit you both."

They offered their thanks and followed her inside.

"I know about your mother, the one they're calling Hollywood. Not even here two months, and she's told half the building she's going to be famous. Pretty enough, but pretty is commonplace in this town. I should know. This city drew me in when I was young and pretty too."

She disappeared into one of the bedrooms and returned carrying a blanket and two pillows. "Are you hungry?"

Sam's eyes grew wide, and he brushed a tongue over his lips.

"If I'm going to feed you, I need to know your names."

"I'm Sam. And this is my sister, Josie. Josie Pictures."

"Pictures? Named for Hollywood, are you?" Her gaze lingered on Josie. "With that hair, you might even find your fame. My grandson told me about you, and he tells me nothing."

"I want to live with my grandparents in Idaho, but they won't take us. Our mom says she's not allowed to go back." It wasn't an answer, but it was the only thing Josie could think to say.

"So, you're stuck just the same as my grandkids." She ran her fingers down Josie's hair the way she did the day they carried her bags. "Josie and Sam, you're fish out of water. But even fish need to eat and sleep. Come into the kitchen, and you can fill your bellies. My name is Francesca, but you can call me Francie. I knew when I first saw you a few weeks ago that our lives would run together. I have a way of knowing such things."

The counters of Francie's kitchen were crowded with food, dishes, and piles of paperwork. It smelled of oil and ripe bananas, but it was the most welcoming kitchen Josie had ever seen. She and Sam were quiet and watchful as Francie heated a small saucepan over the stove. In a few minutes, she served them bowls filled with something that looked like thick oatmeal but had a yellow tint.

"Polenta," Francie said in explanation. She leaned over them and grated some fresh, hard cheese on top.

Josie was worried her brother could hurt Francie's feelings by not liking it. After blowing on a spoonful, Josie was surprised by how much her mouth watered in delight at the creamy, salty taste. By the speed at which Sam inhaled it, Josie knew he liked it too.

As she was finishing, Josie saw movement behind the cracked door of one of the bedrooms. She strained to see who was watching them, but it was dark inside.

"You know my Nicolo," Francie said. "Nicolo, if you aren't going to say hello, go back to bed. You'll be too tired for school in the morning."

There was a shuffle, and the door shut.

"He told me when you came to his class. A blue-eyed girl with hair the color of a flaming sunset."

"I don't know a Nicolo," Josie said. She puzzled over the many still-nameless faces of the boys in her class.

"He goes by Nico with his friends." Francie smiled at the flash of recognition on her face. "He looks just like his father did at that age." She seemed about to say more but gave a light shake of her head and made the sign of a cross in front of her.

Josie knew Nico. She'd had no idea Francie was his grandmother or that he lived in her building. He was the biggest kid in class—tall and slender and quiet. A week before, Josie was paired with him to read a story. He'd stammered in several spots, and she'd pretended not to know some of the words either. His skin was so tan compared to hers, his eyes were stormy gray, and his hair was dark brown and wavy.

"I know him." Josie worried he'd tell the other kids in class that she and Sam had to flee from their mother in the middle of the night.

Sam leaned over the table and yawned.

"To the couch with you both. We all need our sleep."

They didn't take any further convincing. Francie threw a blanket over them and pressed her hand against the tops of their heads. "I know good children when I see them. Sleep, and we'll worry about your mother in the morning."

Sam was asleep in seconds, but only after stretching to take up most of the space. Josie lay in the darkness and whispered a fervent prayer to a god her mother told her didn't exist. She prayed that—if he could hear her—he'd make her mother just a little bit more like Francie. Just a little bit would get them through; she was certain of it.

The apartment grew still and quiet, and Josie waited for sleepiness to set in again, but it didn't. After a little while, the door to Nico's bedroom opened. She held her breath as he approached. He knelt in front of her, balancing on the balls of his feet and resting his elbows on his thighs, reminding her of a crouched tiger.

"Your mother did that?" He nodded toward Sam's scratched cheek.

Josie said nothing, feeling a rare loyalty to her mother.

"My mother never hit," he continued. "She's been gone since I was five. That's when my old man started hitting, but he's locked up now. But it's all good. It's better living here."

"I didn't know Francie was your grandma."

In the darkness, Josie saw a lopsided smile light up his face. "If she has you calling her Francie, then you can come whenever you want. That's Nonna's way."

"I like her."

"Everyone does. She grew up in Italy."

Josie had never met anyone from Italy. All she knew was that spaghetti was her favorite dinner, only she didn't know if that was an okay thing to say to someone whose grandma was Italian.

A silence fell between them. Then he pointed to his room. "Go. Take my bed. I'll stay with your brother."

"I don't need to."

"Take it. Girls need their privacy. Nonna is always saying it."

Josie felt her cheeks grow hot, thinking of her and Sam's shared mattress on the floor. She pushed up to a sitting position and looked at Sam. His breathing was deep and even like he didn't have a care in the world.

"Go," Nico repeated, leaving no room for rebuttal. It didn't surprise her. He was that way in class too.

She left without saying anything else. It was strange getting into his bed. She pulled his covers over her and rested her head on his pillow. She liked the way his sheets smelled. It made her wonder if he smelled the same way.

She finally drifted off, and in the morning, Josie woke up to the smell of bacon and eggs. If Francie cared that Nico had given her his room, she didn't say anything. After breakfast, Francie said it was safe to go home and get ready for school. Francie had been to see their mother while they were still sleeping.

Before they left, Francie told them to hold their shoulders high and not to cry. She said to let their mama do all the crying for them.

Josie thought Francie was wrong; her mother never cried. When they got there, Skye was watching out the window, looking pale and exhausted and biting her nails. She dropped to her knees and hugged them tighter than Josie could ever remember. And then she started to cry. It was one of the few times Josie ever saw her do it.

It took less than an hour at school for Josie to know her and Sam's secret was safe with Nico. He was a quiet boy and not one to tell other people's stories. In the space of a month, he was the best friend she'd ever had. Before long, she loved him almost as much as she loved Sam. One day, a kid in class joked that she and Nico were in love. Nico broke his nose without a second's hesitation and was suspended for two days.

She couldn't comprehend how things between them could ever grow more complicated. And she was too young to consider the implications of being best friends with a boy like Nico, a boy who talked very little, but who everyone listened to when he did. Too young to think about how the world would change all of them when it inevitably began to press in.

Chapter 7

CARTER'S QUADS BURNED FROM exertion by the time he was midway up the Green Street Stairs. Myra wasn't exaggerating with her claim of two hundred steps scaling the bluff from Main Street to the top.

The century-and-a-half-year-old town was a postcard, even at night. Redbrick buildings with soft lights pouring from windows lined the streets and hillsides in the center of town. Myra's place was in a residential area above the massive bluffs, and the steps were the most direct route between them.

Behind him, below the streets and shops, the Galena River became visible as he climbed, glowing glossy black in the night. Maybe it had something to do with the story that had brought him here, but the river reminded him of a serpent that had witnessed one secret after another, century after century. What could the river tell him about the man pulled from it in 1940? Who shot him and why? Who made it his grandfather's watery grave?

Carter climbed high enough that he passed the tops of trees, and it was just him, the endless steps, the bluffs, and the night. His lungs protested, reminding him how ridiculous it was to pick up smoking again in the wake of his stressful breakup. Even if he was limiting himself to a few cigarettes a day. Some habits needed to be quit forever.

An image of Myra on these very steps came to mind. He could picture her, frail and slightly stooped, weighed down with her groceries. A young mother came to her aid and *stayed*. Who did that?

He reached the top not a step too soon. Shaking off the burning in his muscles, he began the final two blocks to the old Victorian mansion. He'd accepted Myra's offer to stay—in spite of an overkill of knickknacks, lace, and doilies—because there was a story here. Most likely, there were a few. For his father's sake, he was committed to staying until he resolved at least one of them.

As he unlatched the wrought-iron gate that led to the impressive front porch, Carter glimpsed the light pouring onto the side yard from the back of the house. He glanced at his watch. Nearly midnight. He guessed that, considering the age of the wedding party, everyone would've gone to bed.

Back at the crowded tavern where he'd been hanging out, talking to a few locals, he'd been buzzing nicely and intended to come back and crash. The stairs had been a buzzkill. Now he was fully awake, sober, and hungry.

He turned onto the crumbled stone path leading to the backyard. He stepped around the corner, blanketed by darkness, and took in the yard. The patio was aglow with candles, and the surrounding yard was lit by lanterns and string lights. Ribbons and bouquets of flowers filled tables and trellises. Coupled with the trees and flower beds covering the grounds, it looked like a fairy tale. No wonder that precocious little kid believed in fairies, growing up in a place like this.

At first glance, the patio seemed empty, but then he spotted Josie. She was tucked into the shadows at one of the tables. His insides twisted the same as they did this morning when he stood at the top of the bluffs where there was no rail looking down on the town.

It surprised him, the way his body reacted to her. He was no stranger to beautiful women. Heck, he lived in Manhattan where they seemed to rise from concrete and stone. He was also fresh out of an eight-year relationship with a former clothing model-turned-activist. But Josie made him feel as if he'd been tucked away in a cabin the last few years.

He reminded himself that, based on his best guess, she was most likely in her mid- to late twenties. At thirty-four, he wasn't looking for the emotional immaturity of anyone that much younger. And on top of that was the whole kid thing. The kid was great, but in terms of relationships, kids equaled heavy. And he wasn't in the space for heavy. Not on the heels of his breakup with Katherine.

If Josie were up for a no-strings-attached romp in one of those lumpy feather beds, there'd be no holding him back. Only, it was clear that wasn't her thing. Pretty clear *he* wasn't her thing either, for that matter. And she had walls around her like a fortress.

But maybe not an impenetrable one. He'd glimpsed that guard dropping when she was showing him his room. A smile had flashed across her face and lit up those remarkable eyes of hers. Whoever that was—that person she kept so guarded from the world—that was the woman he wanted to get to know.

Added to that was her story. And he wouldn't have to unearth secrets from an ancient river in order to learn it. All he had to do was get her to open up. Get her to trust him. *Yeah, right. Getting the river to talk would probably be easier.*

As Carter looked at her, alone in the lantern-lit, fairy-tale back-yard, a yearning tore through his gut—something primal enough to evade words and definition. He told himself to ignore it, to go up-stairs and sink down onto that surprisingly comfortable mattress and catch up on the sleep he'd been missing. When he started moving, he intended to do just that.

Yet, when his feet led him deeper into the backyard, he couldn't say he was surprised. He'd always been one to listen to his gut.

—◇◇◇—

It had been a fabulous day, and an exhausting one. Every bone and muscle in Josie's body needed to be in bed, but her mind was racing a mile a minute. No doubt, it had to do with several glasses of iced mint tea and a late evening cup of oolong as the cake was served.

After Zoe finally crashed into a lump of nonsensical tears and exhaustion after her first foray as a flower girl, Josie had tucked her into bed hours past her bedtime. She could have finished cleaning up in the morning, but there were still dishes left on the patio. If they weren't brought in, the neighborhood raccoons were sure to mess with them overnight.

With the patio empty of guests, the glowing lights and flickering candles had beckoned her to sit awhile after she'd finished cleaning up. She sank into a chair at one of the tables and noticed two card decks discarded there, no doubt left by two of the older men who'd been playing rummy. Without giving it much thought, she pulled out a deck and began shuffling. Back when she and her brother had nearly nothing to their names, sometimes not even a roof over their heads, they'd always had a deck or two of cards, and an intricately built card house had been both a challenge and a distraction.

Half of one deck was assembled into a card house before she realized she was building it. Exhausted as she was, she didn't need the challenge tonight, but the promise of a distraction had its appeal. She didn't want to think about long-lost loves finding one another again. About happily ever afters. Or what happened when happily ever after fell apart.

She was starting a third story of her house when she spotted Carter walking around the side yard. Her fingers froze inches above it, two cards at the ready as he walked up.

"Sitting in the dark building card houses?" His tone was playful and light. "I wouldn't have pegged you as a card house enthusiast."

She sat back, straightening as he helped himself to the seat opposite her.

"I couldn't sleep."

"Mind if I join you?" He winked as he reached for the second deck of cards.

A small huff escaped. "Aren't you supposed to ask that *before* you sit down?"

There was a flickering candle between them, a vase of wedding flowers, and a card house. Nothing else. Josie swallowed her discomfort at the idea of being alone with him. It wasn't just his looks; it was his lopsided grin and easygoing demeanor. Some unspoken promise that, with very little effort, he was the type of guy who could be your best friend. Or, at least, someone you could trust with your spare key. All things that warred with her idea of keeping him at bay.

"Something tells me if I waited for an invitation, I'd have been standing here awhile," he said, his tone light. "And looming over you wouldn't have done either of us any good. Not in that dress you're wearing. Is it vintage?"

"It belonged to Myra's mother, so yes, I guess." She picked up a card to keep from hiking up the low-cut dress. It was a blue, fitted silk with spaghetti straps and flowing toile over a skirt that ended just above the knee. "And I wouldn't have pegged you as an aficionado of vintage clothing."

He gave a little tilt of his head. "I'm not, but until recently, I was engaged to one. Even so, that dress looks like the real thing."

Until recently. As she'd have guessed, he wasn't married. But he'd been close. She wondered what sort of skeletons he hid in his closet. Most of the guys she'd grown up around had a collection of them: drug addictions, cheating, fetishes, the list went on and on. Aloud, she said, "It was a forties-themed wedding. Myra wanted me to wear it."

"Sounds fun. Vintage or not, it could've been made for you." He looked from her to his deck of cards as he shuffled them.

Josie's ears burned hot. When she didn't reply, he didn't pursue the comment. Finished shuffling, he picked two cards from the top and started his own A-frame structure. *He's not seriously going to sit here and build card houses, is he?*

"You don't like my staying here, do you?" He reached for two more cards without waiting for an answer.

In the flickering light, her attention was equally caught by his face and his well-sculpted hands. "You're just…"

"A man?" he asked when she didn't finish.

The comment caught her off guard enough that a small laugh escaped. "I was going for potential threat. To Myra. But if she's okay with you rehashing this story of yours, then so be it."

"I hear you, but sometimes good things come from unearthing long-buried secrets."

Josie was pretty sure there was something pointed in his gaze, but in the dim light, maybe she was reading into it.

"So, how was the wedding?" he asked, and some of the tension left her shoulders at the change of subject. "No one ran for the hills?"

"No, no one ran for the hills."

Holding a card, he waved a hand toward the yard. "This place could be in a magazine."

"Thanks. The credit is mostly owed to Mr. Lange." She pointed down the hill toward the white clapboard house that belonged to their next-door neighbor. "He lives there. He's a retired gardener. We're not sure how it happened, but a month or two after we opened, he was at the bottom of the yard one morning working in the flower beds. Myra walked down and offered him lunch, and since then, it's become a thing. He works in the flower beds, and he gets lunch. The same thing every day. Quiche lorraine and a half grapefruit when it's in season and orange slices when it isn't. He's not very adventurous when it comes to food, but he's a remarkable gardener."

"I love quirky people like that. They're great to write about."

"I bet. We grow our own lavender and many of our own herbs. If it weren't for his help, I'm not sure we'd be able to. And our customers love that we harvest some things here. That, and that most of our produce is grown within fifty miles of here."

"Oh yeah? Cool. And what about the tea everyone's talking about?"

Josie shrugged. "A lot of our tea is shipped in from India and parts of China, though we get some from South Carolina and Oregon too. All our tea is fair trade, though, so it costs more than a typical cup."

Carter worked as he listened, his movements steady and methodical. "I've never been a tea drinker. Except for the sun tea my mom made when I was kid."

"I wasn't either before I came here. Myra sold me on it."

"Tell me, then, why the tea craze?"

She pursed her lips, thinking of the afternoons she'd sat with Myra when Zoe was a baby, enjoying a cup of tea that Myra had blended and listening to her talk of how the herbs and flowers she'd mixed in added to the taste of the tea leaf. It was Myra's passion for tea blending that had given Josie the idea to try the tea garden.

"It's more than a drink, I guess," she said. "It's an experience. Here, at least. Not the heavily processed stuff you grab in a plastic bottle at a gas station. Though it all comes from the same plant, *Camellia sinensis*. It becomes green, white, or black tea, depending on how it's processed. And then there are the blends. Myra's a master blender. She's certified too. She creates almost all our blends."

"I was looking at the menu earlier. It's almost daunting."

"We have thirty-four regular teas, plus seasonal varieties."

He grinned. "And I noticed you don't serve coffee."

"It's not on the menu, but we have a coffee pot. The few times we've served it to tea-averse customers… I have to say our coffee's nothing to write home about."

"I've been drinking coffee as long as I can remember, and it rarely is. Though it serves a purpose."

"If you're up to try it while you're here, we have a blend just for die-hard coffee drinkers. We call it *The Breakfast Club*."

"Oh yeah? I'll give it a try."

Carter finished the second story of his card house before she completed her third, and she'd been working several minutes longer. After a wrong twitch of her index finger, her house toppled into a mound. She gathered up the cards to start again.

"You're quick at card houses."

"I used to go to work with my dad in summer." He hardly paused building as he spoke. "He ran a feed store. When I wasn't loading God knows what into cowboys' trucks, I was sitting in the shade of the porch building card houses. I was an "oops baby," and the youngest of my siblings by thirteen years. My parents are older, and I didn't grow up with limitless entertainment at my fingertips."

Josie straightened her deck before starting again. "Those rural Manhattan cowboys, you mean?"

He smiled but shook his head. "I grew up in backcountry Texas, sweetheart. There was nothing in a hundred square miles but flat, red earth and hardened ranchers. And black coffee and sun tea."

Backcountry Texas. Suddenly Carter made more sense. She'd picked up on the slightest of drawls a couple times, and that flirtatious chivalry of his, none of that screamed East Coast.

"And what about you?" he asked, cocking an eyebrow. "I'd bet everything I own you're not from here. Not that I'm implying this little quiet town couldn't put out something like you."

Josie's newly started house collapsed. This flirting thing—not only was she not going to reciprocate it—it wasn't cool. "The thing is, I love this quiet little town. It's the best place on earth." Before losing her nerve, she plunged ahead. "And since you're going to be staying here another few nights, I should make it clear that I don't take well to compliments, and I take even worse to come-ons."

Carter sank back in his seat, raising one eyebrow slightly. The house he'd built in a short time was three levels and looked sturdy enough to hold up to a light wind. "Points taken. All of them." His tone was playful but his gaze direct. "I guess that's why it's been so challenging to get you to smile."

She swept up her cards and started another house. Her insides were a crazy, rioting mess. She was nervous and angry and exasperated and flattered all at the same time. And doing her best not to show any of it. "I smile all the time." She drew a controlled breath as she started the base of a house. Carter wasn't a bad guy. She could see it in his eyes. She was damn good at reading people. He was flirty and maybe a bit lost or avoidant, but he was kind. Genuinely kind. "The thing is, it's probably best to remember you're here for Myra. I don't make friends easily. And I honestly don't want to. I like my life that way."

Carter nodded slowly and made no move to return to his card house building. It was then that she realized he'd used up his entire deck. He reached out and toppled it with a brush of his fingers, then gathered up the cards to return them to the carton.

It was obvious she'd successfully put him off. And even though she knew she should be relieved, her heart seemed to fall a solid three inches in her chest. *It's what you wanted. Feeling like crap won't make it any better.*

"I'll keep that in mind," he said, standing up and tucking in his chair. "Thanks for the chat, anyway. It was good practice."

He walked around the table and stopped next to her, setting his deck down.

"Practice for what?" she asked, even though she knew the answer.

"I've been off the market a while now. Getting shot down is never easy."

She focused on her card house rather than him. She must not have done something right, because her new house was as unstable as could be.

"Mind if I offer a tip?" He picked up two of her cards and leaned over to overlap them at an angle at the base with the confidence of someone who'd been asked to do so. He was close enough for her to smell a hint of a tavern and that same brush of sandalwood from when she'd fainted. His muscle definition activated her salivary glands, and she fought off the need to swallow.

As she reassessed her newly started house, she realized he'd given the rickety new thing just the stability it needed.

"The thing is," she spat out, "you just showed up here. You could've sent a letter or something. For Myra's sake, I mean."

"True, I could've. Though, there are some things you're never prepared for. But it doesn't mean you shouldn't give them a chance."

Then he was gone, and Josie found herself alone in the big, quiet yard and more unsettled than she'd been in a very long time.

Chapter 8

AFTER A LONG SHOWER early Sunday morning, Josie slipped into the comfy sundress that Linda passed on to her last year after officially giving up attempts at fad-dieting her way back to the size she was before her three kids.

Before heading downstairs, Josie tiptoed into Zoe's adjoining room and pulled the summer-weight quilt back over her. She stood there a handful of seconds in the early morning light, savoring the soft, smooth curve of Zoe's cheeks and mouth and her impossibly thick lashes, and watching the even rise and fall of her chest under the covers. Her small hand was tucked under one cheek. If there was one single thing in the world that had given Josie reason to believe in prayer, it was Zoe.

Hopefully, she would sleep in this morning. With the start of school a day away—*Holy crap, is there really just one day left?*—Zoe had a colossal week ahead of her.

Zoe's new teacher's words from last week's meet and greet raced through her brain. "Oh, what a sweetie. She's the one who didn't go to kindergarten, right? I expect she'll have some catching up to do. They always do when they miss kindergarten."

"She was homeschooled," Josie had replied. "She didn't *miss* it."

Ms. Richard's had offered a light shake of her head as if to show she'd meant no insult. "It's not so much the reading and writing they miss without a formal classroom setting; it's learning to share and play well with others. Stand quietly in line. That sort of thing. But don't you worry, Ms. Waterhill. I'll be sure to take care of her."

Would she though? What if homeschooling Zoe last year was a mistake? Before her thoughts went spiraling, Josie shoved them away. It was too early to think about any of that. She hadn't even had a cup of tea.

She made her way downstairs in the still-quiet house and into the kitchen. Linda was at the kitchen counter, chopping veggies for the wedding guests' farewell breakfast.

She attempted to suppress a yawn as she stepped through the swinging door. "Morning, lady."

"Morning. How late did you get to bed?"

"Not too late." She squeezed Linda's shoulder as she headed for the five-gallon hot water dispenser. Linda lived on a small sheep farm twenty minutes outside of town with her husband and three kids, and Josie admired her more than anyone she knew, right down to the hair she'd chosen not to dye after going prematurely gray in her late thirties.

For a second, Josie was tempted to forgo the tea and have a cup of the coffee Linda had brewed for a couple of the guests but decided against it. The coffee smelled delicious, but as far as Josie was concerned, coffee smelled better than it tasted. Instead, she filled a teaspoon with a serving of *The Soulmate Soiree*, a caffeinated blend they'd created for the weekend.

"I'm so glad you came in so I don't have to face these people all alone this morning."

Linda paused mid-chop on her mushroom. "Are you kidding? They've been running you nonstop all weekend *without* you doing all the cooking."

Josie finished tying on an apron and stretched as her tea steeped. "Anything for Myra, right?"

The house stirred to life as they worked to prep a large farewell breakfast for the guests. Showers ran, floors creaked, and guests grad-ually wandered down for tea and coffee as they waited for breakfast. The sound of a few suitcases being rolled across the floor overhead caught Josie's attention. The weekend hadn't turned out anything like she'd feared, but it would still be a relief to send the guests on their way after breakfast. Except for Carter. He'd be staying another night.

Whenever he came to mind, her thoughts and feelings circled like the winds of a hurricane, too fast and too intense to make sense of.

A little over an hour later, Josie and Linda had eight frittatas baking in the oven, filling the room with the smell of hot butter and cheese. After prepping the rest of the meal, Josie slipped off her apron and headed out to the patio to check on Zoe, who'd woken up and followed Myra outside to talk to the guests. Not to Josie's surprise, Zoe was knee-deep in another sandcastle war. Her face was a mask of fierce determination as she eyed up the competition from the older of the two boys.

Josie knelt in front of the sandpit and swept Zoe's hair aside to plant a kiss on the back of her neck. "Having a good morning, baby doll?"

"Yes. When's breakfast?"

"In about ten minutes."

"Do I still get doughnuts today? Like you promised? Because tomorrow I'm going to school."

"Yes, once everyone leaves, we'll head into town, and you can pick out a few. Be thinking of something special to do today, too, like I said."

"I already did. Myra and Carter already said yes too."

Josie cocked her head in surprise. "Is that so?"

"Yes," Zoe uttered before turning to tell the youngest boy that he was taking too much sand.

Still kneeling, she scooped Zoe's chin into her hand so that she'd look in her eyes. "Why didn't you ask me first, Zoe?"

"Because you said I could have my pick, and my pick depended on who would come. So, I asked."

"And when were you going to share this with me?"

"When you finished being busy."

Josie pressed her eyes shut for two full seconds before replying. She couldn't argue the truth in that. "Okay. What is it you want to do today?"

"Have a picnic in the park by the river, then go to Chestnut Mountain and go down the mountain slide."

The slide wasn't a surprising request. It had become Zoe's favorite activity this summer. But asking Carter to come was something else altogether. "And you asked Carter to join us?"

"He makes me happy," Zoe said matter-of-factly before threatening the little boy with, "If you take any more sand from my spot, I'm going to tell your mom."

The knot twisting inside Josie had nothing to do with hunger. Zoe was longing for a father figure. She knew it. Myra knew it. Linda knew it. Before Carter came, it just wasn't so obvious. But truth was truth, and she might as well not deny it.

Even so, her throat locked surprisingly fast. For some reason, Zoe's wish of companions this afternoon had scraped her insides raw and had her eyes stinging.

Blinking away the sting, Josie watched as Zoe dropped her scoop and army-crawled over to the oldest boy. "You aren't supposed to scoop from my side."

When the boy aptly complained that Zoe's side was much bigger than his, Josie helped carve out a more reasonable middle ground. She reminded Zoe to share like the big girl she knew she could be, which brought Ms. Richard's words to mind again. What about those all-too-important kindergarten lessons that Zoe missed out on? *Wait, isn't there even a book about that? Oh God, Zoe's screwed.*

"Hey, I've got to help finish breakfast." Her throat constricted so much that her words came out short and choppy.

She made it to the kitchen where Linda was setting everything on trays. "Grab those last five frittatas out of the oven, will you?"

Not trusting herself to speak, Josie grabbed a mitt. She slid them out one by one, and by the time she reached for the fifth, her eyes were so blurry from unshed tears she couldn't see a thing.

"What is it?" Linda asked, spying the glossy wetness of her eyes.

Josie shook her head. "Not now."

Linda frowned, setting her hands on her hips. "Girl, you can't carry the mountain all the time."

Her mouth opened, but she pulled the words back before they tumbled out. The urge to unleash it—all of it—was suddenly pressing in harder than ever. Instead, she stamped her foot. Then, when it helped just a bit, she stamped it again.

Linda released a sigh. "If you're not willing to let yourself have a good cry, then I have just the thing. There's a five-pound bag of walnuts that was delivered last week that was supposed to be chopped, but instead it's halves. Why don't you have a go?" She fished a mallet and cutting board out of the drawer and handed it to her. "They're in the pantry. I can get breakfast served without you."

Josie gave a nod of surrender, though she had a suspicion that by the time she was done with the walnuts, the kitchen was going to look like a test lab had exploded.

Chapter 9

AN HOUR AFTER THE weekend guests left, Josie sank onto Myra's plaid blanket. They were at the park overlooking the Galena River on the south side of town. After getting Zoe her own plate of food, Josie picked up a plate for herself and piled on everything that looked appetizing, from hummus and sliced cheese and fruit to the leftover tea sandwiches. She'd gone from hungry to hangry in the last half hour, not having carved out much time to eat for the third day in a row.

"Aren't you hungry?" Josie asked, seeing that Myra hadn't reached for a plate. "I'm starving."

"It was such a wonderful breakfast. I think I'll just sit awhile and enjoy the view and the company."

After three bites of her sandwich, Zoe abandoned her lunch and let her plate tilt sideways, sending a handful of grapes and a few pretzels cascading to the blanket. She was fixated on a man flying a kite along the riverbank to the delight of his two kids.

"Can I go watch, Mom? I won't try to take over."

"I didn't think you would." Josie swiped a strand of hair out of Zoe's eyes. "How about you finish your lunch first?"

"It'll be crashed by then. I'll just go for a minute, and I'll be right back."

Knowing Zoe would be hard-pressed to eat another bite until she'd satisfied her curiosity, Josie consented. "Stay close so you can hear if I call."

Discarding her plate, Zoe popped up and flew across the lawn, stopping short of the two kids by ten or twenty feet.

"She's a cute kid," Carter said after finishing a cracker piled with cheese and turkey salami. "Really cute." He watched her for a moment, then sprawled back on the blanket and closed his eyes. "I'm not as young as I used to be; I'll tell you that."

"Anytime I find myself thinking that, I follow it with a reminder of how I'm younger than I'll ever be again," Myra said.

Eyes still closed, Carter cocked an eyebrow. "True, but a decade ago, I could party most of the night without losing a minute of productivity the next day. Last night, I had four beers, and today I feel as if I've been wandering around lost in the desert. I'm sure it doesn't help that, after eleven years of not smoking, I made the stupid decision to buy a pack of cigarettes last month. I was hooked again with that very first one. I've been trying to limit myself to one or two a day, but I'm way too focused on trying to decide when's the best time to have them."

"It sounds as if you're getting better at listening to your body. It'll tell you when you're treating it well and when you aren't," Myra said. "And how old are you, anyway? Thirty-four? Thirty-five?"

"You're good. Thirty-four, closing in on thirty-five."

"Then you've finally reached the age when life starts to get interesting."

Carter sat up and chuckled. "I won't argue about the last few months being anything but dull."

It was Myra's turn to raise an eyebrow. "I've been wondering why you and your fiancée broke it off; I'm hoping you're about to tell us."

After nearly choking on the bite of cucumber, turkey, and cream cheese tea sandwich she was chewing, Josie shot Myra a look.

Myra responded with a wave of her hand. "I'm too old to be courteous. He can answer or opt not to. No harm is done by those who question the order of the universe."

Carter leaned forward, resting his elbows on his knees, locking his gaze on Zoe. A few dozen feet away, she was still mesmerized by the kite flying.

"I've been asking myself if it matters whether or not the reason we split is one big one or a million little ones. Maybe the only thing that really matters is that it's over."

"And what have you decided?"

As if contemplating Myra's question, he picked up a gnarled twig at the side of the blanket and snapped it. "That it's time to move on."

"If you've given it your best," Myra continued, "then, most likely, that's a good decision."

Feeling like she was eavesdropping on a private conversation, Josie grabbed her stainless-steel water bottle and headed over to check on Zoe. The kite-flying dad smiled a welcome from ten feet away.

"I'm only watching, Mom," Zoe said. "Did you see it bang their dad on the head? It didn't hurt him, and it didn't break either. It's really flying now."

"I saw that," she said, offering the father a half wave. "Don't you want to eat, Zo?"

"A little longer. *Please.*"

Josie glanced at the father, who'd been relaying instructions to his oldest child. "We don't mind her company."

The man was easy to talk to. When he learned that Zoe's first day of school was tomorrow, he unleashed a stream of praise about how happy he and his wife were with the school and how Ms. Richards had been both his kids' favorite teacher so far.

Relief washed over Josie at this unsolicited praise about Zoe's first teacher. Even so, the conversation had her stomach doing somersaults. She was going to miss the days when it was just her and Zoe, Myra, the other staff, and the guests at Myra's tea garden.

From now on, they were going to be much more connected to a world she'd done her best to avoid.

They were safe here, she promised herself. Enrolling Zoe in school had been the right decision. *Wasn't it?*

As if in answer, the kite skittered in a gust of wind and nose-dived to the ground. The kids, Zoe included, broke into gales of laughter.

Josie forced a smile and reminded herself that foreshadowing was for stories, and fate was what she made it. Staying in control was the one thing that had always gotten her through.

When they returned to their picnic spot, Myra and Carter were deep in conversation. It irked Josie the way they fell silent at her and Zoe's approach. Swallowing a wave of jealousy over how easily Carter was drawing Myra in, Josie sank to the blanket and picked up a second tea sandwich.

Rejecting her partially eaten sandwich due to an ant, Zoe heaped a mound of red grapes onto her lap while giving Carter and Myra a play-by-play of the kite flying. When Carter laughed at her animated descriptions, Zoe beamed and said for the second time since they arrived that she was happy he came.

"I'm glad you invited me." He reached over and ruffled her hair. "In fact, I can't think of anything else I'd rather be doing."

When Josie met his gaze, he offered her a wink that caused a jolt of energy to circle all the way down between her hips. She did her best to look indifferent, but her cheeks betrayed her and flamed hot.

As if letting her know he'd caught it, he added subtly, "Well, maybe one."

Thankfully, Carter's poorly camouflaged innuendo seemed to fly over Zoe's head as she folded over to study the ants who'd invaded her plate. Josie seized the opportunity to flick a cracker at him, though, as soon as she did it, she realized he'd be just as likely to assume it was a flirtation as the rebuke she'd intended it to be. It smacked him on the thigh before falling to the blanket, causing his lopsided grin to widen.

An hour and a half later, once they'd wrapped up the picnic and made it to Chestnut Mountain, Josie's big meal was sitting like a lead ball in her belly. Having been cramped in the back of Carter's bright blue Mustang GT hadn't helped either.

As she, Zoe, and Carter headed up in what was normally a two-seater chair lift to the Alpine Slide, Josie pressed the bar tighter against her. She'd ridden the slide enough that she ought to be used to the lift. She glanced behind them in hopes of seeing Myra, who was watching from the bottom, but she was no longer in sight. Off to the side, two concrete runs snaked through the green grass below them, seeming much further away than the thirty or forty feet they were.

"What a view," Carter said as they neared the top, and he took in the rolling countryside below them. Chestnut Mountain was far enough outside of town that no development interrupted the view; the wintertime ski resort was currently an expanse of brilliant green hillsides dotted with trees and cattle and the Missouri River in the distance.

"You can see five states from the top, right, Mom?" Zoe leaned into her as they prepared to get off.

"Three, they say, when the skies are clear like today."

Zoe reached for both Josie's and Carter's hands before jumping out of the lift. *So, this is what it'd be like to have someone on Zoe's other side. Like a real family.* As soon as they'd hit solid ground, Josie dropped Zoe's hand like a hot potato. Safely out of the way of the lift, she bent over to fiddle with her sandal, collecting herself. A real family. Something she and Zoe would never have.

Unaware of her turmoil, Carter paused, taking in the view. "I tell you what, Zoe. You can't get fresh air like this in New York City, that's for sure."

"New York City is where the great lady lives."

"What great lady?"

"*The* great lady."

"The Statue of Liberty?"

"Yeah, her. We have a book about her. It's Myra's."

"You'll have to read it to me later."

"I can't read very well yet. Myra and my mom read it to me."

Carter glanced at Josie; she held his gaze only a second before looking away.

"Something tells me she won't read it to me, so maybe you and I can read it together."

Suppressing a snort, Josie shook her head. "Ready, Zo. We shouldn't leave Myra waiting too long."

They filed into the line to go down the slide behind a dozen others. Only one slide was open today, but the wait wasn't long.

Bubbling over with excitement, Zoe jumped up and down, then wiggled like a worm. "Can I go with Carter the first time, Mom, so he's not afraid?"

Josie ran her fingers through Zoe's hair. She expected as much the way Zoe had doted on him all afternoon. "Sure, baby."

"I don't want to put you out," Carter said.

Rather than acknowledge the compassion in his gaze, she looked down the long hill. The truth was, he was half the reason Zoe was glowing from ear to ear today. "I'm fine going solo."

"I don't doubt it."

Just before her and Carter's turn, Zoe buried a kiss against Josie's cotton sundress. After another wiggle of her hips, Zoe loaded onto the front of their sled. She squealed in anticipation as she and Carter waited to be cleared to go down the mile-long concrete run.

Carter and Zoe whooped in unison as they took off. Josie stood there listening to them holler their way down the mountain. When it was her turn, all last traces of muddled irritation had vanished. The speed and wind in her hair was a rush. By the time she serpentined to the bottom and slid to a stop, even the sight of Carter standing next to Myra and Zoe like he perfectly belonged didn't seem off.

Myra and Zoe clapped in unison. "Isn't it the best thing ever, Mom? It's my favorite thing in the world!"

Carter offered his hand to help her up and, even though she didn't need it, she decided it wouldn't hurt to take it. It surprised her a bit, the feel of a man's hand. It had been so long, she'd all but forgotten it.

She was pretty sure Myra was giving her a knowing look, but she refused to glance her way in confirmation.

Carter let go once she was on her feet, but the tips of his fingers brushed hers, igniting her skin along the way. "You know, Zoe, I didn't realize how beautiful your mom is when she forgets to lock up her smile."

Josie's heart walloped involuntarily as Zoe's eyebrows wrinkled into a knot. "I don't even know what that means."

"That's all right. You're only six. What do you say we don't worry about it and go up again?"

Chapter 10

When the alarm went off at 6:15 Monday morning, Josie resisted the temptation to linger under the cool comfort of her sheet. As her disjointed dreams retreated into the shadows, she remembered the reason for having set an alarm for a Monday, when the tea garden was closed. Today was it: Zoe's first day of school.

Her insides feeling as if she'd swallowed a fish, she sat up, wide awake. In the adjacent room, past the propped-open french doors, Zoe slid out of bed and trotted over to the small dresser where her new outfit was folded on top.

Wednesday through Sunday, days the tea garden was open, Josie's alarm went off at 5:00 a.m., and Zoe slept right through it.

"Morning, sweets. You don't have to get up yet if you don't want to. It's almost two hours until your bus comes."

"But I want to be first to the bus stop."

Sitting up, Josie stifled a yawn. "You know, there's plenty of room on the bus for everyone. Even if you aren't first."

"But I *like* to be first."

Josie got out of bed, stretched, and walked over to Zoe. Their rooms had been designed for child and nanny. Zoe's room, about half the size of Josie's, had been the nanny's quarters.

When Zoe finished yanking off her smiley-faced marshmallow nightgown, Josie pulled her into a bear hug, savoring the feel of her smooth, youthful skin. "I love the way you smell when you're clean."

"Then that's clean you like and not me. I smell like Zoe."

"You smell like childhood and possibility and garden fairies." Before letting her go, Josie buried her nose in Zoe's hair and took an exaggerated whiff that made Zoe giggle.

"How can you know what garden fairies smell like when you don't even believe in them?"

"I believe in you, Zo. That's what matters. And how about listening to some advice from someone who's been through school and learned a thing or two?"

Zoe stuck out her hip and pointed a finger in a mock-authoritarian pose. "Is this going to be boring?"

"I'll keep it short." Josie chuckled. "How about when you catch yourself being worried about being first—whether it's first in line or to the swings or whatever—you try taking a breath and giving yourself permission to just be you and do things on your own time?"

Zoe tugged her shirt over her head, and Josie swept her hair out from under the collar. "Then what if I end up being last?"

"Last for what? The bathroom? When you stop and think about it, a lot of these things don't really matter in the long run."

She thought of Zoe's father, of how much it had mattered to him to be first at everything. First or best. Of how that never changed and what it led to. A shiver ran up her spine, and she shoved back a flood of memories.

As Zoe finished up in the bathroom that was built into the east corner of Josie's room when the house was about a century old, there was a familiar scratching on the bedroom door. Tidbit only scratched on Josie's door to be let out in the morning on the few days Myra slept in past six.

Zoe rushed over and let him in with still-wet hands. She dropped to the floor and buried her head and hands in Tidbit's fluffy fur, offering him a long string of adoration. Tidbit soaked up the praise but didn't let it deter his morning stretching routine, a good stretch of the hips followed by a downward-facing dog that accented the shortness in his legs and length of his back.

"Not so loud, or we'll wake everyone," Josie whispered, thankful that there were only two other people in the house today compared to the overflowing numbers of the weekend. "Let's get Tidbit out back. Then you can make all the noise you'd like."

Tomorrow, after Carter left, it would just be her, Myra, and Zoe again. After the fun of yesterday afternoon, the thought gave Josie a surprising twinge of disappointment. Even though her life seemed so much safer before he'd stepped into it, it would be quieter without him.

Too quiet, she thought before pushing it away.

Tidbit led the way downstairs, accomplishing the impossible task of making his descent look easy despite his squat legs and long body, and Zoe followed, holding onto the banister so she could hop down one step at a time. Josie trailed after them, attempting to lock in the sight as a memory on Zoe's first morning of first grade.

They were headed down the hall toward the back door when the swinging door to the kitchen pushed open. Carter stood in the doorway, and the sight of him sucked the breath from Josie's lungs. The way he'd tied one of the aprons around his hips, drawing her attention to his toned torso, didn't help. "Morning."

"Carter!" Zoe dashed forward and wrapped her arms around his waist in a bear hug. She buried her head against his hip and closed her eyes with the same exuberance as if she were hugging Santa.

"Morning, kid." He ruffled her hair when she stayed locked around his waist. "Ready for your first day of school?"

"Yep! I wanna be the first one to the bus stop." She ended her death grip of a hug and balled her hands into hopeful fists in front of her face. "Are you still making me pancakes?"

Josie's insides twisted at witnessing how much Zoe was idolizing him—at how much she was craving a father figure. *My dad left when*

I was so young. I barely have any memories of him, and I'm doing just fine. In answer to her thoughts, she found herself questioning how fine was fine.

"I made a promise, didn't I? And this is perfect timing. I was just wondering what you like in your pancakes."

"Chocolate chips and bananas." She clasped her small hands together. "Can I help?"

He looked Josie's way. "So long as your mom doesn't mind."

Josie offered a one-shoulder shrug. "Sure. I didn't think you were awake yet. I was going to hop in the shower after I let Tidbit out."

After a quick sniff of Carter's ankles, Tidbit had planted himself by the back door; his ears were perked forward, and his tail wagged to the pulse of the second hand of a clock. Josie bet that, even more than Tidbit needed to pee, he wanted the early-bird chance to chase the two feral cats that had been hanging around the backyard when it was empty. No doubt they were hunting sparrows and mice drawn in by crumbs missed by twice-a-day terrace sweepings.

Carter's gaze brushed over Josie's thigh-length nightshirt and legs without lingering long enough to be brazen. "Take your time. We've got this. Tell me first, how do you like your pancakes?"

"Um, anything you two decide is fine by me."

"Then I'll go with my specialty and surprise you."

There was something in his gaze, something just a bit flirty again, and Josie did her best to ignore it. She reminded Zoe to cover her new clothes with her apron, then headed outside with Tidbit. The temperature had dropped lower than she'd expected last night. The cool wash of air blanketed her skin like a damp cloth, causing a shiver to run up her spine.

The feral cats were nowhere in sight. After a full circle of the yard and scent-marking on half a dozen plants and trees, Tidbit was ready to head back inside.

Through the swing door, she could hear Zoe giving a play-by-play of all the things she'd learned about her school day when they'd met Ms. Richards last week. Josie pushed the door half open and offered a reminder that she'd be upstairs if Zoe needed her, then headed up to her room.

Probably hoping some scraps of food would hit the floor, Tidbit opted to stay behind and sprawl out near their feet.

She savored a bit more time in the shower than normal, knowing Zoe was occupied. Afterward, she dressed and was about to head back down when she paused by Myra's cracked bedroom door. Hearing a soft shuffling, she pressed it open and headed in.

"Morning. Sleep okay?"

"As well as these bones will grant. What's that smell? Bacon?" Myra asked as she tied her robe shut.

"Yeah, I'm guessing. Carter's making Zoe pancakes."

"Pancakes and bacon. What a treat. I haven't been this hungry in days. Nice man, isn't he? Handsome too."

Myra's tone was just pointed enough that Josie rolled her eyes. "Myra, you're like plastic wrap, you're so transparent. He leaves tomorrow, though, so you might as well quit while you're ahead."

"Didn't he tell you he's staying longer? A few weeks at least?"

Josie had been fiddling with Myra's statue of Ganesh that rested atop the side table, which seemed a touch ironic next to Myra's worn family Bible. She froze with the tip of her finger on the elephant trunk. "No. Why on earth would he do that?"

"Because I've hired him. He's freelance, after all."

Her chest constricted enough that she struggled to take a full breath. "Myra, that doesn't even make sense. He's a writer, not a handyman."

"If I needed a handyman, I'd hire Stan from the market. What I need is a writer, and lo and behold, a writer shows up at my door."

"If this is a joke, it isn't funny. I haven't heard you say a single thing about wanting to hire a writer."

Myra pursed her lips. "Some of the things we need most, we don't even know we need until they're upon us."

Carter couldn't stay another few weeks. Not even a few more days. "Myra, he *can't* stay. Haven't you seen how Zoe's all over him?"

"That's a good thing, if you ask me, and if you remember, I've raised a few children too."

"And when he leaves, and it crushes her to pieces, then what?"

"We'll cross that bridge if we come to it."

"No, Myra, we have to cross it now, for Zoe's sake. He's a *New Yorker*. He isn't going to stay. And what's that going to do to Zoe when he leaves?"

"I invite you to consider whether you're talking about Zoe or you." After a direct look that said they were both thinking of a different New Yorker who'd proven to have no staying power in Josie's life—Josie's father—Myra added, "And as I said, my instinct tells me we should cross that bridge when we come to it."

"Life isn't that simple, Myra." Josie lowered her voice even though they couldn't be overheard downstairs. "Besides, what if he starts poking into an entirely different story than the one that brought him here?"

"I trust it'll be in your highest good if he does," Myra said with a characteristic wave of her hand. "And life *can* be that simple when it comes to matters of the heart."

Josie growled in exasperation. "Myra! Are you even listening? I don't want you playing cupid. That man downstairs isn't for me. If we aren't careful, Zoe could get trampled on in the process of you figuring that out."

Myra straightened. "Zoe's tougher than you're giving her credit for. And I know what I'm doing, Josie. Trust me."

Hot anger flowed through her veins. In five years, she'd not fought with Myra. Not even once. And now this. "I'm not having this conversation."

She stalked out of the room and closed the door harder than she meant to. She stood in the hallway, sucking in several deep breaths, angry at Myra, angry at Carter, angry at herself the most, only she couldn't piece out exactly why. Tears burned against her eyelids for the second morning in a row, but she blinked them away.

Feeling more acutely isolated from Myra than she had since her arrival, her knees nearly buckled underneath her. The smell of bacon and pancakes and the sounds of laughter rose from the kitchen, filling the hall with a touch of home that Josie realized wasn't really hers to claim.

An almost imperceptible frown formed on Zoe's face as she saw she was nowhere close to first in line for the bus stop. *You're just like your father*, Josie almost blurted out. He hated being last at anything. But she never talked to Zoe about her father. Not yet, anyway. How could she when the truth was so complicated?

Zoe's frown settled in deeper, but she kept it together. "It was a good trade," she mumbled more to herself than to Josie. Her delicate eyebrows knitted into peaks as she watched the older boys chasing each other in circles, having dropped their backpacks to mark their places in line.

"What was a good trade?"

"Everything back home. For being last."

Her voice was so soft, it tore through Josie. She slipped her hand around Zoe's small, moist one, and nodded to a group of one father and several mothers she had no intention of chitchatting with. "Those pancakes were good, huh?"

Carter had made two batches. To the first, he added bits of crunchy bacon. The second batch was Zoe's favorite, chocolate chip and banana. He'd turned hers into objects. A horse. A dog. A school bus. Even a pencil that had reminded Josie of a penis. "You understand he'll leave in a few weeks, don't you, Zo?"

Zoe dropped her hand. "I'd like it better if he'd stay."

"His life is elsewhere. He has his own home. Just like we have ours."

"He's gonna help me build houses for the fairies in the garden."

Swallowing back a comment, Josie changed the topic to Zoe's day ahead. In the distance, she heard the low drone of a bus, and a tidal wave of anxiety washed over her.

Her thoughts flashed back to the bus ride that started her and Zoe on this journey here to Galena—to Myra and the tea garden. Now fully in the memory, Josie's back itched in anticipation of a searing pain she never actually felt.

Zoe had been so impossibly heavy in her arms when she'd spotted a city bus a few blocks ahead, innocently loading the last waiting passengers. In a moment of wild desperation, Josie had made the decision to run for it. She'd broke from cover behind the cars where she'd crouched moments before and dashed for the bus, Zoe's tears starting up fresh. There'd been yells in the distance and the rapid popping of gunfire.

Dredging up every ounce of strength, Josie ran even when she thought she couldn't run anymore. The doors of the bus pulled closed when she'd reached fifty feet of it, but she kept running. Panic had washed over her as the bus started to pull away. She'd screamed as loudly as her spent lungs allowed.

Thank God someone inside had spotted her. The bus lurched to a stop, and the doors opened. Josie flew on, up the steps, and the bus pulled into motion a second time. That was the beginning of her journey here. To this place. To this world that was so different than the one she left behind.

When Zoe's bus rounded the corner, Josie's lungs were all but locked up, and her hands were shaking.

We're safe now, she'd told herself a thousand times since. Even if someone was still looking for them, she'd broken all ties to her past. To Los Angeles. To the few people she'd once loved so unconditionally.

The school bus came to a stop in front of them. Josie's palms broke out in a blossom of sweat when Zoe got into line without so much as looking at her.

"Hey, I almost forgot." Josie pulled Myra's point-and-shoot camera from her back pocket just as the line of kids began to move. "How about a smile first?"

When their eyes met, Zoe's plastered-on smile became a real one. Her missing front tooth tugged at Josie's heartstrings. Her hands were shaking so wildly, it was all Josie could do to snap a couple pictures. "I'll see you on the flip side, Zo."

"Bye, Mom."

The doors closed, and the bus pulled away with Zoe waving to her from the second window from the front.

After it turned the corner, Josie let out a breath she hadn't realized she'd been holding. She didn't need any reminders to know she'd forever be indebted to a driver whose name she'd never learned and a city bus that had arrived twenty minutes behind schedule.

Chapter 11

CARTER ITCHED WITH ANTICIPATION as Myra joined him at the far edge of the patio. It seemed she was ready to share what she knew of her mother's connections to his grandfather. But she wanted Josie with them when she did. Close to half an hour ago, they'd heard a school bus in the distance, but Josie hadn't gotten back yet.

While waiting, he'd been writing and soaking up the early morning sunlight. A pair of tabby cats, one orange and the other gray, had been hunting in the big yard. While they were too wild for interaction, they hadn't been deterred for long by his presence on the patio. After watching him for a bit and flicking their tails, they ignored him and went back to stalking the flower beds and occasionally chasing one another around the grass.

He had enough freelance work, including the new project Myra was giving him, to stay busy for a month, but his thoughts kept trailing to the murder mystery he'd completed a rough draft of a few years before. He'd been wanting to get back to it for a while now, but a full-length manuscript wasn't a quick turnaround on top of the demanding projects that kept him afloat. The longer he delayed it, the more the plot had been morphing. He'd intended to set it in present-day upstate New York, but now that he was here, he couldn't help thinking this sleepy town might make a better setting. It would be more work up front, but the idea of setting it during the Depression was becoming more intriguing too.

If he did set it here, he was going to write in a pair of mischievous feral cats. And maybe a red-haired, blue-eyed young heroine with a chip on her shoulder would be the one to find the body.

Or maybe not.

"What about calling her cell?" Carter suggested as Myra settled into the chair across the table from him. Tidbit, who'd followed her outside, must have caught wind of the cats because he abruptly dashed off into the yard as fast as his short legs would carry him. Carter had zero doubt in the cats' abilities to outrun him.

Myra let out a huff in response to Carter's question. "She doesn't carry one. Hasn't in the five years I've known her."

"Doesn't carry one or doesn't own one?"

"Doesn't own one."

"Huh." There were only a few reasons Carter could guess for someone Josie's age having no interest in a cell phone. Adding what he'd learned about her past to her standoffish demeanor, the likeliest reason was that she didn't care to be reached. This made him even more curious to find out what she was hiding. The longer he was here, the more Galena seemed to be a good place for burying secrets.

And for rejecting technology. How they ran a tea house with no Wi-Fi, he didn't know. He'd been using his phone as a hotspot when he worked on his laptop, which got him through, but the cell reception wasn't great either.

All of it combined really made him want to set a story here.

Pushing thoughts of the manuscript aside, Carter noticed a worn, leather-bound book on the table in front of Myra and read the title upside down. *Prayers for the Christian Housewife.*

Huh, he almost murmured again.

Noticing the direction of his gaze, she held up a finger. "It'll have a clearer meaning soon. But if you don't mind, I made a pitcher of lemonade. Will you carry it out? It's on the kitchen counter."

"Sure thing." Carter was pushing back his chair when the door at the back of the house opened and Josie stepped out. She must've stopped in the kitchen first, because she was carrying the tray of lemonade balanced over one hand, practiced from serving the tea garden customers. Tidbit, who'd just gotten comfortable at Myra's feet after his fruitless dash about the yard before the cats slipped through openings in the wooden fence, trotted over to greet her.

Myra let out a satisfied chuckle. "She knows my needs before I do, half the time." As Josie neared, she asked, "How was the bus? Did she make it on all right? No tears?"

"No tears," Josie said, with a nearly invisible shake of her head.

She lowered the tray and placed the pitcher and two glasses on it but paused before setting down the third glass. "I'm not much in the mood for lemonade. And I want to go for a jog."

Myra raised the prayer book high enough to draw Josie's attention. "I was hoping you'd sit with us. What I want to tell Carter, I'd like you to hear too. In fact, I suspect you'll be instrumental helping me shed light on something I've put off far too long."

"What does this have to do with your prayer book?"

"It was my mother's. I was only eleven when she died, so I can't say for certain, but I suspect she was an atheist, or perhaps a lackadaisical Christian with a derisive sense of humor. And oddly matched with my father in that regard; I can't remember him missing a Sunday sermon, even in the last stages of his life."

Carter's curiosity was piqued. The leather binding was old and branched with hairline cracks. Josie's curiosity must've been piqued too. She slid the empty tray onto the adjacent table and sank into the open chair between him and Myra.

Myra looked like someone about to dive into untested waters. "I've ignored this book's contents too long. Had it not been for you coming here, Carter, I'm not sure I'd have gotten the courage to unearth this uneasy bit of my family's past."

"I don't understand." Josie looked between them. "What could your mom's prayer book have to do with Carter's grandfather?"

"That's about to make sense." Myra ran her fingertips over the smooth leather. "She entrusted this to me shortly before she died. 'For another time,' she said. 'When you're older.' But the older I got, the more I kept putting it off. So, here I am. A bit later than she might've anticipated. I'm hoping it doesn't matter how old we are when we learn these lessons as much as it matters that we learn them."

When neither Josie nor Carter had a reply, Myra opened the book.

"Have you seen your grandfather's picture, son?"

"Yeah, back when I was a kid. He looked a lot like my father."

Myra flipped open the back cover and tenderly pulled at the seam. Carter sat forward in his seat in anticipation as he realized a secret pocket had been sewn into it.

"She took such care to hide them that I knew this photograph and letter had to be of great importance to her." Myra pulled a thin stack of folded paper from the hidden pocket. With a slight tremor in her hands, she opened the yellowed paper to reveal an angular, handwritten cursive trailing across an unlined page. As she did, a tattered, sepia-toned photograph fell onto the table, landing right-side up.

A gasp escaped Josie, who had a better view.

"It's startling, isn't it? One day, several years before she died, I caught her looking at this photo. Tears were streaming down her cheeks, and afterward, she took to bed. When I asked why she was sad, she said she'd lost something dear to her." Myra passed it over for Carter see. "Carter, meet your grandfather as he must have looked when he came to Galena. The genes he passed on must certainly have been dominant ones."

Carter stared at the picture in silence. It was a photograph of a man about his age, from the chest up; a slight hint of a smile curled the man's lips. A chill passed over him, snaking down his spine. The fact that this man may have died from a few shots in the chest and then been dumped in the river suddenly carried a bit more significance. "You'd be hard-pressed to deny the resemblance."

Myra humphed. "It's an uncanny likeness to say the least."

Shaking his head, Carter passed the picture to Josie for a closer look. A flush colored her cheeks as she studied the picture. "How old do you think he was when this photo was taken?"

"Early thirties, most likely, if it was taken here," Carter answered.

"The photo is yours to keep, Carter," Myra said. "I committed it to memory in my youth after this book was passed on to me."

Josie offered it back to him without meeting his gaze.

"Thanks, I'll give it to my father."

"As for the letter, she went to some length to keep it hidden, sewing in a hidden pocket and writing in her native tongue in the event it was found."

"That letter is written in Italian?" Josie's tone relayed the surprise Carter felt.

"Yes, and it's addressed to me. I rarely heard her speak it, but she learned the language as a child. Her parents immigrated here when she was a baby."

"May I see it?" Josie asked.

"Of course." Myra passed it her way. "It's my hope you're the key to helping me unlock whatever it is my mother wanted me to know."

Carter watched Josie's eyebrows knit together as she studied the writing.

After a minute passed, she offered Myra a pointed look. "Are you sure you want to do this?"

"Very sure. Whatever secrets that letter holds, it'd be my honor if you could bring them to light."

"You're fluent in Italian?" Carter was as surprised by this as he would've been to discover she had a second career as a software engineer, given her lack of enthusiasm for technology.

"Not fluent, but I can carry on a conversation." Josie flipped through several more pages. "I'm better at speaking it than reading it. Still, I can understand this, most of it. I'd need an Italian dictionary for some parts, but I could translate it fairly easily. So long as you're certain you want to know, Myra. No matter what it says?"

"Yes," Myra said with a nod. "The disservice in not knowing all these years has been to me as much as it has been to her." Myra looked back and forth between them. "So, where do we go from here? A trip into town to buy Josie an Italian dictionary and an afternoon to see what she can come up with?"

"The trip into town isn't needed," Carter said, pulling up an Italian to English dictionary and sliding his laptop Josie's way.

"That's it then?" Myra's tone carried a bit of incredulity. "A few hours of Josie's time and a computer, and my mother's longest-hidden secrets will be unearthed?"

Carter ran two fingertips over his lower lip. "Your call."

Myra nodded more to herself than to them. "I'm ready. Finally. My mother's words have waited a lifetime to be heard. And, Josie, I was never one to coat my medicine with sugar. Whatever it says, it says." To Carter, she added, "Whatever becomes of this, I trust our newfound friendship can prevail, don't you?"

Carter went over to help her up, trying not to pay attention to how thin and frail she seemed. "Myra, I respect the hell out of you, and nothing in this letter could change that."

"Then so it shall be. Josie, no rush. My bones are aching this morning. A short rest may do wonders."

As Myra headed for the house, Carter stepped to the side of Josie's chair. "Want me to show you a few things?" he asked, leaning over her. "Since it seems technology hasn't made it to High Street quite yet." Damn it anyway that he couldn't keep his desire for her in check. He couldn't put his finger on what exactly it was, but he was flayed open by her.

"I know how to search the internet." She gave the slightest shake of her head. Maybe she was trying to pull back that tiniest hint of flirtatious response that seemed to slip out in response to him. The one that awakened a slumbering fire inside him. "But thanks for the use of your laptop."

He shrugged and reached over her for the photo. "Help yourself. I'll leave you my phone so the internet will work. So, you think I look like him?"

"If anyone but Myra had pulled out that photo, I'd have bet it was a hoax."

"Yeah, well, considering he met a watery grave here, let's hope that bit about history repeating itself isn't true."

Chapter 12

THE CRATES SAM AND Nico took from behind the bakery were stacked to the ceiling. They had been used to create a wall through the center of Josie and Sam's bedroom, leaving a narrow entry space on one side.

Staring at them, Josie frowned. Once the sheets were fastened on, one side—the windowless one—was going to be a cave. "If you two are going to do this to my room, I'm going to need the window."

"You can't just call the window. It's my room too."

Nico had pushed the creation of the wall even more than Sam. Josie was thirteen; Sam was twelve. Nico insisted Josie have privacy, and Sam, who'd announced last week that he'd found the first hairs on his privates, agreed.

"If the window was in the middle, you could share it, but it's not, so you're going to have to decide who gets it," Nico said.

"If the window was in the middle, these god-awful crates would cover it completely." The idea of sleeping in a makeshift twelve by six–foot room was getting to her. "And I'm not willing to do something stupid like draw straws for something as important as a window."

"What, then?" Nico asked.

"I'll do your homework and laundry for a month." She knew Sam hated those two things more than anything else.

"A *month*?" Sam kicked at his mattress in protest. "No way."

"Two, then."

"A year. And not a day less."

Knowing she did the bulk of the work anyway, Josie agreed but made it seem as if she was relenting. "Fine."

Sam dipped his head. "You have a window, sis."

Wound up by his win, Sam tackled Nico, unsuccessfully attempting to take him down.

Josie left them to their wrestling and headed into the kitchen. Her stomach was rumbling loud enough to draw attention. She glanced again at the note her mother had left telling them to grab dinner on their own. Skye had a chance for a part in a sci-fi movie and was going to hang out with a few of the guys from special effects to see if they'd put in a good word for her. Not surprisingly, she didn't know when she'd be home.

Josie wadded up the note and tossed it into the trash can. Grab *what* for dinner? The kitchen was emptier than it'd been the day before when they had cleaned out the last of the Ramen Noodles.

They could go to Nico's. Francie would feed them. Like always. But Josie was tired of imposing on her and giving her nothing in return.

Having smashed her brother into a pancake, Nico walked in, his hair disheveled. Josie blinked away the tears brimming in her eyes. There was no fixing this. She and Sam were growing up in crappy public-assistance housing with a makeshift bedroom just a little bigger than a shoebox. Her mother was an alcoholic dreamer who'd never get her act together. And her father was never coming back.

"S'up?" Nico asked, yanking her ponytail.

"Just hungry."

"Liar."

Sam rounded the corner, shifting his shirt back into place. "What's there to eat? I'm starving."

"There's some tuna and crackers."

"You can put that away." Nico leaned against the counter. "We're going out. My bro's gonna hook me up at his uncle's place. All the fried chicken I can eat. For free. You two can come."

"Why would he do that?" She searched his eyes for the truth.

"'Cuz I'm his homie."

"What do you have to do for it?" Not a day went by that Nico wasn't being hit up by an ever-expanding group of kids who'd dropped out of school and were turning to drugs—using and dealing. In the nightmares that woke Josie even from the deepest sleeps, he'd found their offers too tempting to resist and joined them. School was hard for him, all of it. The sitting all day, the homework, the rule-following.

"You wanna know what I have to do for it?" He leaned in so that their noses were almost touching. "I have to eat chicken, that's what I have to do. Now, you coming or not?"

Her empty stomach cramped in anticipation at the promise of freshly fried chicken. Besides, it might be worth the trip to see what Nico really had to do for it. "I'm coming."

They'd made it four blocks and were cutting through an empty parking lot when the shooting started. Sam had just spotted an abandoned baseball and dashed to the other side of the lot.

The bullets erupted from two cars on the street nearby. Josie felt like they'd stepped smack into the middle of a fireworks display, only instead of shouts of appreciation, there were screams of panic from people nearby. Bullets ricocheted everywhere, pinging against metal, shattering glass, and thudding into pavement.

Josie felt herself being shoved forward onto the asphalt, and her chin slammed against the ground. Searing pain ripped through her as her upper and lower jaw smashed together. Nico dropped on top of her, covering her and draping his arms over her head.

In a daze, she struggled to get free to find Sam. Nearby, a scream of fear turned into a scream of agony.

"Sam!"

Nico forced her to the ground. "He found cover," he yelled in her ear. "He's okay."

Sirens started up in the distance. Another burst of shots went off, then tires screeched as both cars raced away. An eternity passed. The sirens grew closer, dulling the agonized moans that sounded like a bizarre lullaby.

Nico rolled off her, and Josie was able to look around. Sam was crouched behind an abandoned car with his arms still covering his head, a baseball grasped in one hand. She looked at the street and saw the aftermath. Windows of storefronts were shattered. People were huddled where they'd found cover. A woman was bent over an old man who was splayed on the sidewalk. It didn't take any guessing to know how much pain he was in.

Standing proved too much. Josie leaned forward, gripping her knees. Blood from her chin dripped relentlessly to the ground.

The sirens grew closer, and Nico grabbed her arm, pulling her upright. Seeing her chin, he cursed. She brushed her free hand over it and found it covered in blood from a cut she couldn't feel.

"We gotta go."

Nico dragged her across the lot to Sam, who was still crouched behind the car. He yanked Sam to his feet. "We can't be seen talking to the cops or those guys will come for us later." Half-shoving, he led them down an alley and out of sight before the first police cars arrived.

It took forever for the shock to wear off and for Josie to realize what Nico had done for her. When it did, she was sitting on the couch in Francie's living room. The three of them were still alone, and not one of them had so much as thought about food since the shooting started.

Sam was planted on the floor, lost in a video game. He'd started up with it right when they came in, making Josie wonder if it was his way of processing what had just happened. *Or not processing it.* She sat on the couch watching him, thinking how the bullets in *Grand Theft Auto* didn't sound like the real thing. Her chin was swollen and raw, but the cut was small and hopefully wouldn't scar.

Nico sat next to her, not talking, not sharing whatever was going through his mind. Like always. He'd risked his life hoping to save hers. In the space of a single second, he'd made that decision. Before she'd even realized what was happening.

Josie dropped the ice bag from her chin and wrapped her hand around his wrist. "Promise you'll never do anything like that again."

"Like what?"

"Trying to save me and not you. That was so stupid."

"Of the three of us, you're the only one who got hurt."

She twisted to look at him face on. "I mean it, Nico. I couldn't live knowing you died for me."

From the floor below them, Sam pulled away from his game long enough to scoff. "Toss me some ear plugs, will you? You douchebags make me want to puke."

Nico whipped a pillow at him. "You're just pissed because I wouldn't have covered you if it'd been you next to me and not Josie."

For the first time since they'd met, Josie found herself wondering what she actually meant to Nico.

Chapter 13

IT TOOK LONGER THAN she anticipated, but Josie was able to translate every word of the four pages of precise, distinctive script in Abigail Moore's letter to Myra. She sat still after she finished, taking in the weight of what she'd translated. Her imagination was roaring like a wildfire and famished for more, and her mind was racing so fast she felt disconnected from her body.

She picked up the loose-leaf pages she'd written on and reread her freshly translated words, somehow hoping they'd answer more of her lingering questions.

My dearest Myra,

I envisioned telling you this over a cup of tea out in the garden after you had grown into a woman. In the face of my declining health, I cannot risk waiting. Yet, my pen freezes over the paper at the thought of telling you my most-guarded secret. If I don't, I fear you'll grow up on gossip and assumptions. When we are dust, we are nothing more than our children and our stories. You should know the truth of this one.

Searching for words to do this story justice, I gaze out the window at the gray and white of winter and remember a summer that was the most significant of my life.

Close to a year before it, I met the man my mother and father intended for me. I was fifteen. The man, Francis, wasn't much younger than my own father, and the idea of entering his bed was horrifying. Still, I knew the path expected of me; my father's fortune was dwindling even before the Depression came knocking on our door. If I wanted to live the life I'd been brought up to embrace, I would need to marry well.

But my body wasn't stirred by the promise of fortune. As our wedding date neared, I lived on stolen kisses under arbors and in quiet corners at parties. When I turned sixteen, at my parents' urging, I married your father. I was brought here to live in this house that has been in his family for so long. From the first day I laid eyes upon it, I loved this house and its gardens—far more than I ever loved any of those boys.

With the money that came to me by marriage, I began to dress smarter and had my hair styled as the women do in Bazaar. And I imagined every man, single and married alike, to be wildly in love with me.

By then, the Depression had stormed into Galena, as it had the rest of America. Shops and banks had closed. Homes were boarded up. Vagrant men, and even families, filled street corners. Bread lines were long, and not enough loaves available.

One summer afternoon, I was walking in town and spotted a newcomer sitting on a bench, his head and shoulders hung low. I paused, as was my habit—long enough to allow him to take in the shortness of my hem and the shape of my calf. He was handsome enough, though at the time, my only interest in him was that he looked my way longingly, even if only for a few seconds.

But he didn't, even when I circled back the opposite direction. I walked on, wondering what it would take to get the stranger's attention, to have him look at me as other men did. I wandered along the banks of the river and passed by him again in town on my way home. When he still didn't notice me, I spoke to him. He had the most remarkable eyes I'd ever seen. Bright blue-green and full of sorrow. He answered my question—I don't remember any longer what it was—and looked away.

A challenge rose within me then. I wanted this man to see me. He was handsome and young and broken, and in that moment, my life had a purpose again.

But who is there in our youth to tell us that, once some thresholds are crossed, life will be forever changed? Such are the big chapters of my life. Wife. Adulteress. Mother.

On my wedding day, my mother wrapped flowers in my hair and sprayed perfume on my wrists, but she spoke nothing of the ways of the heart. I doubt I could have stopped myself from loving him even if she had. Myron O'Brien, God rest his soul.

Myron needed work, and I needed a carpenter. The house always needed repairs; there were rooms that needed painting and papering. Bricks needed tuck-pointing.

My love for Myron grew like a puzzle coming together. The polite way he took his tea. How he stood in the rain one afternoon and turned his head and palms to the sky, the world around him glowing like a halo. The courteous nod of his head when our eyes met. The hint of a smile he couldn't suppress at certain jokes I told. The security I felt when my heel broke and he caught me up in his capable hands. The smell of his skin: soap, sawdust, sweat, and cologne. The hearty sound of his laughter the few times he allowed it to escape.

Soon, I experienced a yearning for him deeper than anything I had known. I cried myself to sleep believing there was no greater wrong in the world than keeping me from this man I had grown to love. As fate would have it, the day came when

I realized the man who'd become the center of my universe was also treating me as the center of his.

But if our love was fated, it was a shooting star.

By the time I realized I was pregnant with you, I was attempting to walk in two very different worlds. Your father, I think, knew about my love for Myron even before I told him. He was willing to forgive me for my infidelity so long as I never saw Myron again.

Gentleman that he was, Francis kept my affair quiet and allowed me the duration of my pregnancy to decide on my path forward. I spent those months reflecting on my choice. To raise you in this home, I would have to shut myself off from my heart. To leave Galena with the man I loved, I would have to walk away from the only life I had known. I would have to leave everything safe and familiar and never see my family again. Leave these comforting walls and the remarkable back-yard that's aglow with lightning bugs every July.

But love is an untamable thing. It grows like a vine and defies attempts to uproot it. Those months of my pregnancy, I didn't know which man your father was. My decision might have been easier if I had.

It wasn't until I held you in my arms for the first time and saw Myron in you that I knew. In that delirium of profound motherly love, I confided the truth to my mother, believing she would understand. I would leave Francis, leave Galena, leave my mother and father. Myron and I were meant to be together. You were meant to be raised by the man whose seed had created you.

But that was not to be. The next morning, I sent a letter to Myron at his room in town but received no response. I sent another letter and another. Days passed into weeks, and I began to fear he had abandoned me. Recovering from your birth as I was, no rumors of his disappearance reached my ears. Not until his body was found over three weeks later. The rumors that created became so thick, they pressed in through the windows and walls.

In a twist of fate, it was Myron's murder that enabled the man you know as your father and me to grow closer. I could tell you a hundred lovely things about Francis that I've learned in the days since, but I know there is no need. Your father—by nurture if not nature—is a good man, and you will know his worth and kindness without my proclaiming them.

Do trust, Myra, that your father had no hand in Myron's death. He was upstate hunting with my father when you were born a month early and Myron was killed.

I would never have believed who pulled the trigger had Myron's murderer not confessed to me. To this day, my mind races in disbelief that the woman who raised me to keep my back straight and elbows off the table and to triple knot my thread in cross-stitch, shot to death the man I loved. She claimed it was a bout of insanity, fed by the belief she was saving my life.

There was at least one witness to my mother's crime, a vagrant who helped her get Myron's body to the river in the dark of night. I can only assume she paid him well, because he never came forward despite a generous reward offered for information leading to the arrest of Myron's murderer.

You will have no memory of my mother. From the day of her confession until this one, I have never again spoken to her, nor will she have any role in your life after I am gone. Francis has promised as much. Yet, blood proved thicker than water; I did not turn her in for her crime.

This, my dearest Myra, is the story that weighs on me so

heavily. In the quiet of fall afternoons when the dry leaves salute the sky before dropping off their branches, I hear them whispering to me to tell you. I hear the same whispers in the wind that whips around the house in winter storms, and in the tapping of spring rains on the windows.

Two honorable men have enabled you to spend your care-free afternoons playing in the garden. One gave you life, the other offers you pieces of himself every day. Will you blame me for staying here in the wake of Myron's passing? Without Myron, I was lost. In Francis' willingness to forgive me and to love you like his own daughter, I found a friend who has carried me through.

In you, my dearest Myra, I found a love as great as the love I had for your namesake. I hope you will believe me when I tell you I would take every step again to bring you into this world.

For all else, I hope you forgive me.

Love,
Your mother

Knowing there was nothing to do but tell Myra the truth, Josie headed inside.

Myra was with Carter at the kitchen table. They were finishing off slices of leftover wedding cake, a lemon pound cake topped with buttercream icing, fresh mint, and raspberries that everyone had raved about.

"Hungry, dear?" Myra asked. "We debated bringing you a sandwich, but you seemed entirely transfixed. I thought best not to disturb you."

In the face of everyday conversation and leftover wedding cake, Josie felt like a bat who'd flown out of a cave into bright sunlight. "I'm not hungry right now, and I was."

"Well then, how'd it go?"

Your father isn't your father. Josie's mind was going to be reeling for some time. *The irony of it.*

"Was it difficult?"

"Not really. Some of the words threw me, but I was able to figure them out." She remembered the look on Nico's face when she'd asked him to teach her Italian. Skeptical but intrigued. They'd been friends for a few months, and she'd already picked up a handful of everyday words. Even though Francie had been in the United States since she was fifteen and was fluent in English, she preferred speaking her native language at home. Nico had learned it as a child when Francie was babysitting him.

"Your fluency in Italian, mind if I ask where it came from?" Carter asked, sitting back in his chair and wiping his mouth. There was an unmasked curiosity on his face that made her adrenaline spike.

"Rosetta Stone." Josie eyed him as coolly as she could. She'd played Two Truths and a Lie enough to know not to look away too quickly.

He cocked an eyebrow but said nothing.

"Well, shall we?" Myra asked into the silence lingering between them. "How about we join you on the patio?"

"Sure. I left everything out there."

Carter trailed out the door behind Josie. "So, how long did it take to reach complete fluency like that?"

"Not long. It was something I wanted to do."

As they took a seat, it occurred to her that translating those words and saying them aloud were two different things.

Myra placed a hand over hers. "I want you to give it to me straight. Word for word, as accurately as you can."

"I will." She cleared her throat. Carter and his grandfather—with their uncanny resemblance—had practically blended into one person in her imagination.

Moving the prayer book aside, she clutched the loose-leaf paper in hand and began to read. She hardly dared to pause, even when she read Myron's name aloud the first time and saw, out of the corner of her eye, both Myra and Carter shift in their seats.

When she finished, Josie locked her gaze on the lined paper in front of her. Reminding herself that she didn't bear any blame as a translator didn't relieve her guilt over being the one to bring this news to them.

"As she mentioned, my mother was just a few weeks shy of seventeen when she married my father," Myra said finally. "He was forty-one. Even back then, I'm certain their marriage was a scandal. But I don't know that I accept that she could be so certain of his lack of paternity based on one glimpse at an infant. Or that the wonderful man who raised me wasn't my father."

"It's possible she was wrong," Carter said, his tone soft and compassionate.

Myra wiped at a few stray tears. "My father was a good man. The kindest father, friend, and brother he could be. And he taught me to appreciate a good cup of tea. A cuppa, as he called it. To think he raised me so selflessly; I can only love him more."

Josie gathered the nerve to look at Carter. An uncharacteristic frown was visible on his face, but he said nothing.

"I'm sorry about your grandfather's fate," Myra said, looking at Carter. "To think his life ended at the hand of my grandmother, I can hardly grasp it."

"It isn't your fault, Myra. And it wasn't your mother's either."

"My parents are long gone, obviously, but Carter, those DNA tests I hear talk of, would they be able tell us if we're related?"

He nodded. "Definitely. If that's a step you want to take."

"If my mother's belief is true, it would make your father my half-brother." She placed a hand over Carter's. "And you my nephew. There's so much to take in right now. It may take me a few days to gather the courage, but most certainly, it's a step we should take."

Josie couldn't say why, but it seemed as if a rug was being swept out from under her. And she couldn't help but wonder if things were ever going to be the same again.

Chapter 14

CARTER MIGHT NEVER UNDERSTAND what led his grandfather to Galena that summer, but Abigail's letter had given him a bigger glimpse into Myron's life. The man Abigail described first seeing on the bench had been a dejected one. Carter felt safe to assume his grandfather had been weighed down by both his decision to leave his wife and child and by the people who'd lost their livelihoods after he'd closed the doors of a company who'd supported so many.

Only, what had made him stay here? Had Myron been pulled in by Abigail from the start, or had he been too ashamed to return home? Or something in between? Carter would never know.

And maybe it was because he was crushing on her, but Carter hadn't been able to get the image of Josie as Myra's young mother out of his head as Josie read the letter. Without meaning to, he'd memorized the exact light-red shade of her hair, the curve of her chin, the silky, clear sound of her voice, of her words, as she read. And none of this made it easier to digest the fate of his grandfather. Putting out his third cigarette only halfway through it, he headed up the sloping hillside and inside through the back of the house. Josie was in the kitchen at the sink, drying the glass pitcher from their lemonade.

Carter tossed his cigarette butts and the rest of his nearly full pack into the trash can. "If I don't stop this now, I'll be up to a pack a day in no time."

"I've heard that about how easy it is to get hooked again." There was a softness to her tone he'd not heard before. Not directed toward him, anyway. Maybe this foray into Abigail's hidden life would chip away at those walls of hers.

"Yeah, well, do me a favor, will you?" He worked to keep his tone lighter than he felt. "If I cave and bring another pack into the house, will you toss them for me, then slap me in the face?"

A small laugh bubbled out, and she shook her head. "Happily."

"I mean it, too, you little sadist."

"So do I." Maybe it was primal, and she didn't even notice, but he could sense her responding to his banter. She wanted him as much as he wanted her. The more he got to know her, the more certain he was. "But right now, I'm heading out for a run," she added, drying her hands with a towel. "If you succumb in a moment of weakness while I'm gone, I'll have to slap you later."

"A run? Want some company?"

Her eyebrows lifted in surprise, and she shook her head. "Uh, no, not at all."

Her tone was too light to put him off. "Come on, you could very likely be saving my life. If I can get back into jogging, maybe I won't cave into the nicotine cravings." When she seemed to be considering it, he added, "And if I go jogging alone, I could get lost and end up in the wrong end of town."

"There's no wrong end of town here," she said, laughing. "Besides, you just chain-smoked a half-dozen cigarettes. You aren't in any shape to run."

"Maybe, but I'm betting I've participated in more runs and tri-athlons than you have years on you. So, there's that. Even if it has been a while."

It took her a second to answer. "Fine, but when your lungs seize up, I'm not going to let you slow me down. I've got to change first. If you're set on this, you can meet me out front in five."

He winked. "It's a date."

Her lips pressed into a line for a split second. "No, it isn't. It's not even close."

While waiting for her to change, he headed out front. After walking down to the base of the front-porch steps, he turned to appraise the house. Was his grandfather's craftmanship still evident in places? Most likely, it was. After Abigail's letter, Carter could envision a young man who'd been as enthralled with the remarkable house—and the young woman within it—as much as he was.

But Josie wasn't married. At least, he assumed she wasn't. As secretive as she was about her past, she could be hiding anything.

When she stepped out of the house, her knee-length leggings and clingy tank had his imagination spinning into overdrive. She might not be a perfectly packaged beauty like Myra's mother seemed to have been, but he liked that even better. She'd not made any effort to catch his attention. It was the opposite, in fact.

But caught it she had.

He couldn't help but wonder what something between them could lead to. He hadn't come here to stay more than a night, two at most. Hell, he'd expected to be on the West Coast driving along Route 101 by now. But Josie and Myra and the house—the whole town, in fact—had a surprising draw. Enough to write off getting to California this year.

Still caught up in his grandfather's story, it didn't hurt to remind himself that he wasn't Myron, and Josie wasn't Abigail.

"You know, I wasn't kidding when I said I don't like company on my runs." She swept her red-gold hair into a ponytail. When he mocked being hurt and clasped his hand over his chest, her lips pressed into a tight line, but her stifled smile still lit her eyes.

"If you ask me, you might be too stubborn to admit what it is you really like. Maybe even to yourself."

"And I suspect *you're* so perfectly attuned to me that you have the answer?" She used the stair above her to tighten her laces. Her back and legs were long and had all the right curves, and he ached to close his hands over her hips. He was about to answer when she stood up again and held up a finger. "That was rhetorical, Carter. Let's go if you really mean this." She hopped down the rest of the stone steps and moved straight into a jog.

After a few strides, Carter matched his pace to hers. "Do you treat every guy who walks through your door like this?"

"No, but honestly, most of the guys who show up at Myra's tea garden are married, seniors, or gay. And the only thing they're looking for is a good meal and some harmless conversation about the tea, quiche, or the weather."

"Point taken."

For close to a minute, there was nothing but the sound of their rhythmic breathing and their feet hitting the pavement. The century-and-a-half old houses and towering trees above the bluffs made for a scenic jog.

"So, uh, about Zoe. To be honest, I can't quite figure out why you glare at me like I'm the devil incarnate when she's talking to me."

Josie sidestepped to avoid a puddle, and her shoulder brushed against his arm. After a silence long enough that he wondered if she'd answer, she said, "Before you came, it wasn't so obvious she was missing, you know, a father figure."

"And now that I'm here, you've realized you want the male influence in her life to be null?"

"You really are a New Yorker at heart, aren't you?"

"Because I call it as I see it? Look, I don't know what you have against New Yorkers, but as I said, I was raised in Texas. Once a Texan, always a Texan. I moved to New York when I was twenty. But none of this has anything to do with Zoe."

Ahead of them, a sprinkler was soaking the sidewalk. When Josie made no move to avoid it, he didn't either.

"She's had enough loss." She spoke quietly enough he almost couldn't hear her over the pounding of their feet.

Carter suspected that short confession was the most honest she'd been with him. "What if I promise to tread carefully? Maybe you didn't want me knocking on your door, but I'm here. And I'm giving serious thought to Myra's offer to stay on a few months. Maybe even through winter."

"Through *winter*?" She whipped around to look at him and caught a toe on an uneven slab of sidewalk. She would've gone sprawling if it wasn't for him locking a hand around her elbow to catch her.

"I thought Myra told you," he said after she'd found her stride again. The sidewalk was narrow enough that he had to jog a half step behind her in places. When he did, the smell of her shampoo or bodywash—something light and flowery—washed over his nostrils. "She's offered me the room as long as I'd like it. I've been thinking about using this as a sabbatical. I've had a rough half draft of a novel waiting for me for a couple years. Add that to the fact that I'm between apartments and looking to get away from at least one person in New York, and Galena seems like the perfect place to clear my head."

She shook her head abruptly, disrupting the rhythmic sway of her ponytail. Fueled by fresh fear or anger or excitement—whatever it was his words had stirred up—she picked up her pace. He forced himself to match it even though his lungs protested as she led them into a part of town he'd not yet explored.

"Thoughts?" he said into her silence several minutes later.

"What if Zoe gets attached? What happens when you leave?"

"I'm not just going to walk out the door one day and never look back."

Pain flashed across Josie's face, making Carter suspect his words had hit home in a way he'd not intended. She retreated into silence as she led them in a circle back toward Dodge Street, following the sloping road downhill into town and across the Galena River on the pedestrian bridge.

After another mile, they circled back toward town. Carter was more than ready to slow to a walk when he noticed Josie was heading straight for the Green Street Stairs.

"You've got to be kidding me."

"You can't be a runner *and* a smoker, Carter. You'll live longer if you choose the first."

"If I don't die of a heart attack first."

The smile she flashed made him step out of rhythm. "Run these steps every day, and you won't want to dig through the trash can for that pack of cigarettes."

The first twenty stairs were a killer. He'd walked them twice now, but jogging them was a different story altogether. How many steps did Myra say? Upwards of two hundred?

He made it close to six flights before he was forced to stop and catch his breath.

"Damn cigarettes. I can't believe I'm letting you outpace me."

"Take your time while I ignore that sexist comment," she called over her shoulder. "I'll wait for you at the top."

"If you don't see me in twenty minutes, call an ambulance, will you?"

"More runs and triathlons than my years, isn't that what you were saying?"

Most days, somewhere about two-thirds of the way up the Green Street Stairs, Josie's lungs started to burn like fire and her thigh muscles turned to cement and she was forced to walk the rest of the way up. Today, thanks to the extra adrenaline from having Carter on the run with her, she made it to the top with only a slight drop in pace. Her windpipe felt like it had been sucked dry from the exertion.

As she dropped to a walk to wait for Carter, stepping from the stairs to the sidewalk, a spasm of fear locked up her step at the sound of a long, low growl. Even breathless and with blood pounding in her ears, it was menacing. Fifteen feet ahead, a dog was blocking her path. And not just any dog. It was a massive animal, a hundred pounds, easily. It was sprawled across the sidewalk, panting. She couldn't think of the breed offhand but knew it was something similar to a Saint Bernard.

It wasn't the first time she regretted reading *Cujo* when she was twelve.

As she looked closer, she was startled to find a long streak of blood under his chin and matted blood covering one ear. She winced as she took in more cuts on his legs.

She was no expert, but it didn't seem like he'd been hit by a car. Maybe the animal was a stray and had gotten in a row with a pack of feral dogs. Or maybe he'd been fought by some asshole and then dumped and disregarded.

She latched onto the banister, pity and fear coiling her muscles into uneasy knots. Her taxed lungs constricted even more, making it a struggle to pull in air. Thankfully, Carter seemed to have found his stride again; she could hear him hammering out the last dozen steps. When she kept frozen in place as he reached the top, he stepped around her, following the direction of her gaze.

The dog had lifted its head off the concrete again and was watching them warily. Carter gave a light shake of his head and pulled his mouth into an "o" as he worked to slow his breathing.

"He might be feral," Josie said between breaths.

As if in response to her claim, the dog curled his lips back in a second, long growl.

"He's hurt." His attention still locked on the dog, Carter closed a hand over Josie's shoulder. "Look at those cuts. They're all over him. I'm betting...he was fought," he rasped.

With Carter at her side, Josie felt the truth of the safety in numbers expression wash over her, and her lungs began unclamping, making it easier to talk. "There are reports of feral dog packs around here sometimes. Either way, I bet he's dangerous. We should go down the way we came. If we meet someone along the way, we can have them call animal control."

"We can't leave him here. He needs our help. And he's friendly," Carter argued. "Look at those eyes. He's just scared...and hurt."

"He could be rabid for all you know."

"Hopefully not, but just in case, I'll make sure not to get bit." He gave her shoulder a squeeze before letting go. "Trust me. I'm good with dogs."

She clamped a hand tight over her mouth as he headed up the path, his steps slow and deliberate. When the dog pulled his lips back in a snarl, Carter continued to close the distance between them, talking low and easy all the way. Josie's hand went from her mouth to her eyes, loosely covering them. She wanted to warn Carter that he was going to end up with a series of rabies shots, but her throat had turned to cement.

"Hey, boy, easy there. Easy now," he chanted as he drew close.

When the dog went from snarling to something between whining and a growling, and Carter didn't withdraw, Josie mumbled under her breath, "Oh my God, I can't look."

"Easy, boy, easy there. Easy, now," Carter chanted. He sank to his knees, never having altered his pace or his tone.

Josie clamped her hands over her ears and turned away. Her muscles had gone as rigid as steel, like she was waiting for history to repeat itself. When nothing penetrated the muffled silence, she peeked their way again.

Her knees buckled and tears stung her eyes to find the dog quietly licking Carter's arm.

"He's in worse shape up close. We've got to get him some help." Carter's gaze was fixed on the dog, but his tone was so calm it blanketed her with reassurance too. "Go get my car, will you? And my wallet. It's on my dresser with my keys. My room's unlocked."

"I…I can't drive. Not really, anyway."

"A stick? Then get Myra's big beast and a blanket. She won't care."

"No. Not at all."

This pulled his attention her way. "At all?"

She shook her head.

"You've not yet failed to amaze me, you know that? Stay with him then, will you? I'll be back in a few minutes."

"Okay, but I'm not you; I'm not getting any closer."

"That's fine, but if he decides to take off, I'd appreciate it if you'd trail him." He rubbed the dog gently behind the ears before taking off at a jog toward Myra's.

Josie kept her distance as the stray whined after Carter, then lowered his chin to the sidewalk. He flicked his gaze between Carter and Josie until Carter was out of sight, then turned his full attention to her. He'd stopped growling at her, at least.

He was such a giant dog. Dark brown and black with patches of white and fluffy hair matted with blood. Staring at him, Josie noticed shadows from her past rising up, taunting her, blending with the dog in front of her and causing her to break out in a whole-body sweat.

In her mind's eye, her brother, a bundle of endless energy, zig-zagged in front of her as they headed down the sidewalk. He was maybe six or seven; she couldn't remember. Sam's laughter rang fresh in her ears.

She'd seen the approaching dog too late. His head was lowered menacingly as he watched Sam's spasmic flight. His owner, a hard-ened man with gold chains jangling around his neck, was wrapped up in a phone call. Too far away to stop him, she'd frozen in fear as Sam leaned into the stranger's dog, wrapping it in a bear hug.

Her brother's tinkling laughter melted into screams as the giant dog's white teeth sank into Sam's neck. Twenty-nine stitches and a series of rabies shots was what Sam's encounter with the dog had cost him. And scars that he wore with pride as he grew into a teen. And through it all, Sam remained a dog lover. She was the one who'd begun crossing the street when anything larger than a beagle headed her way.

A shudder raked through Josie, and her sweaty arms broke out in goosebumps.

Not all big dogs were dangerous. She knew that. But a feral beast who'd either been mutilated by his pack or fought and dumped could only be trouble.

As if the injured dog was reading her mind, a deep, guttural growl resonated through the air. Josie's brother's voice rose up from the swell of memories flooding her, telling her to relax. To let go. To trust.

"You were wrong, Sam," she said aloud. "You were wrong about so much. And look where it got us."

The dog whined at the sound of her voice and pumped his tail, as if beckoning her over.

"Not a chance, big guy. Carter's coming for you. You have no idea how lucky you are he came on this run." She stopped and swallowed, fighting back the deluge of tears that had been fighting their way to the surface for a very long time. "If it had just been me, I'd have gone the other way."

Chapter 15

AFTER THE PARKING-LOT SHOOTING, things between Josie and Nico got physical. Once the kissing and touching started, they had appetites for one another like a hot-burning fire, always needing to be fed another piece of wood. Except for going all the way, they did just about everything their hungry bodies could conceive. The older they got, the more creative they became.

Some days, Josie felt like she was standing at the edge of the ocean, bracing herself for a massive wave rushing her way. It wasn't so much Nico but the kids around them who were pressing in, changing things. The looks she got when he wasn't around, the comments… It seemed that, because she had a claim on Nico, everyone hated her.

"What's gotten into you?" Nico asked. He'd turned sixteen a month after Josie's fifteenth birthday.

They were in ninth grade and walking to school alone since Sam was still in junior high. From his grades to his attendance and behavior, Sam was spiraling downward without her in the same school to watch over him. He was smoking pot daily and drinking sometimes too. He promised he wouldn't do anything else, but he was so damn impulsive. Josie had nightmares about it.

With Nico, it was different. He smoked sometimes, but Nico liked control. Josie wasn't worried about him getting swept away in a moment of indulgence the same way she was worried about Sam. No, if Nico got involved with drugs, he'd be the one doing the sweeping.

"Girls," she replied after a pause. It was a one-word answer for a problem that was way bigger than one word.

"How so?"

"Things they say to piss me off. About you."

He nudged her with his elbow. "Go on. I wanna hear you say it. Every word."

"Shut up."

"You think I'd cheat on you?"

"What I think is that everyone hates me because I'm with you."

The playfulness in his expression fell as they neared the entrance. They walked the rest of the way in silence before a group of guys swarmed Nico, high fiving him. "'Sup, brah?"

A few hours later, Josie was still thinking about the best way to tell Nico all that was really bothering her. She was in the bathroom, trying to swipe a loose eyelash from the corner of her eye when she was cornered by a group of girls that she attempted to avoid like the plague.

There were six of them—ninth- and tenth-grade girls who, in Josie's mind, had similar odds of finishing high school as the earth did of being hit by a giant meteorite. Most of them were already using heavily and sleeping with guys who'd dropped out to sell drugs or who were in juvie.

But the one guy they wanted, the guy everyone wanted, in one way or another, was Nico.

Nico wasn't the only freshman taller than six foot with wider shoulders than the gym coach, but that didn't matter. With Nico, it was his presence. He was never going to take shit from anyone.

And Josie was the one person keeping him unavailable.

Josie had no doubt that each one of the girls was more than capable of kicking her ass individually. She turned her back against the sink and faced them. *Let this just be a threat. Please, please, please.*

She knew not to try for the door. Running would make it worse.

Isabelle, the leader, closed the distance between them, something close to evil blazing in her eyes. She was twenty or thirty pounds heavier than Josie and wore fake nails that looked like daggers.

"I never did anything to you," Josie spat.

"That's because all you do is sit around and do homework and think you're better than the rest of us. Well, you're not. And it's time you know it."

They started in on her at once, grabbing her hair and pushing her to the floor. They kicked her, tore at her clothes, clawed at her, and slammed her face onto the dirty tile. She fought back as best as she could.

By the time they backed off, Josie was barely conscious, and her body had gone numb except for the ringing in her head.

Isabelle shoved a phone in her face. "He's Jena's now, bitch. See for yourself."

Without moving her head—it had to weigh a million pounds—she looked at the photo on the screen. It was taken in a dimly lit room and centered on Nico. He was sitting on a couch, his eyes closed, his head tilted up to the ceiling. Even though it was almost too dark to make out, she knew what the girl kneeling in front of him was doing.

Isabelle gave her one last kick, and they walked out as silently as they entered.

Josie vomited on the tile floor. The heaving motion sent a searing pain over her torso, closing off her lungs. After that, she gave into the gray fatigue sweeping over her, the image of Nico burning into her mind.

Sometime later, she woke up in a hospital bed, a thick cloud of fog making it hard to process. Outside the window, the sunlight was so bright, it was painful. Attempting to cover her eyes, she realized two things: she was hooked up to an IV and scratches covered her arms. She could feel the same lines of itchy pain on her face and neck.

Her limbs went rigid as she remembered the girls closing in on her.

"Hey, sleepyhead." Her mom was in a chair beside her. Sam was sitting on the floor, texting someone on his phone. She struggled to sit up as her mom offered her a cup of water. "Are you thirsty?"

"Yeah, really thirsty."

Sam came over and sank onto the edge of the mattress, sending a dull wave of pain across Josie's ribs. "How much do you remember?"

"Enough." She sipped on the straw and winced. No doubt her lips were pulverized. "How long have I been here?"

"Since yesterday. You've been in and out of it. They've got you on some heavy meds."

"I feel like I'm in a fog. Everything's sort of numb."

"That's the meds," her mom said.

Josie brushed her fingertips over her face.

"Don't touch it, Josie." Her mom stopped her hand.

"How bad do I look?"

Skye looked down. Sam shrugged one shoulder, then dropped his gaze too. "Not so bad."

"Anybody got a mirror?"

After a pause, Sam pulled out his phone and snapped a picture. "Just remember, bruises heal. So do cuts."

"Your doctor said the scratches won't scar if you stay out of the sun," her mom said. "Considering it's January, you should be good. They've been putting creams on you all the time too."

Josie reached for the phone, but Sam paused, holding it just out of reach. "Maybe you should wait awhile."

"Sam, you're freaking me out."

Begrudgingly, Sam passed her his phone. It was a trick, she thought, staring at the blurry stranger on the small screen. Her lower lip was twice its normal size and split in two places. She had one purple-black eye and one green one. The bridge across her nose was swollen and exaggerated, making her look like the beast from *Beauty and the Beast*. Four long scratches ran down the length of her right cheek from temple to chin.

She fought off the urge to cry. "I guess you're not going to tell me I look like Rita Hayworth anymore, are you, Mom?"

Sam huffed. "You'll be good in a week. You're only here because your concussion was so bad."

Josie passed back the phone and closed her eyes. A thousand thoughts raced through her clouded mind, including how they'd ever pay for the medical bills.

Acting more like a typical mother than Josie could remember, Skye closed her hand around Josie's wrist, caressing her gently with her thumb.

"Those girls were suspended for a month, except Isabelle. She was expelled."

"What about Nico? Have you heard from him?"

Sam dragged his fingers through his hair. "Hungry? I'm starving. Want me to head down to the cafeteria and sneak you something better than the nasty Jell-O on your tray?"

"Sam, I'm not a four-year-old you can sidetrack with the promise of a piece of candy." She pressed a finger over her lips. Talking was splitting them open. "Where is he?"

Sam looked at her mom, and Skye shook her head. "She won't stop until someone tells her. But it's going to have to be you. I need a cigarette. I'll stop by the cafeteria on the way back and see what I can drum up."

"What happened?" Josie asked again as her mom walked out.

"Everybody knows about that picture. Even Nico."

Her stomach lurched. "I *hate* him."

"Yeah, me too." Sam sank onto the bed, stretching out his legs her direction. "This bed is about the only comfortable thing in this room. I think they do that so visitors don't stay too long."

"I wish pain meds could take away memories too."

"No, you don't. Don't say that. Think of mom, idiot."

"I guess you're right."

"If it makes you feel any better, I took a couple of good swings at him last night."

"It doesn't."

"He didn't even fight back. He just let me hit him, which kind of took the fun out of it."

"Where did you see him?"

Sam huffed. "He was here. Don't you remember? You were yelling at him to leave, but you were pretty drugged up. I told him not to come back. Ever. If it's the last thing I do, I'll get him back for hurting you."

For the first time, Josie noticed the knuckles of Sam's right hand were bruised and swollen. "It isn't your fight, Sam. It's mine."

"Yeah, whatever. If Isabelle wasn't a chick, she'd be dead right now. I heard that last night, Isabelle's guy, Ty—he dropped out a few years ago—well, he and Nico got into it. Nando says Nico put a knife in Ty, but I heard Ty showed up at work today, so who knows, you know?"

All Josie knew was that the world had never felt so dark. Eventually, she drifted off without knowing it and woke up some time later to find her mom and Sam gone. Her mom's tableside note promised they'd be back in the morning. With nothing else to do, Josie gave in to the fog hanging over her and dozed again.

When she awoke, the sky outside was dark, the lights were dim, and Nico was in the chair next to her. She inhaled sharply at the sight of him, sending a ripple of sharp pain across her lungs.

"What are you doing here?" Using her hands for support, Josie attempted to push herself into a sitting position.

"Don't," he said. He was on his feet immediately, offering support by grasping her under the shoulders.

"Don't touch me!"

He flinched at her words. After she was resting against the head-board, he let go and stepped back. "Yeah, okay."

"Sam heard you knifed Ty. Is it true?"

Nico frowned as he stared at her. "It kills me what they did to you. Those bitches. I should've killed every last one of them."

"Don't say that."

"Why? It's true. If they'd been guys, they'd all be dead right now."

"Shut up! You can't say that. You have no right to. Not anymore. You have no idea how much I hate you."

"I'm pretty sure I do. And believe it or not, that's good. They'll leave you alone now. I'll make sure of it."

"All this," she said, running her hand over her body and face, "this will heal, Nico. What will never heal is seeing that—that *picture…*"

He stopped her by leaning forward and pressing his lips against her forehead. "You *have* to hate me, Josie. It's the only way." He sat down on the bed, facing her, his movements considerably more careful than Sam's had been.

"*What's* the only way?"

"Promise me one thing, all right? You keep your head down and keep focused and get you and Sam out of here the first chance you get."

"What are you talking about, Nico? What are you doing?"

"My grandma, she loves you. You and Sam both. She'll take care of you. Whatever you need."

Josie pressed her palms against her temples as the pain resounded through her head. "Whatever idiot plan you've got cooked up, drop it."

"The thing is, I can't risk anything like that happening to you again. Ever." He leaned forward and brushed his lips against hers without applying pressure.

Josie turned her head and pushed him back from her. "Tell me what you're planning. *Please.*"

"There's just two more things I can tell you. The first—the first is that I love you. I have since you knocked on my door in the middle of the night back when I was too much of a kid to understand what it meant. I know you know it, but I thought you should hear it aloud in case you're tempted to forget it."

He stood up and dragged a hand through his hair. "I don't know if I should tell you to take care of Sam or Sam to take care of you, but I guess you've always been best together, anyway."

Josie wanted to run after him as he headed for the door, but she was hooked up to an IV. Besides, when Nico made up his mind, there was no stopping him.

"*So that's it?*"

He turned toward her and smiled a thin, foreign smile. His expression had become cold and impenetrable so fast it was startling. "No, there's still that second thing. That picture of Jena and me—you should know she wasn't the first. She won't be the last either. That's the thing about life on the streets, Josie. There's always bitches to keep you company."

Then he turned and walked out of her life completely.

Chapter 16

Josie shifted the purple gift bag from one hand to the other as she waited under the shade of a towering walnut tree that had dropped hundreds of ripening walnut husks along the road, grass, and sidewalk. The large group of parents who'd come to see their kids off this morning was absent this afternoon.

The only other people waiting were three moms huddled in a circle near the stop sign. Their voices were low and intimate, and Josie knew by their hushed "Nos!" and "I-had-no-ideas" that they were exchanging bits of juicy gossip. Aside from offering a quick hello, Josie had no interest in getting to know them better.

She recognized the trio from the tea garden. They'd lunched there several times last year while their kids were at school. Two of the women ordered the lowest-calorie offerings on the menu, complained about the taste as they ate, and rarely finished their plates. The third woman, who was hardly any less fit than the other two, ordered something carb-laden while profusely apologizing for her lack of willpower.

When the bus finally pulled around the corner, Josie scanned the windows for sign of Zoe. A weight lifted when she caught her beaming down from one of the front windows while the bus screeched to a lumbering stop. Zoe clambered down the big steps—her narwhal backpack making her look small and big at the same time—and Josie's throat grew tight.

"How's my girl?" She squeezed her. "I can't wait to hear all about your first day, you first grader!"

Zoe was grinning ear to ear when she pulled out of the hug. "I love Ms. Richards. She's the best teacher in the world! And she's so beautiful. And I have a best friend too."

"Oh, really? What's her name?"

"It's a boy. His name is Andrew. And he didn't have a dad, either, but now he does. He has a big sister too. I wish I did. Oh, and I got a green apple for being good." Zoe locked hands with her as they headed toward Myra's. "It's the opposite of the way I like them. You get a green apple when you're really good. A yellow one when you're sort of good. And a red one when you're bad."

Josie hoped that Zoe's summary was marred in translation, and the school made it clear it was the student's behavior that needed correcting, not that the child was "bad." "Well, good for you for listening and paying attention, Zoe."

"Everyone got a green apple today, but some of the boys should've gotten red ones. I told Ms. Richards that, and she said we should give them a chance, since it was everyone's first day."

"That sounds fair."

"Mommy, is that for me?" Zoe asked, eyeing the bag in Josie's hand.

"As a matter of fact, it is. Just a little something to celebrate your first day of elementary school."

Zoe reached for the bag and pulled the handles apart, peeking inside. Her eyes lit up as she pulled out a stuffed calico kitten Josie had bought last week and kept hidden for today.

Zoe hugged it to her body. "I love it the most of all my stuffed animals! I do, I do!"

Josie laughed as they neared the house.

A hint of a frown formed on Zoe's face as they neared the house. "Mommy, where's Carter?"

"He's out for a bit."

"I know, but where?"

"Errands. And how did you know?"

"His car's not out back. I could tell when the bus passed on that street. I can see from my window."

"I didn't know you paid attention to which cars were at the house."

"It's the best way to know if someone's here. Unless it's you, 'cuz you don't have a car."

"Huh, you have me there," Josie said as they headed up the front steps. "Myra's in the kitchen. She's making you the official after-school snacks she made for her kids."

Zoe whooped and flew up the last steps into the house. Leaving the door open behind her, she charged inside.

When Josie walked in, she spied tears twinkling in Myra's eyes as Zoe engulfed her slim waist in a hug.

"Eeewww! Is that celery?" Zoe said as she pulled out of the hug and spied the peanut butter and celery sticks with raisins that Myra had set on a plate next to a glass of milk.

"Nope," Myra replied. "Those are logs and they're carrying ants and you get to eat them all up."

Zoe wrinkled her nose. "I don't eat ants. Even if they look like raisins."

"How about you give it a try before you decide? After you wash your hands."

After washing up, Zoe puckered her lips but nibbled at one tentatively. After a few more hesitant bites, she began devouring them. "Try one, Mom."

"I had one before I left to get you. And I like them too," Josie said, taking another one.

"Did your mom make them for you?"

"No, but I've had them before. At friends' houses."

"What did your mom look like?" Zoe asked, crunching on a celery stick and cuddling her stuffed kitten close to her with her other hand.

"Like me, I guess. Just older. That's what everyone said who knew us." She tensed at having to answer so coolly. Zoe knew Josie's mom was in heaven, but that was as much as she'd been told.

Zoe's gaze flicked to Myra. "I'm glad Myra looks like Myra. I wouldn't want her to look like you."

"I wouldn't mind," Myra said. "Your mother is beautiful."

"So are you, Myra," Zoe said, wiping a dab of peanut butter onto her new pants before Josie passed her a napkin.

A car rumbling onto the parking pad next to the detached garage at the back of the house caught their attention. Leaving her kitten on the table, Zoe ran outside. Josie crossed to the window as Zoe yelled out Carter's name and dashed across the backyard. When she didn't stop, Carter caught her in his arms. He even planted a kiss on her forehead. Watching it stabbed Josie's heart.

"Myra, it's only been four days and look at her." Her fingers gripped the edge of the sink. "I tried to talk to him, but he doesn't get it."

"Have you considered that maybe he just sees a potentially different outcome to all this than you?"

Josie shot her a look of desperation. "Even if he does, it doesn't mean he's right."

"I'm sorry, Josie, but he's welcome to stay as long as he has a mind to. I can see the good in it, even if you can't."

When she looked out the window again, Carter had the blanket he'd wrapped the dog in under one arm. His free hand was locked around Zoe's as they headed toward the house.

"I know you're concerned, but I'm asking you to trust me." Myra placed a hand on her shoulder, and all Josie had time to do before Zoe and Carter filed into the kitchen was offer a defeated nod.

It was Myra's house. And even without a DNA test to prove it, Carter had just as much claim on Myra as she did. Like it or not, he was going to be a fixture here as long as he wanted.

And the thing was, a part of her *did* like it. More than she wanted to admit.

Carter was filling Zoe in on the story of the dog in an edited-for-a-younger-audience way, and her eyes were big and round as she listened. Josie and Myra waited as he caught Zoe up to speed and then started to talk about what he'd learned at the emergency vet clinic.

"He's got cuts and bruises, but it's likely he wasn't a stray. His weight and muscle tone are good." Carter's bright blue-green eyes settled on Josie. "The vet suspected it's the scenario we thought of."

So, some asshole had fought his or her dog and dumped him. Josie wasn't convinced there was a hell beyond what some people experienced on earth, but if there was, she hoped there was a special room for people who intentionally hurt children and animals.

"He's sweet though," Carter added. "Mild tempered like the best of them. No wonder he wound up like he did."

"What's going to happen to him?" Zoe and Myra asked in unison.

"Well, he's there a few nights, most likely. He needed over sixty stitches, and they want to make sure he didn't pick up a virus from another dog. The office staff is going to be on the lookout for anyone claiming to have lost a Bernese mountain dog, in case he was yanked out of a yard or something, which happens. If no one's found, it'll be up to me to take him, or he'll go to a shelter."

"Can *we* keep him, *please,* Myra?" Zoe begged, clasping her hands in prayer.

Tidbit looked up from his cozy spot on his bed and barked, as if he understood what was on the table.

"No, Zo," Josie answered on Myra's behalf. "I know you'd love a dog of your own but, trust me when I tell you, this isn't the one. Besides," she said, looking pointedly at Carter, "Carter isn't staying forever, and I'm betting he wouldn't want a dog that size in New York."

"You never know," Carter said, refusing to take her lead. It took her a few seconds to realize she didn't know which part of her claim he was answering, the forever part or the New York part. "But I wouldn't mind giving him a shot—so long as he stays as gentle as he was today, which I'm betting he does."

A short silence fell over the kitchen, and Zoe looked around at all three of them, trying to determine if things were playing out in a way that might bring a second dog into their home.

"If he stays as gentle as you say he was today," Myra said, breaking the silence, "I'm fine with you figuring out what's in the dog's best interest, and in yours. But if he's as big as Josie says, he won't be able to roam the grounds the same way Tidbit does while customers are here. We have paying guests to think of, and not everyone is a fan of large dogs." The way Myra's attention turned toward Josie at the end, it was obvious who she was referring to.

"It's hard to be a fan of big dogs when the last one you came across nearly took…someone's head off."

As soon as the words were out, Josie clamped her lips shut. She almost said Sam's name. She never mentioned him aloud. She hardly allowed herself to think of him anymore. She needed to find the courage to start though. No matter how badly it tore her apart. Zoe was getting old enough to learn the truth. Old enough to start hearing his stories.

Just not today.

"Look, Josie, whatever experience you had, I'm sorry, but this dog…trust me," Carter said. "I know dogs, and this one is going to be spectacular."

There was a look of compassion on Carter's face that created a knee-jerk reaction in Josie. She did her best to swallow back the wild storm inside her that made her feel like her insides were full of shaken-up carbonation. "From just one meeting? You're honestly going to tell us you know everything important about him in that short of a time?"

"Yeah, I am." For the second time in a few minutes, Carter's remarkable blue-green eyes were drilling into hers. "Sometimes that's all you need to learn the important stuff."

Chapter 17

A STORM WAS ROLLING in; Carter could smell it in the wind. It would be his first one in Galena, and he wanted to savor it but was fighting off a tidal wave of fatigue after a late night writing. After pressing Save, he closed his laptop and sat back in his chair on the lower terrace where he'd taken up residence most of the afternoon the last several days. He couldn't decide between heading into town for a large cup of coffee and heading upstairs for a quick nap as the storm passed over.

A glance around the patio showed the last of the diners had spotted the dark clouds to the west and were finishing up their lunches. Josie, Linda, and one of the servers were collapsing the table umbrellas and collecting cups and dishes.

Carter stood up and closed the umbrella at his table and neighboring ones too. As he did, he spotted a glimpse of one of the stray cats in one of the flower beds down the hill. He'd been leaving small handfuls of Tidbit's food at the bottom of the yard where they seemed to hang out most. Carter had gotten within five feet of one yesterday evening, but a noise had scared it off at the last second.

"You're making friends who will miss you when you leave," Myra had said. She'd been referring to the cats but, quite possibly, not only them.

Vacations weren't meant to last forever. Even knowing this, Carter was leaning toward unpacking the last of his things and staying on like he'd told Josie he would. There were a thousand things he loved about New York. And there were a thousand others he longed for that evaded him in a city with over eight and a half million people, like the quiet expansiveness he felt in the vicinity of more trees and animal life than people.

The small-town upper Midwest might not be the sprawling plains of the west Texas of his childhood, where the most populated thing around was the star-filled night sky. But he experienced a peace here that eluded him in New York. Back there, he'd been so busy living, he thought it hadn't mattered. In the never-ending buzz of the city, he was productive and focused. It took stepping away to realize that came with a cost.

Three months ago, he'd missed a train at lunch and had a dead cell phone and decided to walk the twelve blocks from his client's back to his apartment on West Tenth. During that thirty-minute walk, he sidestepped to avoid a puddle and ended up glancing through the window of an Indian restaurant. He was stunned to spot Katherine at an undersized table for two having lunch with her old boyfriend.

Even though they'd never met, Carter knew right away who the guy was. He'd seen a dozen pictures of him on Katherine's social media accounts in the early months of their relationship. The prick had his hand over hers, and she was smiling and staring into his eyes and not pulling away. And Carter knew in an instant that things between him and Katherine had been over for months, though neither of them had had the courage to acknowledge it.

He'd kept walking, not because he was afraid to make a scene and bust up their rendezvous; he needed to process all the shit he'd been shutting out that was suddenly rushing at him like a freight train.

She came home late that evening and he confronted her. Eventually, she admitted to cheating on him that very afternoon. Her excuse was that things hadn't been the same between the two of them for a while, but she wasn't entirely sure she wanted to break off their engagement. They still had something; didn't he think so?

Carter didn't.

After she'd taken off to find somewhere else to stay for the night—her old boyfriend's, he had no doubt—he'd gone to the drugstore for a bottle of Jack and a pack of cigarettes. A few weeks of walking the city and letting in thoughts he'd been too busy to acknowledge, and he knew he wanted—needed—to get out of New York for a while. Quite possibly forever. Rolling up his sleeves and helping his dad find out more about his grandfather had seemed like a perfect distraction while he figured out what he wanted to do next.

And all of that had led him here. To this place that seemed to be lagging behind in time by a few decades. To Myra. The tea garden. Zoe. And Josie.

He was done smoking now. Done being angry at Katherine. Done with her altogether. Ready to get on with his life.

And part of figuring out what that entailed included getting a handle on what he was feeling for Josie. And what she was feeling for him.

He'd not planned on meeting anyone. Not for a long time, and certainly not in this backwater town. But he couldn't escape the thought that he'd sidestepped that puddle and looked into that window a few months ago for a bigger reason than he'd first realized.

When he wasn't writing or interviewing Myra and sitting in awe of her strength and her dynamic life, he was either in town searching for mention of his grandfather in the Galena archives, convincing Josie to let him tag along on one of her afternoon jogs, or playing Uno with Zoe after school.

And he wasn't eager for any of it to end.

The reopening of the tea garden proved interesting. There was Mr. Lange, the neighbor who poked around in the garden every morning, deadheading flowers and trimming plants, then wandered up the hillside for an early free lunch. Carter ate lunch with him on Wednesday and was intrigued enough by Mr. Lange's eccentricities to want to put him in a novel.

It was something Carter could count on, the way a dozen things a day presented themselves as story fodder. In Mr. Lange's case, it was the meticulous way he both gardened and ate his lunch, quiche lorraine with half a grapefruit, five days a week.

The whole place proved to be a bit of an anomaly, and an intriguing one.

On days with the nicest weather, the tea garden sold out of the most popular items on the menu before closing. No one seemed to care that, with a little more effort and preparation, they should be able to considerably increase their profits.

There was a plus side to selling out each day, Carter was beginning to realize. He was doing his arteries a favor by not getting in the habit of eating leftover quiche for dinner every night. And as he became intent on extending his stay beyond the end of summer, the more important that was. It wouldn't do to eat like he was on vacation indefinitely.

While she'd seemed against his staying on at first, as the week passed, Josie seemed to be laying down her guard a bit. She'd been letting Carter jog with her, and earlier, when their hands brushed as she handed him a glass, she'd not jerked away like she had the first time or two they'd touched. She was also including him in conversation, looking at him more, laughing at his jokes here and there.

Baby steps, he reminded himself as he gathered his computer and slipped his paperwork into his laptop case. *Baby steps to what?* He didn't know the answer. The only thing he knew with any certainty was that his questions about her were still lining up like dominoes. And the more there were, the more he was drawn in.

An attention-grabbing rumble of thunder rolled across the darkening skies. Deciding to hold off on the coffee, Carter headed upstairs. He'd doze a bit but not long enough to miss heading out for a jog with her, so long as the rain let up in time.

Josie curled up on her bed after changing out of her rain-wet clothes, listening to the angry storm. If there wasn't a pile of work waiting for her downstairs, she'd lie down until it passed, letting her mind wander wherever it wanted, even if that meant to thoughts of Carter.

Finally, knowing the money wasn't going to count itself, Josie headed downstairs to tally the day's receipts and compare them to the cash and checks on hand. How long they'd be able to get by as a cash- or check-only restaurant, she wasn't sure. Most of the customers her age kept trying to pay with their phones. And hardly anyone carried a checkbook anymore.

Carter stepped into the kitchen when she was halfway through counting.

"You going for a run before Zoe gets home?" He stifled a yawn as he joined her at the table, sinking into the seat next to her. Aside from Linda, who was in the pantry finishing inventory, the rest of the small staff had gone for the day.

Josie attempted not to notice how the back and side of his hair was just a touch disheveled like he'd been napping and how it was more than a bit endearing. "Does it look like it?" She meant for her words to come out more playful than they did. And possibly to make more sense. She was dressed in capris, a cornflower-blue tank, and tennis shoes. Clearly, she did look ready for her afternoon jog.

Carter didn't seem fazed. "Yes, but it's still raining. Hence the question."

"When it lets up," she conceded. The blowing winds and thunder and lightning had moved on, but a quenching rain persisted.

"Great. I'll join you."

She huffed. He wasn't even *asking* anymore. He'd run with her

almost every day this week. It was clearly getting to be a "thing."
"You know, my favorite time to run is after a storm passes. So, if you
don't mind, I'd rather go alone." She glanced up from counting for a
second to make a point.

In answer, he scooted his chair closer to hers and leaned over.
"You sure about that?" The feel of his breath on her neck made her
skin burn. "You know there's a dozen benefits to jogging with a
buddy."

"She isn't," Linda said from inside the pantry.

Josie pressed her eyes shut a brief second. Shouldn't Linda's
loyalty be to her, not Carter? In order not to lose count of the cash,
she scribbled on the register tape. Then, she scooted her chair so her
and Carter's shoulders were no longer touching. "Carter..." What
did she want to say?

With that devilish grin lighting his face, he scooted close again
and nudged her with his shoulder. "Want me to name them?"

A half snort escaped before she could pull it back. It wasn't flirting, she told herself, when she locked one hand over his shoulder
and the other on his waist in attempt to scoot him further away.
She giggled when she ended up pushing her own chair away in the
process and further from the pile of money.

"That's basic physics for you, sweetheart. I've got forty or fifty
pounds on you, at least."

"Carter, *pleeeeease*," she mimicked Zoe. "You have no idea how
annoying you are."

"Annoying or vexing?"

"They're the same, aren't they? Except that no one under the age
of ninety-nine uses the word 'vexing' anymore," she said, leaning to
reach for the stack of bills. "If I don't finish this, I'm not going to
have enough time to jog before Zoe gets home, assuming the rain
does let up."

"Fine, I'll leave you to your money and go change. I have a good feeling about beating you up those stairs today," he said, rising from his chair. "But want to know the difference first?"

"What difference?"

"Between annoying and vexing."

"There isn't one."

"There is. People you don't like *annoy* you. People you like just fine but who've gotten under your skin *vex* you."

Josie rolled her eyes, but the truth was it was as if there as a balloon welling up in her chest, making her almost weightless. "I don't think you're right, but if you are, then I was right to go with annoying."

"She meant vexing," Linda added from deep in the pantry.

The phone rang, and Carter headed over to the counter to answer it.

"Myra's house of vexing, perplexing, and often-interjecting women." He grew quiet. "Yeah, sure. She's right here." He walked the phone to Josie.

Josie's heart skipped a beat when Mark Wington, the principal of Galena Elementary, announced himself on the other end of the line. It was a minor incident, he explained, but Zoe had been brought into his office after a scuffle on the playground that resulted in another child being hit.

"Zoe hit another kid?" Adrenaline dumped into her system. "You're certain it was her?"

"I'm sorry, but there are witnesses," he said. "Teachers even. Listen, school's nearly out. Why don't you swing by, and we'll talk about it? She's a good kid. I have faith this'll be a one-time incident."

When Josie powered off the receiver, she sat in disbelief for several seconds, processing the principal's words. Zoe had hit another child. And now Josie was being called in for a visit to the principal. *In her first week of school.*

Suddenly she remembered that Myra had left twenty minutes

ago to visit a friend who'd had a hip replacement last week. This left Josie either to embark on the several-mile trek to Zoe's school on foot or hitch a ride. Finally, she pulled herself together enough to give Linda a pleading look. She'd stopped her inventory and was standing at the threshold of the pantry with a concerned look on her face.

"Seems like Zoe's in a bit of trouble. Can you give me a ride to her school?"

"Sure, but I've got to pick Melly up from volleyball at four. Think Myra will be long? Could you stick around and wait for her to pick you up on her way home?"

"I'll pick you up," Carter offered.

"You don't know where Zoe's school is." Jogging with Carter was one thing; involving him in something like this was entirely too much.

"I'll Google it."

She debated a few seconds before realizing beggars couldn't be choosers "Yeah, okay. Thanks. Linda, I can finish the inventory tonight if you're ready." Then she looked back at Carter. "There's a spare booster in the front closet. And I don't have a cell, so why don't you just head up to the school in half an hour? But please don't come inside. I'm not ready to explain you."

Carter's mouth pulled into a lopsided grin. "Yet."

Ignoring his banter, Josie dashed upstairs to grab her purse and tug on a light-gray sweater. In less than a minute, she was back downstairs and trailing out the back door after Linda. "Can you put the money back in the cash box for me?" she asked Carter, who was walking them to the door. "Just leave it on the top shelf in the pantry."

When Carter agreed, she headed into the rain, shuddering from the cold drops that soaked through her sweater before she climbed into Linda's van.

"I can't believe Zoe hit someone during her first week of school." She felt like a tire with a slow leak, her shoulders sinking.

Linda gave her knee a reassuring squeeze. "It probably doesn't seem like it, but a single punch in the first grade isn't as bad as you're thinking. Trust me. I've been through this rodeo a few times."

Josie buried her face in her hands. "You know what they say. You can take the girl out of the country, but you can't take the country out of the girl."

"Meaning?"

"It's just that, knowing her father, this won't be the only time Zoe punches someone." She knew immediately that even saying this much would stir up questions she didn't care to answer. Not even to Linda. Linda knew the same story Josie told anyone curious enough to ask about her past. She'd grown up in Seattle but had wanted a quieter life for Zoe. Only Myra knew the truth.

"Temper, I take it?"

"Not a temper, per se," she admitted. "He was just impulsive." *Was.* Did Linda pick up on it? If she did, she didn't press.

"If you ever need an ear, sweets, I'm here."

Josie squeezed Linda's hand. "I know. And right now, that's enough."

"Josie…"

"Yeah?"

"I never told you, but I got pregnant when I was seventeen. I was a junior in high school, and I didn't even have a committed boyfriend. I was leaning toward adoption, my parents toward abortion. When I see you with Zoe, how natural it is for you, and how good you are at it, well, I realize I could have done it too."

Josie stayed quiet, soaking in her words. *A natural.* She thought back to her early days with Zoe when everything was a battle and nothing she did felt right. "I rose to the occasion, that was all," she said finally.

"Yeah, you did. As for me, I ended up miscarrying in my eleventh week, so I didn't have to make the decision after all, though it tore me up for months. Longer, if you want the truth. Then, seven years later, Kyle came along, and I stepped into motherhood for real."

Linda flipped on her blinker as she pulled into the school and rolled to a stop in front of the main doors. "Call my cell if you need anything."

"Thanks, Linda." Josie said, pushing her door open.

"When you go in there, keep your chin up. We all know that girl of yours is about as genuine as they get. If she hit someone, the kid deserved it. And whatever you do, don't apologize for her. Zoe did it, *not* you." Linda gave Josie a mischievous smile. "And if you ask me, you have an entirely different fish to fry when you get back home. A man like that doesn't come around often. Hardly ever, actually. But I'm pretty sure you know that."

Josie frowned. "Yeah, well, knowing something and being ready for it aren't the same thing, are they?"

"It's been my experience that the most significant things don't wait for us to be ready for them."

Chapter 18

JOSIE SETTLED INTO A worn, padded chair in Principal Wington's office. His desk was crowded with knickknacks. A fuzzy-haired troll, an empty M&M's jar, and several photos of his family—a middle-aged wife and three kids all older than Zoe—caught Josie's attention. The pictures were from the same photo shoot, a fall day in a rustic park.

She tucked her hands under her knees and waited for him to get settled. He'd gotten up to meet her at the door and was now checking something on his computer. Zoe was coloring at a kindergartener-sized table in the corner next to a crowded bookshelf. She'd mumbled a hello as Josie walked in but hadn't stopped coloring.

Josie's heart went out to her; like Linda said, this wasn't Josie's first rodeo either. When her mother wasn't reachable, Josie had been called in more than once to help create game plans that might corral Sam's unruly behavior.

When Principal Wington finally started talking, Josie was as familiar with his spiel as he seemed to be.

"I hope you don't mind my asking," he said as he wrapped up, "but you're the only parent listed on Zoe's registration papers. You'd have made the office aware if there was a custody battle of any sort?"

"What's a custody battle?" Zoe asked, looking up from her drawing for the first time since he'd started talking.

The principal glanced Zoe's way and drummed his fingers on the desk. When Josie made no move to give him an out, he said,

"A custody battle is a disagreement parents sometimes have when it comes to their children."

"I wasn't born with a father," Zoe replied. "I've only got one parent." She dared a quick glance at Josie before looking back at her work.

Zoe's words scraped Josie like a knife, and she straightened defensively in her chair. The world was full of children growing up in atypical homes. And not everybody had two parents, not even close. "I have sole custody over Zoe. In case of an emergency, I included two contacts aside from myself on her paperwork." Myra and Linda, but she didn't need to tell him that.

"Of course." Mark Wington's cheeks reddened, and he turned his attention to Zoe. "Zoe, I'd appreciate it if you'd be willing to share a little more about what happened on the playground now that your mom's here. Both Ms. Richards and I have heard Andrew's recount of it. It'd be good to hear yours too. All you said earlier was that he was being mean. If you could explain what you meant by that, it could help us understand what happened today."

Zoe paused with a purple crayon three inches above her paper. She looked from the principal to her mother, then back to her drawing. "He lied about being my best friend. Best friends aren't ever supposed to be mean to you." She lowered her head low enough so that her soft brown hair tumbled forward, covering her face.

"The thing is, Zoe, sometimes our friends can hurt our feelings without meaning to. That's why I was talking to you about other ways to express your feelings when people hurt them."

"I *know* that." Her voice pitched.

Principal Wington seemed to pick up on the fact that Zoe was close to tears. "How about showing us your drawings?"

Zoe shook her head determinedly. "I don't want to."

"Zoe, honey." Josie crossed over to the low table and swept Zoe into a hug. "Principal Wington can help if what's bothering you has to do with Andrew."

Zoe's frayed composure broke like a dam. "Andrew wasn't being nice at *all*." Large tears spilled down her cheeks, and her chin quivered wildly.

"How so, Zoe?" Principal Wington asked, concern evident on his face.

"He said my idea was stupid."

Josie's own eyes stung as she swept back Zoe's long, silky hair. "What idea, baby?"

For a second or two, she seemed about to answer, but then she buried her head in Josie's chest and sobbed.

Clearly concerned, Principal Wington crossed over and flipped through Zoe's abandoned pictures.

"I've only got three weeks to find a daddy!" Zoe bawled into Josie's chest.

Josie pulled back to get a better look at her. "What do you mean, Zo?" Gently, she lifted Zoe's chin and brushed the tears on her cheeks dry.

"Everybody has a dad to bring to Doughnuts with Dads but me. I know because they all said so!" Her words were muffled and broken up in a torrent of sobs and sniffles. "I told Andrew I was going to put up signs like people do for lost dogs, but he said that was stupid. He said I have to wait for you to find a daddy for me. Only you're *never* going to do that."

"That explains this," Principal Wington said, holding one of Zoe's pictures for Josie to see.

Dade wontid.

Myras tee gardin.

Nise won onle.

"I'll tell you what, why don't I leave you two alone for a few minutes?" He smiled at Josie sympathetically before stepping out and shutting the door.

Josie pressed her cheek against the top of Zoe's head. Zoe's tears were soaking through her sweater just as the rain had done. There was so much she needed to say, but she couldn't summon the words to save her soul.

She remembered that feeling of being scraped raw inside after her own father left. She was young—not much older than four. It surprised her, the strength of the sorrow that returned with the memory, even after all these years.

She survived. Sam survived—that, at least. Kids all over the world survived without fathers. It hurt, but you got over it. You moved on. Grew stronger. Learned to need people less.

Zoe had no idea how good she had it—the love of the wonderful people all around her—right down to the regular customers who brought her Christmas and birthday presents. She was loved. Protected. Doted upon.

Life could be worse. Much worse.

Principal Wington returned with a sympathetic look on his face and a bag of popcorn and a carton of apple juice in his hands. He smiled sheepishly as he passed them to Zoe.

"Here you go, Zoe. For you. But you have to do me a favor and not tell any of your classmates. If all my students thought you got popcorn and juice every time there was a scuffle on the playground, it'd be utter chaos at recess."

Zoe wiped her nose on her arm and nodded, sniffling heavily.

"Did Ms. Richards explain that Doughnuts with Dads isn't only for actual dads?" he said. "Anyone can attend—grandpas, uncles, cousins, friends of the family—so there's no need to put up posters. I'm sure you and your mom can come up with someone once you put your heads together. I've even attended a few with some of the kids over the years. So has Janitor Mike. What's important is that we'll make sure you aren't eating doughnuts alone, okay?"

"Okay," Zoe muttered.

Josie wanted to thank Principal Wington for his kindness, but her throat was dangerously tight. This was different than it had been with Sam. An entirely different ballgame. This *hurt*.

"We'll talk to Andrew's parents again after we get the kids out the door and onto the buses. Thankfully, he's no worse for the wear. And tomorrow morning, hopefully you can apologize, and the two of you can make up."

"I don't think he'll want to be my best friend anymore." Zoe sucked on the paper straw of the apple juice box.

"If you ask me, I think it's better not to have a best friend, at least not right away. Sometimes it's better to give everyone an equal chance to be your friend."

The principal was about to say more, but he was silenced by his walkie-talkie going off. Amidst the static, Josie overheard one of the secretaries give a five-minute warning call for dismissal.

"Well," he said, looking from Zoe to Josie. "Duty calls."

Josie glanced through the window toward the front at the row of busses that had lined up. Carter was standing on the front steps, looking down at his phone.

"Are we okay to go? Our ride home is here. I asked him to meet us outside."

Zoe slid off Josie's lap and ran to the row of windows facing the front of the building. "Carter!" Without pausing to ask permission, she plopped the popcorn and empty juice on the table and dashed out the door.

"Zoe!" Josie stood up, her hand covering her mouth in humiliation. "I'm so sorry. She's just…"

"Unencumbered?" he finished. From the window, they watched Zoe fly down the front steps. She dashed over to Carter and wrapped her arms around his waist in a bear hug.

"Looks like you have a candidate for the doughnut breakfast after all," the principal said, slipping his hands into his pants' pockets. His eyes were kind, but the way he said it made Josie's cheeks flush.

"He's…a New Yorker." *A New Yorker? Yeah, Josie, that makes everything crystal clear.*

"Well, I meant what I said. Neither Mike nor I like to pass up the opportunity for doughnuts and coffee."

Josie thanked him and reached for Zoe's drawings. "If we're excused, I should go talk to her about not running out of a school building without permission."

"Yeah, of course. I'll walk you out. I have bus duty."

They reached the front door as Carter and Zoe rounded the top step.

"Mom, I have to get my backpack." Zoe tugged on Josie's shirt as they met up on the wide front entryway.

"Okay. Want me to go with you?"

"I can go by myself." Zoe wiped her nose with the back of her hand and dashed into the school as the bell rang.

"I'm Mark Wington," the principal said, holding out his hand to Carter.

"Carter O'Brien."

"I hear you're a New Yorker."

"That I am," Carter said, glancing at Josie curiously.

"Big fan of the Giants?"

"Of course."

"Me too. And the Yankees. I used to summer in upstate New York every year."

Josie turned away to flip through the rolled papers in her hand. The second drawing was another version of the poster she'd already seen but with some of the words crossed out as a result of Zoe struggling with the spelling. The third was a picture of a smiling Zoe in her bubbly cartoon drawings standing next to a man. *Kartr* was written beside it.

As she rolled them up, Josie spotted Zoe through the propped-open doors shuffling through the lobby with her narwhal backpack strapped to her back. She was sandwiched in the middle of a mass of kids heading for their buses. Her eyes were puffy from crying, but there was a happy grin splayed across her face. *Oh, Zoe...* she thought. *How come nobody prepares you for this stuff?*

———

Josie buckled in and shut the passenger door of Carter's Mustang after getting Zoe tucked into the back. Beside her, Carter flipped the ignition, and the car rumbled to life.

Twisting in her seat, Josie turned to study Zoe. "We can wait until we get home for the whole story. But I will want it. All of it. And I'm sure you understand there will be consequences for hitting one of your classmates."

"Did the girl hit back?" Carter asked.

"It was a boy," Zoe interjected. "My best friend, Andrew."

"Oh. Then how come you hit him?"

"He was being mean. I felt bad after, especially when he started crying."

"Was he picking on you?" Carter glanced Josie's way and dropped his voice. "If he was being mean, maybe the kid deserved it."

"He wasn't picking on her at all."

"Mommy, don't tell him!" Zoe blurted out, near hysterics once again. "You'll ruin it. I know you will!"

Josie let out a controlled breath. She was getting a bad feeling about this whole thing. "We'll talk about this when we get home, Zoe."

"I know, Mom."

They rode in silence for a few blocks before Josie noticed Carter was taking a wrong turn. "You're going the wrong way."

"Actually, we've got one more passenger to pick up along the way."

"Oh, no," Josie protested. She heard him telling Myra earlier that the dog could be released today. "You're not planning on putting that giant of a dog in this cramped car with us, are you? There's no way I'm letting him ride in the back seat with Zoe."

Carter cocked an eyebrow. "Who says you'd get the front seat over him, anyway?"

"Funny," she mumbled, but she realized it was the only solution she'd ever be comfortable with.

A half hour later, Josie found herself crammed into the confining back seat next to Zoe, who was grinning ear to ear. The newest addition to Myra's home—even if he was a temporary one—was leaning his head out the front-passenger window, his dark-pink tongue flailing in the air. Stitched up, rested, fed, and bathed, he was even more giant than he'd first seemed.

He was mostly black with a white chest and brown patches on his cheeks, paws, and above his eyes. Now that he was cleaned up and Josie was so close to him, the small patches above his eyes gave him an added level of expression she'd never seen on Tidbit.

He'd wagged his tail vigorously as he was brought up from the back of the office and spotted Carter, something Carter said was worth every bit of the $1,200 vet bill. He was a good man with a soft heart that he hid behind humor.

Unable to contain her happiness, Zoe clapped her hands and scrunched her shoulders together.

"This is the best day ever," she said, wriggling in her seat.

Seated behind Carter, Josie reached forward and poked him on the back of the shoulder. "You do get that this totally negates any punishment she receives, don't you?"

"Sorry. That's timing for you, isn't it? When I was a kid, I'd have guessed it was divine intervention. But then again, I suspect my father's punishments were a bit more physical than yours." After stopping at a light, he turned to appraise the dog, who looked his way and panted, releasing a single drop of drool on Carter's leather passenger seat. "He's a good-looking dog, isn't he? What do you think we should call him, Zo?"

Josie frowned at the sound of Zoe's nickname rolling off his tongue so easily.

"Buttercup," Zoe replied without a bit of hesitation.

"Really? I was thinking something more masculine, since he's a boy."

"I always wanted a dog named Buttercup. My whole life."

Your whole life of six years? Josie had never heard her mention the name, but she wasn't about to give Carter this out either.

"A hundred-pound Bernese mountain dog named Buttercup, huh?" Carter said. "Think the other dogs at the dog park will make fun of him?"

Zoe cupped her hands over her mouth. "Buttercup!" She called loudly enough that the dog turned his head toward her. "He likes it! He likes it!"

"What's your mom think?" Carter asked as the light turned green and the Mustang's engine thrummed to life.

"Buttercup's a great name," Josie said, working to suppress a smile as their eyes met in the mirror. "I'd go with it if I were you."

He chuckled, then reached over to rub the dog at the nape of his neck. "You'd better learn to come when I whistle, boy, because I'm not calling you Buttercup in public."

A minute later, Carter pulled into Myra's driveway at the back of the house. The dog turned from the window and licked him eagerly on the cheek. "Welcome to Myra's, Buttercup."

Chapter 19

"I SIMPLY CAN'T UNDERSTAND why anyone would want to watch a dog fight another dog." Myra shook her head from where she sat at the kitchen table next to Zoe, who was making an apology card for Andrew. "How can that vet be sure he didn't escape from his yard and end up in a scuffle with another free-roaming dog?"

Carter was splaying his legs on the floor against the far cabinets, feeding Buttercup pieces of dog chow by hand. "Mostly he was basing it on the degree of the cuts and bites. It's hard to tell. He's a healthy, purebred dog in his prime. If he'd had a caring home recently, you'd think there'd be posts on the lost-dog alert sites. The clinic staff has been checking, and there hasn't been a single report matching his description all week. He wasn't microchipped either. If someone does end up coming forward to claim him, they'd better have a good story as to how he got away."

"Well, it's a shame to think a gentle dog like him might've been forced to fight another dog for someone's twisted pleasure." Myra tsked loudly.

Josie, who was chopping up kale for a salad to go with tonight's dinner of oven-baked chicken, made an effort to keep her thoughts to herself. While she couldn't think of a worse form of animal abuse than dogfighting, she wasn't convinced Buttercup should be labeled gentle after one afternoon at the house. Timid and cautious could also be good descriptors, couldn't they? And neither of those traits inspired her unending trust. Her hope—and commitment to herself for agreeing to let an unfamiliar dog his size reside in a home with Zoe—was that Carter would remember his promise to keep Buttercup under watchful eye. At least until the dog had actually earned a reputation as trustworthy.

Even so, she'd been a touch surprised how well Buttercup's introduction to Tidbit had gone this afternoon. The two different-as-could-be dogs had been interested but not overly concerned with one another. Where Tidbit liked to be a part of everything, Buttercup seemed considerably more chill. At least for the moment.

Out of precaution, while Buttercup was eating dinner, Tidbit was shut away in Myra's room. Though a dog sharing his home would be new to Tidbit, dogs often accompanied their owners on the outside terraces while dining at the tea garden, and Tidbit enjoyed their company. So as long as Buttercup continued to treat Tidbit like he did today, Josie suspected they'd be easy roommates.

Carter slid the dog's dish behind him and held out his hands to show Buttercup they were empty. Clearly still hungry for more of the food in the bowl, Buttercup calmly took to licking Carter's hands and wagging his fluffy tail.

"Can I feed him like that?" Zoe asked, losing interest in her apology card once again as she watched the activity on the floor.

"Not yet," Carter said. "Your mom's right about one thing. We have to build up trust with him slowly, especially when it comes to small fries like you. Just because he's easily obedient to me, doesn't mean he'll naturally be that way with you."

"Why?" Zoe rubbed her index finger back and forth across her nose.

"Because it's in a dog's nature to want to establish his place among his pack members—in this case, the people he lives with—as high up as he can. That means the few areas a dog is the least willing to share—his food, toys, and his bed—need to be off limits to you until he earns our unconditional trust. Understand?"

"What's unconditional?"

"It's another way of saying absolutely always with no exception," Josie interjected.

Zoe's brows furrowed into a knot. "So, he can't sleep with me?"

"No," Josie said. "Absolutely not."

Zoe's shoulders sank. "Can I at least *help* you feed him?"

A hint of a scowl formed along Carter's forehead. Josie was about to answer when he looked at her in earnest. "So long as your mom agrees."

Josie frowned. "I'd say no, but I'm worried she'll try it when no one's looking."

"I was thinking the same thing." He pushed himself up so that he was balancing on the balls of his feet and motioned Zoe over. "Come stand on this side so I'm between you two."

When Zoe was on the opposite side of Carter as Buttercup, Carter said, "I'll put one piece into your hand at a time. But you have to promise you'll never do this without me."

"I won't, but Buttercup won't hurt me. He's my friend."

Josie suppressed a grimace. It was quite possible Buttercup could be trusted more than Zoe at this point.

Carter patted the big dog confidently, then dropped a piece of kibble into Zoe's hand and guided her hand toward his mouth. Buttercup inhaled the kibble with an almost imperceptible flick of his tongue.

Zoe giggled. "That tickled."

"Want to do it again?" Carter reached behind him for another piece.

They'd done the same process another few times when Buttercup shoved forward and began licking Zoe's face. Zoe squealed with delight, her hands flying out to grab his neck in an embrace.

"No, Zoe!" Josie lunged forward instinctively, knocking the bowl of salad fixings to the floor in the process.

Surprised by the crash, Buttercup whipped around, tucking his tail and whining.

Zoe patted his hip, her fingers burrowing into his thick fur. "Mommy, you scared him!"

She's okay. Josie's knees nearly buckled underneath her as memory melted into the present. Sam's helpless scream rang in her ears. She could picture her mother's face too—white as a ghost—as clearly as if she were seeing it on a screen. Her lips had been moving in a fervent prayer to a God she insisted didn't exist. It was the only time Josie ever saw her pray.

It's over. Josie let out a shaky breath. Sam survived. He grew and healed and remained a dog-lover for life. He did all those things. Just not for long enough. Not nearly long enough.

As the memory receded, the soft commotion in the kitchen pressed in. Myra ushered Zoe back to the table and her artwork while Carter offered Buttercup the rest of the kibble in the bowl.

Josie sank onto her heels and began to scoop the mess of kale back into the bowl. Her fingers were shaking, and her blood was racing like she'd been standing in front of a firing squad. Carter walked over and squatted beside her.

"I've got it." She didn't want his help. Especially not right now.

He took her by surprise by cupping her chin in his hand. His eyes held hers, his expression earnest. "If you can't do this, I want you to know, I'll work something else out."

Crunching a mouthful of food, Buttercup trotted over and sniffed the kale on the floor, then Josie's hair. His tail wagged innocently, and his warm, brown eyes seemed solemn and friendly.

Josie understood it then; he wasn't a bad dog. Maybe there were *no* bad dogs, just bad owners. Whatever the case, so long as they proceeded cautiously, the dog would be fine.

Rather than letting her go, Carter's thumb remained at the rim of her jaw.

"I'm okay. We just need to take it slower than this."

"We'll take it as slow as you need."

Buttercup trotted back to his dish, and Josie stood up to dump the pieces of kale into the compost bin. She knew they were both talking about the dog, but the way he'd been looking at her, it was as if he meant something else too.

Somehow, she made it through dinner without ever being more than half-present. Thankfully, it was so close to the end of a long first week that Zoe was exhausted and ready for bed early. After Zoe's bath, Josie curled up in her bed and half listened to Zoe's whispered prayers.

"Zoe," Josie asked when Zoe was finished, "why did you hit Andrew today?"

"I told you why."

"Yes, but I've got the feeling there are still some things you aren't telling me."

Zoe turned onto her side and curled toward her. "How come I can't pick out my own dad? How come I have to wait for you to do it?"

"Not everybody has a dad, Zoe."

"Andrew says everybody has to have a dad."

Josie frowned into the darkness. She couldn't go there with Zoe today, but she needed to. Soon. "You have so many people who love you, Zo. More than you even realize. All week customers have been asking about you."

"I want a *dad* though. They're different than you and Myra. I like the way they smell. And the way they have those short, rough hairs on their cheeks and under their chins. And the bigger hairs on their hands and arms."

Josie's father had walked away so long ago, Josie wouldn't have guessed Zoe's words could conjure up an image of his stubbly chin and cheeks, and the way they'd felt against her palm. She'd not known it then, but that smell on his breath, it had most likely been bourbon or scotch.

"You still haven't answered me. What aren't you telling me?"

Zoe reached out to run her fingertips down Josie's neck. "It's like a birthday wish, Mom. The ones you want the most, you aren't allowed to tell."

After a moment of reflection, Josie said, "You don't have to tell me anything, but there's something I need you to hear."

"What?"

"Carter. I know you like him, but you have to remember he's not going to be here forever."

Zoe pulled her hand away from Josie's neck and tucked it into a fist under her chin. "I know, Mom."

"You say that, Zoe, but you need to believe it too."

"I believe in fairies and you don't, but you never said I can't believe in them."

Josie brushed back Zoe's bangs. *Shit.* For the thousandth time, she wished there was a fail-proof guide to raising kids.

"That's true, but I'm not worried about fairies—or the lack of them—hurting you."

Zoe stayed quiet for so long that Josie wondered if she was drifting off.

"Mom," she said finally, her voice an easy whisper, "maybe you just shouldn't worry so much."

Chapter 20

"CLARIFY ONE THING FOR me, will you?" Carter said the next night as he flipped over the ignition, and his car purred to life.

"That would depend on the thing."

"About you and not driving," he said. "Is it that you can't or won't?"

"Or don't want to," she offered. "A blend actually."

"Want me to teach you?" He cocked an eyebrow her direction.

Josie clicked her buckle in place and shot an apprehensive glance through the darkness toward Myra's house as he backed out of the drive. "No thanks… Well, maybe." She wasn't in any hurry to learn to drive, but if she intended to stay planted in rural mid-America, sooner or later she was going to have to. "Can I think about it?"

He chuckled. "I'm here if you want me."

Of course he would say that. Josie already had full-on fishbowl stomach at the idea of being alone with him, away from the security of this place. It wasn't that she was worried about Zoe needing her; after her first full week of school, Zoe was out like a light. And Buttercup was closed in Carter's room for the next few hours. Though, none of that calmed her nerves.

Rather than turning toward town, Carter got on Highway 20 East, which led out of town toward not much else but farmland.

"Where are we headed, anyway?"

"A little dive I heard about. Supposedly it has great food and good music."

"That sounds more like a bar than a coffee shop."

"No one will stop you from having a coffee, or tea, in your case, but it's eight o'clock on a Friday night, and I've been writing at a tea garden all week. I'm in the mood for a drink that isn't served with a saucer."

Josie failed to suppress a snort of laughter. This was day eight of Carter in her world. It was safe to assume he was never without a joke or wry comment.

It was Myra who'd convinced Josie to go tonight so Carter could get her input on some of what he was writing for her. "You'll never open up if you're worried about me overhearing," she'd insisted. They hadn't needed to leave for that, Josie knew. She and Carter could've sat out on the terrace after Myra and Zoe went to bed.

But somehow, she'd found herself agreeing anyway.

The bar was a good fifteen minutes outside of town. Nestled atop a gently sloping hillside and illuminated by landscaping lights up the winding entrance, it was surprisingly inviting. The parking lot was nearly full, and Carter parked in an open spot at the end. A muffled Lady Antebellum song greeted Josie's ears as she got out of the car.

She couldn't help but notice Carter headed around the car empty-handed. "Where's your laptop?"

"Back at Myra's."

He was in jeans and a long-sleeve, button-down shirt that was tucked in and drew her attention to his waist. Again. It didn't seem as if he had his well-worn moleskin notebook on him either.

"How are you going to remember anything I say if you don't write it down?"

"I haven't forgotten a single thing you've said, and I don't plan to start tonight."

As they got closer to the building, Josie could feel the thrum of the music reverberating in her chest. "If I didn't know better, I'd say this is a bait and switch."

He held up his hands. "Us getting out of the house was Myra's idea. I'd have been fine to hang out on the terrace. I've been craving a big fire in one of those fire pits, and it's about cool enough tonight to appreciate one. If you want to head somewhere else, we can, but I say we give it a shot since we're here."

Josie shrugged off her apprehension as Carter pushed through the entry doors. Inside, it was intimately lit, and there was a large dance floor on one side filled with couples who were clearly adept at Western moves. After a quick scan of the room, Josie guessed she and Carter were the only two people not in cowboy boots.

Carter's hand locked over her elbow, and he guided her to the side farthest from the dance floor.

"Nice place," he said, sliding into a seat at an open booth.

Josie sank down across from him. "Quite the change of pace from your Manhattan scene, isn't it?"

"True, but as I said, I lived the first half of my life in west Texas, sweetheart. This feels closer to home than anything in Manhattan. Hell, if you don't mind me saying it, I lost my virginity in a joint like this."

Josie suppressed a snort. "Aside from being TMI, I know you're lying. You can't go to bars until you're twenty-one, and I'm never going to believe you were that old when you—you know. Besides, you said earlier that you moved to New York when you were twenty."

"All true, but I started going to bars like this when I was seventeen. You could get by with stuff like that in my hometown. And I know what you're thinking—seventeen's old for a prime specimen like me. But I'm not afraid to admit I was a terribly awkward teenager. Gangly as all get out and with my share of acne. And a god-awful retainer. My first time was probably more out of pity than anything else."

"I don't believe you for a second." Josie pressed her lips into a tight line and shook her head but still couldn't shake off a laugh. "But we're here to talk about Myra, not your teenage prowess," she said as she recovered. "Or lack of it. So, what is it you want to know?"

Carter drummed his fingers atop a name carved into the table. "Has anyone ever told you it isn't easy to break the ice with you?"

Josie cocked her head. "Weren't we just discussing your virginity a second ago?"

"I was. But you were locking up your smile."

Josie buried her face in her hands, shaking her head. "Myra. Please. What do you want to know?"

"Ah, things I can't come up with on an identity search, I guess. For starters, tell me more about her kids. Have you met them?"

"A few times. They don't come home often."

"Why? Any bad blood there?"

"Not that I've seen. Not toward her, anyway. Her son eyes me like I'm the devil incarnate whenever he comes home. It's my guess that he thinks I'm trying to whittle away Myra's fortune, which I'm not. Obviously."

"Obviously."

She wished something would catch his attention and distract it from her. The intimate lighting, tall booth, and the way he was focused on her mouth—probably to understand her over the music—stripped away at her composure.

"You helped Myra stay in her house with your idea to open the tea garden. That's hardly taking advantage of her."

A server showed up with two bottles of beer, both Stella Artois, and set them on the table along with menus. *So that's what he'd said to the server as we walked over.*

Carter lifted a beer to his lips and slid the other Josie's way.

"What if I don't like Stella Artois?"

"Then I'll drink it, and you can order your tea when she comes back."

Josie chewed on the inside of her cheek before deciding to take a swig. It had been a while since she'd had a beer. She enjoyed a small glass of wine every so often, but considering the affinity her mother had had toward anything addictive, Josie had always thought it was better not to test fate.

The beer proved more refreshing than she'd have anticipated as it rolled over her tongue. She took another sip and turned her attention to the dancers who were moving in impressive rhythm to "Whiskey Glasses."

"So, I'd love to hear how you two met."

Josie's discomfort heightened instantly. She didn't want to talk about anything related to her arrival. "There's not much to say. We met in town. I was new to Galena. She needed someone to help her open the tea garden, and I needed a job."

"So, it was just business then?"

"No." She dropped his gaze almost as soon as she looked at him. "It was more than that."

"Yeah, I know. She loves you like family, and it's obvious you feel the same way."

Josie shrugged. "She's easy to love."

He sat back, stretching out his legs. His jeans rubbed against Josie's bare calf.

"Did Myra tell you I'm taking her to New York with me next weekend?"

Josie's jaw dropped. "No, she didn't." *Myra's going with him to New York?* "Why?"

"I need some of my things since I'm staying on, and I need to make sure the rest gets into storage. It isn't much after Katherine took what she wanted, but it's worth keeping."

"But why are you taking Myra?"

"She's never been to New York. She wants to go. You're welcome to come if you'd like."

"Thanks, but no way." Josie had never been on a plane in her life, and the idea of being in a city that size made her limbs lock up. And though a part of her would like to see New York someday, even if it was just to see for herself the city that had drawn her father away, she'd not yet put her fake ID through any real tests. She certainly wasn't going to start at an airport.

"She said you wouldn't come with us."

"She knows me better than I know myself most of the time."

"I guess we'll see about that."

Josie felt a challenge in his words, innocent as his tone was. "What do you mean?"

"She wants Zoe to come with us."

"With *you*? To New York?" She huffed. "Not a chance."

"Myra will be there."

Josie shook her head adamantly. "No."

"She said you'd say that. But the thing is, Myra would really like to see it with Zoe. She loves that little girl a great deal. Almost as much as she loves you."

Josie flattened her hands against the seat of the booth. Cool as the leather was, she suddenly craved something much colder against her skin. She'd known this would happen. Her life was like a spiced apple cake mix that had separated out. The thin, easy stuff was at the surface, and the heavy stuff had settled to the bottom. And Carter was stirring shit up.

"She's hoping you change your mind once you've had some time to think about it," Carter added into her silence. "And I've got no doubt Zoe would eat it up. Lady Liberty. The Brooklyn Zoo. Yankee Stadium. Times Square. You name it."

Josie's skin was growing clammy. "Can we *not* talk about this?"

He was quiet a few seconds. "Yeah, sure."

She swiped a loose strand of hair behind her ear and took a swig of the beer. "What are we doing here, Carter?"

Carter tapped his thumb against the table. "Good question.

Dancing, I hope." His reply was light and playful as if he'd picked up on the tension locking up her insides. "Have you ever done any of these line dances? They're fun. Come on."

He stood up and paused at the edge of her seat. When she didn't move, he scooped up both beers in one hand and wrapped his other hand around her wrist. "Come on, Josie. Let's dance. I promise not to embarrass you with my moves."

Still holding her wrist, he stepped back a foot or two so that her arm was extended.

She considered pulling away, but her body wasn't listening to her mind. "Carter, a thousand wild horses couldn't drag me out there, so you might as well stop trying."

"A thousand wild horses wouldn't drag you anywhere; they'd stampede you." He took another few steps back and pulled so that she began to slide across the bench.

"Carter!" she groaned as she reached the edge. In an easy swoop, he pulled her to her feet. She bumped against his chest. "You're invading my personal space, but I think you already know that." She stepped back, fighting a smile. "You don't want to dance with me. I have no idea know how to line dance, or whatever this is."

"You don't have to know; I'll show you."

"Look, if I humiliate myself with one dance, will you promise not to say another word about Zoe and New York?"

"Cross my heart."

She nodded slowly. "Okay. One dance, and we're both going to look like idiots, because I'm going to be bad enough to bring you down with me."

—⁓—

Carter hadn't brought Josie here to dance, and he'd half expected her to shut him down when he pulled her off the bench like that. He hadn't line danced in years, but when Kenny Chesney's "Get Along" started playing over the speakers, and he led her to an open spot in the corner, it all came back. He passed her one of the beers and wrapped his free hand around her arm.

"It'll be considerably less painful than hauling it up those stairs like you do every day, I can promise you that."

He broke the steps into a series of simple moves. The music was booming; for her to hear him, he leaned close and spoke into her ear. His mouth brushed against her hair, and he forced himself not to think of how much he wanted to lose his hands in it. Only one beer in, he had the strength to refrain from attempting it.

Her outfit didn't help him any; a dress, something formfitting at the top and stopping an inch or two above the knee, called his attention to her toned calves. Halfway through the second song, they sat their empty beer bottles on a nearby table, and she shed her jean jacket and hung it over one of the chairs. Without the jacket, his attention was drawn to the top half of her body as strongly as it had been to her bare calves.

Most of the time he thought of her as an enigma, someone whose shell he'd never crack, no matter how many ways he tried. Then he'd brought up New York, and she'd looked vulnerable and exposed in a way she'd managed to keep hidden so far. It was obvious that a part of her wanted to let Zoe experience New York; she just found the thought terrifying. It made him even more committed to finding out what—or who—she was afraid of.

Fear seemed to have been getting the best of her for a long time. He was more and more committed to helping her shed it.

By the time the song switched to "Save a Horse, Ride a Cowboy," she had the pattern down, though she still tended to turn the wrong direction a quarter of the time. "You've got moves." He flexed his hand to keep from locking it around her waist. Her little smile had widened into a big one, and he didn't want her shutting down.

The next song that came on was Kenny Chesney's "Me and You."

As if a giant magnet had been aimed their way, couples all around pulled close together, and the floor became dotted with tightly paired bodies tangled in hungry arms.

Josie stepped back involuntarily even before Carter reached for her. "Thanks. That was more fun than I thought."

"Then stay awhile." He held out his hand, palm up.

She shook her head. "I don't do slow dances."

"Don't, can't, or won't?" he said, bringing it around to their earlier conversation about driving.

"Considering it won't change my answer, I don't think it matters."

She looked like a deer debating whether to stand frozen or take flight, so Carter closed his hand around her arm slowly. "Come on, just one."

Her eyes seemed to shut involuntarily, but she didn't attempt to pull away.

Not letting go of her arm, he stepped closer, and was a bit surprised when she didn't back away. As they began to move to the rhythm, he wrapped his arms around her waist, carefully, at first, then more confidently.

As sure as he was that he could pick out her body in a lineup of a thousand other women's, he was still surprised by the way she fit against him, thighs, breasts, hips—all parts he longed to explore.

Gradually, Josie's body relaxed into his, and Carter slowly began to trust this unspoken truth more than any declaration she'd made at the start. Releasing his hands from where they'd been locked around the small of her back, he allowed them to slide over her hips and up the sides of her body, stopping just under her arms. He craved to explore her more, but that was a trust he needed to earn.

Her eyes closed again, but she didn't step back. Her dress was so thin, he could almost envision it being flesh upon flesh.

And he was certain it wasn't just him. As the song went on, she melted closer into him. When he glanced over at the couple next to them who were well into their seventies and had the smoothest moves on the floor, his lips brushed against Josie's forehead.

He was damn certain in all his life he'd never wanted to kiss anyone more. He raised one hand and traced his thumb along the ridge of her jaw, then let it trail over her lips. For a second, he was impossibly close to doing so, and from the way her lips parted as she looked at him, he was confident she was going to let him. Then, it was as if she remembered something—or someone—and the longing in her gaze shut like a curtain.

She stepped back and tugged at one earlobe. "I told you I..." Her eyelids pressed closed a second. "I'm sorry, I just can't do this."

She took off without waiting for him, heading back toward the booth they'd abandoned to dance. Halfway across the room, she switched directions and headed to the bar. By the time he collected her jacket and made it over there, she was flipping through one of the vertical drink menus.

"A chocolate martini," she said to the bartender. "Two actually."

"Thanks, but I'll just have another Stella," Carter said, resting an elbow on the bar, facing her. "Seeing as how I'm driving and all."

Josie shot him a look. "Just because I ordered two, doesn't mean one is for you."

He took a second to read her. Her defenses were back up. "Thank you kindly, Dr. Seuss."

The bartender overheard and chuckled. "Would you two like to start a tab?"

"No, we'll be leaving soon," Josie said, clearly realizing she no longer was wearing her jacket by the way her hand froze halfway to her nonexistent pocket.

Carter had already pulled out his wallet and handed over his credit card.

"You don't need to get mine." Josie eyed the jacket draped over his arm without reaching for it. Maybe she still felt too raw to initiate any form of touching too.

The bar was packed, and Josie shifted from one foot to the other as she waited.

"Why don't you have a seat, and I'll bring it to you?" Carter offered.

She didn't argue. She took off for the bathroom, and they met up at the booth seconds apart.

"Two chocolate martinis," he said, setting them down. The thin, angular glasses were decorated with swirls of chocolate along the side, and the drink was topped with chocolate shavings. "I didn't realize you had such a sweet tooth."

"I don't. Usually. Nothing else sounded good." She took a cautious sip of the first one. "It's good."

He swigged his beer and watched as she had another few sips, twirling the glass in a slow circle when she wasn't drinking. "So, mind telling me what the objective is here? While you're still sober?"

Josie frowned. "I just—I need you to understand that I can't do this. Not now. Not ever."

He took a minute to respond. "Do you want to tell me why, at least?"

She was halfway through the first martini. She wanted to get drunk, that much was clear. When she wasn't drinking, she was using the plastic pirate sword to scratch away at the syrup stuck to the inside of the glass. *What is it you're trying so hard to keep buried, Josie Waterhill?*

"Because the thing is," he said when she didn't answer, "I kinda think we could be good together."

She winced at his words and gave a light shake of her head. "When this is all over for you—when you're done unearthing whatever else you can about your grandfather's story and you've written whatever it is Myra wants you to write for her and you leave—you're going to be like the syrup in this glass. You're going to leave behind a residue."

A slow grin spread across Carter's face. "A residue, huh? I've gotta say, I can't remember being compared to residue before."

"Myra will remember you," she continued undeterred. "Zoe will remember you. *I'll* remember you." Josie shook her head. "But none of that means you belong here."

She raised the first glass and finished it off. When she sat it down, Carter reached out to wipe away a smudge of chocolate under her lip. "It might not be any of my business, but two of those will probably put you on the floor."

"We'll see about that." She wasted no time moving to the second martini. "I can't do this with you. Can you just tell me you agree?"

"Do *what* with me, Josie?"

"Dancing. Sex. All of it."

"What if we put a few more steps between dancing and sex?"

She shook her head and swallowed a few sips of the second martini. "You aren't as funny as you think you are."

He closed one hand over hers. "How about giving me a chance, at least?"

"I can't. How could I do that? For goodness sakes, Zoe said you smell like doughnuts and special days."

Carter shook his head. "That's touching, but I don't see how the way I smell has anything to do with this." It was obvious a buzz was hitting her hard, and he suspected the decent thing to do was table the discussion until tomorrow when she was sober.

"She's wrong," she added, pointing a finger his direction and blinking heavily.

"How so?"

"You smell like Santa."

He chuckled softly. "You mean like Scotch tape and freshly baked cookies?"

She set the half-finished second martini down and looked at him, her head cocked sideways, and her lips parted slightly. Her red-gold hair spilled over her shoulder, beckoning him again. "Is that what your Santa smelled like?" Her words were just a whisper.

"I can't say I ever thought of it before, but that's what came to mind. Why, what did your Santa smell like?"

She traced one finger over his hand and stayed quiet a long time before answering. "Like hope and disappointment."

He shifted in his seat, her words stabbing him in the heart. "Are you going to tell me why?"

"Because I used to be little enough to believe he could fix everything. To think that, if I was good enough, for long enough, he would."

"And Christmas came, and he couldn't?"

"Most of the time, it just came without him."

What would he take on to fix that for her? To make sure nothing like that ever happened to Zoe? No wonder Josie didn't want to let anyone in. "Not everyone leaves, Josie. Not everyone disappoints."

She turned his hand over and traced the lifeline of his palm. Her gentle touch heated his blood again. "Everyone leaves sooner or later. Especially the ones you want to stay."

Carter closed his fingers around hers, stopping her caress before his blood boiled too hot. With her free hand, she raised the second martini and swallowed down the last of it. Her eyes drifted closed and stayed that way for close to a minute.

"Will you take me home?" she asked when she opened them.

"Yeah, sure."

"Carter?"

"Yeah?"

"If I get any drunker than this, I'm either gonna fall asleep in the car or come on to you. If I do that, will you turn me down?"

"Is that a question or a request?"

"No wonder my mom never cared to be sober," she said, her head dipping to the side again. When she saw him watching her, she said, "Did I say that out loud?"

"Yes, and a few other things."

"Oh." She fell quiet again. "Carter?"

"Yeah?"

"Out there on the dance floor, it was nice."

"I thought so too."

"I didn't realize martinis were so strong."

"How about a glass of water?"

She shook her head. "No. I don't think I should put anything else in my stomach right now. Can you take me home?"

"Yeah, and if you come on to me, I'll do right by you. Promise."

She nodded and lifted one of the glasses to lick at the chocolate on the rim which was somehow both sexy as hell and endearing at the same time. "I'd have put money on you being a gentleman."

He stood up and reached for her hand. "Come on, Josie Waterhill, let's get you home."

Chapter 21

As Josie walked back into her apartment living room, the ice water in the bowl she was carrying sloshed over the side, splashing her bare feet. The frigid water helped pull her back from the shock she'd been in the last hour.

Sam was still curled on the floor at the foot of the couch, a sweaty, disheveled mess. He didn't even seem to notice the tirade of words, senseless numbers, and phrases slipping from his lips.

Stepping over him, she took a seat on the couch and dipped a raggedy washcloth into the bowl, then wrung it out. She pressed the washcloth over his forehead, securing it with her hand.

"Sam. Sam…" She shook his shoulder. "You need to tell me what you took."

He was sweating, but his teeth chattered uncontrollably. "Shit. Eight. Fifty-two. Forty-seven. Son of a bitch. Thirty-one. You're the best, Josie. Don't leave me. Shit. Shit. Sixteen. Sixteen is best. That's it. Sixteen."

Five minutes ago, she'd been hopeful he was coming out of it, but now he was slipping back in. When he recovered, she'd kill him. Somehow, she'd make him see what he was doing to himself. To his future. To her.

For now, all she could do was help keep him calm. Get him through until morning. Minutes passed like a line of dominos waiting to come crashing down.

During his calmer moments, her thoughts went back to Nico. Her arm still burned from his touch. For the last two years and three

months, she'd had little more than bits of wild gossip and two quick
sightings in passing, similar to tonight's. Those sightings had left her
longing for some deeper reassurance that he wasn't the lost soul he
was rumored to be.

Only tonight had been different. They'd spoken. Sort of. And
he'd promised to send help. What had he meant? Maybe he'd just
said it to get her back in that cab and away from that house with Jena
inside, glaring at her from the window.

Sam had called her three hours ago as she was getting ready for
bed. At first, she'd thought he was wasted. But it was worse than
that. After a bit of cajoling, he'd spouted off an address. She'd never
have believed for one second Nico had been there too. The party
was forty-five minutes out at an over-the-top Redondo Beach house,
where cars had been lined up a half-mile away, and music had
boomed from its windows.

Leaving the cab driver idling out front, using up all the money
she'd saved for groceries, Josie had headed up to the house and let
herself in without knocking. No one would have heard had she tried.
Some people had been dancing. A handful of couples had been getting
it on in corners. Others seemed to have been quietly riding out a buzz.
She'd been scanning the crowded living room for Sam when she spotted
Nico. He was sitting on a couch staring right at her, Jena at his side.

Surprised as she was to see him, she'd stood there, gawking at
him until he acknowledged her with a slight nod of his head toward
a nearby hall. That was when it hit her. He'd known Sam was there
and hadn't bothered to help.

Her feet had unstuck then, and she ended up finding her brother
on a dirty bathroom floor curled in a ball against the bathtub, muttering incomprehensibly. It took a bunch of coaxing and a promise
of no hospitals to calm him down and get him to his feet. Once
standing, he leaned heavily against her, and she dragged him out and
into the hall.

"Potluck," he'd mumbled.

Halfway to the front door, he'd dropped to his knees and doubled over, refusing to budge. She'd been attempting to haul him to his feet when she noticed Nico was standing a foot away, his expression an unreadable mask.

"Let me help you get him outside."

He towered over her, all the muscle and height and power that his body had once promised to become. He was eighteen now, closing in on nineteen.

Anger had rushed through Josie's veins to know he'd been sitting on the couch while Sam had OD'd thirty feet away. She'd thought of Francie, all this time, all the long nights of worrying if her son was alive or dead or causing others harm. And Nico sat around at parties like this and got high.

Before she'd even knew she was doing it, she shoved him hard in the chest. "Asshole!"

He'd recovered with the grace of someone accustomed to considerably bigger blows. In the space of the time it took him to plant one foot behind him and steady himself, everyone was staring at her.

"You gonna teach that bitch some manners or want me to do it?" some guy had yelled.

Nico had raised his hand to ward off Jena, who'd jumped to her feet and was crossing the room with a string of angry curses.

"I've got this. Sit your ass back down."

After hoisting Sam over his shoulders like he weighed no more than a big bag of dog food, Nico had shoved Josie toward the door.

After smacking the front door shut behind him, he locked his free hand around the back of her arm. "Don't look back." His words had been gentler than they'd sounded inside. He headed for the cab without even clarifying that it was hers.

He got Sam splayed across the back seat before turning to her.

"When he wakes up, tell your brother if he steps foot into one of these houses again, I'll kill him myself, you got that?"

Busy reliving the cruelty in his words the last time they'd spoken in that hospital room, it had taken her a few seconds to respond. "Screw you for not helping him!"

"Who do you think dialed your number? He was too wasted."

"The Nico I knew would've gotten him out of here."

"The Nico you knew isn't shit anymore. He got his ass handed to him."

She'd been debating how to respond when he opened the passenger-side door and tossed the driver a hundred-dollar bill from a wallet padded with money. In her heart, she'd known he was dealing, but somehow, seeing all that cash still crushed her.

"If anybody follows, take them straight to the hospital," he directed the driver. "If no one does, take them home."

He'd turned toward the house without looking her way and had taken several steps when he spoke again. His back had been to her, and his words had been muffled by the blare of the music. So much so, Josie was beginning to doubt what she'd heard. "As soon as I can get away, I'll bring help."

Josie glanced at her phone. That was nearly two hours ago now. Maybe she'd heard him wrong.

A handful of drowsy minutes passed. She was refreshing the washcloth when there was a burst of knocking at the door. Her body tensed as she debated if she had a better chance of it being Nico, the police, or someone worse—someone Jena had sent—on the other side.

She put a finger to her lips as Sam jerked his head up from the floor. "Quiet, Sam, let me see who it is." Keeping a finger over her lips, she stepped over her brother.

Still delusional, Sam grabbed her calf and screamed, "No! Stupid bastards. Kill you! Kill you! No!"

The door blasted open like a bomb had gone off. Splinters of wood around the dead bolt flew across the room. Sam clawed at her to get her out of the way as two men burst into the room.

Josie screamed as a bear of a man—someone she'd never seen before—reached Sam, flipping him onto his back and pressing his knee against Sam's chest.

She knew the arms that grabbed her even before she could focus on his face. Nico.

"Stop that screaming," Nico directed the guy. To Josie, he asked, "Is anyone else here?"

"No. It's just us. Tell that man to get off my brother!"

Sam's captor was a massive man with thick arms covered in tattoos. She blinked a few times as it sank in what he was holding. He had a gun in one hand, pressed sideways against Sam's shoulder as he held him to the floor. A medic bag had fallen out of the other hand and was on the floor next to them.

"We brought meds. Douglas is an EMT. Off duty. He can get Sam sedated enough to keep him calm until it passes."

Slipping out from Nico's grasp, Josie sank next to her brother. She had to twist his head to get his attention off the man and onto her. "It's okay, Sam. They're here to help."

"Don't let them shoot me up with anything," Sam spat. "Can't take no more of this. No more. No more."

She smoothed back his damp hair. His hazel eyes were still so dilated their color had all but vanished.

"It's just something to help you sleep," Douglas said.

Sam nodded. "Sleep. Thirteen. Twenty-seven. Eleven. Sleep is good."

Nico shot Douglas a look. "Let's just do this."

"You're sure it's safe?" Josie asked.

Douglas assured her it was. Whatever was in the syringe, Josie was surprised how well it worked. In the span of few minutes, the tension lining Sam's face slipped away the same way water dripped off soaked sycamore leaves in the front of her building.

Afterward, they moved Sam from the floor onto the couch. Josie would've thought his nod was one of thanks until he said, "Seven. Don't know what I was thinking. Seven is best."

"Think he's picking Lotto numbers?" Nico paced the room as Douglas packed up. He took his time eyeing her stack of homework, her backpack, and other things that made her feel like a kid who'd been stuck in a time capsule while he'd kept aging.

She sat on the edge of the saggy couch with Sam's feet on her lap. No one talked, making her wonder what sort of connection there was between Nico and Douglas. Had Douglas come along out of friendship or debt?

The memory rushed in of the last time she and Nico had been on this couch, hands exploring each other, legs entwined. She wondered if he was having similar thoughts. Then she remembered that wild pain from when he'd walked out of her life and did her best to shove the memory from her mind.

Exhaustion, blame, and disbelief circled through her. She didn't know where scientists stood on the whole nature versus nurture thing. Regardless, she still blamed her mother. If not for the genes Skye Pictures had passed to her son, then for letting her kids wind up in foster care after she'd overdosed enough to nearly kill herself. Josie had been eight; Sam had been seven.

Josie remembered the Sam before foster care, happy and playful and caring. The Sam who came back didn't look people in the eye and he bit his nails to the quick, and he ground crayons into waxy clumps. How long had it taken him to laugh again? Josie couldn't remember. She was so young then; she hadn't understood how dark the world could be.

Not that her mom was even around to take the blame. She hadn't been home in three days. She'd landed a bit part in a made-for-TV historical and had made friends with the casting director, which Josie took to mean she was sleeping with him.

Douglas headed for the door, and Josie slipped out from under Sam's feet. "Thank you for coming. For helping him."

"Yeah, well, just remember, I was never here."

Nico offered a single nod to Douglas and said, "I'll catch up later."

Leaving Josie to close the busted door, he headed, uninvited, into the kitchen. When she walked in after him, he was standing at the sink, helping himself to a glass of water.

She stopped in the doorway, her heartbeat increasing from the slow thud of exhaustion to a stuttering tap against her rib cage. Nico belonged to the streets now. To drug trafficking. To guns and violence. Not in her kitchen, holding her favorite glass, drinking water that never forgot to carry the taste of iron.

"I won't forgive you for being there and not helping him. I won't forgive you for any of it."

His smile was soft, but she could see the anger brewing in the tension lining his jaw and in his stormy eyes. "You could blame yourself a little too. Maybe he'll grow up when he doesn't have you directing his every move."

He set the glass in the sink and wiped his lips with the back of his hand. She didn't budge from the doorway. He paused in front of her, sucking up all the air. She was reminded of the way the Santa Ana winds carried an angry heat in late summer that made it hard to breathe.

"I heard you stole a car with an old woman in it," she spat out. "Heard you threw her out and left her on the side of the road." His hands tightened into fists, which, for some reason, only made her want to provoke him more. "Do you know what these rumors do to Francie? Do you even care?"

It gave her a brush of satisfaction, being able to anger him. She'd built up a fear of him over the years, but it was falling away like a layer of skin she was shedding. In its place, anger and a humiliating love vied for first place.

When he didn't defend himself, some of her satisfaction waned. "Most of the time I wish I'd never met you," she said into his silence.

One of his hands locked around the side of her jaw so fast she didn't have time to flinch. His thumb pressed into her chin. "Me too. It would all be so much fucking easier."

There were things she knew before their lips touched. Everything she believed in would be contradicted in a relationship with him. Worse, she'd be ushering in a bigger mess of danger than Sam was. And any romantic ideals she'd held over the loss of her virginity were girlish fantasies. But somehow, no matter how far away he'd seemed, she'd always known it could only be Nico.

Pressing in and quieting everything else was the faint whisper in her gut that it would end badly. Experience told her that, with Nico, there was no other way.

And still it didn't stop her.

Chapter 22

THE SQUEAK OF JOSIE's door had her eyelids fluttering open. Startled by the bright light pouring in through the windows, she sat upright. Or attempted to. Her head pounded, her tongue was thick and dry as a salt lick, and nausea rolled over her in a slow wave. *Welcome to the other side of that drinking thing.*

"Morning, dear. I thought you might want something to eat." Myra stepped into her room, Tidbit at her heels. She was dressed and bright-eyed and balancing a tray in her hands, making Josie feel even more out of sorts.

Rubbing the sleep from her eyes, she glanced over at Zoe's bed to find it empty. "What time is it? And where's Zoe?" She cleared her dry throat and added, "She didn't wake me up. And is Carter watching Buttercup?"

"Everyone's just fine, dear. You can give yourself the gift of a minute to wake up peacefully. Sometimes I forget you were raised to think your middle name is Atlas."

"I wasn't raised with a middle name at all," Josie said, rolling her neck. There was an awful crick in it, which meant she'd slept at a terrible angle.

"I guess Josie Pictures says all it needs to say."

Josie shot a look toward the partially closed door and frowned. She hadn't heard that name spoken aloud in years. Myra had said it aloud a time or two, but that was a month or so after they'd met, after Josie had gathered the courage to tell her everything there was to tell about the life she'd left behind.

"No one heard. They're both outside," Myra said with a wave of her hand. "It's a beautiful morning. The patio's half-full, but it's one of those fortunate days when no one's in much of a hurry, and everyone's having a nice time."

A glance at the alarm clock showed it was a quarter to ten. Josie couldn't remember sleeping in this late in all her life. "Linda doing okay? I needed to help prep this morning."

"They're fine, and the last of the quiches and scones are coming out of the oven as we speak. And no one's any worse for the wear. Except you maybe. I'm guessing you have a headache."

"A splitting one."

"Have a sip of tea. It's chamomile. It'll calm and rehydrate you more than anything with caffeine would." Myra set the tray on Josie's lap and sank carefully beside her. From his spot on the floor, Tidbit shuffled backward, then took a running jump, just making it onto the bed. He scrambled over Josie's legs and over to her other side where he settled down into a beg, paws planted, ears forward, offering an almost imperceptible whine.

On a plate next to the tea was an apple-cheddar scone, warm and with a lump of butter on the side. Josie's mouth watered in anticipation of the dense, salty-sweet scone. After a few sips of tea, she pinched off a piece and nibbled cautiously, doing her best to ignore Tidbit's cocked head and hopeful stare. Her wary taste buds exploded at the sharp flavor of cheddar and the tart apple. Somehow, it was exactly what her rioting stomach wanted.

Sometime in the middle of the night, she'd woken up and felt miserable enough to head to the toilet. She'd been thankful when she didn't throw up. But maybe doing so would've gotten some of the toxins out of her system.

One or both of her parents had been alcoholics. She didn't know enough about her dad to say with any certainty. All she knew was that, whenever her mother had spoken of him, she'd referred to him as "that worthless alcoholic." Whether it was true or not, last night made it clear Josie had every reason to ward off alcohol for good. Carter's hands on her body on that dance floor had woken a sleeping dragon of desire and a fresh tidal wave of fear along with it. One beer in, she'd been just tipsy enough to believe a few more drinks might send those feelings into the depths of oblivion. No surprise, they'd only heightened them.

Josie pulled a pillow behind her and rested against the headboard. "Where's Zoe?"

"With Carter. They're in the shed working on the fairy houses he promised to help her build."

Of course. Seeing Myra's inquisitive look, she said, "I didn't sleep with him if that's what you're wondering."

"I wasn't, but I'd only have applauded you if you had. It's rare that women allow themselves the gift of wild abandon, especially after taking on the role of motherhood as you have."

Josie rolled her eyes, but she couldn't deny her skin still tingled where Carter's hands had been on her body. When they'd gotten home, she'd leaned on the hood of his car during a wave of queasiness. He'd ended up carrying her all the way up here to her bed. On her side of their connected room, Zoe had been sleeping like a log and hadn't so much as stirred.

A fresh wave of embarrassment rolled in as she remembered something else. She'd gotten back up after Carter tucked her into bed. She'd tugged out of her dress—and out of her bra—while he was standing a foot away. How much had he seen in the dark? Considering he'd helped her into her nightgown, there was little hope much had been left to his imagination.

Instead of getting back in bed, she'd stepped close and tucked her head in the crook of his neck and draped her arms around his waist. How long had they stood like that? She had a terrifying feeling she'd asked him to stay with her. Dear God, *what* had she been thinking?

No wonder her mother had had a new guy every month. Alcohol certainly broke through barriers.

"Why are you going to New York with him?" She took another cautious nibble of the scone.

"You may not have noticed, but I'm getting up there in years. It's not every day a woman my age gets an offer to be chaperoned around such an amazing city. I went once in my youth, but I barely remember it. I'd love it if you came with us."

"I can't, Myra. I can't risk it."

"You have to test that ID sometime."

"Not in an airport. And not yet."

"It's a long trip, but maybe the four of us could drive. Though Zoe would miss much more school that way."

"It's okay, Myra. You know how I feel about big cities. And there's the tea garden to run."

"I didn't hold out much hope I'd be able to convince you. But will you let me take Zoe?" Myra let out a small breath and locked one bony hand over the other. "Please."

It wasn't a question but a plea, a raw, vulnerable one. Josie met her gaze, and her heart sank at the sadness in Myra's pale-blue eyes.

"It's that book," she added. "The one about the Statue of Liberty. We've read it together dozens of times. 'The Great Lady,' she always says. I want to be with her when she sees it. If I had a bucket list, this would be at the top of it. And all she needs to fly is a social security card. Which she has, thanks to that man we found."

Josie clamped her hands around her warm cup. Myra never asked for anything. How could she possibly refuse this one request from the woman who'd given her and Zoe everything?

"Okay." It came out small and feeble and helpless. Before now, she'd never thought of okay as the worst of the four-letter words.

Myra brushed unshed tears from the corners of her eyes. "Thank you, Josie. She'll be in good hands."

An image from last night filled her mind. Carter was a good man, and an honest one. And she trusted Myra with her life. Zoe would be okay. "Have you said anything about it to her yet?"

"Not about her going of course, but this morning she heard that Carter's taking me. I think she's bubbling over at the hope you might let her go along as well."

"How soon are you thinking?"

"The weekend after next if the tickets aren't too steep. Thursday afternoon through Sunday or Friday through Monday. Depending on whether you want her missing two days of school or just one."

"Being without her that long is going to be harder on me than it is her."

"Carter said he'd leave you his iPad, and something or other about an upgrade and unlimited live video time."

"That might help."

Josie let the thought settle in as she dropped a few crumbs in Tidbits reach. He inhaled them with a flash of the tongue.

So, Zoe was going to New York, to all those fun places Carter had mentioned. Josie had no doubt that letting her go was the right thing to do. It was a solid step toward living a life that Josie was afraid to lead. At the very least, she could raise Zoe not to carry her fears. However rough Zoe's start might've been, she didn't have to carry those scars. God only knew if the memory of any of it was buried into the recesses of her young mind.

"Thank you." Myra brushed Josie's hair back and planted a light kiss on her forehead. "I know I don't have to tell you this means a great deal to me, but it does. Now eat and rest up. Take a bath maybe. Our world won't stop without you being our fearless leader for one morning."

Chapter 23

ONE OF THE THINGS about being six meant that Zoe still looked angelic in her sleep. Thick eyelashes, full lips, and a face not yet lined by experience or time. Rather than waking her, Josie slipped into bed beside her and draped an arm around her petite frame. They still had a few minutes before Zoe needed to get ready to head for the Dubuque Regional Airport, where she, Myra, and Carter would be catching a short flight to Chicago in two hours.

Zoe twisted in her sleep and curled into Josie automatically like she had when she was younger and had trouble sleeping. Josie brushed Zoe's silky hair back from her forehead and allowed a few more minutes to tick by until she heard Carter rolling his and Myra's suitcases to the top of the stairs. A big part of her was terrified to let go like this, but something else—coming from somewhere deeper—told her this was the right decision.

"Hey, sleepyhead, it's time to get ready to go," she whispered finally.

Proving for the umpteenth time her ability to move from zero to sixty in seconds, Zoe popped up as soon as her eyes were open. "I'm going on a plane. A real, live plane right into the sky." She threw off the covers and clambered over Josie, accidentally kneeing her in the privates before hopping down to the floor and heading straight for the toilet in Josie's room.

"And you're going to love every minute." Josie trailed along after her.

"For sure there are windows, right? Make sure to look up when we're in the sky."

"I will, baby, and yes, there are windows."

"I wish you were coming. Are you for sure you aren't going to be sad without me?"

"I'll miss you, Zo, but I'm only going to be happy for you. My only concern is that you listen to Myra at all times like we talked about. No wandering away even a little bit. And always hold her hand if you're near a street or on a busy sidewalk, okay?"

"What if I want to hold Carter's hand?"

"That's fine, but Myra's known you since you were a baby. You stick by her."

"Okay, Mommy." Zoe flushed the toilet and splashed a trickle of water over her hands before Josie reminded her to wash them fully and brush her teeth.

When she was finished, Josie sat on Zoe's bed soaking in the dark-gray light of early morning as Zoe tugged on the clothes that had been laid out last night. Afterward, they gathered her suitcase and backpack and headed downstairs.

Josie's heart began to tap out a faster rhythm as she spotted Carter's and Myra's luggage by the back door. They were at the kitchen table having cups of tea and coffee and day-old scones. Linda would be arriving any moment, but she wasn't here yet.

Buttercup rose to his feet as Josie and Zoe walked in. Tall enough to be nearly face-to-face with Zoe, he went from a sniff of her hair to a lick of her nose, making Zoe giggle. Tidbit was nowhere in sight. It was Josie's best guess that he was still curled in Myra's bed protesting this early morning activity.

Carter locked eyes with Josie and nodded toward Buttercup. "Sure you're okay caring for him this weekend?"

Maybe because her palms were starting to sweat in anticipation of watching Zoe drive away without her for a long weekend, it was all Josie could do to bite her tongue about it being too late to change plans. It wasn't Buttercup's fault, but she was still hesitant around him. More than hesitant. He scared the crap out of her several times a day. She was pretty sure the dog sensed it and was standoffish around her as a result. "We'll make it through."

Carter had been relatively reserved since their night at the bar, compared to his earlier charismatic and flirtatious self, at least. Josie thought maybe he was being respectful, things having gone the way they did. She'd tried her best to put it from her mind entirely, but every so often, little whispers of memory rose to the surface like the soft tapping of late-summer rains on the windows. The desire that accompanied them—nearly knocking her off her feet—wasn't sexual. Not really. It was the sense of security, of being cared for, that she'd gone her entire life without that had threatened to be her undoing this last two weeks.

"Feel free to shut him in my room when you're busy if you don't want him wandering around," Carter said as if picking up on her hesitation. "And what do you want to do about his leash?" He was referring to the fact that he had Buttercup following him around indoors and out without one. All he needed to do was give a light click of the tongue or snap of the fingers, and the dog trotted over as if he'd been conditioned to listen to Carter's direction all his life.

Considering she'd had incredibly little to do with the giant of a dog since his arrival, it was unlikely he'd behave as well for her. "Do you want to practice putting it on him while I'm still here?"

Clearly, Carter knew it too.

Josie was disinclined; her pulse was racing fast enough knowing she was about to see Zoe off. Maybe it would be easier if she'd broken down and petted the dog before this. Given him some treats. He'd been here two full weeks, and she hadn't so much as touched him. He'd sniffed her several times, but each time she'd frozen, and her hands had locked into fists.

Zoe buried her fingers in Buttercup's thick fur. "He's the best dog in the world. You're going to love him, Mommy."

"You know what they say, wonders never cease." Seeing Zoe's unmasked adoration, a real smile lit her face. "You'll remember your homework, Zo, right? You don't have much, but you're missing two days of school."

Zoe mumbled that she'd remember, and Myra rose from her chair. She headed for the sink and set her and Carter's cups in it. "We'll check in frequently."

"I know."

All too fast, they were headed out the back door, then Carter was putting the suitcases in the trunk of his car. Josie was glad the morning was still a dark silver-gray. Hopefully it would hide any worry spilling into her eyes. Beside her, Zoe yawned heavily but somehow managed to do so without her grin dissolving.

Carter opened the driver's-side door and disappeared inside. A second later, the engine revved to life. Buttercup had followed them out. After relieving himself, the big dog lumbered over to Carter's side of the car and sat down on his haunches expectantly. Josie got the sense he was waiting to be let inside.

Josie hugged Zoe tightly and planted a dozen kisses on her cheeks. Zoe giggled and dragged a hand over her face.

"It's going to be all right," Myra said, hugging her. "Don't worry about a thing."

"I won't. She's in good hands."

"Yes, I've noticed," Myra replied, glancing inside the car.

"Yours, Myra. You're the one I trust with her."

"I know, dear."

After another round of hugs, they filed inside—Zoe to the back seat, Myra to the front. Josie shut the passenger door and stepped back, folding her arms across her chest.

Carter popped out, heading toward the trunk. Rather than stop at it, he kept walking until he reached her. So, he wasn't *not* going to say goodbye. Josie opened her mouth, but the words stuck in her throat inexplicably.

Before she registered what was happening, he leaned in and pressed his lips boldly against hers. Startled, she started to pull back just as one of his hands wrapped around the back of her head. He locked his other hand around her hip, drawing her closer into him.

It was a real kiss. Deep and hungry. And it set her insides on fire. For the first time all morning, she wasn't thinking about planes or fake social security cards or crowded city streets.

Something inside her registered that she should pull away or slap him or something. Even if the feeling of his mouth on hers was perfection.

Finally, it occurred to her to question whether Zoe was witnessing it from inside the car.

He ended it before her body finished warring with her mind and she decided how to react. He pulled away just enough that his mouth was mere inches from hers, and he rested his hands atop her shoulders.

A playful smile formed on his lips, and his teeth gleamed white in the silvery light. "With any luck, that'll keep you preoccupied until midway through the flight at least. Before you know it, she'll be safely on the ground, and you'll be able to enjoy the long weekend."

He dropped hold of Josie abruptly and headed back to his side of the car like it never happened. He stopped by Buttercup who was still staring at Carter's door as if he were waiting for him to pop the seat forward so he could hop in. Carter stopped to ruffle his fur. "Good boy, you. Be good for Josie, will you?"

"That's it?" Josie's words came out in a squeak.

He turned and winked at her in the silvery light. "For now."

Then his door was shut, and the Mustang was in reverse. Josie and Buttercup watched them go with, no doubt, the same confused looks on their faces.

Chapter 24

IT WAS BUTTERCUP'S SOLEMN brown eyes that threw her. That, and the humanlike way his eyebrows raised as he watched her move about the house after the tea garden closed and everyone left for the day. So different from Tidbit, who hadn't yet seemed to notice Myra's absence; he'd napped and chased the cats and hung out on the terrace most of the day with the customers, hoping for handouts. Now he was dozing again.

Buttercup was less like a dog and more like a person circling through the life of a dog. A bit surprisingly, Josie had gone ten hours and had managed not to touch him yet. His tail had brushed against her leg, and his cool, moist nose had pressed against her bare calves a few times, but he seemed to have picked up on Josie's determination to keep this thing between them as much of a business transaction as she could.

She'd worked through breakfast and lunch—she'd not been in the space to acknowledge hunger until she'd heard Zoe was safely on the ground in New York. While she and Linda had finished prepping for tomorrow and cleaning up from lunch, she nibbled on a handful of grapes. Now that everyone was gone, Zoe was safely on the ground, and Josie had time to herself, she was starving. She heated up a large slice of today's special quiche, kale with shallots and goat cheese and a sweet-potato crust, and a cup of tea—she'd chosen the *Missing You Matcha*—and headed to the terrace with Myra's mother's prayer book in hand.

She couldn't say exactly why, but she needed to reread Abigail's letter. Myron's picture was no longer with it, which Josie found to be like a peanut-butter-and-jelly sandwich without the jelly. She read Abigail's original version rather than her translated one, marveling again over Abigail's precise and distinctive penmanship. After the hours she'd spent revising it, Josie knew every next word before her eyes landed on it, and still, it left her wanting.

Sitting back in her chair after she finished, Josie ate another bite of the mouthwatering quiche, savoring the buttery, salty, flaky layers of the sweet-potato crust in a way she normally didn't. Great food, sex, the unadulterated bliss of a child, birdsong, sunsets, the loyalty of a trusted dog at your feet. They were the first fleeting pleasures that came to mind, but the list was endless. And none of them could be held onto. Whenever anyone tried, pleasure faded into the dullness of routine.

She'd first thought it was Carter who was the interloper here. Even though they were still waiting on the DNA results to come back, for the first time, she found herself wondering how different *she* was from Myron. She'd come here a vagrant with an infant in tow, and she'd been swept away by this house, by these grounds, by the love of, and for, a charismatic Moore woman. She worked day in and day out on these grounds and attempted to hold onto a beauty that didn't belong to her.

What if nothing belonged to her at all? If, in fact, it had been her fate to die that day in LA with her brother. To never have gotten Zoe out. How long could someone stay hidden on borrowed time? How long could you avoid your fate?

As if sensing her turmoil, Buttercup, who was splayed on his side next to her chair, hauled himself to his feet with a grunt. The big dog was so tall, he was almost at shoulder level. Thankfully, his cuts were healed and hardly visible in his thick fur.

"Do you remember what happened to you, Buttercup? Do you

dream about it and wake up sweaty and terrified of what might be about to burst through the door?"

That's total personification, Josie. Besides, dogs don't sweat. They pant.

Like he'd done with Zoe, Buttercup abruptly shoved forward and swiped his giant, pink tongue fully across her mouth and over the tip of her nose.

Coughing, Josie turned her face and dragged a napkin over it. "Please. No tongue. Never tongue. I see you licking your privates when no one's looking."

Undeterred, Buttercup pressed in and rested his giant furry head on her thigh, his eyebrows raised as if to say, "Really, you haven't petted me yet? What's holding you back?"

"Fine," she said, placing one hand cautiously over the top of his shoulders. "But don't take this to mean we're friends."

His fur was so much softer than she'd imagined. Thick, silky, and inviting. No wonder Zoe couldn't keep her hands out of it. She ran her hand along the length of his back, and he wagged his tail and shifted sideways so she had an easier reach. She ran her hand down his back over and over again, surprised to find it as rewarding for her as it seemed to be for him. "You and me, we're the interlopers here, you know. Waiting to see if someone comes to claim us. Or if we get to stay."

A quarter moon was sinking in the west as Josie walked through the gardens early Monday morning. The long day ahead might've felt less daunting had she been able to sleep in, but she'd opened her eyes at a quarter to six like every other day. With the tea garden closed today, she had nothing but the dogs and her thoughts to fill her time until Zoe, Myra, and Carter returned around 6:00 p.m.

It was September, and the garden was still in bloom with the last of the summer and early fall flowers and herbs. As she walked the grounds, Buttercup hung by her side, leaving only to do his business in the far corner where Carter had been training him to go. Tidbit, who was finally seeming a bit lost without Myra, trotted about, sniffing this and that, popping his head into bushes in hopes of spotting a squirrel or stray cat.

The whole grounds seemed to be basking in the long hush of night as the sky lightened in the east. A heavy dew covered the bushes, flowers, and grass, soaking Josie's bare feet, and one or two birds were starting to trill erratic morning songs. She inhaled deeply through her nose, savoring the earthy garden scents.

After Buttercup made his way back to her, she paused to inspect one of the three painted fairy houses that Zoe and Carter had placed around the flower beds. Reminiscent of a Smurf house but painted in a rainbow of colors, the little house sat on a wooden stilt just above a carpet of white daises.

Inside its latched half door, a trail of ants was devouring a peanut-butter cookie. Josie opened the door and swept the cookie to the ground. Buttercup inhaled it—ants and all—with a single swipe of his tongue.

She'd not thought about him getting bitten, but when he didn't seem fazed in the slightest, she figured his tongue was thick enough to keep him safe. She headed to the other two houses in other beds and swept them out, giving the cookies a shake to free them of any ants and dropping them so Buttercup could catch them in midair. On the other side of the yard, Tidbit was too busy sniffing around one of the birdbaths to notice Buttercup's special treatment.

"So, what should we leave in return?"

Buttercup cocked his head and stared at her as if he were trying to figure her out.

Jewelry maybe, or some fun little trinkets, she decided. She would head into town later this morning to see what she could find.

The part of her that would forever be her mother's child warned it was ridiculous to feed this fairy nonsense any more than she already had.

But what was the harm in indulging Zoe in a bit of fantasy? Too much work had gone into the houses not to have them catch a hint of something. So, after a lazy breakfast with the dogs on the terrace, she jogged—and missed Carter razzing her along the way—showered, and then headed into town to shop. She took her time, browsing through more than a dozen shops on Main Street. After a bit of deliberation, she returned to three different stores to purchase her favorite finds: a miniature gold pot with a four-leaf clover on its front, a small turtle with a diamond-shaped shell made of jade, and a miniature glass puppy figurine that could pass for a young Buttercup.

By the time Zoe, Carter, and Myra had landed in the Dubuque Regional Airport, gotten their bags, and were driving home, Josie had survived the long, quiet day, filled the fairy houses, and had Zoe's favorite dinner of homemade chicken fingers, smashed red potatoes, cheddar-cheese biscuits, and a salad with extra peas and tomatoes ready and waiting for all of them.

Her heart skipped a beat when she heard the rumble of Carter's Mustang as it rolled onto the parking pad next to the detached garage. Thanks in part to her focus on being separated from Zoe and getting used to Buttercup, Josie had been distracted enough that she'd not come to any resolution as to how to address that kiss of Carter's.

Determining to pretend it never happened until they were alone and she knew what she wanted to say, she jogged around back to greet everyone. Tidbit and Buttercup dashed to the edge of the yard and trotted back and forth by the back gate, just as anxious to greet everyone as she was.

Once Zoe was in her arms, it was as if they'd never been separated. "Oh, my little sweets, I think you grew. And I'm so excited to hear all about your trip!"

"It was so fun, Mommy," Zoe said, launching into a litany of her new favorite things.

With Zoe still on her hip, Josie hugged Myra, careful not to trip over Tidbit who was running around her in circles. "How'd you hold up?"

"It was the weekend of a lifetime," Myra said. "My only sadness was that you weren't there to share it with us."

Zoe slid off Josie's hip to wrap an excited Buttercup in a bear hug—the sight of which didn't even have Josie flinching. She credited her new comfort with the giant dog to his hopping onto her bed the last few nights at bedtime—like there was no question whether he had equal rights to it—and snoring the night away. His endearing sleepy-time demeanor had warmed her to him just as much as his daytime habits of patiently following her everywhere she went.

"But none of my new favorite things are better than Buttercup," Zoe added, burying her face in his thick neck once more. His tail pumped in response, and his pink-purple tongue burrowed into her ear. "Except Lady Liberty, maybe," Zoe said, drying dog kisses off her ear with her shoulder. "And the big lion at the zoo, but you couldn't get close enough to touch him. Only Buttercup's going to be with us forever, isn't he, Mom?"

Josie looked at Carter, who was pulling their luggage from the trunk. The more days they went without someone coming forward to claim him, the more it seemed he was Carter's for certain. But would he want to take him back to New York?

Her mother's voice was somewhere under the surface, attempting to ruin the moment by insisting nothing was forever. Fighting it back, she said, "You know, Zo, he's here now, and they say it's always better to celebrate the things you have than to worry about what you get to keep."

A bit to her surprise, her words caught both Myra's and Carter's attention. They turned at the same time to appraise her.

Zoe debated her mom's answer for a second or two and seemed to accept it. "We saw ten hundred dogs, but none of them were as sweet as Buttercup."

Once they were inside the gate and halfway to the house, Zoe remembered the fairy houses. She dropped her backpack in the middle of the walkway and made a beeline for the closest one, exclaiming that, surely, they'd had a visitor by now.

Josie bit her lip as she watched. Sure enough, Zoe's whoop of joy carried across the yard as she wiggled her hips in a victory celebration. "The fairies came! The fairies came!"

Carter glanced Josie's direction again as they headed over with Myra to check out Zoe's find. "You're full of surprises today, Josie Waterhill."

Josie shrugged her shoulders in attempt to downplay his compliment, but heat rushed to her cheeks all the same. She made eye contact with him for the first time, locking her gaze away from his mouth, since the sight of it would almost certainly make her want another kiss badly enough to lose focus on anything else.

Inside, at dinner, Zoe talked nonstop about their weekend, only pausing to chomp little bites of food and to let Carter and Myra chime in. Zoe's favorite highlights included Central Park, the Statue of Liberty—as if there'd been any doubt—and the Brooklyn Zoo. The hot-dog stands and subway system also ranked high on her list. Her only dislikes were the smelly streets and crowds of people walking about not having any fun.

By the time she'd eaten enough to warrant being finished, the first signs of exhaustion had clearly set in. After a giant yawn that went uncovered, and which Myra warned was big enough to catch flies, Josie suggested it was time for a bath.

Surprisingly, Zoe didn't argue. "Can I have bubbles tonight?"

It was early enough that Josie didn't mind. She'd been making her own lavender-infused bubble bath and bath salts since Zoe was three and showing early signs of a struggle with hyperactivity. On bubble-bath nights, Zoe liked to linger. That was less than ideal when they were in a rush. Tonight, Josie would have no complaints if she did. Giving Zoe a bath and massaging her little scalp was as calming for her as it was Zoe.

Afterward, when Josie was tucking her into bed, Zoe pushed up and threw off the covers. "I didn't say good night to Carter and Myra."

Josie couldn't help but notice how Zoe called out for Carter first when she stepped into the hall. Carter was downstairs in the parlor setting up a full-sized computer he'd flown back in his luggage.

She trotted downstairs and came back a few minutes later, stifling a big yawn. Josie had been trying not to listen, but she heard "I love yous" proclaimed by Zoe for both adults.

Once Zoe was tucked back in, she snuggled next to her until Zoe's face was calm and her breathing was deep and even, then she headed to Myra's room.

"I'm sure you're wiped," Josie said, shutting the door and stretching out on Tidbit's side of Myra's queen bed as Myra slipped underneath the sheets on the other side. "Can you handle a few more minutes?"

"For you, for certain. But if that girl needs to sleep in in the morning, I hope you let her."

"I will." Josie tucked the spare pillow underneath her head and curled around Tidbit, who'd gone from a tight ball to spreading out as long as his short legs would allow as if declaring that this side of Myra's bed belonged to him.

Myra closed a hand over Josie's arm. "You should have been there."

"I know, I'm sorry I missed it. I wasn't ready."

"Next time then."

"What makes you think there's going to be a next time? Didn't he get what he needed?"

"I saw the kiss, Josie. I wasn't spying, but I saw it in the side-view mirror."

Josie pressed her eyes shut. "Please tell me Zoe didn't see it."

"She talked right through it. I have no idea what she said, mind you," Myra said, chuckling. "It was some kiss."

Josie didn't need Myra to tell her that.

"It's not every day a man comes around who'll kiss you like that," Myra added.

Josie snorted but pressed her lips together as Myra pointed a stern finger her way.

"This isn't about sex, so you can stop giggling like a schoolgirl, Josie, although you could use a lecture on that too. What I'm talking about is a connection that goes much deeper, and I know that you know what I mean."

An image of Nico rushed to her mind, shoving her to the pavement and covering her as gunfire exploded all around. Yes, she did.

"It was just a kiss," Josie said, her voice barely a whisper.

"*Just*. It's my opinion that people use that word when they want to undermine the importance of something that shouldn't be undermined."

Josie sat up, tucking a strand of hair behind her ear. "I was happy, Myra. Before he came—I didn't *want* a man."

"Survival and happiness are two very different levels of living. Now, be a dear and hand me my tote bag over in the corner, will you?" Myra pushed herself up to a sitting position. "There's something I want to show you, and you're more limber than me."

Josie got it for her and waited as Myra sifted through it. She pulled out a folded-up brochure and passed it to her.

"I found him tossing it into a waste can as the movers were putting his things in storage."

It was a flyer for a farm for sale in Connecticut. Josie skimmed the description and took in the storybook pictures. Rolling hillsides.

A hundred-and-ten-year-old fully restored farmhouse on twenty acres. White fencing and flaming-red maple trees all around.

"How does this have anything to do with Carter?"

"He didn't share at first, but the picture caught my eye. Turns out it was a dream of his. He was trying to convince his ex-fiancée to move out of the city so he could write, and they could raise a couple of kids. Thankfully for us, it turned out that it was only his dream, not hers."

Josie passed the flyer back to Myra, trying to close off the strange bubble of emotion in her chest she wasn't ready to define. "I could picture him there."

"Funny, but I could just as easily picture you and Zoe there too. Someday."

"I'm never leaving you."

Myra smiled softly. "Some fledglings take a little more convincing to leave their nests than others."

"Chirp, chirp," Josie said, leaning over to press her lips against Myra's forehead. "Good night, Myra. I can't help but wonder if you were this bad with your own kids."

"Sadly, I never thought my own children had such agreeable prospects. But the truth is, so few of us get it right with our own kids. By the time our grandkids come around, we start to understand the gravity of our mistakes." Myra waved a hand dismissively. "But I won't lose sleep over it. I'll see you in the morning, dear."

Josie shut Myra's door and paused at the top of the stairs, looking down. From here, the golden-yellow light spilling out of the parlor was warm and welcoming. The old writing desk Carter had taken over was out of sight from where she was standing. Buttercup was in full view, sprawled out on the floor watching as Carter assembled his computer. Hearing her, Buttercup thumped his tail but didn't lift his giant head.

The urge to head down into the light and warmth and life was almost overwhelming. Before Carter came, the house was weighted by silence after Zoe and Myra were asleep. In the three and a half weeks he'd been here, she'd gotten into the habit of drifting off to sleep lulled by the sounds of life he added.

Her hand curled around the banister's smooth newel cap. Twenty steps were all that separated her from a night of solitude to one of warmth, light, and—who knew what else. The memory of his lips on hers flooded in full force, warming her blood.

There was no denying the itch in her bare feet to descend the steps. With nearly five and a half years of being the last one awake, she'd had enough solitary reflection to last a lifetime.

But her breath had gone shallow from fear more than it had excitement. Carter was an all-or-nothing kind of guy. If she let him in, he'd want to see behind doors she was doing her best to keep bolted shut.

When it came to a choice between fear and pleasure, she wasn't her brother. Had they both suffered from the same poor impulse control, God knew, their volatile world would've fallen apart even sooner.

But Sam wasn't here anymore. He hadn't grown up enough to make safer choices. And the one thing Josie knew was that she wasn't going to let the same thing happen with Zoe. Dropping her grasp on the newel cap, she turned away and headed into her room, shutting the door and allowing the too-comfortable blanket of seclusion to envelope her for another night.

Chapter 25

ON TUESDAY MORNING, ZOE woke up wide-eyed and eager for school, so getting her dressed and on the bus was a breeze. Oddly enough, Josie was a bit disappointed. She missed having Zoe around all the time and wouldn't have minded her going in late. Had she treasured those formless days before Zoe's school years enough? From now on, all she'd have with her were summers and holidays. Before she knew it—God willing—Zoe would be even busier with normal kid and teen things like after-school sports, hanging out with friends, getting a job, driving a car, going to prom, heading off to college.

After waving goodbye as Zoe's bus pulled away, Josie headed back to Myra's. Nothing about her own life had been normal or ordinary. How old had she been when she'd taken on the role of making sure she and Sam made it to school on time? Eight, maybe nine. Those years blended together, a mix of sweet pleasure during her mom's good days and sadness and fear during the bad ones. Josie had heard enough horror stories about her over-the-top Jehovah's Witness grandparents to wonder, if her mother had had a kinder upbringing, things might have been different for her and Sam.

Linda, who'd been prepping today's special when Josie and Zoe left for the bus stop, had stepped out to the porch for a phone call. She held up a finger as Josie passed by. "Be in in a sec," she whispered.

Josie heard Carter's low voice coming from down the hall as she stepped inside the house and shut the front door. Until he came,

Josie hadn't craved a thing. Not a damn thing. As far as she'd been concerned, she and Zoe had lived in a dream world.

Now, Zoe was drawing "father wanted" posters, and Josie was doing her best not to notice how her blood was pooling in her nether regions like a long-slumbering volcano waking from dormancy.

Knowing she couldn't avoid the kitchen just because he was in there, she kicked off her shoes and headed barefoot down the hall, savoring the cool floor against the bottom of her feet.

She couldn't help but notice how Carter and Myra's conversation stopped as she soon as she pushed open the swinging door. *So, they had secrets now?* A sharp prick of jealousy stabbed at her.

"Hey." She headed for the sink and filled a glass with water, even though she wasn't thirsty.

"You running today?" Carter stood up from the table and carried over his empty coffee cup, setting it in the sink. Damn it if some part of her didn't long to lean close and soak in his smell. He wasn't like some of the guys, young and old alike, who came here to dine and had an invisible cloud of cologne surrounding them; Carter's scent was subtle enough that she only caught it when they were this close or it wafted over on a breeze.

"At some point," she said, stepping back half a foot to put a smidgen of distance between them. "Probably not until later. Did Stump's call with the delivery time?"

"Between ten and ten thirty," Myra answered. The majority of the week's food and supplies were delivered every Tuesday before noon.

"Good, because I still need to rotate the inventory this morning." As careful as everyone was, when they got busy, things shifted out of place over the course of the week, and Josie needed to rotate what remained, bringing the oldest items to the front.

Resting against the counter, Josie sipped her water and looked over at Myra. Myra's lips were pursed tightly together, and she seemed to be looking anywhere but at her.

Josie hadn't been wrong when she'd walked in; there was a weird energy in the room. Carter lingering at the sink next to her didn't allow her any mental space to figure it out either.

"What's going on?"

Myra looked down at her mug of tea before turning to Carter. "Have you told her yet that the results came in?"

Carter cocked an eyebrow. "Spoiler alert, but the email came Saturday. We're related."

Adrenaline dumped into Josie's system. Myra and Carter had made the trek to a DNA-testing lab a little over a week ago, and even though she'd suspected as much, having confirmation was something else altogether.

No wonder Myra was acting strangely. Her father, the man who'd raised her and given her a love of tea and left her this home, hadn't contributed to her DNA.

"Myra's your aunt, then?" She looked back and forth between them, feeling as if a canyon was forming, shoving her apart from them. "Congratulations, both of you. Even if it is a bit nontraditional how it came to be. Have you told your dad?"

"Not yet. I'm going to give him a call today."

"It *is* a congratulations," Myra said, "a big one. I couldn't be more thankful to learn it, even at my age."

Josie knew she shouldn't feel anything but happiness for them. And she was adult enough to know this news wasn't going to change Myra's love of her and Zoe. It was Carter's significance here that was throwing her.

He wrapped his hand around the rim of the quartz counter just a few inches from Josie's hip. Even though she was doing her best to look anywhere but there, she caught a good enough glance to notice the defined muscles lining his forearm, the bump of bone on his outer wrist, and short, scant hairs on his arm.

She cleared her throat and stood straight. "I'd better get this pantry organized."

"Want some help?" he asked.

There was no way she could handle working side by side with him in the crowded pantry. Not right now. "I'm good, thanks." Just then, Linda walked through the doorway. *Saved by the bell.* "And I'm sure you've got writing to do."

He nodded just a little too slowly. "We'll catch up later, then."

Later, then? Josie had a sinking feeling he had his own agenda for talking to her today, and she suspected it had to do with that kiss.

All too soon, lunch was over and the skies were clearing up and it was either time to head out for a jog or pretend she was too tired. She wasn't ready to face Carter alone. Not with that kiss still to talk about.

But when they met up in the kitchen and he said he could really use the run, she didn't have the heart to back out. He was stretching by the front stairs when she finished changing and met him out there. His mouth pulled up into a half smile when their eyes met; the lightness in his mood surprised her a bit. She wasn't sure what she'd been expecting, but it hadn't been the playful, carefree Carter who'd been the first to get under her skin.

At a loss for words for the second time in a few hours, Josie started down the steps and fell into a jog.

He nudged her elbow as they rounded the end of the block. "I'm beating you up those stairs today."

She huffed lightly. "You haven't run in four days. Don't you think that'll have set you back? That, and all those hot dogs?"

"It was only one hot dog and more pizza and pasta than I've eaten in years, thanks to that kid of yours, so I guess we'll see."

However far they ran, it always came down to who was going to make it up the stairs first. They'd been evenly matched their last few runs, but Josie had somehow found it within her to haul it up the last few just a brush ahead of him. She'd been running them for five years. She wasn't about to let him outpace her in a matter of weeks, even if he had quit smoking.

He hadn't been exaggerating about that marathon thing, it turned out. He'd run the New York City Marathon when he was twenty-five and the Philadelphia Marathon at thirty. Now that he was closing in on thirty-five, he was thinking of doing another. And he'd been dropping hints about how they could train together.

Josie wasn't about to agree to something like that. Her jogs were somewhere between three and five miles, and even him jogging with her was enough of a change of routine to challenge her stride. God forbid she try to run with a crowd.

Just the thought brought back a memory of the first time she'd run. *Really* run. Her thighs had turned to lead, and her lungs had burned like fire. She'd taken up jogging after she made the decision to stay on here, and it hadn't been easy. Back in LA, she'd thought she was fit enough, but it turned out she was just thin. She would never find herself in that situation again. All brains and no body was just as bad as the other way around.

Suddenly she realized he was glancing over at her like he was waiting for an answer. If he'd asked something, she'd not heard it.

"Zoe said the pizza there was her favorite ever," she said, appreciating how even though his natural stride was several inches longer, he'd set it to match hers.

"It's good. You'll have to try it."

It wasn't exactly an invitation, but it was still something she didn't dare follow up on. They lapsed into silence for the better part of a mile as they settled into the rhythm of the run and their lungs and muscles warmed up.

She was just beginning to feel like maybe that smile really had been just about the stairs when he spoke again. "Whatever your reasons for not going with us, I'd still like to show it to you sometime."

It was enough to make Josie lose a beat in her stride. How did she answer that? It took her nearly a full block as they circled toward town to come up with a response. "I'm sure it's something to see."

"I doubt I'll live there again. You know that piece 'live in California once, but leave before it makes you soft, and live in New York once, but leave before it makes you hard,' or something like that?"

"Not all parts of California make you soft." It was out before she could pull it back. She gave a little shake of her head and reached up to tug her ponytail. "But I can see where you might not want to stay in New York City forever," she added, hoping he'd glaze over the first bit.

"You're from California?"

"I didn't say that. I just said...not all parts of California would... make you go soft." Maybe it was nerves, but her lungs were locking up, making it difficult to talk and jog at the same time.

"True. I think it's Northern California, anyway. Memory fails."

"Where would you live, then? After here?" She asked it more to get his attention off her and California than anything else.

"Good question, but one I'm in no rush to figure out."

Josie figured he was trying to bring it around to them again. They were approaching the town, and without asking, she chose the shorter run and crossed the road, heading into the center of town toward the Green Street Stairs. She wanted to get home. She wasn't ready to deal with any of this today.

"So, you going to tell me where you're from?" he asked into the silence.

Rather than answer, she shook her head and hoped he'd get that she was out of breath. The way her lungs were today, it was either run or talk, and just maybe he'd forget and never bring it up again.

After another half mile of silence and flat sidewalk, and her breathing was under control again. As they neared the bottom of the stairs, Carter began building his speed and nudged her with his elbow. "You ready for this?"

Josie increased her pace to match his but didn't reply. Their feet smacked against the first step in unison. After the first dozen or so stairs, it was clear he was going to win. There was a power in his stride that wasn't sustainable to her today.

"You aren't giving up? Come on, Jos, you got this."

She gave it her best but couldn't keep up. She dropped behind and waved him on when he started to slow. About halfway up, she found a bit more juice and pushed hard, reaching the hundred-and-ninetieth step just fifteen or sixteen steps behind him.

She doubled over at the top, her lungs searing in pain. "Impressive," she breathed, sucking in ten or so deep breaths before she stopped seeing stars.

"Maybe it was all those carbs," he panted. "Or the nitrates."

A breathless laugh escaping, she stood up and was completely taken off guard when he stepped in and closed his mouth over hers. Instinctively, she began to pull back, but one of his arms locked around her waist, and his other hand cupped one side of her jaw.

Surely there were more romantic moments to kiss a girl than when she was red-faced, sweaty, and struggling to catch her breath. She debated pulling away to tell him so, but everything seemed to be moving in slow motion. Without his support, she had a feeling she'd tumble to the ground. Blood pulsed in her ears, making it sound as if she had giant seashells pressed against them.

Her hands locked around his strong shoulders, and she came to her senses enough to break off the kiss and look him in the eye. It was a touch intoxicating, experiencing the rise and fall of his chest against hers. "You aren't supposed to kiss a woman without asking, you know."

"Something tells me if I did that, I'd never have a fighting chance with you. So, you're going to have to look me in the eye and tell me you don't want me kissing you. And I'll promise not to do it again."

As if to ensure she knew exactly what that entailed, he leaned in and brushed his lips against hers, softly until she opened her mouth to it. Then his arm tightened around her, and she felt the brush of his teeth and tongue against hers, setting the v between her legs on fire.

Just when it started to feel like she was floating in a pool of water, he drew back five or six inches. His remarkable blue-green eyes seemed to be telling a joke of their own. "How about it? Are you going to give me permission to kiss you, Josie Waterhill?"

Kissing him was extraordinary—his was the kind of kiss that, if she experienced too many times, learning to live without would be like living without an appendage.

Her lips parted, but nothing came out. She needed to step out of his embrace to clear her head, but she might as well be standing on rubber legs.

"Because, the thing is, I sure as hell could get used to it."

Finally, her defense system stirred to life, doing the job she'd trained it to do. "Carter, I can't do this. It isn't that I'm not interested; I just can't."

"Can't, won't, or don't want to?" he asked, and suddenly she was back on the dance floor with him again, and Myra's earlier words ran through her mind on auto play, "*With a little interest from you, he might very well stay on forever.*"

Would he leave if she turned him down? She didn't want him to go. Not anymore. She wanted him to stay.

Which was exactly why she needed to tell him no.

When she had no answer ready, he leaned in again, pulling her close enough that she could savor every bend and line and bit of muscle pressing against her.

Rather than closing over her mouth, his lips brushed against her neck, sending a wave of goose bumps down her spine. Her knees turned to butter as his mouth traveled over her skin. If it was sweaty, he wasn't complaining. To keep standing, she tightened her grip on his shoulders. Something between a grunt and a moan rose from the middle of her throat.

He'll leave you, just when you need him.

She was fairly certain the voice was her mother's—coming to her out of nowhere like it always did. Would she ever be free of it? Those early years, the ones that had shaped her more than any others ever could, those years her mother had had free rein of her developing mind. Of her psyche.

No doubt, the answer was no, she'd never be free of it. But it didn't mean she had to listen to it.

You could give him a chance and see for yourself.

That thought came from somewhere else entirely—the same place that had told her it was safe to follow Myra home, all those years ago.

Suddenly it occurred to Josie she'd heard that voice for the first time right at the top of these steps that looked out on the most beautiful view she'd ever seen. That first time she'd looked down on the town, impossible as it seemed in the moment, she'd wanted to make Galena her home.

As it had turned out, doing so hadn't been that impossible at all.

She stepped back a foot, separating herself from the enticement of Carter's mouth and arms so quickly a chill swept over her.

He stayed quiet, watching for whatever was coming. She looked from him down the street toward Myra's, then out toward the town below that was framed by trees brushed with the brilliant red and yellow hues of early fall.

Her life had changed once right here at the top of these stairs. Her heart raced at the idea of giving it permission to change again.

"You're either really smart or really lucky, you know that?"

"Why's that?" he asked, one side of his mouth pulling into a grin.

"Because, if you'd kissed me anywhere else but right here, I think I'd have told you no."

He dragged his fingers through his hair as his smile widened. "Can I take it that's a yes?"

She bit her lip. "I'm not all that confident in the yes, but it isn't a no either."

When he stepped in to kiss her again, she met him in the middle.

Chapter 26

JOSIE WOULDN'T HAVE THOUGHT it possible how much she began to look forward to the quiet hours when Zoe and Myra were sleeping, and it was just her and Carter and Buttercup. Certain things about Carter were becoming wonderfully predictable. Like how, when he was writing, he sat back in his chair and let out a long breath when he was working through a string of words that was evading him; as they began to form, he drummed his fingers on the desk a second or two, then his fingers danced along the keyboard once again. And how, when they watched one of the DVDs in Myra's old movie collection, he draped his arm over her back and smoothed the bare skin above her waist with his thumb, sending her into a comfortable trance.

Josie's favorite nights were when they headed into the kitchen for a late-night cook-off. He wasn't a talented cook by any measure, but he didn't seem to care. He'd add too much salt or liquid or burn something to a crisp and get her laughing so hard she'd nearly pee her pants.

Tonight, after their fourth cook-off, she said she thought he was ruining his food on purpose. "You're just letting me win because you want in my pants, aren't you?"

"I wouldn't put that past me." He waggled an eyebrow and pushed his failed omelet aside for another bite of hers. "But it sounded like they would taste well together." He'd added both capers and jalapeños and had overcooked it too.

"To you, maybe," she said with a laugh. She'd made a veggie and goat-cheese omelet, and they ate it together. Halfway through, she leaned close to nibble on his neck. "You can get in my pants anyway, you know."

That was all it took to get his attention off their late-night snack. After a kiss that melted her insides into goo, he said, "What do you say I wrap it up and save it for tomorrow?"

"Wrap *what* up?" she teased. She loaded the dishes into the dishwasher while he put the omelet and the rest of the ingredients in the fridge. She was putting away the olive oil and a tea canister when she noticed that he'd followed her into the pantry empty-handed.

While the pantry wasn't the first spot they'd broken in outside of Carter's bedroom, it was the most crowded. Her mind raced with half a dozen reasons not to, but her body responded with a hell, yes. She ended up braced against the only twenty-four inches of empty wall not lined with shelving and her legs locked around Carter's hips.

She credited it to his ability to read her, but they climaxed at the same time. Afterward, he continued to brace her against the wall and rest his forehead against hers as their breathing slowed.

"I could get used to you, you know."

She ran her hands through his thick hair, over his ears, and along the stubble lining his jaw but didn't respond.

"That's a lie," he added. "It isn't just that I could get used to you. It's that I *want* to get used to you. I want this; I want *you*. For more than just today. I know you don't want to talk about it, but it doesn't change anything."

Josie felt the familiar walls inside her begin to close tight, like a giant ocean clam when a predator was near. Damn him anyway to bring it up when they were intimate like this—when he was still *inside* her.

The first night they were together, almost three weeks ago now, she'd asked him to keep to the present. "If you want me to be able to handle this—and believe me, *I* want to be able to handle this—promise me you'll leave my life before this out of it," she'd said. "I'm here. Zoe's here. You're here. If there are things you want to share about your family, about your past, I'm happy to listen. But my family's here. My life is here. Nothing before my coming to Galena matters."

She could tell he hadn't been satisfied, that he'd been swallowing back a mountain of curiosity, but he'd wrapped his hand around hers and agreed.

"There's something else," she'd said. "It's the same in the other direction too. If it's further than a week or two out, I'm not going to want to talk about it. Here, this, now. It's all I can handle. And trust me, it's a stretch."

Again, he'd agreed. Probably because he'd wanted in her pants a second time.

Suddenly, Josie felt trapped by the nearby shelves, the cramped space, his body pressing against her, holding her up. "Carter—don't. Please. You promised. I'm here. You're here. It doesn't have to get any more complicated than that."

He swallowed and lowered her to the ground, accidentally knocking over a can of crushed tomatoes in the process. He was either mad or hurt, but Josie wasn't going to press to figure out which.

She was reaching for her wadded-up yoga pants when she felt something wet and sticky between her legs.

"Carter!" she said the same second he said, "Shit!"

"Did it tear?" she asked. Panic flooded in. She had a prescription ready to get on the pill with the start of her next cycle, but until then, they'd been relying entirely on condoms.

"Yeah. Completely. No wonder it felt so good."

She grabbed her pants and made a mad dash for the hall bathroom. She didn't quite know what to do other than sit on the toilet and hope gravity could work a miracle. She forgot about closing the door, and Carter appeared in the doorway. He leaned against the frame but remained quiet. He was probably doing the same thing as her, counting out the days since the start of her last period. How long had it been? Fifteen or sixteen, she guessed. It was quite possibly still in her window of ovulation.

"What are you looking at?" she asked, noticing he'd pulled out his phone.

"My calendar."

It was eleven-thirty on a Wednesday night. The odds were slim anything was open, but she asked anyway. "Can you see how close the nearest all-night drugstore is? And can you give me a minute to clean up?"

He stepped away and shut the door behind him without saying anything. When she came out a few minutes later, he was coming down the stairs. Buttercup was awake and looking back and forth between them as if he'd picked up on the subtle panic emanating across the room.

Carter's keys were in his hand. "Everything around here is closed. If you're in the mood for a drive, it looks as if there's one in Dubuque."

"What if Zoe wakes up?"

He ran his tongue over his lower lip but said nothing. Josie blinked as she looked at him. There was something in the set of his shoulders—he wasn't panicky like her. Well, maybe a little. More so, he seemed mad and working to keep it under control.

"Want to wake up Myra and tell her?" he asked.

Josie did the math in her head as she tried to remember bio class and the facts she'd learned. How long did it take those little suckers to break down a wall? An hour? Two? If she waited here for him to come back, she could very well be playing with fire. If Zoe did wake up, which she rarely did, and she couldn't find Josie, no doubt she'd find Myra. Rather than waking Myra up, Josie dashed into the kitchen and wrote a note, then jogged upstairs and set it by Myra's nightstand.

When she came down, Carter was waiting by the front door with Buttercup at his side. Josie closed a hand around one warm, furry ear, and Buttercup leaned into it, pressing into her leg.

Outside, the night was beautiful and crisp, and a zillion stars studded a moonless sky. Carter drove in silence for over ten minutes as Josie gazed at the stars and Buttercup sprawled across the back seat, calmer about the night ride than he was during the day.

Finally, Josie asked if Carter was going to tell her why he was mad. "Is it because I want to take this pill?" She remembered him saying he'd been raised Catholic. Even though it didn't do anything but prevent an unfertilized egg from being fertilized, maybe he disapproved of it.

"No, it's your body and entirely your prerogative."

"Then what is it?"

He was quiet another minute, then finally he let out a breath of air. "You don't want things to get complicated, Josie. You don't want me to feel what I'm feeling. You don't want to talk about the past, and you don't want to talk about the future. You can do your best to slam shut every door around you, but life is complicated. The way I see it, the only thing to do with complicated is talk about it." He drummed one thumb against the steering wheel.

"Case in point, look at tonight. We're committed to being careful and still this happened." He shifted in his seat and his arm brushed against her, making her crave his touch even though she didn't reach for him. "I guess what I'm saying is, eventually, you're either going to have to ask me to ship out, or you're going to have to start talking."

Josie stared out into the darkness and watched a thin row of trees and fence line slipping past. She needed to say something in response, needed to tell him that hard-to-manage feelings were rising inside her too. And they were big enough to be terrifying.

Her throat locked up at the thought of broaching it, but there were things she could tell him about her past—about Zoe—that would help him better understand her fears. She could trust him with the truth. She'd known that even before they started sleeping together.

But it didn't mean she was ready to say any of those things aloud. Maybe she was like her mom that way, clinging to an illusion she wanted to be true.

When she opened her mouth, the only thing that came out was that she'd forgotten her purse and could she borrow a bit of cash.

She didn't have to pick up on the disappointment in his single-word response to know she'd let him down. After that, neither of them said anything at all until they'd gotten to the drugstore.

The ride back was just as quiet with the exception that Josie commented on the remarkable, starlit sky. She still marveled over the difference between the sky here and in LA. Here, the stars glowed, brilliant and white. Carter agreed it was magnificent, and a few minutes later, he pointed out a falling star she wasn't fast enough to see.

When they got to the house, it was just after one o'clock. Leashless, Buttercup clambered out from the back and trotted to a patch of grass, peed a forever-pee, then trotted ahead of them around the house to the front door. Clearly, the easygoing dog had no complaints about this being his new home.

"You'd, uh, better get to bed considering you've got only four hours till your alarm goes off."

Carter was right; Josie would be tired tomorrow. She'd been cutting into her sleep most nights now, but never this much.

Halfway up the stairs, with Buttercup a few steps ahead of them, Josie wrapped her hand around Carter's and pulled him to a stop. She didn't want to separate like this. Even if it was just for a handful of hours.

"Carter, I'm sorry. What you said in the car—I heard it. I know what I need to do to make this relationship work. And I *want* it to work." She clamped her mouth shut and cleared her throat. Once the urge to break out into tears resided, she continued. "Can you just give me some time?"

She didn't know who moved first, but his arms locked around her just as hers did him. He pressed his lips against the side of her temple. "I'm sorry, too, and yeah, I can do that."

"Thank you."

Seeing they'd stopped progressing up the steps, Buttercup made his way back down and planted himself on the step next to Josie, letting out a yawn that sounded as if it belonged to an old man.

Josie's bare feet sticking out from under the oversized flannel blankets were the only thing that prevented her from sliding from a light doze into a deep sleep. Shifting, she attempted to wiggle them under the covers without having to sit up and expose any more of her body to the chilly night air.

It was the perfect night for a fire in the fire pit. The star-filled sky was cloudless, and there was little to no wind to whip the smoke around. And it was chilly enough to breathe out clouds of steam.

Carter had come outside to build the fire as she'd gotten Zoe to bed. He'd brought out a couple of long-neck beers, and Josie had had just enough of one to cop a light buzz, then get drowsy.

There were four chairs and two chaise lounges surrounding the stone fire pit on the far side of the lower terrace. Josie and Carter were sharing one of the chaises while Buttercup was stretched across the second one, dozing as his front feet paddled through the air as if he were in an easy lope.

"You getting cold?" Carter's arm was draped over her back, and he ran his hand along her side.

"I'm fine so long as you don't have to get up again. You're better at putting off heat than an instant hand warmer."

"If you ask me, this is great sleeping weather. I could stay out here all night." His voice was thick and heavy, and Josie guessed he was as drowsy as she was. "Have you ever taken Zoe camping?" he asked after a sleepy pause. "Maybe we could head out to a state park for a night or two this fall."

Josie took a few seconds to consider her reply. "Maybe. She's always wanted to try it. I bet we could borrow a tent from Linda."

She'd never been—no surprise—though, after an eviction, she and Sam had slept in their mom's old Accord in gas-station parking lots so many nights in a row that she had sufficient experience staring at the sky as she fell asleep. Though staring at light-dulled LA night skies out the window of a car that reeked of Camel cigarettes while her mother hit up strangers for her next fix wasn't a bit like sitting around a campfire, eating s'mores, and having fun with a family that loved and supported you.

As Carter spoke of a few parks he'd come across, doubt swept over her. Not for the first time, she wondered how a girl who'd stolen bananas from the fruit stand and boxes of Little Debbie's from the open door of a delivery truck so she and her brother would have something to eat could ever really fit into this life.

Carter's hand on her back suddenly felt like sandpaper. She pushed up and savored the wash of cold air that pressed in, erasing the trails of heat from his body.

"I have to pee."

She headed inside and used the bathroom. Afterward, she stared at herself in front of the mirror for what felt like forever. *It's like Myra says, you're never going to heal unless you talk this shit through with someone who can help you process it.*

Josie doubted there was a therapist alive she'd trust with some of her secrets.

Before heading back outside, she went into the kitchen and grabbed another beer for them to share and a handful of the glazed walnuts that were a staple in the spinach salad. Buttercup had awakened and lifted his big head; he thumped his tail and watched her return. Josie paused to give him a quick rub with the back of her hand that was holding the beer.

After a few sips, Josie handed the beer to Carter and settled back under the blanket next to him. "Walnut?"

Carter ate one off the tips of her fingers. As his lips brushed her fingertips, she kissed his temple, then his neck.

It had been almost a week since the accident with the condom. After dialing their lovemaking back for several days afterward, their last two make-out sessions had escalated into the full thing, including earlier tonight while snuggled under cover of the blankets, serenaded by the crackle and pop of the fire.

It wouldn't take much effort on her part to get something started again. The part of her that craved him now, at all hours of the day, wanted to, but her train of thought had dropped her in the deep end of doubt.

So, instead of giving her hungry lips and hands permission to arouse him, she took another swallow or two of beer and burrowed under the blankets beside him. She closed her eyes and breathed him in. If he disappeared tomorrow, would she remember this smell? This solid, inviting feel of muscle and skin covered by a thin layer of sweatpants and a hoodie. The gentle rise and fall of his chest.

He yawned and pulled her closer; his breathing was slow and relaxed, showing he was close to sleep. With her hand on his chest, she savored the easy rhythm of it.

She must have drifted off again because she jerked awake sometime later. She bolted into a sitting position, a new version of a familiar nightmare still clinging to her. Carter had been in it this time, along with Sam and Nico. As always, she'd been the bystander, watching her world collapse into chaos while she fought for control of sluggish, slow-to-respond limbs.

So much of the dream was still hauntingly vivid. Sam's eyes had

had the hollow, sunken look of when he'd been struggling the worst with the heroin addiction as he had in their last years in LA. Dream Sam had been tugging her around the corner of a building, and tiny drops of blood had been dripping from his mouth, nose, and ears, but he'd not seemed to notice. Before they rounded the corner, so she could see whatever it was he wanted her to see, the small drops of blood had become large ones and then a trickle and then a stream. Josie had been trying to dab a towel at his face, but it had been so hard to hold up her arms. Finally, they'd trudged around the corner just in time to see Nico put a bullet in Carter's forehead, and Josie had bolted awake.

"Hey, you okay?"

Carter was awake, and Buttercup was sitting up on his chaise watching her with one paw draped over the armrest. The fire had burned down to the passive glow of embers, and the temperature had dropped another few degrees.

Judging by the burn in her throat, her scream hadn't just been in the dream. "I, uh, fell asleep."

"That was some nightmare."

"Weren't you asleep too?"

"I woke up ten or fifteen minutes ago. You were sleeping so soundly; I didn't want to wake you."

She felt even more vulnerable, knowing he'd witnessed it. "It's over."

Carter sat up and placed the flat of his hand on her back. "Want to tell me about it?"

"No."

"Josie, you have it almost every night, don't you? That same dream?"

She got up, grabbed a poker, and stabbed at the fire, sending a cloud of glowing embers into the air.

"About three or four in the morning," he continued. "I've come to your door a few times, but you've slept through it. Until tonight."

"How do you know? Do I scream?"

"Tonight, you did. Mostly it's just muffled moans and cries." He got up and squatted next to the fire pit, resting his elbows on his thighs, facing her. "Who's Sam?"

Josie's insides turned to ice at the sound of her brother's name on Carter's lips. She poked at a glowing log, sending more embers into the air. The mountain that was her past pressed in, breathing over her shoulder the same way Zoe did when she was waiting for an answer. She shook her head and swallowed.

"Did you love him or fear him? I can never tell when you say his name."

"I'm not going to talk about this."

"We *need* to talk about this. Maybe I can help. Whatever it is, I doubt it'll get better until you talk it through with someone. How about you give me a shot?"

A huff escaped. Josie dropped the poker on the edge of the fire pit and faced him. "You're a good man, Carter. A really good man. But you can't help me with this."

"What if you're wrong? How about try me and we'll see. If some guy hurt you—or wants to hurt you…"

Anger surged through her veins. She saw it clearly for the first time; he was never going to stop asking questions. And she couldn't even blame him; she was a poorly hidden enigma. Anyone who got as close as he had would never stop wanting to tease out the answers.

"I'm going to bed. Do you need help with the fire?"

"Josie, don't shut me out. Please."

As if he'd picked up on the tension between them, Buttercup woofed decisively and clambered down from the chaise. He looked back and forth between them, wagging his tail.

Josie shook her head. "Don't open my door when I'm asleep, Carter. I mean it. If I have to lock the door to keep you out, I'm not having sex with you anymore."

She took off up the hill, adrenaline surging through her body.

"So that's all we've been doing? Having sex?" he called after her. "Because that's not how I work. Now or ever."

Josie whirled around, anger and sorrow blending with the fear racing through her veins. "He was my *brother*, you ass!"

On the ground next to her was a large limb that had fallen off the big oak. She picked it up and threw it down into the yard with a satisfying "Urgh!" It traveled further than she'd anticipated, crashing into one of the lower beds, and most certainly making a mess of the plants and flowers.

Buttercup trotted a few feet down the hill after it but stopped and whined, then looked back at her.

Without waiting for a response, Josie fled for the quiet security of the house, her body and hands shaking from unspent adrenaline. Buttercup was at her heels when she reached the back door. "No." She held out her hand to stop him from following her inside even though she was certain it caused her more pain than him. "You're Carter's dog, not mine." She shut the door to his whine, the tears she'd somehow managed not to shed the last month running down her face. What had ever made her hope this might work?

Chapter 27

AFTER SEEING ZOE OFF on the bus, Josie made her way up to Myra's bathroom before getting to work in the kitchen. She would be helping Linda with today's special, a savory butternut squash soup, a perfect match with the cold front that was moving through.

Myra had plans for breakfast in town and was standing in front of the mirror wrapping curlers into her hair. Josie collapsed onto the rim of Myra's tub and let out a long breath, one that didn't escape Myra's notice. The fact that Josie's eyes were still puffy this morning probably didn't help matters.

"Had your first spat, did you?"

Leaning against the wall, Josie tucked her knees into her chest and wrapped her arms around her shins. She hadn't needed to tell Myra when she and Carter first slept together either; she'd read it on her face the morning after.

"You're too big to be sulking on the edge of a bathtub, Josie. Unless you're finally regressing and letting yourself experience the youth that was stolen from you."

Crying was supposed to be restorative. But Josie felt worse this morning, not better. A mother of headaches was practically splitting her skull in half, she'd barely slept, and there was a long day in front of her. It was early October and the start of the county fair, so they were sure to be packed to the gills today unless the gray clouds and cold front moving through kept customers away.

"If you're not going to talk, why don't you help me wrap my hair—what little I have left, anyway."

Josie shoved off the tub and began sectioning off small swathes of Myra's silky gray hair to wrap into the curlers. "You look beautiful with straight hair, if you ask me."

"I look old, that's how I look."

"Who are you meeting again?"

"Bob Waxler. My friend who tempted fate by sending Carter here, remember? I thought he was due for an update on what he made possible. I have a wonderful nephew who I never would have known had it not been for him. Only fate—or the universe or whatever they're calling it these days—wasn't only sending Carter *my* way, was it?"

Josie opted not to answer. Earlier this morning in the kitchen, when Carter had closed a hand over her back and said he was sorry, she'd wanted to melt into his arms and tell him everything.

A part of her did, at least.

The other part—*that* part—wanted to send him packing and bolt the doors behind him. And she wasn't sure which part of her was going to win.

"So, are you going to tell me what's bothering you, or have you decided you'd rather sulk?"

While debating whether she was ready to unleash the flood of all that she was holding in, Josie accidentally twisted a curler a little too tightly.

Myra winced. "I need all the hair I have left, dear."

"Sorry." Meeting her gaze in the mirror, she said, "I can't even sleep next to him without having nightmares, Myra."

"Don't you have nightmares regularly, regardless of whether you have a man in your bed?"

Josie pursed her lips. "I can't believe Zoe sleeps through them if they've been waking you up again."

"My sleep has been fitful for years, and thankfully, that little girl of yours can still sleep without a care in the world."

"I think my being with Carter is making them worse."

"You need a good therapist, dear. You and I have both known it since you came here. Don't let my nephew slip through your fingers because of a series of mistakes and abuses that are no fault of your own."

Without letting go of Myra's hair, Josie used the tip of her comb to scoot the curler box closer and accidentally knocked over a pill bottle in the process. It rolled off the counter onto the floor.

"I'll get that," Myra said.

"It's fine." Josie let go of Myra's hair and swept up the bottle in her fingers. As she set it on the counter, a New York address caught her eye, and she began to examine it in more detail. The pills were in Myra's name, prescribed by a doctor she'd never heard of and dated the weekend of her trip to New York.

Myra held out her hand for the bottle. "It's nothing, dear."

"You didn't tell me you saw a doctor in New York."

"It was nothing, just a little reflux."

Josie held the bottle a moment longer, staring at the name of a medicine she'd never heard of. Something was off; she knew it even if she couldn't place it. She heard it in the nearly indiscernible tension in Myra's voice and saw it in way she'd stiffened when Josie reached for the bottle. Suddenly she remembered a dozen snippets of conversations that had ended when she'd walked in the room.

Without offering an explanation, she took off with the bottle, heading downstairs to the empty parlor. Carter had been in it when she'd gone up to Myra's room, but now his computer was in sleep mode. But he'd given her his new password, "Zoeinfairyland," and offered her use of it whenever she needed it. It took only a second to pull up seemingly endless entries about the drug. She clicked on a lead article that focused on an emerging new drug being used to fight certain cancers in patients deemed too fragile to handle chemotherapy.

In the background, she heard Myra making her way down the stairs and Carter whistling as he walked down the hall from the kitchen. Ignoring them, she kept reading and skimmed a second article in confirmation.

Finally, she turned from the computer and took them both in. Myra was white as porcelain, though her hair only half set in curlers made her seem a touch comical. Carter was standing next to Myra holding a steaming mug of coffee. From the way he'd gone quiet, it was clear that he'd noticed the pill bottle next to his keyboard. And they were both staring at her as if she were a volatile substance that needed to be treated with caution.

The concern in both their expressions only made her want to shut down even more.

"You have cancer? Why didn't you tell me?" It was harder to talk than she might've guessed; little razors were cutting into the back of her throat.

Myra crossed the room and carefully bent over her, her knees popping in disapproval. She covered Josie's shaky hands in her own.

"I asked Carter not to tell you. It was my hope that in a few months I'd be able to tell you a different story than the one I can tell you right now."

Josie slipped her hands from under Myra's grasp. "What do you mean?"

"I'm old, that's what I mean. Cancer's a bitch, Josie, but I'm eighty. In a perfect world, it's unlikely I'd have another full decade of life in these frail bones."

"Then how many do you have in this sucky one?" Any strength had all but washed from her tone by the end of the sentence.

After giving Josie's knee a single pat, Myra righted herself slowly and crossed to the window. "There's the possibility of surgery in my future," she said, "especially if those pills are able to shrink the tumor. With it, I could easily have five more years. Who knows, maybe longer."

Carter, who'd been watching the exchange in silence, crossed the room and set his coffee on the desk. He squatted in front of Josie and closed one hand over the back of her calf, squeezing it soothingly. He was lucky her body had gone numb, or she'd probably shove him right onto his ass.

She needed to clear her almost-paralyzed throat in order to talk. "And if they don't?"

"A year at most," Myra said after a pause, her voice faltering. "I should know more in another month."

Josie bolted to her feet. "Don't," she managed as Carter stood with her and started to close a hand over her shoulder.

She needed to go to Myra, who seemed exceptionally pale and broken as she watched for Josie's next move. Josie loved her more than anyone except Zoe. She needed to tell her it was okay; she was angry, but she'd forgive her. She'd be here with her. Every step of the way. No matter what.

But back when she'd needed it most, she'd built a fortress around her heart, and it was always there, ready to do the work she'd built for it to do. The walls inside her closed up defensively, just like she needed them to.

"That really sucks," was all she managed before she stormed across the room and out the front door.

Carter jogged out of the house after her as she rushed down the porch steps. "Josie, I'm not saying it was right of her to keep it from you, but please don't walk away from her right now. That woman in there loves you more than anyone in the world."

Who did Carter think he was? He'd gone from prying into her past last night to telling her how to navigate her relationship with Myra.

There was so much she wanted to say in reply. Words of betrayal. Of defense. Of accusation. But they were locked up so tightly, she was certain she'd never get any of them out.

So instead, she looked his way long enough to tell him where to go—long enough to see the hurt register in his eyes—then continued down the steps.

She had no idea where she was headed, so long as it was away from the two of them.

Myra met Carter at the door as he stepped inside. With her hair half full of curlers, the pleading look she gave him made her seem a touch deranged. "You were right; I should have told her after seeing that doctor."

Carter forced himself not to look out the window after Josie as she disappeared down the street. "There's nothing that can be done about it now."

"Nothing but wait her out." Myra let out a breath that seemed to deflate her like a balloon. "She's worth the difficult time you're having breaking through those barriers of hers, by the way. If you're wondering."

"I have no doubt of that."

After a pause, she added, "If only I'd hid those pills out of sight."

The last thing Myra needed weighing her down was guilt over her decision to keep the truth from Josie a while longer. "She had to learn sometime. And now, it'll be out in the open."

"Maybe so. But the thing about Josie, she's frailer than she believes. In some ways, at least. In other ways, she's tougher than kryptonite. I'm afraid I might be one of the few things than can break her."

Carter wasn't entirely sure he disagreed. But he wasn't about to tell Myra that either. "Are you hungry? I could make you something to eat." Outside, the wind was picking up and the sky was clouding over. It was likely to be a slow morning when the tea garden opened.

"I am hungry, but perhaps we could go out instead? There's a breakfast place I enjoy in town. If we stay here, I'll have my ear trained on that door every moment."

"Yeah, sure. I'm good with that." He nodded toward her half-curled hair. "I'm guessing you need a little bit."

"Suddenly the way I look when I meet up with Bob later doesn't seem as important. I'll take these out and brush through the curls. It doesn't take anything more than a light headwind to flatten them, anyway."

Carter chuckled. "I'm ready when you are."

Myra's favorite breakfast stop was tucked into the lower Galena hillside, offering a view of the bustling town around it. Carter got lucky with a close parking spot, and there wasn't a wait to be seated.

Bothered by the chill seeping in from the large windows, Myra kept her jacket on and zipped as they perused menus and were served two steaming mugs of coffee. "She left without a jacket. I hope she isn't too cold."

"Maybe she's back by now." Even though he said it, Carter was doubtful. Josie had had a look that said she wasn't coming back anytime soon.

"I'd be surprised to see her home before the bus," Myra confirmed. "But she'll come back for Zoe. I'm confident of that."

"What happened to her brother?"

Myra dropped his gaze and looked out the window at a group of women passing on the sidewalk. "If she's talking to you about her brother, I'm sure she'll share more with you in time."

"She isn't. She says his name in her sleep. She hasn't told me anything."

"If it helps, she won't share her past with anyone."

"She did with you."

"And I won't betray her. When she first came, her night terrors were much more...chilling. She confided in me more out of necessity than anything else. She couldn't pull out of them easily on her own, and Zoe was a bigger mess than she was in many ways. Josie needed me to know. Her nightmares nearly disappeared for a few years. She felt safer, I think, before you came. Now that you're sleeping together, they've gotten worse. She's like a soda, my Josie. All that pressure bottled up so tightly, then someone comes along and shakes it up. That pressure needs to release somehow."

"Are you saying I should take a step back, if she isn't finished with me already?"

"No, that's not what I'm saying at all. If I wasn't afraid of her running again, I'd tell you to shake her until she explodes. I'm fairly confident she'd still be Josie, just not Josie in a bottle."

Carter took a swig of coffee. "I wasn't planning on her. Not in the slightest."

"The best things in life aren't planned for."

"I can't help but think that I just spent eight years patching together a relationship, and it fell to shambles anyway."

"You can't compare Josie to that woman. She might have her faults, but she'd never cheat on you."

"No." That he knew for sure. Josie was nothing like Katherine. He wouldn't have fallen in love with her if she was.

"You're searching for her online, aren't you? I caught a glimpse of your computer screen the other day. Whatever you do, make certain she doesn't see it."

"Will I find her? Eventually?"

"Yes. She doesn't know it, but I've made a point of running a search on the computers at the library once a year. I endure my own week or so of night terrors every time I confirm that someone out there is still searching for her. Actively too."

Carter's jaw went rigid. "Could you give me her name at least?

Because the one she's using came from a mom-and-pop diner on the corner of Water and Hill Streets that went out of business about six years ago."

Myra's thin fingers closed over her throat. "You're a smart man, Carter. You'll find her soon enough on your own. You're searching for pictures of a young woman who went missing around the age of twenty. That's all you really need to know."

Chapter 28

AFTER A SEVERAL-MILE WALK, Josie hung out at the park in town, watching the gentle flow of the river and using a cove of evergreens as a wind block. At first, it didn't seem as if the soft ripple of the water could calm the unease flooding her the way the ocean had done the times she and Sam had taken the bus to Manhattan Beach. Sam had walked around searching for bits of shells to throw into the ocean while she'd sat on the sand and lost herself to the rhythm of the waves.

As minutes spilled into hours, the first hint of acceptance ebbed in. It wasn't that she'd never considered Myra might not be here one day; Myra was eighty years old. But people were living longer and longer. Myra took care of herself, ate well, and managed her arthritis. Before this morning, Josie had every reason to hope Myra would be here another ten years at least. Realizing she might only have one was unfathomable.

Hunger and the chill in the wind eventually forced her to get moving again. She crossed over the pedestrian bridge and made her way into the center of town. She warmed up by browsing in a series of shops, her attention caught by figurines that Zoe would struggle not to pick up. She staved off hunger with a handful of samples in the old-time market. It came as a surprise when she realized she was close to the spot where she'd first planted herself on a bench hours after arriving in town, almost two thousand miles from the only home she'd ever known.

Even though the already-chill winds were picking up, she made her way over to it. Finding the bench empty, she took a seat, twisting to keep her back to the wind. It seemed like a lifetime ago that she'd sat here with baby Zoe—an angel with her brother's eyes and early signs of his intensity too—on her lap. Josie hadn't had a dollar to spare, and a mess of trouble had been calling her name. Yet somehow, she'd found her way to that magnificent old mansion on High Street with one of the most remarkable women in the world as her friend and mentor.

And she'd built a life that shadows whispered was too good to be true.

A single year left with Myra—that might be all she had before it came crumbling down.

A woman in leggings, high-heeled boots, and a faux-fur jacket passed by her, filling Josie's nostrils with the thick scent of too-sweet perfume. Her thoughts trailed to Abigail Moore and Myron O'Brien. Abigail hadn't mentioned which street she'd been on, but Josie guessed it might well have been this section of town where she first spotted Myron. He'd come here like Josie with little more than the clothes on his back, made a life for himself, and taken a lover. *And ended up dumped in the river.* Who was Josie to hope she'd find her happily-ever-after here when others before her who'd been just as worthy hadn't been so lucky?

She sat still as long as possible, waiting for guidance of one sort or another, but nothing came. Finally, she was shivering so wildly, she couldn't sit still any longer.

And she didn't need guidance to be certain of one thing. Regardless of how much time Myra had left, Josie wasn't leaving her.

She warmed up in a candle store, inside which she realized it would be time to get Zoe off the bus in another half hour. Rather than head up the steps and pass by Myra's along the way, Josie kept to the street and sidewalks, heading the long way up Green Street, approaching the bus stop from the opposite direction.

While still two blocks away, she spotted Carter's empty Mustang parked across the street from Zoe's bus stop. Scanning the area, Josie spotted Carter leaning against the trunk of an ancient oak tree. He was browsing on his phone and either ignoring or oblivious to the mommy trio who were gawking his direction as they talked.

Josie steeled herself as she continued walking. She was angry he hadn't told her, but she knew beyond a doubt Myra would've made her wishes clear. To tell her, Carter would've needed to betray Myra. And knowing him, his silence most likely hadn't been an easy one.

Carter spotted her when she was within fifty feet of him. He slipped his phone into his pocket and strode the final block toward her purposefully. It came as a bit of a surprise, the way she allowed her stride to quicken too. She melted into him, burying her face in his chest and slipping her arms inside his jacket as she soaked in his warmth.

He smoothed back her hair and pressed his lips against the top of her head. "I'm sorry. So very, very sorry. I should've told you."

"I understand why you couldn't."

Her mother had told her men like him were nothing more than actors playing a part—men who treated women with compassion and tenderness and respect. In her mother's world, that might well have been true. But she wasn't in her mother's world anymore.

Even though he'd not said it aloud, Carter loved her. Josie had glimpsed it in a dozen different ways. It was here, now, in his touch and the unmasked emotion in his voice.

Too vulnerable to address it, she turned her attention to something safer. "Why did you drive here? Myra's house is three blocks away."

"She's been worried all day that you're going to take off." His arms stayed locked around her, and his mouth was just above her ear, tickling her as he spoke. "She asked me drive to Zoe's school to make sure you didn't have those kinds of plans. When I saw Zoe get on the bus, I drove here hoping to find you."

"Well, she can stop worrying; I'm not strong enough to run again."

"She can't lose you, Josie. It would kill her faster than the cancer she's fighting."

"I know. I'm not going anywhere."

He let out a long exhale, and Josie caught a hint of mint and lemongrass on his breath. "The thing is, I don't want to lose you either."

Josie pulled back to look at him. "Were you drinking tea?"

"Myra insisted *Peace of Mind* calmed the nerves." He grinned. "But I tell you I don't want to lose you and that's your reply?"

Josie bit her lip. "You don't like tea."

"I'm starting to see where it has its benefits." He cocked his head slightly. "But make no mistake about it; I'm a mug man. So, if there's a blend you're going to ask me to try, you'll have better luck if you don't serve it in a teacup."

Josie brushed her lips against his. "I won't. Promise. And I have the perfect blend for a blustery afternoon like this."

"Blustery, huh?" His grin was cut short when she closed in for a second kiss. She locked her nearly frozen fingers on both sides of his face and opened her mouth to his, savoring the taste of chamomile, mint, and lemongrass on his tongue.

She didn't know why a single cup of tea mattered so much, but it did. It wasn't that she hadn't already picked up on a dozen wonderful qualities. She had. *But Carter was open to change.*

"I love you, Josie," he breathed when they pulled apart.

She felt equal stabs of pleasure and pain. "How can you love me when there's so much of me you don't know?"

"I don't know all of you, but I know enough. I know Josie Waterhill. Kickass mother. Master of card houses. Manager of tea gardens. Maker of exotic tea blends. Loyal friend. Lover of Buttercups. Winner of cook-offs."

Stifling a laugh, Josie buried her head against his chest and closed her eyes. "You forgot one."

"What?"

"Lover of Carters." After a short pause, she clarified, "One Carter, anyway."

Her words were muffled by his shirt, but she knew he heard them by the way his hands locked tighter around her hips.

"I wasn't sure you'd feel safe enough to admit that. Especially today."

"If I hadn't spent the day trying to accept the fact that I might lose Myra, I don't think I could've."

They stayed locked together until the screeching of the bus's brakes forced them apart. When the doors opened and Zoe clambered out, Carter kept Josie's hand locked in his. It was clear Zoe noticed by the way her eyes lingered on them, even though she didn't stop talking long enough to acknowledge it; she had so much to tell them about her day.

───

Carter chuckled over the way Zoe's mouth twisted in concentration as she squeezed homemade Play-Doh through her fingers. The kitchen counter and surrounding floor was a mess of flour, and Buttercup was hanging out nearby, trying to swipe occasional drops of dough.

"I like how squishy it is." Zoe tightened her fingers until all the dough had squirted out in globs. She yelled up at the ceiling for her mom to come see it.

"Maybe we should give her a bit longer, Zo?" Carter suggested. "I think she's talking to Myra."

"You made this with your mom?" she reaffirmed, even though he'd already said so. She lifted the dough to her nose and inhaled deep enough that her thin shoulders lifted.

"Yep. A lot when I was your age."

"I wonder if my mom ever made it. I love how it smells. It's my third favorite smell in the world, just under root beer floats but better than fresh doughnuts."

"Oh yeah? So, if root beer floats are your second favorite smell, what's your first?"

Zoe's eyes grew as big as saucers and she shook her head, sending her brown hair tumbling over her shoulders. "I can't say."

"You don't have to, but just know you can tell me anything."

She kept quiet, dividing her dough and squishing it in her small hands.

Carter moved on to thinking about how quiet it was upstairs. He wondered what kind of mood Josie would be in when she came downstairs, and if he should wind up the Play-Doh foray and get to making dinner.

"You're my favorite smell," Zoe said, taking him by surprise.

He paused with his fingers cupped around the bird nest he was building. He was as moved as when he'd taken her to the doughnut event at her school and he'd overheard her tell one of her classmates that he was more fun to play with than anyone she knew. "Thank you, Zoe."

"For liking your smell?"

Chuckling, he ruffled her hair without thinking, then brushed away at the few dabs of dough that were left behind. "For trusting me enough to tell me."

Zoe dropped her ball of dough and wrapped her arms around his leg, pressing her cheek into the side of his hip. "I want you to be here always."

After taking a handful of seconds to consider how best to respond, Carter lifted her to a clean spot on the counter and brushed her bangs away from her face so she could see him clearly. "I can't promise you to always be here, as much as I might like to be. But I can promise to always be in your life, one way or another."

"What does one way or another mean?"

"It can mean different things for different people. For me, it means if I end up living someplace where you aren't someday, I promise to stay in touch through phone calls and letters and trips. That sort of thing."

Zoe nodded and swept her hair out of her face, leaving a trail of flour across her cheek. "I'd like my way better."

He smiled as Buttercup began to lick her bare toes, which were dangling in the air. Zoe must not have been ticklish because she wasn't fazed.

"You know what? I would too. And I bet Buttercup seconds that." He didn't realize that the door had swung open and Josie was joining them until he'd said it.

Seeing her, Zoe hopped down and dragged Josie toward her mound of dough. It only took a glance for Carter to confirm Josie had shed some tears while she and Myra were talking.

After pulling her in for a hug and a light kiss, he gave her free rein to take over his mound of dough.

"I went to the grocery store this afternoon. You may win every cook-off, but I've got mad grilling skills." He could grill just about anything, from meat to veggies and the occasional pizza or piece of fruit. He'd even done an impressive job with an eighteen-pound turkey. Tonight, he was grilling chicken and asparagus and baking russet potatoes.

"Cooking tonight, drinking tea, and stepping in to help serve at lunch. You're full of surprises today, Mr. O'Brien."

"Mr. O'Brien!" Zoe pulled her hunk of dough apart and giggled. "Just call him Carter, Mommy."

Carter grabbed the wooden crate of potatoes and selected enough for dinner. "It's nice to feel like a productive member of this household."

"What's a household?"

"A group of people who live under the same roof."

"Like a family?"

Zoe was between them, but Carter met Josie's puffy-eyed gaze and raised an eyebrow. "Yeah, like a family."

A bit to his surprise, Josie raised one back at him and agreed.

By the time dinner was finished and they'd eaten, Josie was still a bit puffy-eyed and nasal but considerably better than when she'd first come downstairs. Carter appreciated that, when Zoe finally noticed, she didn't lie about having cried. "Sometimes grown-ups fill up with tears and need to get them out, just like kids," was all she said, and Zoe didn't press beyond asking, "But you're okay now, Mom, right?"

By the fun they had with the Play-Doh while Carter was cooking, Zoe had little reason to doubt she was.

When Zoe realized it was time to go get ready for bed, her shoulders dropped, and she let out a huff. "Mommy, can Carter give me a bath tonight?" She folded her hands in prayer. "*Please?*" she added when Josie didn't immediately respond.

Zoe's nightly bath and story time was her and Josie's special time together. Even Myra never stepped in. He was surprised when Josie asked if he wanted to.

Carter wasn't entirely confident in agreeing to it; he'd made it to nearly thirty-five and had never given a kid a bath before. "Yeah, I'd like that. Just tell me what to do."

"Zoe knows how she likes the water."

"Can I have bubbles?" Zoe jumped up and down.

"So long as you agree to wash them off when it's time to get out," Josie said, sweeping her hair into a fresh knot.

Zoe lifted her hand to high-five them both, something she'd picked up at school and had been doing nonstop for the last week or two.

Bath time was easier than he would've guessed. Mostly, he watched her splash around and answered a dozen or so questions about things he'd not given much thought to in years, like why bubbles were round, what happened to them when they popped, and if he liked to read stories before he fell asleep.

Josie joined them as Zoe was drying off and getting into her pajamas. Buttercup, who'd hung out downstairs with Josie while she did the dishes, most likely hoping to snatch up a few discarded scraps, joined them as well. He sniffed Zoe in earnest as if trying to discern who'd replaced her with someone so clean smelling.

"Can Carter stay while we read, Mom? We could go to your bed 'cuz it's bigger."

Again, Josie surprised him by agreeing. Zoe zoomed over and stripped back Josie's bedspread and sheets as he finished washing out the tub. She crawled in and ushered him in after her. Josie chose the night's selection from Zoe's crowded bookshelf and joined on the opposite side. Barefoot but in jeans and a long-sleeve Henley, Carter settled in, appreciating Zoe's small body pressing against his and the sweet, clean smell clinging to her damp skin and hair.

"You can read, Carter." Josie passed him Zoe's *Frog and Toad* collection.

"I read these when I was a kid."

Wrapping a hand around her mom's arm like a security blanket, Zoe curled into Carter and slipped her small feet underneath his knee. Carter figured he might as well be drawn and quartered; Josie and her little girl had taken a claim to his heart like no one ever had.

Determining they were settling in for a while, Buttercup clambered onto the bottom of the bed and stretched out across the length of it; his back legs draped over Carter's feet.

By the time Carter was finished reading *Frog and Toad All Year*, Zoe was yawning heavily, and Buttercup was snoring.

Too soon, Josie was ushering Zoe to her own bed.

"You're a good reader, Carter." Zoe pressed a small kiss against his cheek, then dragged a hand across her mouth. "Your cheeks are prickly. They tickle my lips."

"Oh yeah? Sorry about that."

"It's a good tickle, not a bad one."

"Thanks for asking me to read with you. Night, kid. I love you."

"Love you too."

Josie walked around to Carter's side to take the book and gave his leg a gentle squeeze before heading into Zoe's side of the double room. "She'll be asleep in seconds if you want to stay."

Carter did. Before tonight, he'd never spent more than a few seconds in Josie's room. The wallpaper wasn't his style—too Victorian, but she'd done things to breathe new life into the room, from the string of soft lights accompanying the crown molding in both rooms to the large framed black-and-white photos of Zoe to the updated bedspread and mattress.

As Josie tucked Zoe in and curled beside her, Buttercup thumped his tail. For a few seconds, he seemed to be considering switching beds but decided against it, leaving his back legs sprawled atop Carter's ankles. Carter adjusted the pillow under his head and closed his eyes. He had no idea he was close to doing it, but he must have fallen into a doze, because the next thing he knew, Josie was curling up beside him. Wrapping his arm around her, he noticed she'd changed into her nightgown.

"She's out that fast?" He cleared his throat and worked to keep his voice low in case Zoe was a light sleeper.

He saw the whites of Josie's teeth in the dark and knew she was smiling. "How do you know it was fast when you were out like a light too?"

"You got me there. Will we wake her?"

"A bulldozer wouldn't wake her, trust me."

He chuckled. "Feeling any better?"

She burrowed into the crook of his arm, resting her head on his chest. "Sort of. After a good night's sleep, I'll be normal again." After a pause, she added, "Thanks for being so good with her. With both of us."

"You make it easy. You both do."

A comfortable silence lapsed between them, extending long enough for him to suspect she was falling asleep. "I don't think I do. But I'll try harder," she said, surprising him with how awake she still was.

"Trust me. You do. Whatever happened to you, I'm here for you."

"That's what scares me."

"I don't understand."

"I know. I'm sorry I can't explain it better." She pressed her lips into his chest. "Will you stay till I'm asleep?"

"Yeah, and longer if you want me."

She gave a light shake of her head. "I do, but the nightmares will be worse if you're here."

A surge of rage washed over him, and he did his best not to let her pick up on it. Whoever had done this to her—if he ever met them… And her brother, Carter could only presume his death hadn't been accidental. The anger flowing through his veins kept him awake until her breathing became deep and even.

Discovering that his feet had gone numb where Buttercup had been lying on them, he rolled his ankles in few circles before standing. He covered Josie and paused at the door, listening to her and Zoe's slightly out-of-sync breathing. Standing there, he knew what he had to do. He needed to find out the truth that was too painful for Josie to tell him.

It took a few hours of searching to realize Myra had all but spelled out what he needed to know. It didn't seem real when he first spotted it, an excerpt of an article on a young woman's disappearance the same day of a string of brutal homicides that took the lives of her mother and brother. It was the brother's name that caused the adrenaline to dump into his system. Sam Pictures.

Heart hammering in his chest, Carter clicked on the link and found himself staring into the eyes of a younger image of the woman he wanted to spend the rest of his life with.

His stomach flipped in a mixture of guilt and relief.

He'd found her.

Adrenaline coursed through him so heavily that he struggled to decipher the words accompanying her photograph. When he finally did, he wished he'd stayed upstairs next to her, soaking in her warmth and her smell.

After reading it, it was hard to think anything would ever be the same.

Josie Pictures. A twenty-year-old young woman whose disappearance was presumed to be related to the disappearance of an eleven-month old girl named Zoe Claire Lehman whose mother was murdered that same day. One of eighteen deaths in a string of gang-related shootings over two brutal days.

It was the only thing he'd never considered. Zoe not actually being hers.

Chapter 29

JOSIE WAS SIX BLOCKS from her apartment at the drugstore where she worked most evenings when Sam came in carrying a whimpering baby in his arms. The sight struck her as insanely out of place; her brother didn't know a thing about babies and had no business looking after one. Even at nineteen, Sam still had a mountain of growing up to do.

She noticed the panic in his eyes the same time as she realized he was gasping for breath, and she stopped thinking about baby care. Adrenaline flooded through her even before she spotted the butt of a handgun shoved into his front pocket.

Sam didn't carry guns. He'd made a million and one mistakes, but he'd never touched a gun. Until now.

"What the heck, Sam?" She was behind the counter and a short line of people were waiting to be checked out. He walked around the counter without a word and grabbed her by the elbow with his free hand, dragging her toward the interior of the store.

She opened her mouth to protest, thinking how she couldn't walk away from the register. Her manager was in back, and she was about to call her for help when Sam stopped her.

"Just shut up and listen, okay? I can hardly think with this kid screaming in my ear." His eyes darted toward the front door.

Dear God, what's he gotten into, running away with someone's baby?

"She's dead, Josie. They fucking shot her."

"Who, Sam, they shot *who*?"

"Jena. I swear I didn't know until today when she called me. It was just one night forever ago."

Jena, dead. It seemed impossible. She'd heard Jena and Nico had had a second child but hadn't allowed herself to think about it until now. Josie had been sleeping with Nico on and off the last few years. Every time she thought she was finished with him for good, something happened to break her resolve, and she'd let him back into her life the way she did the night of Sam's first OD. Since then, she and Nico had gone on like that, not really together but never a hundred percent apart. The string of ODs and close calls and trouble that Sam had gotten into hadn't helped her not to need him.

Josie's throat stung with bile as Sam's news settled in. Jena was dead. The finality of it floated in and out of her consciousness. "Nico's baby."

Wet tears clung to the baby's cheeks, and her fist was crammed in her mouth. The baby's eyes, something about them...

"No, Josie. Not Nico's after all."

The implication of Sam's words struck home. Those eyes, the resemblance was undeniable. "Sam, you didn't. *Not* with Jena."

Jena's brother had been one of the most connected dealers in LA before he went to prison. Everyone who skirted street life like Sam and Nico knew who Jena was. And everyone with any sense knew not to mess with her.

"It's too late for a lecture; she took a bullet in the head an hour ago. *Do you hear me?*"

Josie couldn't find her voice. Ten feet away, customers were calling out in complaint.

"Look," Sam went on, "shit's gotten serious. A couple of guys from Nico's crew caught her in bed with a dealer friend of Ty's. Suddenly everybody's turning on everybody. Nobody's safe."

Panic flooded her. "Do they know you're involved? Are they after you now?"

"I don't know. She called me to her place this afternoon. She wanted my help getting the baby out of the city. She swore the kid's mine, and I guess maybe the timing could be right.

"Then a car pulled up out front, and she dropped the kid in my arms and told me to run out the back. She went to the door and started screaming at a couple badasses that used to run with her brother. Some guy put a bullet in her head before—before—" He shook his head hard before speaking again.

"Someone's got to get this kid out of here. They'll kill her just to make a statement."

"Does Nico know?" It didn't seem possible that he could—that he could be behind any of it. No matter whose kid it was. But the Nico she knew now wasn't the Nico she'd fallen in love with a life-time ago. "Did those guys see you? Can anyone trace you back to Jena?"

He brushed a band of sweat from his forehead. "I don't think anyone saw me; I didn't exactly stop to check. And I don't know who else she told, but I didn't want to go home in case someone ratted me out."

Just then tires screeched to a halt outside the main window, and a series of curses burst out from the customers at the register as they scattered. "Guns," Josie heard one of them yell.

"Shit!" Sam dropped the baby in her arms and shoved her behind him. He pulled the gun from his pocket, and Josie's knees nearly buckled. "Go out the back and run. Now! Whatever you do, don't look back, and don't stop running. I'll find you when things cool down."

"No! Come with me, Sam. I'm not leaving you!"

Sam shoved her into motion. "Hey, somebody up there call the police. Now! Josie, get out of here with that kid! These guys aren't playing. Just run and don't look back. I'll hold them off until the cops come."

The world was moving in slow motion. "Okay," Josie managed to say.

"Go. *Now!* And whatever you do, don't go home."

Josie shot one last glance at her brother. The first shot rang out as she was considering dashing into the break room for her purse and phone in her locker. Hearing the plate-glass window shatter, she bolted out the back door instead, setting off the emergency alarm as she went. As soon as she started to run, the baby began to wail.

Shouts and more gunfire erupted inside as Josie dashed into the parking lot in the fading daylight. A half-dozen shoppers ran out behind her, scattering in all directions. "Run and don't look back," Sam had said.

On legs that felt like rubber, Josie started to do just that.

Chapter 30

MYRA WOKE UP WELL before the sun and knew it would be useless to attempt to fall back to sleep. Whatever good they might be doing, her new pills had side effects, not the least of which was that they made her mouth dry enough to rouse her from sleep desperate for water.

Rather than refilling her cup in the bathroom, she put on her robe and slippers and headed downstairs. She couldn't deny it any longer; the truth was staring Myra in the face. There was another reason she'd not told Josie aside from wanting to protect her.

Somehow Josie's knowing about her condition made it more real. Myra's world suddenly felt like a movie, and life was watching over her left shoulder while death was over the right. And she couldn't help but feel she was just getting to the good part.

She'd lived to be eighty years old, well outliving her mother and father—both fathers, actually, the one who'd raised her and the one whose DNA had created her. But regardless of whether she wanted to admit it, the act of not being here anymore frightened her.

And somehow Josie's knowing stirred up that fear. But as her father had taught her, the only thing to do with such thoughts was quiet them with a good cup of tea.

Halfway down the stairs, she smelled coffee brewing and noticed light spilling from under the closed kitchen door. It wasn't even five o'clock. She stepped into the kitchen to find Carter filling a thermal mug to the brim.

"I didn't expect to find you awake this early." She patted his shoulder as she crossed to the sink.

"Myra...I found her."

She turned to eye him sharply. "Is that so?"

"Yeah."

"Where I expected to see compassion, I find a steely resolution instead."

"What do you want me to say? It never occurred to me that Zoe wasn't hers."

Myra felt her mouth press into a thin line. "Be careful of making accusations about things you know nothing of."

"So, you're saying those articles are wrong?"

"I am saying there's more to this story than you understand after a night of searching through a bunch of internet gossip."

"Yeah, well, since neither of you are sharing anything with me, I've got to find the truth somewhere."

"Wait for it. She'll bring you into her confidence in time. I'm certain of it."

"I'm not waiting anymore, Myra. That independent site, the one you mentioned the other day, who is that searching for her?"

Myra shrugged helplessly. "I don't know. The owner uses a ridiculous pen name."

"Do you think it's Zoe's father?"

Releasing a breath that seemed to deflate her lungs, Myra took a seat on the nearest chair. "You're going to have to ask Josie that. But I can only think of one person from her past who would still be searching for her."

"Well, I'm finding out. Today with any luck."

For the first time, Myra noticed Carter's laptop bag and a backpack on one of the kitchen chairs. "Carter, you're not! You have no idea how dangerous some of those people are."

"That's why I don't want Josie to suspect a thing. I'm asking that you keep my confidence. For her safety, and possibly for mine. If she gets suspicious, she won't be able to retrace my browsing history. I'm going right to the source. We're meeting in St. Louis later today."

Myra inhaled sharply. "You don't know what he's capable of. None of us do."

"Which is why I didn't tell him anything. All he knows is that I'm a journalist from New York, and that I have questions regarding her disappearance."

"I can see the determination in your eyes, so I know there's no talking you out of it. Damn me for giving you that hint, anyway."

"It helped, but I'd have found her eventually."

"Perhaps." Myra would never have expected the morning to take this sort of turn. "Seeing as you're set on doing this, I think you should take a gun."

"I'm representing myself from a newspaper, and I gave a pen name I use occasionally. We're meeting in a public place. I'll be fine."

"I still think you should have a gun. It'll pacify me, at least." She pushed up from the table and waved him out of the room after her. "Unfortunately, the only one I have to give you hasn't been fired in a very long time. Hopefully you can find a secluded place to test it on your drive."

Carter followed her to the library where she sifted through the lowest desk drawer and pulled out an antique pistol hidden in an old cigar box in back.

"I found it years ago buried under a loose floorboard in the corner. Knowing what we know now, I'm sorry to say I suspect the last time it was used, it killed your grandfather. Of course, if I'm right, a whole new set of questions arise, like why it was hidden here in this house and not elsewhere. Perhaps my mother never even knew about it."

Carter sucked in a breath. "Myra, that's a Colt 1911. That's the type of gun they were searching for when my grandfather was autopsied." He held out his hand for it, lifting it into the light to study its craftsmanship. "I'm pretty confident the only luck this gun could bring me wouldn't be in my favor any more than it was in Myron's."

"I for one have always been a believer that luck is what you make of it. Take it with you. At the very least, it could be a bluff if you need it. The bullets are in here." She passed him a small satchel that was hidden in a vase on the shelf. "What am I to tell Josie about why you aren't here?"

"Nothing right now. I'll call her when she wakes up. By then, I'll have had time to think up some kind of story. It'll probably be easier on you if she doesn't know we talked at all."

"There isn't one part of this I like."

Myra sighed as Carter pressed his lips against her forehead.

"Have them call my cell when they wake up. I'll be back tomorrow most likely. You won't have to keep the truth from her for long."

Chapter 31

ADRENALINE KEPT CARTER GOING through the winding country highways, and he reached the St. Louis Gateway Arch an hour sooner than he anticipated. Thanks to too much coffee and too little sleep, he was both groggy and riding a caffeine buzz.

He'd never been to the city before, and the Arch was something to take in. To kill time, he toured the underground museum beneath the Arch, which detailed western expansion, and grabbed a sandwich in the café.

At precisely noon, he headed to the ticket counter and purchased a ticket for the ride to the top, saying his pen name loud enough that the clerk selling him the ticket stopped typing to give him a once over. A movement out of the corner of Carter's eye caught his attention. A guy in a faded-blue hooded sweatshirt was watching him.

After getting his ticket, Carter headed across the wide hallway toward him, fresh adrenaline pumping through his system. "You meeting someone?"

"You, it seems. I expected you to be older," the guy replied, his eyes darting about the room. He was Carter's height almost exactly—six feet, one inch—but with a much slighter build. With the hood pulled over the guy's head, it was hard for Carter to tell much about him other than that he seemed like the typical American twenty-something-year-old white male. Thin as he was and in an oversized hoodie, he looked more like a teen than an adult. And he certainly didn't look the part of a cold-blooded killer. But then again, did anyone?

"Want to go someplace where we can talk?"

The kid scanned the room again before answering. "Let's go outside and walk the grounds." He started walking before Carter answered, heading up the long ramp that led outside.

Carter followed him. "Would you take that hood off?"

"Why?"

"Because I'm a big believer in reading more truth in expressions than in words." That was partly the truth. He was also pretty sure he'd seen the guy before, and he wanted a better look.

The kid paused just outside of the exit and stared at him. Then, after a single jut of his chin, he tugged off the hood. "I guess if you'd been followed, I'd be dead already."

Carter's knees grew weak as he took him in. He felt like he was a few pieces away from finishing an abstract puzzle, yet none of it was making any sense. He could see both Josie and Zoe in the shape of his face, his eyes, mouth, and nose.

"Why are you wanting to write a story about Josie?" the kid said, shoving his hands in the pockets of his hoodie and taking off abruptly down the long concrete path that stretched across the arch grounds. It was cloudy and drizzling lightly, and there weren't many people walking the park grounds. "She's been gone long enough that I thought everybody but me and maybe one other person gave up any real interest in her."

Carter's heart pounded wildly as he trailed after him. "What's your name, because I'm pretty sure it isn't Harry Underball like your site suggests."

A hint of a smile flashed over the kid's face, disappearing so quickly Carter had to wonder if the resemblance was actually that strong, or if he just imagined it.

"I can't see why that matters. What is it you want to know?"

"Why don't I go ahead and start with the biggest one, and ask why you look so familiar to me?"

The kid stopped walking and turned to face him, his intense hazel eyes piercing Carter's. "I didn't come here to talk about me. How come you're researching this story?"

He'd be damned if those weren't Zoe's eyes. Straight on like this, the kid was undeniably equal parts of Josie too. "Are you related to her?"

The kid stepped close, narrowing his eyes. "You've seen her, haven't you?"

Carter raised a hand and started to take a step back before he felt the sharp edge of a knife pressing into the side of his throat. The kid was fast, faster than Carter had given him credit for.

"You son of a bitch! You tell me where she is right now before I cut your throat, you hear? If you touched so much as one hair on her head, you're going to pay like you've never imagined."

Carter reacted on impulse, jerking back and giving a powerful right blow that connected under the kid's jaw, taking him down. As soon as the kid hit the ground, Carter kicked him in the back hard enough to debilitate him a few seconds, then kicked the knife out of the way. Cursing, he closed his palm over the side of his throat. He'd been cut.

He pressed hard but could still feel the blood flowing down his neck. "Christ, that frickin' stings. How the hell did you get that through security?"

The kid wasn't listening as he writhed on the ground, a string of obscenities pouring from him. Two of his words hit Carter like a slap in the face, shaking him so much that he dropped to his knees, his hand still pressed hard against his throat.

"Did you—did you say she's your sister?" Suddenly the puzzle pieces seemed to make more sense. But impossibly so. "Sam? Are you Sam?" Sam Pictures was dead. He'd been shot three times in the chest.

The incredulity in Carter's tone must have sunk in. The kid

rolled onto his back and pushed himself into a sitting position, grimacing as he pressed a hand to the side of his back. Carter had had no restraint when he kicked him.

"You're Sam, am I right? I don't mean to hurt you."

The kid's eyes were on his neck. "Yeah, well, I didn't mean to cut you."

With Carter kneeling and the boy sitting up, they were face to face again. He could pick out Josie's features perfectly. What was a bit more perplexing, considering Zoe wasn't hers, was the way he was looking at him with Zoe's eyes.

"I thought you were dead!"

The kid scanned their surroundings again, reminding Carter of a dog who'd been picked on enough to hold a fear of it.

Their antics had attracted a handful of tourists. Carter suspected a few of them would be calling the police soon if they hadn't already.

The kid pushed up to a standing position, wincing again, and unzipped his hoodie. He had Carter's full attention when he pulled his T-shirt up to his neck to reveal a spattering of scar tissue that covered his chest the same as if he survived a war zone.

"I was," he said. "Officially for seventeen minutes. Then I woke up."

—⁓—

Carter wanted to swallow, but his throat felt unusually heavy as the emergency-room tech sewed the final stitch into the side of his neck. The kid was sitting in a chair at the side of the room, not having left his side in the two hours they'd been at the hospital.

"You're a lucky man, Mr. O'Brien," the tech repeated. "A few centimeters deeper, and you could've bled out on the spot."

Carter didn't need that reminder after looking in the mirror. If he ever had a knife pressed against his throat again, he hoped to do more than act on instinct.

"I recommend taking it easy the next several days. Rest as much as you're able and let pain be the guide for when to lie down."

Like the numbness that had spread over his neck, the whole situation was akin to being half-asleep. The kid—Sam—had overheard Carter's real name as he checked in, and he'd made no attempt to hide the search he'd done on his phone.

All Sam really knew were things that tied him to New York. He didn't know about Galena or where to find Josie. But even though they hadn't spoken in any real depth yet, Carter trusted the kid. He'd driven Carter's car to get him to the hospital. Once here, when he could have taken off, he didn't, even though he didn't know if Carter was the type to press charges. And it was clear his only motivation was to find his sister.

"Where is she?" the kid repeated for the umpteenth time after the tech left to get Carter's release paperwork.

"I'll take you to her myself once we get out of here and you convince me of what I need to know." Resisting the urge to clear his throat, Carter pressed his fingers around the thick bandage that spanned from the middle of his neck to his Adam's apple.

"What do you want to know?"

"Tell me about Zoe. Why did Josie take her?"

Sam's eyes widened in surprise. "She's still got the kid? I thought—I thought she'd have dropped her with Social Services somewhere. I never thought she'd stay in hiding with a kid."

"Aren't you Zoe's father?"

He shrugged. "That's what Jena said. I never laid eyes on her before the day everything blew up."

"Well, kid, I've laid eyes on her, and I'm willing to bet you are. Positive paternity test or not."

Sam turned away and stared at the wall before replying. "That would explain why Josie kept her."

"What happened to make her run with a baby that wasn't hers? What happened to make those gangs want all of you dead?"

Sam tugged at his zipper and shrugged. "The baby's mother was, uh, well connected, I guess you could say. It was East LA if that means anything to you. Her brother was one of the biggest drug dealers in the area. For that matter, her lover got pretty high up there too. This guy—her man—we grew up with him. He was like a big brother to me, and he was in love with my sister ever since they first met in fourth grade. Only, he dropped out of school in high school and started dealing, and she dumped him. More or less. It got to be a vicious circle of who was hurting who, but the chick he ended up with—the baby's mother—she had it out for my sister. This guy and the baby's mom had a kid together awhile back, a boy. They were tied together that way, though neither of them were legit faithful, you know."

Carter noticed how Sam didn't use any names but didn't stop him to question it.

"One day, I guess close to two years before things really fell to shit, I ran into that chick at a supermarket. We'd hung out in the same circles, but we weren't close. She needed money for cigarettes, and I needed a ride. I guess you could say she gave me one. I never saw her alone again until the day she called, begging me to come over. She was hysterical when I got there, saying her kid was mine and a few of the wrong people had gotten wind of it. Minutes later, she took a bullet in the head, and I was holding a crying baby in my arms and had about ten different guys wanting me dead for reasons I hadn't seen coming."

"So, what happened?"

Sam glanced toward the door, still messing with his zipper. Not for the first time, Carter noticed the dark circles under his eyes and the shiftiness of his gaze. He couldn't help but wonder which of the two had a harder five years, the sister who made it out but believed her brother dead, or the brother who was very much alive but unable to locate his sister.

"We'll be out of here soon. We'll talk when we're back in your car," Sam answered.

Carter nodded and closed his eyes. In seconds, he slipped into a doze, the dull burning in his throat pulsing like a lullaby.

———

"So, where to?" Sam flipped over the ignition, and Carter's Mustang purred to life. Carter was out of the running for the driver's seat for a day or so. "Where's my sister?"

"How can I be sure that bringing you to your sister cold turkey is the right thing to do?"

"Look, you dumb shit—no offense." Seeing the look on Carter's face, Sam started again. "Sorry, but you can't possibly know what it's going to mean to my sister to have me back in her life. To have her back in mine. And every fricking minute we waste, it's all I can do not to go apeshit on your ass. Five and a half years is a really long time."

Carter nodded. "Let's go by your place. As you pack, you can fill in the rest of the holes. If you can convince me it's safe to take you there, we'll go tonight."

"I haven't got much, and besides, everything I own is dispensable. And my lease is month to month; I'll convince you as I drive. Wait, there's a cat that comes and goes in my apartment. I keep a window open for him, but I should shut him out if I'm not going to be here."

Sam's place ended up being just a few blocks from the Arch but on a less polished end of town. It was an undersized, refurbished warehouse apartment with a wall of windows overlooking the riverfront. In the right hands, the apartment could have been fantastic. In Sam's, it was wanting. As Sam had said, it was sparsely furnished with items that looked as if they'd come from Goodwill. It also lacked any real personality, making Carter wonder if his stay was temporary. In the main room, there was a beat-up couch facing a giant flat-screen TV and a MacBook on what looked like an old TV tray. At the far side of the couch, curled against a flattened pillow, at first glance seemed to be a poufy cream blanket but was the fur of the biggest cat Carter had ever seen.

There were no pictures on the walls or accessories anywhere apart from a giant map of the United States on one wall. An assortment of pushpins dotted it, from the West moving eastward. A giant pile of newspapers rested in several stacks in one corner of the room.

Carter stared at the map for a long time, nausea flooding him. He'd written a few articles on missing people over the years, but he'd never really imagined what it would be like to walk in the shoes of someone who'd been left behind.

After Sam finished tossing in enough clothes to fill a backpack, he walked over to stand next to Carter in front of the map. "The red ones are towns where I felt like I'd searched long enough to move on. The white ones are still active—were still active, I guess."

"You've been to all these towns? There are over a hundred pins here."

"Yeah, they were short trips. I worked a few towns at a time, and I've moved around a lot. I'd put up signs and place ads in local papers. Will you tell me what town she's in now?"

Having seen this, Carter couldn't keep it from him. Clearing his throat, he pointed out Galena. A few white push pins came within a hundred miles of the town. Sam pulled a lone thumbtack from the top border of the map; it was gold and larger than the others. He pressed it in, nodding to himself.

"I knew I'd find her eventually. I couldn't see another way. I almost gave up a few times since the only calls or emails I ever get are from freaks fascinated with girls who are presumed lost to the world of sex trade or from the Bible thumpers who want me to know they're praying for her. I was bracing myself for you being one of the former." He placed the flat of his hand on the edge of the map as if to steady himself. "When I could tell that you'd seen her, my mind went to the worst place it could go."

Carter dragged a hand over his mouth, taking in the complexity of Sam's search. The kid had done so much more than host a website. "I'm sorry. I was protecting Josie until I knew who you were and why you were looking for her."

"Look, do you have a picture or something? Because a part of me thinks maybe I'm going crazy, and none of this shit's happening."

"I have a few." Carter pulled out his phone and began flipping through his pictures. Josie wasn't big on pictures, but she'd let him take a string of them when they were carving pumpkins with Zoe and a few other ones just because. He offered his phone to Sam. "You can scroll through. I'll use your bathroom before we get moving."

He lingered in the bathroom, gripping the sink to collect himself. When he returned, Sam was on the couch holding his head in his hands. His tears were perfectly silent, but they were streaming down to his chin and dripping onto his jeans. If it wasn't for the controlled shaking in his shoulders, it would've been easy to miss that he was crying.

Carter took a seat at a respectful distance and closed a hand over Sam's shoulder. "It's going to be better now. For both of you. It has to be."

───～───

Sharp claws digging into his thigh pulled Carter out of a doze. He brushed his thumb and forefinger across his eyes as memory rushed in. He was reclined in the passenger seat of his car. He attempted to sit up but doing so sent a stab of pain racing from the side of his throat outward.

The claws belonged to the giant creamy-orange tabby cat of Sam's. After explaining that the cat was a nearly feral mouser he'd found dozing on the hood of his car one day and had brought inside for a meal and ever since had been coming and going out his second-floor fire-escape window, Sam had been ready to turn the animal back out on the streets.

But when Sam had set him down, the giant cat had walked back and forth between them, rubbing against their legs, and Carter had ushered him into the car. He crossed his fingers that Myra would be okay while they figured out the cat-and-two-dogs-in-one-house issue.

He cleared his throat carefully as he extracted the big cat's claws. The animal was purring as loud as a percussion band. As calm as the cat was, when they stopped for a pee break, hopefully they could offer him the same thing on a patch of grass.

"How long was I asleep?"

"A couple hours."

"That explains why it's dark." From what Carter could tell, they were still traveling north on I-55. A glance at the dashboard showed it was six o'clock, yet it felt like the middle of the night. But then again, with the little sleep he'd gotten the night before and how early the sun was setting, his body had the right to a bit of confusion.

"How's your neck?"

"So-so. The numbing shot wore off. So did that Advil."

"We should've stuck around to pick up your prescription."

"I'm not big on prescription pain meds."

Sam huffed. "I've known enough addicts to see why. Myself included."

Carter looked at him but stayed quiet.

"No worries; I've been clean in this life. Not that it's been easy."

"In this life?"

"If you'd been dead for seventeen minutes, you'd understand."

Carter tipped his head. "Point taken."

"Sorry I pulled a blade on you."

"Do you always carry around a switchblade big enough to carve up a deer?"

"Pretty much."

"Is someone after you?"

"I can't say for sure, but it doesn't hurt to be careful."

"You never finished your story. What happened after you were shot?"

"I woke up in the hospital a couple days later. The Feds were hanging around. After all that went down, I'd become a person of interest. For me, it was nark or go to prison. I'm not one to rat someone else out, but they promised to help me find my sister. Promised to get us into a relocation program. Josie was on the run, but they told me they had a lead. So, Sam Pictures was officially pronounced dead, and the information I gave helped them bring down several dealers from a couple different gangs. I heard they got about a mill in the drugs they confiscated, and five or six dealers went to jail."

"But they didn't have her?"

"No, their lead ran cold. I was transferred to a hospital in Seattle for another month. I had taken three hits, all in the chest. I was pretty drugged up most of the time, but there was this one agent I trusted. She promised they were doing their best, and mostly I believed her." Sam regripped his hands around the steering wheel and shook his head. "Josie ran with nothing. Not a purse or phone, her ID. Anything—just a kid she didn't know from squat. One credible witness put her in Vegas. Another put her in San Francisco. If either were true, even for a short time, I knew it wouldn't stay that way. My gut said she'd stick to small towns and stay out of big cities. She'd been ready to get out of LA most of our lives. If I hadn't screwed up so bad, she'd have gotten us out sooner. She had scholarships to three different universities. She was brilliant like my mom, only she was always so much better at keeping her act together."

"Then she hasn't changed much."

"You seriously have no idea. We were dropped in foster care for five or six months when we were kids, but we weren't placed together. The people I was with—I can say it now. They fucked me up bad. When we got back with our mom, Josie was hell-bent on us never getting separated again. I'm bad with time; she was eight, maybe nine. She picked up all our messes so it looked like my mom was doing her job when Social Services same by, and whenever my mom got drunk or OD'd and it looked like she was going to haul off and start hitting us, Josie would get us out long enough to make sure my mom wouldn't leave marks that would arouse suspicion and have some do-gooder pulling us away from each other again."

"At eight years old?" That was just a little older than Zoe; Carter's heart twisted to think Josie's childhood innocence had been lost so young.

"It's true. Every word. My sister saved my ass a thousand times if she saved it once. By the time she was eleven, she was figuring out which bills needed to be paid when so as not to have the electric shut off. She kept me from failing out of school and made sure we had clean clothes to put on in the morning."

"That all sounds like Josie."

It wasn't until Sam flew past a car in the slow lane that Carter glanced over at the speedometer. "Hey, did you notice you're driving about a hundred and five? Mind keeping it closer to eighty-five? Or ninety, tops. They arrest you at this speed, rather than hand you a ticket, and I've got an unregistered gun in the trunk."

Sam cocked an eyebrow as he eased up on the gas. "You don't seem like a gun-in-the-trunk type, but it's your car. And a nice one too. I can't believe you only have a few thousand miles on it."

"I haven't had it long. When I was in New York, I shared a car with my ex-fiancée, a BMW, which she took after we split."

"So, you and my sister, you're a couple, aren't you? I could tell by the way she was looking into your camera when you took those pictures."

"Yeah, we are."

"Judging by the miles on your odometer and the highway miles you've had to have put on it if you drove from New York to Galena and now St. Louis, I'm guessing you're pretty fresh on the heels of that split, huh?"

Carter chuckled carefully, trying not to jar his wound. "We separated in June. I got this car in July, and I met your sister in August."

"You got any kids?"

"No, not yet, but there's a little girl who I've come to love like one."

"Zoe?"

"Yes, though your arrival makes that a little more complicated."

Sam shot him a glance. "Why? Does she think Josie's her real mom or something?"

When Carter didn't answer, Sam said, "Huh." A few seconds later, he added, "Kinda makes me showing up and telling everybody I'm the kid's dad a bit awkward, huh?"

"It might make it a little more than awkward."

"Well, you can relax. I'm twenty-four years old, and I've been told since I was four that I'm immature for my age. I'm not looking to take on the role of a dad, and the only thing I'd do is disappoint the kid if I tried. You don't even know. I can't take care of a cat, man. I remember to feed him two or three times a week, but the rest of the time, he goes in and out of my bedroom window to hunt. Considering he was feral and smelled like a trash can when I found him, I don't hear him complaining."

The giant of a cat was still stretched atop Carter's thighs, making himself at home. Why he wasn't interested in the empty back seat, Carter didn't know. He was just thankful the cat didn't have the typical car-ride hysteria most cats seemed to have.

"What about Zoe's other family? Grandparents or family on her birth mother's side?"

"Jena was a foster kid. Pretty sure her parents are dead. Or in jail. All she had was her brother, and he's in jail for life. Killed three people."

"Damn."

"Not all parts of LA are Disneyland, I'll tell you that." Sam re-adjusted his speed a second time, slowing the car to eighty-five. "It feels like it's crawling at this speed, man," he complained. "So, what about you? You're dating my sister, which makes it fair game for me to hit you up with some questions. Number one, what kind of guy are you? Got any fetishes or addictions? And why'd your fiancée leave you? And are you really a writer or was that bullshit?"

"Ah, let's see," Carter said, grinning with amusement. "I'd like to think I'm a decent guy. I don't have any fetishes or addictions, other than the fact that I gave up smoking for the second time not that long ago. My fiancée left me because, after years of failing to make it work, she found someone better. At least, she thought she did. They've since broken it off. And yeah, I make my living stringing words together, so I guess that makes me a writer."

When he stopped talking, his neck was burning something fierce. He cleared his throat and pressed his fingers gently around the six-inch bandage covering the left side of his neck.

"Last question. You got a temper? Because if you ever hit my sister or that adorable little girl she was holding in her lap in those pictures, I'd have to kick your ass."

"I haven't been in a fight since I was nineteen. Until today, I guess. And I'd never hit a woman or a child. Ever. If it makes you feel any better, I'm willing to bet I love your sister and Zoe as much as anyone is capable of doing so."

Sam pursed his lips. "How'd you meet anyway, with you being from New York and all?"

"It's a long story, but the short of it is one day I showed up at her door kind of like this cat of yours did."

Chapter 32

OUTSIDE THE KITCHEN WINDOW, a few stray snowflakes danced about, whipped by the wind, reminding Myra that the tea garden would soon be closing for the winter. The propane heaters and fire pits could only extend the season so long. Once it closed for diners for four months, they would be selling loose-leaf tea in bulk and quiche, scones, pies, and cakes by special order.

With Josie upstairs readying Zoe for bed and out of earshot, Myra picked up the landline and dialed Carter's number.

"Well, you're alive at least," she said when he answered on the fourth ring. "I was beginning to wonder."

"I'm sorry. I should've checked in again." Maybe it was his connection, but his voice sounded weak. "It's been a bit of a blur since noon."

"A nine-hour blur. That must have been an informative meeting."

"More than I think any of us could have imagined. But it's good news. Phenomenal news. Where's Josie?"

"Upstairs getting Zoe into bed. What is it you found?"

"Can you wait ten more minutes? I'm almost home."

A rush of relief swept over Myra. He was safe, his meeting had gone well, he'd be here to answer Josie's questions. And he'd called this place home. "That'll make Zoe happy to be able to say good night."

"Just do me a favor and see if you can have Josie sitting down when I come in. She's in for a bit of a surprise."

Alarm coursed through Myra's veins. "What is it you're up to?"

"It's going to be good. Trust me, Myra."

She hung up and sank into a seat at the table. "Dear God, Carter. I hope your judgment is as strong as the faith I have in you."

She was still collecting herself when she heard Zoe's tiny feet pattering down the hallway. "I'm all ready for bed," Zoe said as she pushed open the swinging door wearing her s'mores nightgown and her hair still damp. "Can you help tuck me in, Myra?"

Buttercup was behind her, wagging his bushy tail. Tidbit, who'd just settled on the floor around Myra's feet, let out a single bark as if in reminder that he was the dominant animal in the house, even though Buttercup never paid him much notice.

"Of course, but can you do me a favor and ask your mom to come downstairs first?"

Zoe disappeared in a flash, returning a few minutes later with Josie behind her and Buttercup at her heels.

"Everything okay?"

"Everything's fine. I was just wondering if you'd freshen my tea and sit with me a minute?"

Josie frowned skeptically as Myra swept Zoe's still-damp hair off her shoulders. "Carter's almost home," she offered in explanation. "He'll be here in a few minutes."

Zoe dashed out of the kitchen to the back door.

"Not yet, child. Come sit a few minutes. I didn't hear about school today."

"I told you at dinner," Zoe said, coming back into the room.

"That's right. Did you have outdoor recess?" she asked in hopes of holding off some of Josie's questions a bit longer.

After heating Myra's cup of chamomile tea, Josie sank into a seat at the end of the table. She waited until Zoe finished talking about the game of "Everyone's It" to start asking Myra about some of the things that were no doubt racing through her mind. "I thought he wouldn't be here till tomorrow. Did he say why he changed his mind?"

"Thanks for the tea. And no, he didn't, but I expect he didn't want to spend the night away if he didn't have to."

"I can tell you're hiding something," Josie whispered to Myra as Zoe clamped both her hands around Buttercup's fluffy ears, and he swiped his giant tongue across her face.

"I know," Myra admitted, "so it's best not to talk."

Josie frowned. "I hate being kept in the dark."

"So, sit here in the light, and in a few minutes, all our questions will be answered."

Unwilling to accommodate her, Josie walked over to the sink and looked out the back window.

Seeing her mother's actions, Zoe dashed out of the room to the back door again. "He's here. He's here!" She shoved out the screen door and onto the brick patio in her bare feet, allowing Buttercup to run out ahead of her.

"Josie, he wanted you sitting," Myra instructed as Josie headed after her.

Josie shot her a sharp look and headed to the back door. As Myra stood up to follow her, Josie reprimanded Zoe for running out of the house barefoot.

Rather than follow her out, Josie stopped in the doorway, watching through the screen door as Zoe threw open the back gate and ran to the edge of the car pad by the garage. Snowflakes were dancing all around as the Mustang pulled in. "Zoe, give him some space to park," she called.

The engine fell silent, but the headlights remained on, keeping the inside blanketed in darkness.

Then Buttercup, who was standing next to Zoe, let out a long, low growl just as Zoe looked back at the house. "Where's Carter, Mom?"

The driver's door opened, and the interior light came on,

revealing that there were two passengers inside rather than one. Myra clutched at the door frame. "Josie, get inside. I'll get Zoe."

Ignoring her, Josie rushed out barefoot as well, no doubt intent on grabbing Zoe. Myra followed, watching helplessly as the driver stepped from the car. He hung next to the door as Buttercup offered up a second, more pronounced growl. "Easy, dog."

The passenger door opened, and Carter stepped out. "Buttercup, come here, boy."

Zoe had been staring at the stranger—a young man who only had eyes for Josie—but let out a squeal of delight and ran around to greet Carter. Buttercup let down his guard and followed, eager to greet his owner.

It was the whirling snowflakes most likely, but Myra felt a touch detached from her body. At the very least, it was as if time had slowed down. Josie had stopped walking midstep and was staring at the driver as if she were staring through a door that led to a different world.

"What the shit," the young man said finally, a grin spreading over his face. "Five and a half years, and all you can do is stare?"

Myra looked to Josie for an answer, but Josie didn't notice. There was something oddly familiar about him, the shape of his eyes, nose, and mouth. Myra racked her brain, trying to remember if she'd met him before.

The young man started moving, setting time into motion again. He locked his arms around Josie, enveloping her without her consent, smashing her face against his chest.

"It's me, Josie. It's me."

It took a second or two, but Josie's arms locked around him just as tightly, and she was racked by sobs.

Myra grappled for a different explanation than the one rising to the forefront of her thoughts, the seemingly impossible one that might well be the only way to make sense of things.

Josie's brother wasn't dead after all.

Chapter 33

Josie couldn't quite get ahold of her thoughts. Everything from *I'm hallucinating* to *Holy shit, someone cloned Sam* raced through her mind. For a second or two, she even wondered if she'd dreamed up her brother's death in a stress-related breakdown.

But that wouldn't explain Zoe.

"How?" she sputtered, trying to regain control of her heaving lungs. It was as if there were two of her, one who was distant and removed from everything happening around her, and another who was sobbing and losing control of her arms and legs. She stepped back and brushed the tears from her eyes to clear her vision. She looked from his face to the faded scars on his neck left by a long-ago run-in with an aggressive dog. There was no mistaking him. He was older and as thin as when he'd been struggling with a heroin addiction, but the guy holding onto her arms—the one keeping her upright—was Sam.

"If I was my doppelganger, I'd wouldn't be able to remember how off-key you were singing to me to get me to sleep when we got out of foster care that first time." His voice cracked, and he cleared his throat, fighting away tears that had always been harder for him to shed than her. "And now that I've found you, you're never getting rid of me. *Ever*. So, you can tell this overprotective boyfriend of yours that, if he wants to keep you, he's going to have to fill out a set of adoption papers for me too."

Josie doubled over, bracing herself with her hands on her knees and gasping for air. Her feet were burning from the frozen ground. This was real. This was Sam. He was right here in front of her.

"Mommy, what's wrong?" Zoe was beside her, tugging at her shirt.

The fear in Zoe's voice lifted Josie a little above the wave of shock rocketing through her. She stood up and brushed away more tears. "This is my brother, Zoe. I haven't seen him in a long time. I'm just really, really happy to see him."

The flurries had picked up in intensity but were still whipping about the air, adding to Josie's disorientation. Looking around, she noticed that everyone's watchful gaze was fixed on her. Myra, Zoe, Sam, Carter, even Buttercup. Except for Tidbit, who hadn't followed them out.

"I didn't know you had a brother," Zoe said, leaning shyly against Myra.

"I didn't either. Not anymore." It came out in a whisper. She couldn't stop crying, and not just crying, bawling. And her hands were shaking wildly.

"How about we get you inside," Carter suggested, motioning toward the back door. "Where you can warm up and sit down."

"Should I get her some juice like when you came?" Zoe piped up, lifting a foot to brush off the bottom of it.

"Yeah, that'd be good," he said. "Pour a glass for Myra, too, will you?"

Zoe nodded and ran ahead. Buttercup trotted along after, his bushy black-and-white tail hypnotic in the whirling snow.

"Look at you," Sam said, taking Josie's hand and starting toward the house. "I don't remember you being so short. What are you? Like five four?"

"Five six." The reply was automatic, but the words got stuck in her throat. Her jaw was shaking, too, and her tongue felt oddly numb. *Sam.* Sam was walking next to her. Telling her she was short.

Carter, who'd been a step or two ahead of them, stopped. "Your cat."

"Oh, yeah." Sam let go of her hand. "Let me grab him. Josie, I'll meet you inside."

Josie stopped in her tracks and turned to watch, afraid he'd disappear in the blustery snow, and this would all be a dream she'd spend the rest of her life trying to have again.

"I'm sorry," Carter said, coming back to stand next to her. "I should've called. I didn't think you'd believe me until you saw him in person. I should've known how hard it would be on you."

"I can't even believe it now. Carter, *how*? How did you find him?" Pulling her gaze off Sam, she noticed the bandage covering Carter's neck and the stain from drops of blood that had seeped through it. "Your neck! What happened?" A different type of alarm coursed through her veins as she brushed her fingers over the bandage.

"I nearly severed his jugular, that's what happened," Sam called out. Josie looked to him for clarification. He was hoisting the biggest cat Josie had ever seen across his arm and shutting the car door. "Accidentally. I'll come back for the food and litter we picked up at the gas station in a minute."

"That's a slight exaggeration," Carter replied, his voice a few decibels quieter than usual.

"It wasn't far from it, was it? He's supposed to be on bed rest the next couple days," Sam added, joining them with a big-eyed, cream-colored tabby cat over his arm. "So, seeing that he's the one here who's closest to death at the moment, I think we should switch directions and get his ass to lie down. Then, you and I can go back five and a half years and take turns filling in the holes. What do you say?"

Even though Josie wanted answers, the chaos of life pressed in, and she found herself having to wait to get them. Tidbit, whose cat sense must have been on overdrive, met them at the door, barking and whirling in excited circles. Myra walked into the hall from the kitchen, attempting unsuccessfully to usher Tidbit away.

The cat, who was every bit Tidbit's size, looked down from Sam's arms, flattened his ears, and hissed. "I guess the six-hour car ride got under his skin, because he's pretty chill with dogs. I've seen him walk up to a Rottweiler and sniff noses without an ounce of hesitation."

"There's a few stray cats who hang around the yard," Myra said, "too feral to want our company, but they keep the mouse population in check. Tidbit has gotten into the habit of chasing them when he can. Though, I'm confident he wouldn't have a clue what to do if he ever caught one."

Zoe squeezed in ahead of Myra, holding a nearly overflowing glass of cranberry juice out for Josie. "Here, Mom." Her eyes grew as big as saucers when she spotted the giant cat. "Oh, a kitty! Can I pet her?"

"It's a him," Sam said, looking intently at Zoe for the first time. "Let's give him a minute to get used to the place. He's got claws and all. I'd hate for you to get scratched." After a pause, he added, "I didn't think you'd be so big, Zoe."

"I'm six," she replied as if it explained everything. "I'm in first grade too. My teacher is Ms. Richards. And I like cats. But not as much as dogs."

"Same here," Sam agreed. "You know what they say, it's best to just rip that Band-Aid off." Without any more precautions, he lowered the giant cat to the floor. "I'm pretty sure he's a Maine coon," he added. "They're supposed to be good with dogs."

Face to face with a real cat, Tidbit stopped circling in overzealous anticipation and scooted back a foot, the hair along his spine puffing out like it had been electrostatically charged. After a deliberate look around, the cat stepped forward, sniffing Tidbit on the nose and then along his body. Tidbit let out a warning "ruff" and shuffled backward another step or two. He looked up at Myra as if in confirmation that this wasn't how meeting a cat for the first time was supposed to go.

Interested in the newcomer, too, Buttercup circled back from the parlor, stepping over Tidbit for a sniff.

"Hey, I can't vouch for how he is around cats," Carter said, stepping forward as if to grab the cat but hesitating. Buttercup's tail was wagging, and the cat went straight from sniffing him to rubbing along his front leg. Tidbit ducked underneath Buttercup to yip at the cat, and Buttercup responded with a loud and determined bark that sent Tidbit backing up against Myra. Of the three of them, the cat seemed the least fazed by any of it.

"Well, it looks as if this is going to work out just fine," Myra said. "You said you have food for him? Let's give him a minute, and we'll find a quiet place to feed him. I haven't had so many animals in the house since my kids were young. I suspect if walls could talk, these ones would bid you both welcome."

"What's your cat's name?" Zoe asked. "And I want to help feed him, Myra."

"Ahh, I just call him Cat. He's not really mine, at least he wasn't. He kinda came and went out of my apartment when he wanted."

"He looks like a fuzzy blanket," Zoe said, dropping to her knees and extending her hand. The cat walked over and rubbed his cheek against it, a soft purr emanating from him that made Zoe squeal in delight.

The better part of an hour passed before the chaos died down. When it did, Josie tucked an overtired Zoe into bed and said good night to Myra, promising to explain more in the morning when she hopefully understood more. "The one thing I *do* know is that he's the real thing."

Carter, who was clearly both groggy and in pain, pressed a kiss against her forehead and went to lie down for a bit as well. A few of Josie's questions had already been answered, like how Carter had found him, but countless more were rising to the surface.

Even though she'd come out of her shock, Josie still held her breath as she made her way downstairs to find Sam again. *What if this is just a dream?*

It wasn't, she promised herself. And a giant cream puff of a cat had been wandering the house to prove it. She found Sam in the kitchen, standing in front of the commercial fridge—doors wide open—eating a cold piece of today's quiche.

"How come you guys have so much egg casserole?" he mumbled with his mouth full. "It's like crack."

Seeing him, hearing him—a relief swept over Josie almost big enough to buckle her knees. Sam was very much alive and still very much Sam. *And he was standing in her kitchen.* She walked over and locked her arms around him, appreciating the slightness of his frame that was all bone and lean muscle.

"It's quiche," she answered. "It's even better warm. We run a tea garden if Carter didn't tell you. There's so much because the weather was bad, and it was a slow day. And I'm still having a hard time believing you're real."

"So that explains the fifty giant containers of loose-leaf tea in the pantry. At first, I thought you were running a dispensary." He rested his free hand over the top of her head. "And I can imagine it'll take a bit to really sink in for you. It's hard enough for me, and I believed you were alive the last five and a half years. But like I said, I'm not going anywhere."

When Sam took another bite of quiche, and she could feel a few crumbs falling into her hair, she stepped back and crossed over to the counter, brushing it out. "I'm still completely freezing. Want a cup of tea?"

"You got any coffee?"

"We do, but I'd rather make you a cup of tea."

Sam shrugged. "What the hell, I guess we're not in Kansas anymore, huh?"

"We hardly ever had money for coffee in Kansas. And trust me, you'll like it." After pulling out two cups, Josie headed into the pantry and scanned the canisters of tea and tea blends. Sam liked sugar, so she knew he'd be a fan of the *Peppermint Patty*, with its heavy mint and licorice-root flavor.

"You'll like this one."

A few minutes later, steaming cups of tea in hand, they headed for the front parlor where Sam's cat was making himself at home on the couch after eating and exploring the house. Sam was finishing off his second scone; this one pumpkin. "I've pretty much been living on eggs and Ramen Noodles," he offered in explanation, wiping his hands and not caring where the crumbs fell.

He'd probably changed in many ways she'd yet to discover, but his eating habits hadn't changed a bit. The Sam she'd known had been insatiably hungry since he turned thirteen—at least when he hadn't been in the thick of addiction. And he'd left messes like he was leaving a trail.

With Sam's appetite, she guessed he hadn't survived on Ramen Noodles and eggs by choice. Money had most likely been tight.

"Fair warning, you might want to name that cat before Zoe does," she said, watching the cat roll onto his back and blink his eyes closed.

"Yeah, why's that?"

"You asked earlier how Buttercup got his name. Zoe's pick of names likely differ from yours, and she's hard to resist when she's passionate about something." After a short pause, she added, "So, could you tell how much she looks like you?"

"A little. I could see it in the eyes. I think she looks more like Jena though."

"It's not easy for me to picture Jena without thinking of her best

friend pulling my hair and punching me in the face, so maybe I'm
not the best judge."

Sam frowned. "I, uh, never got a chance to explain. I didn't plan
on sleeping with her. She came onto me and, I don't know, it just
happened."

"You don't have to apologize; the very best thing in my world
came out of it. But honestly, I suspect you were a pawn in a game she
was playing that didn't work out in her favor. She suspected something was going on between me and Nico when he stopped sleeping
with her, even if she couldn't prove it."

"Yeah, I kind of figured she was using me."

"All's well that ends well, right?"

Josie wasn't ready tonight to talk about how they should move
forward with Zoe. Of course, knowing Sam was alive, they'd have
to find a way to explain a very complicated truth to a fragile young
mind, but the only thing Josie knew for sure was that her relationship with Zoe was never going to change.

"For us, at least."

Sam started telling her about some of the people from back home
who'd either gone to jail or were shot or killed in the last several years.
Most of them were Sam's friends only, ones he'd made when he'd
begun spiraling downward and mixing more and more with addicts
and drug dealers. But she could put faces with several of the names,
and her insides twisted at so much loss.

They talked through the night. It was after five in the morning
by the time the holes were mostly filled in, and Josie had a better
picture of Sam's life the last several years. The questions that remained
would wait until they'd had some sleep. She'd known all along Sam
had made it out of the drugstore and been shot a half hour later
outside their apartment, but she'd always wondered why he'd gone
back there when he'd told her not to. Thinking he had more time
than he did, he'd gone back to grab some things so they could hide

out a while. With their mom and Zoe. Only he hadn't had as much time as he'd hoped.

Josie only cried once, and that was when Sam promised that he'd been clean and drug free the entire time he'd been apart from her. "It took dying to figure out I wanted to live."

After a final trip into the kitchen where Sam helped himself to another slice of quiche, this one spinach and feta, Josie showed him to the empty room next to Myra's. She flipped on the light and smiled at the skeptical look on Sam's face as he took in the lavender bedspread, lace doilies, and flower-printed wallpaper.

"I don't suppose you've got anything a little less effeminate in this massive place?"

Josie smiled and shook her head. "Most of the rooms were last updated in the nineties, and the bulk of the furniture is a century or more old. This place was a Victorian bed and breakfast for years." She pressed a kiss into his temple. "The seventeen minutes you spent in another world didn't take the Sam out of you, at least." She had a feeling she'd fall asleep seeing the chilling spattering of scars on his chest for a long time to come.

"Not nearly as much as not knowing where you were for so long."

A few tears dampened her eyes, but she blinked them back.

"It'll be better now," he added.

"That's for sure." She was stepping out and about to close the door when she spotted the giant cream puff of a cat heading her way. He sauntered past Josie and pounced on top of the bed, curling up in the middle without so much as acknowledging Sam's presence. "You may not think of him as yours, but he's happy with your connection, however you define it."

"Yeah, well, I didn't want to say this in front of the old lady, but I'm pretty sure he's got fleas."

"We'll get him to the vet this week, and her name's Myra. You'll love her when you get to know her. She's the kindest person I know. And as for the cat, if you and Zoe don't come up with something better soon, I'm calling him Creampuff."

Leaving Sam's door cracked in case the cat needed to get to the litter box, Josie bid Sam sweet dreams and stepped out.

The sky was beginning to lighten to a silver gray. She peeked into Carter's room. She was surprised to find him dressed in yesterday's clothes and sleeping on top of the covers, a Himalayan throw covering half of him. Buttercup was at his feet, stretched across the full length of the bed.

She crossed over as silently as she could. In the dim light, he seemed unusually pale. She closed a hand over his and noticed it was freezing.

He stirred at her touch, lifting his head and wincing. "Hey. What time is it?"

"It's almost six. You're freezing, Carter. Let's get you under the covers."

"I didn't mean to sleep all night." He stood up, moving cautiously and locking his hand over his bandage. "You just getting up, or are you still awake?" he asked, drawing her in for a hug.

She sank against him, soaking in his strength. "Still awake. I'll try to catch a nap after Zoe gets on the bus. It snowed almost four inches last night, so I bet the only business we'll have are deliveries."

"You holding up okay?"

"Yeah. It's sunk in enough now that I'm okay letting him sleep a few hours without being afraid he'll disappear into thin air."

Carter pressed his lips against her forehead. "It'll take time, that's all."

Josie pulled back to look at him. "You had no idea what you were walking into, Carter. It could've been so much worse than Sam and a knife."

"I know. I'm sorry I didn't tell you."

"Promise you'll never do anything like that again."

He stepped back and closed his hands over her shoulders. "I'm kind of hoping I'm fresh out of opportunities." After letting her go, he tugged out of his shirt, moving it carefully over his bandage, then his jeans. As he walked them over to drop in a hamper in his closet, he asked, "Wanna get in with me a few minutes? I don't know if it's more from missing a night's sleep or the blood loss, but I'd be lying not to admit I could really use another few hours' sleep."

"I'm always down for some cuddle time with you." Josie walked around to the other side of his bed and slipped off her jeans.

Seeing her bare legs, he let out a soft moan of appreciation. "Or I could stay awake a bit too."

She'd been about to pull off her shirt to savor the sensation of skin on skin but decided against it. "I don't think that's the kind of bed rest they were referring to."

"Not even if you do all the work?"

Josie's blood warmed instinctively, but she shook her head. "We'll survive a few days, I'm sure."

"Speak for yourself."

Not having moved off the bed, Buttercup hoisted up onto all fours, came over to sniff her, then returned to the foot of the bed and flopped down on his opposite side. "How do you stretch out with him taking up the bottom of the bed like this?"

"There's usually a few inches I can claim on the edge. Or he lies across my feet, and when I wake up, I just have to walk out the pins and needles."

She giggled. "You're a beautiful person, Carter. And in case you're wondering, I knew that even before you found my brother."

"Yeah, well, you're pretty okay by me too."

Josie ran her palm down his ribcage, letting it come to rest on his abdomen, savoring the rise and fall of his breath. "I won't ever be able to thank you enough. I never would have found him. I never would have *started looking*. I thought he was dead. I saw his obituary, Carter." A fresh chill swept over her.

"You may not have found him, but he'd have found you. Eventually."

From what she'd heard tonight, he had a point. "You don't know him yet, but Sam—he was abused in foster care. And in a different way by my mom. Severely neglected, at least. I guess we both were. But Sam, he has pretty severe ADHD too. I'm saying this so you'll understand when I say it was hard for him to accomplish much of anything—from homework to studying for tests to cleaning his half of the room. And that was before he started doing drugs. What he explained downstairs, his process of looking for me, I was speechless. It took an attention to detail and focus I'd never have believed he was capable of."

"It was impressive for sure. That map he had—I wish I took a picture."

"He's going to have a guy he knows clean out his apartment. He can take a photo." She shook her head in disbelief. "I swear, tonight I kept thinking about how once, when he was recovering from one of the times he OD'd, he told me I should stop helping him because he'd never be able to help me if the tables were turned." She cleared her throat. "I guess neither of us knew what he was capable of."

"He can have a fresh start here. Who knows what he'll be able to do now that you're together, all three of you."

"I've been thinking about him and Zoe. I suspect it'll take a bit for him to bond with her. He always said he'd never have kids; he didn't want to bring someone into his chaotic world. But Zoe's here regardless, and now he has a chance to see things in a different way. The whole thing's so complicated; my mind keeps racing about how I'm going to explain it to her."

Carter smoothed his hand over her back. "Complicated is a good word for it. Josie, are you sure Jena had no other family that could try for custody?"

"Positive. That's the only looking back I ever did after I got here. I knew she and her brother were raised in foster care, but I confirmed that there's no immediate family. Her brother is serving three life sentences, and her mother died when she was little. She had put up a Facebook post once about not knowing who her father was. She had no living grandparents either."

"That's sad, but it makes everything cleaner on your end. And Zoe's current birth certificate…"

"It's forged, obviously. Myra and I found a man in Chicago to do it so she could start school."

"Can I ask, did you list a father?"

"No. It's just me." When he didn't follow up his line of questioning, she asked why.

"I have a feeling you're going to tell me I'm moving too fast, but if we get to the point that you're thinking of adding one, I'm ready to petition."

Josie went still as his words sank in, then she raised up, bracing herself with one hand. His expression was as earnest as she'd ever seen it. "What are you saying?"

"That I love you. And I love her. In a no-going-back way." He raised up a bit, bracing himself with his elbows. "If you were hoping for a romantic proposal, I'm afraid you drew the short straw. Today, at least." He grinned. "I'll make it up to you when this bulging jugular can handle a bit more excitement. When I was in the emergency room, and I realized how close that could have been, the one thing I knew with any certainty was that I'd like to spend the rest of my life with you."

Josie sat up the rest of the way, crossing her legs and allowing her limp hands to fall into her lap. The silver-gray sky was brightening to a yellow pink, creating a surreal glow in the room. For the second time in less than twelve hours, Josie seemed to be moving through a dream. "Carter, there's so much you don't know," she breathed.

He sat up as well, wincing from the movement that undoubt-edly jarred his wound. "I know the important things. My internet searching—more than anything, it was because I wanted to protect you. I still do. But I'll wait for the rest of your story until you're ready to tell me."

Josie closed her eyes and counted to three. Sam being here, and now this, it was too much in one day. The fortress she'd built around her heart threatened to slam shut. Everything that had helped her survive had her wanting to shut him down. Send him away.

Only damned if she was going to let it.

As if he'd picked up on her turmoil, he closed a hand over her knee and squeezed it gently.

"What about Sam?" It wasn't a yes, but it wasn't a get the hell out of here either.

He cocked an eyebrow. "I've always been open to having a big family. I just never pictured my oldest child to be twenty-four."

A half-snort escaped. "You have no idea." Josie leaned in and pressed her lips against his, then pressed a half dozen more on his forehead, cheeks, and chin. "I love you. That same way. I know what you want, and I want it too. I just… Can you give me time?"

His lips pulled into a half smile. "Yeah, I can do that."

She nodded and let out a breath. "Thank you. And one thing's for sure, it would be a lot less complicated adding you on her birth certificate than it would be my brother."

Chapter 34

THE FIRST TIME JOSIE could remember having something other than a spread of double cheeseburgers and cold fries from McDonald's on Thanksgiving was after Francie had taken her and Sam under her wing. Francie prepared for her extended family's meal for days, and Josie had gawked at the towering pile of food in disbelief. From a golden-braised turkey stuffed with pancetta and herbs to a giant bowl of homemade ravioli, a platter of antipasto, and stuffed artichokes to numerous decanters of wine, there was an Italian flair to the feast, though most of the traditional dishes had been spread around the table too.

Since Josie's arrival in Galena, Thanksgiving meals had been on the traditional side, with stuffing, sweet potatoes, and green bean casserole making an appearance, but on a smaller scale. Myra's children, living in three different states, had established the routine of coming home between Christmas and New Year's each year but not in November for Thanksgiving. As a result, Josie had passed her last five Thanksgivings quietly with Myra and Zoe.

This year, with Carter and Sam in the house, Myra insisted on putting together a feast on a scale similar to Francie's. Close to three weeks after Sam's arrival, Josie still had waves of disbelief wash over her as she sat at a table full of people who had such big claims on her heart.

After the meal was finished and they'd all pitched in to clean up, Carter, Sam, and Zoe threw on a few extra layers and headed out into the first big snowfall of the year. Too chilled to savor being outdoors for any length of time, Myra promised to watch from inside. Josie hung back, sitting beside her on the rattan couch in the all-season sunroom behind the library. A heavy blanket was draped over Myra to cut her chill. Having been ignored while Myra and Josie were busy cooking, Tidbit sandwiched himself in the six inches of space between them, burrowing into the blanket like it was a nest and shoving his feet against Josie as if trying to push her away.

"When will they know if the tumor's shrinking?" Josie wasn't sure if it was her imagination, but Myra seemed to be resting more, eating less, and commenting more and more on the chill in her bones. The doctor she'd seen in New York had referred her to one in Madison who was also participating in the study.

"They'll do another round of scans after the first of the year. For all my complaints of those pills making me cold, I'm hungrier and having less stomach pain."

"That's good," she said, even though she wasn't sure she agreed about Myra's appetite.

"Josie, whenever it is that I go—in one year or many years— knowing that the group out there in the snow is here to stay gives me comfort, right down to those monsters of a dog and cat. And what a cat your brother brought! Whoever saw a feline trudge through the snow like a dog?"

"Sam's says he's a Maine coon, and I'm pretty sure they thrive in snow. But I don't want to talk about you not being here. Especially not today."

"Then how about we talk about you and Carter?"

"What about us?"

"Has he proposed? I keep waiting to see a ring on that finger of yours."

"Nothing's official," Josie said, running her hand along Tidbit's spine and down his tail. Outside, they'd finished up a snowman's body and were balling snow into snowballs. "But we've been talking about the future. About marriage and stuff."

"By 'and stuff,' do you mean children? I'd love to know Zoe will have a sibling before she's much older."

If anyone but Myra had asked, Josie wouldn't have answered. "That's been one of the topics of discussion."

Myra kept quiet, but the way her eyes stayed on her, it was obvious she was waiting for more.

"He's basically ready now; I want to wait a year. Since it's obvious you want details, one of the topics of discussion is whether I should get on the pill, or we wait it out with condoms."

Myra nodded and brushed her thumb and forefinger over Tidbit's silky ear. "Well, if your discussion goes to committee, no hard feelings whose side I take."

Josie huffed. "No surprise there, but don't hold your breath." As soon as she said it, she wanted to take it back. Myra wanted to welcome Zoe's brother or sister into the world. She wanted to be here to do it.

"I trust you'll know when it's time." Myra reached over and squeezed her hand. "There's a snowball war on the horizon, it seems. Why don't you get out there while you can have your pick of forts? I've got Tidbit to keep me company."

More because she'd promised Zoe than because she was ready to leave Myra, Josie tugged on her boots, coat, and gloves, and headed into the swirling snow that was transforming the backyard into a wonderland. Buttercup was the first to notice her. He bounded over and dropped into a play bow, barking for her to join in the fun.

Josie clamped her hands over her knees and "ruffed" back at him, which made Buttercup dash around her in circles, kicking up chunks of snow as he ran.

"Someone likes the snow. I've never seen him with so much energy," she said as she reached Carter.

"And he's not alone in that." Carter pulled her in for a kiss as, a few feet away, Zoe complained that kissing was gross. As the kiss ended, Carter smashed a snowball on top of Josie's head that he pulled from his jacket pocket.

Josie squealed from the cold chunks cascading down her neck, back, and into her bra. "Oh! You're in trouble—that was so mean! And *so* cold!" Only she couldn't say it with a straight face.

He winked. "Sorry, babe. You know what they say, all's fair in love and war."

"Love sucks, but I'm all for war," Sam agreed, pelting Josie in the shoulder with a giant snowball of his own.

"We haven't even picked teams yet!" Josie shielded herself the best she could, then pointed at Zoe. "I call Zoe. You two unchivalrous men are going down!"

"But Mom, I want to be on Sam's team," Zoe argued. "He's going to win because he's got the most snowballs."

"Good foresight, kid. Though I'd win even if I had the least." Sam swiped another snowball from his pile behind a bare rhododendron and hurled it at Josie. It smashed against her shoulder.

"That's pretty good for a California boy," Josie said before charging at her brother with her best "Aargh!" She pummeled full-speed into him as he went for another snowball, taking him down and landing on top of him, undoubtedly giving herself a few bruises she'd feel later.

She was laughing so hard she nearly peed her pants. "How can someone who eats as much as you be so bony?" She splayed her hands as Sam rolled her over and started shoveling snow in her face. "Mercy! Mercy!"

Thankfully, Zoe and Carter came to her rescue and began a joint attack on Sam. Josie hadn't even been outside three minutes, and she was soaked and freezing. She finally wriggled free and stood up, brushing the snow out of her face, hair, and neck. She hadn't put on enough layers for this sort of snow play.

As she swiped at her eyes, she noticed a flash coming from a car parked a hundred feet away on the side street. In the hazy, snowflake-filled world, it struck her as odd that she even noticed.

Looking closer, she inhaled sharply. A man was stretched across the front seat toward the passenger-side window of a silver sedan. The window was fully open, and a long camera lens was pointed right at them, one big enough to capture them in detail. She made eye contact with the driver just before he dropped the camera and started the car. In seconds, he was rolling away into the falling snow.

Limbs frozen, Josie stared after him in disbelief. At her feet, Carter and Sam struck a truce and got up from the ground, pulling Zoe up with them. Even though she was certain she'd never seen the man before, she knew beyond any doubt what his presence in front of her house meant.

Like she'd feared but had been too afraid to voice, Nico had been monitoring Sam all along.

Josie's mother might as well have been standing over her shoulder with her classic "I told you so" smirk, the one she'd worn when she was sober and angry at the world and looking for her next fix, be it drugs or alcohol or a man. Josie wanted to crumple into a ball on the floor; her energy was zapped, and not just from a long day of cooking and getting pelted in the snow.

What had made her think she could reach for happiness and actually receive it? Happiness was meant for people with better breeding and more cohesive families. People with a knack for picking the straw that wasn't the short one.

It had been naive to hope Nico had stopped looking for them. Not after the bad blood Sam had created by sleeping with Jena and, unknowingly, creating strife between rival dealers and gangs that led to over a dozen people dying and a handful of key dealers going to jail.

When Sam had told her that he'd used his old comic book pen name, Harry Underball, as the administrator on the missing person website he'd created for her, she'd known Nico would have understood the significance. Sam had drawn dozens of comics in that favorite series of his while hanging out at Francie's. She'd hoped—naively—that since Nico had left Sam alone for the three years Nico had been out of jail, he'd all but forgotten about it. Forgotten about all of them.

But now Josie was convinced that Nico had been monitoring Sam's site all along, waiting until they found one another before he made any sort of move. Even though Sam believed he and Carter hadn't been followed, she was certain someone had been watching on the grounds of the Gateway Arch and had traced them here.

At first, she was terrified that the stranger could have pulled a gun right there while they played in the snow. But if Nico wanted Sam dead—wanted her dead too—he wouldn't send someone to do it for him. He'd come here himself.

Only Josie wasn't going to wait around in hopes that wasn't the case.

While everyone lingered in their rooms after changing out of their snow clothes and showered—or, in Zoe's case, played with her animal and fairy figurines—Josie snuck downstairs to use Carter's computer. Sam had told her that Nico was the sole proprietor of an after-school center for troubled kids in East LA, and a dozen articles popped up confirming it. On the first page of the center's website was an announcement that the center would be open and serving Thanksgiving dinner to the families of kids in the program.

She jotted down the number and snuck into the kitchen, blocking her number by dialing *67 before making the call, a trick she'd learned years ago that she hoped still worked. Even though it had her breaking out in a cold sweat, it seemed worth the risk to confirm whether he was still in LA.

She hadn't said his name aloud in over five years and nearly froze up when a teenage boy answered with a "'Sup?"

"Is, uh, Nico there?"

"Hold on." A few seconds later, Josie heard the kid scream, "Hey, Nico!" She hung up fast, rubbing her palm like she'd been holding a burning-hot poker.

That man outside in the snow—she still had zero doubt he was reconnaissance. Sanctioned by Nico. She stood in silence for several minutes, waiting to see if the phone would ring back. When it didn't, she gradually began to breathe again.

She didn't so much as debate for longer than a few seconds whether to tell Carter and Sam. Sam would dismiss her as being paranoid. And Carter, he'd prevent her from doing what was suddenly clear she needed to do.

Lost in her racing thoughts, Josie feigned exhaustion to explain why she was unusually quiet the rest of the night. After getting Zoe to sleep and staying long enough to savor the gentle rise and fall of her chest, her impossibly thick lashes, and soft cheeks, she pressed a kiss onto her head and left. She headed straight for Carter's room. He was in bed, reading a thick book by a physicist she'd maybe heard of.

"I didn't know you like physics," she said, curling up next to him but keeping on top of the sheets.

"I have varied interests," he said, letting his hand slide down her back to her ass as his lips met hers.

"You okay?" he asked when he pulled away. "You seemed a million miles away tonight."

She swallowed. Face to face like this, it was harder to lie. Instead, she went with a partial version of the truth. "Before I came outside, I had a heavy talk with Myra."

Closing his book, he nodded slowly. "I'm sorry."

She pressed her lips against his cheek, savoring the hint of stubble that had grown in since he'd shaved this morning. "It's not your fault. Have I told you that you're a good man?" She planted a few kisses along the ridge of his jaw and earlobe.

Setting the book aside without so much as a glance as to where it landed on the nightstand, he rolled on top of her, rising to tug away the covers that separated them. Josie knew what he wanted, and she wanted it too. After their clothes came off, and Carter was reaching for the condoms in the nightstand drawer, she wrapped her legs around his hips. "Not yet," she said, stopping his hand.

He looked at her sharply.

"For a little while," she said, making her intentions clear.

"You know I'm game. If you're sure?"

With two worlds crashing together, all she wanted at this moment was to feel him inside her. She wanted—needed—to know what it was like for their bodies to join together without a barrier. She nodded. "Just pull out, will you?"

He answered with a kiss that conveyed his eagerness. For the first time all afternoon, her thoughts slowed until it was just her breath and his body inside hers and a rhythm that reminded her of the waves in the ocean.

When it was over, she cleaned up and dozed beside him until he was in an even, steady sleep. The lamp was off, and the snow-covered trees and gleaming clouds lit the room, making everything glow white blue. She dressed in the dark and pressed the lightest of kisses against his forehead.

She paused at the door, losing her nerve. A part of her wanted to crawl back into bed and sleep beside him and pretend she'd not seen what she'd seen.

Gradually, the energy to keep going snaked upward from her feet. "I'm going to fix it. I promise."

She snuck back into her room, made a quick job of packing some things in a weekend travel bag that wouldn't be noticed as missing and slipped out, pausing by Sam's door. After confirming that he was snoring softly, she headed inside and swiped his cell phone off the nightstand. She left a note on the dresser that said she borrowed it and to call her using the house phone. She crossed her fingers he didn't find out until morning.

Unlike the journey that brought her and Zoe here from LA, she wasn't leaving empty-handed. She headed to Myra's Crown Victoria parked in the garage loaded down with her weekend bag, a purse, Sam's phone, over five hundred dollars in cash, and one of Myra's credit cards. Just in case. She also took time to pack the trunk with a coat, gloves, a flashlight, a shovel, Myra's gun, and a bag of cat litter, courtesy of Creampuff.

Her hands had broken out in a cold sweat, and she needed to make several attempts to get the ignition to turn over. The old car was nearing seventeen years old, and Josie could only hope it would stand up to the over nineteen-hundred-mile journey.

She wished she'd gotten around to more of Carter's driving lessons. She'd taken four so far and was getting confident on un-crowded roads. She'd never driven in snow, though, and even though she knew how to conceptually, the idea of doing so terrified her.

Proving she had every reason to be worried, she fishtailed twice in the first mile. But being able to pull out of it and keep driving gave her a bit more confidence. Fishtailing didn't necessarily mean skidding out of control. And, like every time she'd driven before, she kept well under the speed limit—this time even more so.

She said a prayer that, once she made it to US 151, the roads would be plowed, and driving would be easier.

Spying the cleaner roads ahead, she fishtailed again turning onto the ramp to US 151, this time enough to get the back tire stuck in the embankment. Once she got control of the wave of panic flooding her, she put the car in neutral and got out to throw some cat litter under the wheels and push, something she'd done more than once to get Myra unstuck over her years here. She was soon joined by a man who'd been clearing the roads with a big diesel plow truck. With the two of them working, they had her mobile again in a few pushes.

"I don't know what kind of early-morning deal you're hoping to find, but if you ask me, no Black Friday sale is worth traversing these roads."

The man's assumption gave Josie an idea that might buy her much more of Friday than she'd hoped for. The last thing she wanted was Sam coming after her. With any luck, she'd be in and out of LA before he realized what she was doing.

What exactly are you doing? an inner voice chided.

"I've got nineteen hundred miles to come up with a plan, so cut me some slack, please," she answered it aloud.

After merging onto the highway, she breathed a sigh of relief. As she'd suspected, the wide lanes were better plowed, and there were thick strips of clear pavement where cars had traversed.

At regular speed, Google Maps put her trip around thirty hours of drive time. The first few hours of imperfect roads and the occasional swirling snowflakes forced her to stay just below 40 mph, adding even more time to her journey.

By the time she reached Des Moines, the snowflakes had dried up completely, the roads were better, and she was feeling like a seasoned highway driver. She stopped at a gas station, refueled, and bought a large coffee and a doughnut. She chose a chocolate long john, one of Zoe's favorites.

As she was heading out, it occurred to her that Nico could have gotten his confirmation and already be on the move for Galena.

Returning to the car, she fished Sam's phone from her purse. Nico had been in jail for two years. What reason did she have to think he'd still have the same cell number? After giving it some consideration, she decided she was too afraid to attempt to block the number on Sam's cell. Instead, she fished out as much change as she could find and headed over to the gas station's grimy pay phone. Holding her breath, she dialed it.

Nico answered on the fourth ring, his voice still very much the same. "Yeah," was all he said into the line. For a second or two, she was frozen, his voice burning her ear like acid. Then abruptly she hung up, slamming the receiver into its base loud enough to draw a man's attention who was walking past into the gas station.

She got back in the car, locking the door and shoving her hands under her thighs. The last snowflakes disappeared into nothingness before her hands stopped shaking enough to drive again.

She was going home, and Nico was waiting for her. He'd been waiting a very long time.

Chapter 35

JOSIE WAS GETTING DROWSY again when Sam's phone rang out, causing her to jerk reflexively. She'd made it the whole night without him calling. She pulled over to the side of the highway and shut the ignition, answering just before it was lost to voicemail.

"Hey, what the shit?" It was nearly nine in the morning in Galena, and by the sound of Sam's voice, it was clear he'd just woken up. "Why'd you take my phone?"

"Because I don't have one, and it's Black Friday," Josie said, trying to seem like she had more energy than she felt. She was going to have to find a safe place to pull over and nap soon. "I decided to shop last minute, and I didn't want anyone getting worried."

"Yeah, about that, I keep meaning to ask you. Why the hell don't you have a cell phone? It's like you're one of those people who dropped off the grid or something. Oh, wait, you were."

"Is Zoe around? Because you're not watching your language if she is."

"I'm in my sissified room all alone missing my phone."

"I'm sorry. I won't take it again."

"Yeah, whatever. Where are you? I'll join you."

"You can't; I'm Christmas shopping."

"Fine. I'll play Uno or Lincoln Logs with Zoe. I can't believe I didn't pack my Xbox. I should never have let my buddy have it when he was packing up my stuff. It's weird not having anything to obsess about or anything to distract myself from obsessing."

"Uh, you and Zoe playing together, want some advice or just want to figure it out?" Not to her surprise, Sam was pretty much just Sam regardless of who he was around. Unlike Carter, her, or Myra, he didn't understand how to set up a six-year-old for success.

"I'll figure it out, Mommy." He was clearly unconcerned, and Josie figured if Zoe had a meltdown, one or both of them would grow from it. "Hey," he added, "so, uh, don't answer my phone for any number but Myra's. You really don't need to hear what the freaks sound like who call wanting to talk about how you've probably been pulled into the illegal sex trade."

Josie shuddered. They'd decided to keep the site active in case Nico or any of his friends were monitoring it. Only now it seemed it no longer mattered. "You don't need to convince me of that."

He told her to stay safe before hanging up.

"I'll be as safe as I can," she said aloud after the connection ended. "I have every reason in the world to be."

Twenty minutes later, the phone rang again, showing Carter's number on the caller ID. This time, Josie opted not to pick up. Instead, she pulled off at an exit ramp to find a safe spot to check the voicemail a few minutes later. She tensed upon hearing Carter's voice, calm and steady with just the slightest hint of concern bleeding through. "Hey, Jos, Sam said you're Black Friday shopping, which is great. I figured you were down in town, but we noticed Myra's car is missing. I'm having a hard time deciding which is more likely—it having been stolen or you taking it." After a long breath, he added that, if she'd taken it, to enjoy her day and finish shopping, but to give him a call before heading back. He and Sam could drive together and pick her up. "I've been in the car with you every time you've driven, Josie," he finished. "You don't have a license yet, and in that car with this much snow, you'd be asking for trouble you don't need."

To buy more time, she texted back.

Got your message. All fine here. Yep, I drove but your idea makes sense. Will call this afternoon. And technically, I have a license. 😊

Putting the phone down, Josie stepped out of the Victoria to stretch and get her blood circulating before getting back on the highway.

She had a feeling that, somehow or another, Carter and Sam would put the pieces together soon enough. She needed to put as many miles as she could between her and Galena before they did.

———

Carter was sitting cross-legged on the parlor floor finishing up a game of Candy Land when Zoe's giant yawn reminded him it would be her bedtime soon. Myra was on the couch, working on a piece of embroidery under the light of the side table lamp. Tidbit was curled up next to her, and Buttercup was stretched out next to him, taking up the rest of the couch. The cat, Creampuff as he was being called against Sam's preference, was on the floor next to Zoe and Carter, lazily batting at their game pieces whenever they advanced across the board.

In the ten hours that had passed since they'd talked to Josie, she still hadn't given them any idea where she was so they could drive out to meet her. He hadn't expected her to be gone this late into the day, but the snowplows had done a pretty thorough job throughout the course of the day. The truth was, if she took it carefully, she could make it back on her own. Besides, it wasn't as if his rear-wheel drive Mustang handled great in the snow either.

Mumbling to himself, Sam walked in and grabbed Carter's phone off the side table, shoving it Carter's way for him to insert the code. Sam was tapping his fingers erratically on the side of his leg, and Carter figured he wasn't the only one with tension mounting.

"What're you texting her?" Carter asked, unlocking his phone and offering it back to Sam.

"That, if she doesn't pick up my calls soon, I'm going to kick her a—pple," he added after a glance at Zoe, who was watching him intently.

Ten minutes later, as Carter was packing away the game and Zoe was rolling around on the rug with her body long and her arms straight overhead, reminding him of a rolling pin, the house phone rang. Zoe, Sam, and Carter all jumped for it at the same time. Sam, who was pacing the room, got to it first.

"Dibs," he said, grabbing the receiver and turning his back to them. "What the shit, Josie, you've been gone all day."

Gritting his teeth, Carter waited through a string of complaints and a few expletives of Sam's that Zoe didn't need to overhear. "That's not cool," Sam said as the short conversation ended and before passing the phone to Zoe. "Zo, your mom wants to say good night."

The first thing out of Zoe's mouth was to ask when her mom would be home. After that, as she started relaying the highlights of her day, Carter looked to Sam.

"What's up?"

"She says she's staying the night at some hotel. Next to the mall. That she'll come home tomorrow."

"What mall?"

"The flipping Mall of America."

"The Mall of America," Carter repeated, dumbfounded. He pulled up his phone. "That's five hours from here. You're saying she drove five hours in the snow to go shopping? After only having driven four times? That doesn't sound like Josie."

"It doesn't." Sam stopped walking and drummed his fingers rapid-fire over the thin line of his tightly smashed lips.

Zoe asked her mom if she could sleep in Carter's bed, since she wasn't going to be home.

After a pause, Zoe looked his way and asked, "Will you sleep in my mom's bed, so I'm not scared?"

"Sure thing, Zo."

"And can Buttercup sleep on my bed?" she added, still looking at Carter.

"Ahh, maybe. He's kind of a space hog."

Zoe was saying good night and repeating she would pass the phone to Carter when Sam shook his head abruptly. "She doesn't do *anything* on a whim. And she doesn't break the law, not even driving without a legit license—for very good reason, at least."

"What are you saying?"

Suddenly, Sam smacked his palm against the mantle. "Oh, shit no." He strode across the room and swiped the receiver straight from Zoe's outstretched hand.

"You're telling me the truth right now, do you hear me?" Sam sputtered. "You're going back, aren't you? That car yesterday— who the hell was that? I saw you looking after it. I saw your face go white. I figured you were just being paranoid. But you saw someone, didn't you?" After a short pause that Carter took to be silence on Josie's end, Sam added, "Well, you're not doing it! You're turning around. Do you hear me?" Sam went silent again, listening. "Josie? Josie!"

He hurled the receiver at the wall, smashing it to pieces. Zoe burst into tears and ran to Myra, burying her head in Myra's lap.

Carter pointed a finger at Sam. "Get it together right now or get out of sight." He pulled out his cell and dialed Sam's number. It rang forever and then went to voicemail. He called again three more times to receive the same results.

Then he got a text.

Hey, the service here is terrible. Tell Sam I couldn't hear him. Give Zoe a kiss, and I'll check in in the morning.

Then, a half a minute later, another one came.

I love you all.

Carter sighed and pressed his fingers into the bridge of his nose. Hearing Zoe's sniffles, he crossed over and sank into a squat, rubbing her back. "Hey, Zo, it was just a misunderstanding. Your mom's fine, but she has bad phone service. She said to give you a kiss and that you should get to bed."

He looked pointedly at Myra who looked as worried as he felt. "Think you can start her bath, and I'll be up in a bit?"

Myra nodded and ran her fingers through Zoe's hair. "Come on, Zoe. Let's see if the dogs will follow us up."

As soon as they were making their way up the stairs, Carter crossed to his computer and pulled up Google Maps.

"What are you doing?" Sam asked, coming to stand behind him.

"Seeing how long it takes to drive to LA."

"She left before any of us woke up this morning. We'd never catch up in time to stop her."

"No," Carter said calmly. "But I'm pretty sure I can catch a flight that, at the very least, will put me in the city at the same time as her."

"I'm going with you."

"If Josie wanted to bring her little brother back into a war zone, she'd have woken you up before she left. You should stay here with Zoe and Myra."

"She didn't wake you up, either, did she? Besides, you wouldn't last five minutes alone in the hood. Hell, I almost took you down in two at a national monument."

Carter shot him a look. "Geez, you're cocky, kid."

"So I've been told. But you need my help to find her, and you know it."

Carter had thought of that, but he also knew what Josie would do if he brought her brother back to the troubled neighborhood that almost took his life. Then again, she wasn't exactly making herself available for consultation either.

Suddenly it struck him to check the library where Myra kept the old Colt 1911 pistol stashed away. Not explaining himself, he took off with Sam following at his heels.

"Look, the way I see it," Sam said, "we're getting two tickets on whatever flight you find, or you're literally leaving here over my dead body."

Carter waved him off as he flipped on the library light and headed over the desk and opened the bottom drawer where Myra kept the gun hidden. Even though he wasn't surprised, adrenaline flooded his veins to find it missing.

"It's not dead bodies in Galena I'm worried about, kid."

Chapter 36

THE PANIC IN SAM'S voice gave Josie the adrenaline she needed to make it through most of the second night on the road. Earlier in the afternoon, she'd dozed while sitting at a truck-stop diner, charging Sam's phone since Myra's car didn't have a charging dock. Now, nearly twelve hours later, she was passing Las Vegas and close to dozing off at the wheel. With Sam having put two and two together, she had even more reason to keep driving.

Even though she cringed at the idea of giving herself over to the vulnerability of sleep on the outskirts of Sin City in the middle of the night, she knew it wasn't safe to drive any further without a second nap. She got off the highway and parked in view of the front doors of a gas station that seemed to have more slot machines than brands of potato chips.

Keys in hand, she curled sideways into the seat and fell into a doze almost instantly. An hour and a half later, she was jolted awake when a truck's engine revved next to her. She winced and grabbed her neck, her head having pitched forward in sleep. It took a bit to orient herself, and once she did, she clambered out and headed inside the gas station. The women's bathroom had an assortment of condoms and sex toys for sale in dispensers and a pink-and-gold slot machine. *Because who wants to touch a slot machine that basks in bathroom aroma all its life?*

She splashed water on her face and brushed her teeth, then headed to the food aisle where she meandered around, choosing an early breakfast of a banana, string cheese, a large coffee, and a large bag of Gardetto's. On the way to the register, she picked up a ceramic fairy figurine for Zoe.

Even though it was still well before dawn, she became more energized and happier as the lights of Las Vegas faded into nothing more than color on the horizon behind her. This section of I-15 in the Mojave National Preserve was something to experience, even in the dark. The sky was blue black and star-studded, and the uninhabited dessert was expansive and seemed mostly barren with the exception of tumbleweeds and the occasional silhouette of a Joshua tree in the distance.

She was looking over her shoulder at the stars when a movement in her peripheral vision snapped her attention back to the road. She slammed the brakes, narrowly missing a coyote that was crossing it. The startled animal scampered away, turning back to look at her as it ran. Josie stared, transfixed at its eyes; they glowed from the beam of her headlights. They were the last parts of the animal she could see as it disappeared into darkness.

It certainly wasn't her first coyote sighting; she'd grown up in LA where they'd become a carnivorous pest. But it was the first time she'd nearly killed one. She remembered Francie saying something once about how, in Navajo legend, a coyote crossing your path was a bad omen.

What about almost killing one?

It was no matter; there was no turning around now.

At six thirty in the morning, with the sky lightening behind her, she found herself less than two hours outside of LA, and adrenaline was starting to kick in. Her hurriedly completed internet search had resulted in two addresses for Nico. One was for a house a few miles from the housing complex where they'd lived in their youth. The second was for a refurbished warehouse that was revamped two years ago into the after-school safe house that Nico was now associated with.

She'd been thinking about him and the safe house a lot as she'd driven. And what she'd decided was, just because it seemed as if he'd turned a corner and was dedicating his life to a very worthy cause didn't mean it wasn't a front. For all she knew, the safe house was something to keep him out of the eyes of the law and out of jail again. And even if it was legit, and Nico was no longer traversing the LA drug world, that didn't mean he didn't want Sam dead. Or her either. Not after the way things had gone down.

The closer Josie got to LA, the more her palms began to sweat. By eight thirty in the morning, she reached the outskirts of her old stomping ground. Strange as it was, parts of what she saw tugged at her, like the eclectic blend of architecture, the palm, citrus, and fig trees, and the bird of paradise flowers and jasmine bushes, so different from the nineteenth-century homes and non-coastal plant life in Galena.

For a minute, she debated finding somewhere to sleep and heading in after it got dark, but as soon as the thought crossed her mind, she dismissed it. She'd be safest in broad daylight. And the earlier in the day, the better. If anyone still wanted her dead, odds were none of them lived lives that made them early risers.

Realizing she'd not thought about a disguise of any sort, she stopped at another gas station and paid a ridiculous amount for a pair of oversized sunglasses and a too-big LA Dodgers hat. Back in the car, she knotted her hair into a ponytail and pulled it through the opening at the back of the hat, then slipped on the thick-rimmed sunglasses. The person staring back at her in the rearview mirror looked a bit ridiculous, but hopefully, it was enough of a disguise to keep from being noticed.

Because Nico's safe house was further from her old stomping ground than the house titled in his name, she decided to start there. Ignoring the missed calls on the silenced phone and not opening the texts from Carter in case he could tell they'd been read, Josie navigated to the address. Her palms were still sweating, and her heart was thumping wildly. With any luck, Carter had calmed Sam down and they would give her through this morning to explain herself.

And with a bit more luck, she'd be able to, after she confronted Nico face to face. *Assuming you aren't dead.*

She did her best to shut the thought down. If Nico was intent on killing her—or any of them—he'd find the time and place to do it. She wasn't going to wait around hoping that wasn't the case. No doubt, it was something she'd learned from her mom. "You wanna mess with me? Okay, let's do this," had been her mom's attitude from as early as Josie could remember.

When she got to the refurbished warehouse that was the safe house, she circled once and saw that the building was dark. When she came around again, she parked a block and a half away, across the street from a neighborhood Latino market. It seemed far enough not to be seen, but close enough to be able to watch for anyone coming or going.

Despite the extra adrenaline coursing through her veins, she felt calm and even-headed, which wasn't something she'd have guessed on stepping into the lion's den. Maybe it was because she'd chosen to find Nico on her terms rather than waiting for him to come to her, bringing along any Armageddon he might want to unleash. Or maybe it was one of the few good qualities she'd inherited from her mother.

After rubbing her palms up and down her jeans, she popped the trunk release under the dashboard, got out, and went around to the back where Myra's old handgun was hidden in a blanket underneath her other supplies. Maybe it was ridiculous to bring it with her. It wasn't even loaded. But somehow, it seemed like it would be a comfort to know she had it. At the very least, she might be able to hit him over the head with it in a scuffle.

"I'd be careful, shuffling around in your trunk like that in this neighborhood." The voice was deep and guttural, and it came from directly behind her. "You don't want people thinking you've got something worth hiding."

Josie froze with her hand on the bag of kitty litter that was covering the blanket. Whatever had made her think she could outsmart Nico on his own turf? Breath locking in her lungs, she turned, wondering if she was moving in slow motion or if it just seemed that way.

Nico was six feet away, holding a to-go cup of coffee and leaning on the hood of a parked car directly behind Myra's Victoria. How had she not seen him ten seconds ago?

Josie's strength leaked into her toes as she took him in. Like Sam, he'd aged. Become a man. Only he was so much bigger and stronger than the last time she'd seen him. Like a bodybuilder. He was in activewear with sleeves that were tight around his biceps, shoulders, and chest. His wavy brown hair was gone, shaved so short it was almost nonexistent.

"You look like a fricking tourist in those big glasses and that hat."

Josie shook her head; her voice had abandoned her just like the rest of her body wanted to.

His steady gray eyes pierced into her as he took a sip of coffee. "I'm not sure what I expected you to be driving, but it certainly wasn't an old Victoria. It took you long enough to get here. Now I see why."

"How…how'd you know I was coming?" Her voice sounded thin and far away.

"Same way you knew I was looking for you, I expect. Though I had a bit of confirmation from your brother in the middle of the night when he called and threatened to gut me like a fish if I so much as touched you."

"You talked to him?"

"Can't say I did much talking. After I tracked that hang-up last night to Cedar Rapids, I figured you were coming. Until he called, I didn't know if you were alone or if one of them two jokers was with you."

So, Carter hadn't talked Sam off that cliff. She hadn't expected Sam to call Nico. Everyone back home was probably crazy with worry. She needed to call and explain herself. And soon. "What is it you want?"

He cocked one eyebrow. "Same thing as you, I expect."

Her blood was going from cold to hot, and things didn't seem to be in slow motion anymore. She suspected she might be able to outrun him with the adrenaline coursing through her, but then again, she'd driven all the way here to confront him, so that didn't make sense.

He reached into his pocket to click a remote, and the car underneath him blinked unlocked. It was a new model silver Dodge Charger. "What do you say we go someplace we can talk?"

Josie gave a stern shake of her head. "No. No cars, Nico. We stay here. In public."

His smile deepened, and he walked forward so that he was mere inches from her. He was so close she could feel the warmth radiating from him. "Josie Pictures, if I wanted to kill you, you'd have been dead before you even parked that big boat of yours."

She collected herself, waiting out the space of several heartbeats before answering. "I'm still not getting in a car with you."

"Would you prefer to walk around the hood while we talk? Maybe rekindle some old memories. Personally, I suggest we hop in my car and get out of here for a bit. Clear some stuff up."

"*What* do you want from me?" she repeated, attempting to step back but prevented by the trunk.

"I'd like you to take those ridiculous glasses off so I can see your eyes. And after that, I'd like to give you something I've owed you for a long time. So, how about getting in the car before somebody takes a shot at you just for looking like a damned tourist in the hood?"

Josie looked around as his words sank in. For one reason or another, they had in fact drawn the attention of the half-dozen people in view.

Refusing to take the glasses off, she stared at him for a full half minute. He wasn't angry. And he wasn't afraid. She caught a glimpse of the boy she'd known underneath the layers of muscle and the shaved head, the same one who'd shoved her to the ground and covered her when the bullets started flying, the one who'd tried to give her everything except for the one impossible thing he couldn't—safety.

She didn't know she'd been holding her breath until she released it. She gave a single nod and walked around to grab her purse and phone from Myra's front seat. She locked the doors even though she knew it wouldn't keep out anyone who was intent on getting in.

She sank down onto the passenger seat of Nico's Charger and closed the door. Her palms were sweating again. The interior smelled like leather and Nico's cologne.

Nico took up every bit of the driver's side; his shoulder pressed in against hers. Josie shifted to lean toward the door. There was a surrealness—a blending of past and present that made her feel as if she was losing herself.

"Relax, Josie, this is going to be good. I promise." He started the ignition and pulled away from the curb.

"I get that you were monitoring Sam's site, but how did you find us in Galena?"

"It took a bit, but it wasn't hard. I had a buddy in St. Louis who got a picture of the plates of that Mustang, and I had someone else trace them. They were registered to a New York address. That guy, Carter O'Brien—your man, it seems—he had his mail forwarded a couple months ago. So, I asked another buddy in Chicago to check it out. Took him a couple weeks to get there, but he did. And now here you are."

"Seems like you have a lot of buddies."

Nico huffed. "That's one thing I've got."

"And Sam? How long did you know he was alive?"

"I was searching for you when that site popped up. Believe it or not, the great state of California lets its prisoners have limited internet access. When I saw the name of the administrator, I couldn't think of anyone else it could be but him."

"He figured you would know."

"Yeah, well, when I decided I wouldn't get the kind of satisfaction I was hoping for by putting a bullet in his ass, I figured it wasn't important where he was, so long as I knew he still hadn't found you. I wouldn't have given him credit for so much persistence. But he kept working town after town, putting ads in papers and monitoring that site. It just took a weekly search of your name to know the towns he was covering. I had an IT guy break his ID and password, and I've been watching the email he receives for when someone real finally bit. It was surreal, how completely you dropped off the grid. Even the FBI couldn't find you."

Nico made a series of turns that led to the interstate, and suddenly it occurred to Josie that it was the first time she'd been in a car he was driving. "Where are we going?"

"You and I, all the things we did together, we never saw much beyond the asshole of the world. Thought I should take you to where I go to step away, to find myself. It's not far."

Josie stared out the window at the houses visible from I-105. They were getting bigger and more elaborate the closer they got to the ocean.

"You know, even before I had proof, my hunch was that you kept the kid and that was why you kept a low profile." He shot a glance her way as he switched lanes. "Especially with her being Sam's kid and all."

"Nico… He didn't know. Not until the day everything blew up."

"I figured as much. But it doesn't mean he didn't disrespect me, does it?"

Anger flared, sharp and hot. "Kind of like when you started fucking her? After what her friends did to me?"

Nico fell quiet and stared at the road until more than a minute of silence had passed. "I spend a lot of time talking to donors now. When they look at us, at this place, from the outside, they try to solve our problems like a puzzle, like they're solvable. Turn this, move this here, flip this over, connect these three pieces—look at that, all better. What they don't get is how we can only take so much before we implode. Before life becomes as cheap as oranges in the year of a good crop."

Nico's words settled in, stirring up a rawness she'd done her best to forget about, to leave behind on her long runs and her busy schedule and in a hundred different ways to blend tea. Life here was a knot so tangled, there was no way to unravel it. Who had wronged who first or worst? Sometimes all that was left was anger and sorrow and, like with her mom, the off chance to numb it beyond oblivion.

There was no fixing this place, not from the outside and not by throwing money at it. It was Dante's *Inferno*, and the way up and out was the journey itself. Kindnesses like Francie's were life-sustaining and gave people the strength to keep going. But in the end, the decision to leave—to heal—came from within.

"You could leave. You don't have to stay here. It isn't like this everywhere."

Nico pursed his lips. "True. But this is home. For years, it was the home where I'd been planted. But now it's the home where I choose to put down roots."

Josie wasn't surprised. She couldn't imagine Nico anywhere but this part of LA.

"You know," he said, "that's how I knew you and I couldn't make it. You saw a way to get out even when we were kids, and I didn't have the foresight to see beyond my fist. You with your calendars and your calculations and those books. You saw the way out, only you waited because you wanted to bring your brother with you. Me, too, when you weren't too busy hating me."

"Sam said it took dying to understand he wanted to live."

"That sounds like something he'd be crazy enough to pull off." He switched driving arms, draping his left wrist across the steering wheel and squeezing her hand with his other. "The thing is, what I learned in prison—thanks, I'm betting, to your brother helping put me there—is when you make hell a part of your life's purpose, it doesn't have the same hold anymore."

⌇

The strip of beach Nico brought them to wasn't one where Josie had ever been, back in a life that suddenly didn't feel as distant as she'd believed. Halfway across the sand between the parking lot and the shore, she stopped to roll up her jeans and pull off her shoes. She started carrying them in one hand, but Nico reached for them without asking, balancing each shoe on the tip of a finger and reminding her of the boy who'd once done his best to carry loads that weren't his to carry.

They walked to the spot where the waves rolled over the sand and it was easiest to navigate. They headed south in the same comfortable silence they'd once known as Josie drew in breath after breath, savoring the briny smell of the saltwater and seagulls. She'd taken off the hat and glasses and left them in the car, and her hair whipped in the soft wind, so much so she needed to keep pulling strands from her mouth.

"I forgot how calming the ocean is," she said as a wave washed over her feet. It had taken a few rolling waves to get used to the chilly water, but now it was nothing but invigorating when a wave washed up on shore.

"That town of yours, Galena, what's it like besides unpopulated as shit, full of old people, and about as far in the States as you can be from an ocean?"

"I see you looked at the census info," Josie said, laughing. "It's quiet. You can see the stars. Most everybody knows everybody, except we get a lot of tourists. Most of the buildings are on the historic register. And they're almost all brick. And there's a river. It's a quiet one, as far as rivers go, but it's still water."

"And the kid?"

"Zoe?" She ran her tongue over the back of her teeth as she considered how best to describe her. She hadn't been around Nico back then enough to know how involved he was in Zoe's first year. She suspected he wasn't very. "For starters, she's the best thing in my life. She's precocious and the light in the room. Always has been. I guess you could say she's a better-adjusted version of Sam. She's six now. She was just eleven months old when Sam dropped her in my arms. She doesn't remember Jena. I'm the only mother she knows."

"Does she know about Sam?"

"Being her father? Not yet. He doesn't want to—well, in some ways, he's still the Sam you knew, I guess. He says he doesn't care if I ever tell her, but she needs to know."

"How'd your boyfriend like that technicality? You and Sam being mother and father, brother and sister?"

Another wave came up, washing over their feet, joining them in water and sand. "He's stepping up in ways Sam can't."

Nico nodded and stopped walking, turning to face her. "Good, because I'm not in the habit of kicking ass anymore, Josie Pictures. Though I could take it up again if needed."

"No ass-kicking needed. And it's not Josie Pictures anymore."

"You going to tell me what it is, or are you keeping me in the dark in case I decide to come after that nark of a brother of yours someday?"

"Not funny, and it's Josie Waterhill."

"*Josie Waterhill?* Huh. That sounds a lot more Midwestern than Josie Pictures."

"Technically, it is," she said, smiling a little. "My turn. What about you? That clinic, that's what you do? Full time?"

"If that's your polite way of checking if I've still got one foot in the street, I don't. Not that way. I keep my head down to keep an eye on about a dozen boys skirting the life. And I still get guys trying to recruit me just about every week. But those twenty-two months in prison were enough. Now I spend my days trying to keep as many kids off the streets as I can. If I save a few from getting lost in these wars, then my life should count for something."

Josie's heart twisted. "Nico."

He shrugged a shoulder. "What can I say? Losing you changed me. It just took a while for me to notice. In jail, I finally found Francie's God she'd been ragging on me about forever, and I got a GED. And I'm thirteen credit hours away from a bachelor's in social work."

"Wow, I'm impressed. Very impressed." A few seagulls circled overhead, spying something in the break of the waves.

"Enough to leave that skinny-ass New Yorker and stay with me?"

Josie pressed her lips together and shook her head. "Nico…"

"Just yanking your chain, Josie. I've got a real decent girl now. Went through a string of wrong ones, I'll admit. We've been together almost a year. You'd like her. She likes math like you. She helps me keep my books straight."

"That's great."

Nico closed a hand over her back. "Want to know one of the reasons I brought you here?"

"I thought you wanted to talk?"

"Yeah, but specifically, there's something I never could tell you, and I thought you deserved to know."

"Okay." She shrugged a shoulder. "What is it?"

"Maybe a month before you came into my life, I saw this nature show on TV."

"I never knew you watched nature shows."

"Yeah, well, it wasn't by choice. Nonna couldn't pay the cable bill, and it was on the only channel with good reception." He turned his back to the ocean as a wave broke over their feet, motioning toward the sandy beach. "There was this special about sea turtles, and this one turtle's journey in particular. It showed her dig a nest, lay eggs, and head back into the ocean. Weeks later, the baby turtles hatched. Apparently that short trip from their nest in the sand across the beach until they make it to the water is the most dangerous of their lives. There were dozens of them, popping up from the nest and digging their little flippers into the sand to get moving. But there was this one albino one the narrator said was extremely rare. It had pure-white skin and blue eyes, and the cameraman panned in so close, its little face filled the screen. It had this upturned beak like a smile. More than anything I can remember, I wanted that little turtle to make it to the ocean."

"And did it?" Josie said, folding her hands together in anticipation.

"Yeah, but barely. I'll spare you the details, but the damn seagulls were everywhere. Because that turtle was so rare, the camera stayed panned in on it as it scrambled across the sand, sometimes a foot or less from one of those merciless gulls. When it made it to the water and started swimming, I cried like a baby."

Envisioning a stressed-out young Nico, Josie locked a hand over his arm.

"I still thought about it when you came to our school, and I knew right away with your fair skin, blue eyes, and that hair of yours, you were that sea turtle, Josie. And I knew your journey in that ghetto was going to be just as tough."

"So, you befriended me because I reminded you of an albino sea turtle?" She teared up and laughed at the same time. "That's the sweetest thing I've ever heard. Absolutely the sweetest."

He stepped back a foot and she got the sense he wasn't offended, just keeping a certain distance between them. "I'm not trying to be sweet. I just thought you needed to hear it."

"You did everything you could, didn't you, to make sure I made it to the ocean?" She remembered so many times he tried to protect her, to keep her safe, that the tears brimming in her eyes spilled over.

"Yeah, well I figured the ocean needed a creature like you in it."

Chapter 37

THE TENSION KNOTTING CARTER'S chest was so intense he was certain he'd lose it in the face of any additional triggers. The meticulously slow movements of the rental car salesperson, added to her whistly, nasal breathing, had Carter about to snap. Behind him, Sam's continual pacing and muttering under his breath wasn't helping.

"Why don't you go to the bathroom now, so we don't have to stop until we find her." It came out sounding far from a suggestion.

"You aren't my boss," Sam said but headed there anyway, commenting on the giant Mountain Dew he'd chugged after landing.

By the time he returned, Carter had turned down enough extra services in such a clipped voice that the woman finally went quiet and handed him the keys. Rather than relaying the aisle number of their rental, she pointed to the far corner of the parking garage with a slight roll of her eyes.

"That went well," Sam muttered under his breath as they head out the door. "Bet she saved us her finest with that attitude of yours."

"Shut it, will you?"

Sam yanked the keys from his hand without asking. "I'm driving. I can get us where we're going a lot faster than you, and you know it."

"So long as you don't get us arrested along the way."

"I won't." Sam clicked the remote. Across the garage, a yellow Kia Soul blinked in reply. "We are so getting shot at in that," he protested.

A half hour, several rolling stops, two no-right-on-reds, and no tickets later, Sam pulled up in front of the house that was registered in Nico's name. It was a small, square stucco ranch set into a gentle, sloping hillside.

"This is near where you lived?" Carter asked.

"We weren't this lucky. This is 90210 compared to our place. We were a couple miles closer to hell. But don't let that make you think you can't still get shot at here. We're in the ghetto. Don't disillusion yourself there."

"Just so we're on the same page, any chance you packed that knife of yours in your luggage?"

Sam huffed. "That knife was for the defensive side of the court. Offensively, I'm willing to bet it's better to walk into the lion's den unarmed."

"And you really think the best plan is to just knock on this guy's door?"

"I'm hoping Nico had time to cool his jets. We were like brothers once. It wouldn't be easy for him to kill me. Still," he added, looking up at the house, "whatever happens, we should stay outside where there might be someone to call for help."

Carter followed Sam up to the porch but moved in front of him after Sam rang the bell.

"I don't need a bodyguard."

"There are scars from three bullets on your chest that make me think otherwise."

A shuffling could be heard inside, and Carter held his breath, suspecting they were being observed through the peephole. After a pause, the door opened slowly. A petite, older woman stood in the frame, looking past Carter, her eyes fixed on Sam.

"Step aside so I can see him." Her voice was barely a whisper and her eyes were welling with tears. "Let me touch you, *piccolo*. My eyes tell me you're real, but my mind says this is a lie."

Carter stepped back. That look on her face wasn't anger or anything close to it. It was love.

"Francie," Sam said huskily as she drew him in a tight embrace, the top of her gray head reaching his chest. Carter peered inside the half-open door. The main room seemed empty aside from a kid who was nearing his preteens.

"You were too long in coming home."

"I'm sorry, Francie. I should've called you. I don't know. I was afraid."

"Nico said he thought you were alive, but I never could believe it. Not until now. I held your hand and watched as they tried to revive you. You were lost to this world." She let out something that was between a sob and a laugh. "God has plans for you; there's no other way you could be standing here."

She brushed the tears from her cheeks and ushered them inside. When Sam didn't object, Carter raised an eyebrow skeptically.

"Just go with it."

It was dark inside. The blinds had all been drawn. Carter took in a picture of the Virgin Mary hung above a simple couch facing a TV. The kid, a sloppy-haired boy with big eyes, sat below it, barely acknowledging them, lost in a video game.

"I want you to meet my great grandson. Enzo, stop your game and welcome our guests."

Enzo groaned but pulled his attention from the TV screen. "Hi."

"You've never met him, Enzo, but this young man here is like a grandson to me just as his sister is my granddaughter." She squeezed Sam on the arm again. "His name is Sam." Then, looking at Carter, "And you are?"

"Carter O'Brien."

"My name is Francesca. If you are a friend of Sam's, you may call me Francie. Enzo is my oldest great-grandchild, and the only one who lives with me. Or I live with him, I should say. He has been in my and my grandson's custody since his mother died five years ago. He's ten now."

"He's Jena's child?" Sam eyed up the boy. "I met you once. You were little."

"Her first child," Francie said. "Her second, I was told, has a closer connection to you than any of us imagined when she entered this world."

Sam cleared his throat and nodded at the boy as he went back to playing his game. "Nice to meet you." To Francie, he said, "I can see the resemblance."

"To Nico or Jena?" Francie asked, still holding Sam's arm as if afraid he would disappear.

"To both. And to Zoe."

"Me too," Carter added. "To Zoe."

"Sit. Please. You must be tired. You both certainly look it. I'll get you something to eat and drink. I know how my Sam likes my cooking."

"We can't stay, Francie. We have to find Josie."

"Have a seat. I'll call Nico and see if he's found her."

"He's *looking* for her?" Carter said, the tension thick in his voice.

Francie frowned. "I don't know you, and you don't know my Nico, so I'll forgive the accusation in your voice. If my Nico has found her, she's safer than she would be with anyone else in this town, including the two of you."

"Call him, will you?" Sam asked. "She needs to know we're here. She had my cell with her, but either the battery died, or she shut it off."

Carter kept standing as Sam headed over to the couch and planted himself next to the kid, asking what the kid was playing. As they started talking about video games, Carter shook his head. His thoughts were clouded with fatigue and another receding adrenaline rush. But one thing was for sure, this whole thing was more complicated than he'd assumed.

A garbage truck passing behind Nico's car jerked Josie out of her doze. Before conscious thought kicked in, she was startled to find Nico in the driver's seat next to her. They were in a parking lot and headstones dotted an expansive cemetery, stretching out in three directions. Josie had asked him to drive her here but had dozed off on the way.

"I fell asleep." She cleared her throat. She needed a strong cup of coffee and a shower. And a bed tonight.

"You pushed yourself, driving all that way without stopping."

"I napped a couple times."

"You know, you being here is bringing that day back for me. I kept seeing it as you slept."

"A lot of stuff has been coming up for me too." She shifted, stretching her back. "I heard about the day from Sam, but if you want to share, I'm all ears."

He gave a one-shoulder shrug. "What can say? Play with fire, and eventually you'll get burned. It fell apart so fast when it happened—like a grenade I forgot I was holding. Suddenly it exploded and everything was a wasted mess."

"Sam said it was guys from Jena's brother's gang, not your friends, who killed my mom and shot him. He said you took a bullet too."

"I wouldn't have let it play out the way it did had I been conscious. I wouldn't have let those guys take down your family like that. You have to know that."

Josie nodded and stared out at the graveyard. "I know. I think I always knew. I just didn't trust myself enough to believe it."

"Francie would've been dead, too, had she gotten home fifteen minutes earlier. I'm not going to tell you I wouldn't have put a cap in Sam's ass myself, him disrespecting me like that, but I'd have died for him still, had I been there."

For the second time that morning, Josie found herself near tears.

"Like I said, everything fell apart all at once," he continued.

"Everybody had their own agendas. I took a hit through the shoulder a couple miles from home. I passed out and someone took my gun. When I came to and made it home, there were cops and medics everywhere, and Francie was kneeling over Sam, crying like she was breaking in two."

"Oh, Francie." She shook her head, willing away tears that wanted to press in. "She was so good to us. Right from the start."

"You were good to her too."

Josie released a long, controlled breath and nodded toward the cemetery. "Which one is my mother's?"

"Over there," Nico pointed. "Sure you don't want company?"

"Not for this, thanks. And Sam's got an Uber account on his phone, so don't worry about me getting back. I'll see you at your place in an hour or so. You'll be there?"

"All day." He turned the car back on. "Jena's buried here too. She's diagonally south of your mother twenty or so stones."

Josie stepped out, offering a wave of thanks. Jena was here. She hadn't thought that her mom and Jena might be buried in the same place. As she walked from the parking lot onto the grass, it occurred to her she'd never been to a cemetery before. The few kids she'd known who'd died had all been cremated. Only a handful of people dotted the graveyard, and a few hundred feet away, an older man operating a backhoe was digging a fresh grave. Josie wondered what he thought of death. Had he lost his fear of it, working alongside it day by day?

She spotted her mother's nondescript stone while she was still two rows away. She was surprised to have expected more, but the bareness of the stone stood out in contrast to so many others. It was inscribed with only her name, Skye Pictures, and the years marking the beginning and end of her life. No vows of sorrow or devotion marked it, and no faded flowers or trinkets adorned it.

Josie's stomach pitched at the realization that the woman who'd brought her and her brother into this world—the woman who'd come to Hollywood to create a legend that would immortalize her forever—had vanished from its surface almost unnoticed.

As Francie would say, *such is life.*

Josie's knees nearly buckled as she noticed the grave to the left of her mother's. It was marked for Sam Pictures who'd supposedly left this world at nineteen. It was just as plainly inscribed but was adorned with a handful of faded, plastic flowers and a figurine of Jesus on the cross. Items left by Francie, no doubt.

"You don't get him yet," Josie said to her mother's stone, her voice lined with anger and sorrow. "Forever, if I can help it."

If Lady Justice were weighing the memories Skye had left her children, the sad, dark, and fearful would outweigh the shiny, happy ones. Josie had no doubt about it.

Most certainly stirred up from this morning's beach visit on the heels of Thanksgiving, she could remember, as clear as day, being eight or nine and sitting on the beach at sunset with Sam and her mom. Her fingers and mouth were greasy from their annual Thanksgiving Day picnic of McDonald's double cheeseburgers and fries. She'd been thirsty, but their sodas were empty. The wind had been up, and she and Sam were chilled. After they'd finished eating, Skye draped the picnic blanket around them as they watched the sunset and called out things they were thankful for.

Josie had watched the big orange disk slip below the ocean horizon, wishing that this mom—the one who'd not given up the search when their usual McDonald's was closed and who told the best knock-knock jokes and who wasn't even griping at Sam for his never-ceasing fidgetiness—would stick around forever.

Where would we be now if she had? Would Sam still have spiraled like he did? Josie and Sam wouldn't have needed Francie the way they had. Maybe she wouldn't have grown to be inseparable with Nico all those years. And Sam would never have been shot.

And maybe Zoe wouldn't exist.

The only thing she knew for sure was that her mother had run out of opportunities to realize there was more to life than chasing a dream that would never have filled the hole inside her.

Digging through her purse, Josie fished out the ceramic fairy figurine she'd bought for Zoe in Vegas. There was always the trip back home to get another one.

"You'd have loved her," she said, remembering her mom's affinity for people and things that were bright and bigger than life. "On those good days when you could appreciate things." After unwrapping the figurine, she used the base to dig away at a bit of grass and wedged it in against the headstone. The bright colors stood out starkly against the trimmed grass and plain stone, making it seem even more barren than before.

She stared at the fairy, whose hands were raised in front of her lips, blowing at a handful of petals that were morphing into butterflies as they blew into the air. Right now, this unintended gift was as close as she could come to forgiveness.

"I'll tell her about you someday," she said, her voice just audible. "And I'll try to remember more of the good things."

It wasn't until Josie had visited Jena's grave and was headed back to the parking lot that she realized the battery on Sam's phone was dead. Her internal clock was so messed up from lack of sleep, she could only guess at the time. Ten or ten-thirty possibly, and with the two-hour time difference between here and Galena, no wonder it seemed like the middle of the day.

She sent up a silent prayer that everyone back home was calm. She'd not meant to go this long without calling. Her whole body ached to hear Zoe's soft voice on the other end of the line, prattling on about one thing or another.

Without Sam's phone to order the Uber, her only way back to Nico's was the bus. *Talk about full circle.* She'd not been on a bus since she'd left here with an eleven-month-old Zoe crying in her arms. There was a half-mile walk to the nearest stop, and then a ten-minute wait. And the whole time, she kept thinking about the run she'd made.

She'd not recognized any of the people who'd been following her, and it was still hard to believe that local drug wars could escalate to the point that the life of an infant was intentionally in danger. Had Zoe's life been a test by some power-hungry mongrel working his way to the top?

How those two guys could've been so inhumane to pursue her when she'd been unarmed and had a baby in her hands, she'd never understand. But as Sam had said, there were things he'd said and done as a heroin addict that he'd never thought he would do.

The bus stopped a block away from Nico's center, and just hours after worrying that going there could turn into the worst decision she'd made, she headed toward it without fear.

She was fifty feet away when the door opened, and a man stepped out. In a split-second glance, she noticed that he was fit and attractive—and familiar.

She stopped midstep and stared. Impossibly familiar. Her stare transformed into a gawk. She blinked and waited for her head to clear, clouded with fatigue as it was.

The last reserves of adrenaline dumped into her system. "*Carter?*"

Her feet refused to move, so Carter had to walk to her. He looked tired and tense and relieved at the same time. He stopped a foot from her, his thumbs shoved into his jeans pockets. Josie looked from him to the building, but no one followed him out, and the glass was too reflective in the sunlight to see inside at this angle. It was crazy to worry about it after the forgiveness Nico had shown her, but some instinctual, untamed part of her was still terrified he wanted to hurt the people she loved, and she had to talk herself down from it.

"How—how did you find me?"

"Everything's searchable nowadays."

"Nico?"

"He's inside."

"You met him?"

He nodded but added nothing.

Of course, he's angry. You stole Myra's car and drove across country without so much as telling him. The voice she'd gotten from her mother answered that he'd sort of done the same thing to her a little over a month ago.

He was wearing a button-down shirt that was open at the collar, a checkered blue one that set off his eyes and exposed the fresh three-inch scar on his neck courtesy of Sam's knife. Something about the sight of it, the way it reminded her of the raw vulnerability of life, helped her unstick. She jumped forward, burying her face in his chest and locking her arms around his shoulders.

"I'm sorry. I was afraid—I was afraid of everything, most especially that the people I love were going to end up hurt, and we wouldn't even see it coming."

Carter's arms locked around her and he pressed a kiss into her temple. "You're okay. That's all that matters."

Josie was about to reply when the door jangled open again. "If you ever do anything so stupid again, I'll kick your ass, and I'm not even kidding."

"Sam?" Josie was just as dumbfounded to look around Carter's shoulder and spy her brother headed their way.

And Nico was right behind him, a ghost of a smile lighting his face.

Practically shoving Carter out of the way, Sam clasped his hands on either side of her face, his voice kind but blaring. "I spent over five years looking for you. You can't just vanish like that. *Ever.* You don't know what it does to me."

Tears stung her eyes. "I'm sorry, Sam. I needed to know you were safe."

"You could've asked me. Like I told you before, if Nico wanted me dead, he'd have shown up in one of the cities I was working while I was looking for you."

"It's been a long couple days for everyone." Carter closed a hand over Sam's shoulder; Josie was half surprised when the action calmed Sam down rather than bringing out his defensive side. Another sign he was growing up.

"It really has," she agreed. "Did you drive here?"

"No, we flew."

When she looked over at Nico, who was joining them, a woman was at his side, eyeing her with undisclosed interest.

"How 'bout we all agree that the only bullets flying today will be stray ones?" Nico looked at Sam. "After I introduce your sister to my girl and show her around, we can start that game you wanted to play. Though I don't know how much of a challenge it'll be playing your ass, skinny as it is." Nico paused, then looked at Josie as he jutted his thumb toward his girlfriend. "Josie *Waterhill*, this is Cristina Torres."

Nico's girlfriend was older than Josie might have guessed, mid-thirties maybe, with light-brown skin and long, curly brownish-black hair that was tied in a low ponytail, and she was fit enough to look like an athletic Barbie to Nico's hulky Ken.

Cristina offered a hand. "I refuse to fit in the jealous girlfriend category, but I've heard a bit about you this last year we've been together. Welcome home."

"It's nice to meet you." And it was nice. Josie still loved Nico; she always would. But it was a different love. It had morphed into the familial love she had for Myra and Sam. "Nico said you help him keep this place running smoothly."

"She does." Nico winked at Cristina and waved them inside.

"Come on; I'll give you a tour, then we'll play a game before we head over to Francie's."

Josie's heart constricted in anticipation of seeing Francie. Countless times, she'd wished she could've called and let Francie know she was okay. But knowing she couldn't answer any questions Francie might ask, she'd never had the nerve.

Her brother hooked his thumb toward Nico as they filed inside. "Guess it's good he's forgiven me, because he's a frickin' tank, isn't he?"

Josie made eye contact with Carter before answering. "I'm guessing he's upped his protein intake a touch."

"It's all spinach," Nico said with a laugh.

Seeing Nico and Carter just feet apart, the stark difference in the two lives she'd led struck Josie. She wondered if Nico and Carter would even really understand each other, coming from such different backgrounds. The friendliness in Nico's tone as he showed them around his center gave her hope they might.

Josie wasn't sure what she'd have expected on a Saturday, but the building was full. There were more than twenty kids in the building, mostly boys but a few girls. They were all ages, sizes, body types, and races. And within a few minutes, it was clear that all of them were enamored with Nico.

A smile spread across her face. Nico had found his passion and was making a difference in the lives of kids like the ones she'd grown up with.

When the basketball game started, some of the older boys were asked to play, four on Nico's team, and three on Sam and Carter's. To keep it fair, Nico let Sam choose his team first. The three teens didn't flinch at the opportunity to play against Nico, though they said the odds were in the favor of the opposing team even though it hadn't been picked yet.

After changing out of his button-down shirt into one of the

extra gym T-shirts, Carter nodded his head toward Nico. "Think I could take him if I had to?"

Josie bit her lip. "Uh, I just think it's a good thing you don't have to."

"I guess what matters is when it's all said and done, you're going home with me. At least, I hope you are."

Josie's mouth fell open just a touch. "Of course, I am. I love you. But do you really think of it as home now? You aren't just using Galena as a reference point since we're sitting on the edge of one of the most dangerous neighborhoods in LA?"

"You, Zoe, Myra—even Sam," he said, closing an arm around her back. "You're my home now. That's what matters, isn't it? Being with the people you love most."

Stepping in front of them, in a fit of bravado, Sam yanked off his sweatshirt. "Ready to beat some ass?"

He was too thin still but already looked healthier than the boy who'd driven up from St. Louis. The scars from the bullet wounds on his chest and back drew more people's attention than Josie's. They would never tan and never fade, a forever reminder of the miracle her brother was.

"You meant it when you included Sam?" Josie asked as her brother got in one of his teammates' faces, double fiving him and promising that they were taking Nico down. "You aren't just saying that? Because I don't think he's going anywhere for a long time."

Carter grinned. "It wouldn't be the same without him."

"Trust me, it wasn't. It really wasn't."

Chapter 38

AFTER FRANCIE SPENT MOST of the afternoon preparing it, Josie had no doubt dinner would be every bit as good as the special holiday meals she'd prepared when Josie was a kid. When Francie was finished cooking, the long dining table was hardly visible underneath fresh bread, a platter of antipasto, flank steak, pasta, minestrone, vegetables, and cannoli for dessert.

In addition to Cristina, Francie's granddaughter Sofia and her two children joined them as well, making their party total ten in all.

From the moment Francie's tableside prayer ended, there wasn't a second of quiet. From the clanking of forks on plates and the playfulness of Sofia's young kids to the conversation of the adults, it reminded Josie of the first big family meal she'd had at Francie's. Back when she'd not known families could be big and loud and chaotic and still be loving and supportive the way Francie's family was.

Josie had a hard time keeping her attention off Enzo, Nico's son and Zoe's half-brother. The ten-year-old boy listened intently and seemed neither eager to add to the conversation nor too shy to do so when he had something to say. Like Nico, Enzo seemed quiet and introspective, the yin to Zoe's yang, and Josie very much wanted to get to know him more.

When she found out he'd yet to see snow, she said, "You should talk your family into visiting us this winter. Something tells me you'd love playing in snow."

Enzo smiled, revealing a single deep dimple that matched his father's. "Can we, Dad?"

"Yeah, maybe," was Nico's response.

When Sofia's kids got quiet enough that it was easier to speak over them, Francie told Carter of the first time she met Josie and Sam—how they helped her carry her groceries to the third floor when the elevator was broken—and how she knew when she looked into their eyes that their lives were meant to run together. Carter was clearly moved when Francie talked about how Josie had helped her in just as many ways as she'd claimed to have been helped by Francie. From keeping both Sam and Nico on top of their homework to cleaning and helping with laundry, Josie had been a godsend to Francie.

"Before I met Josie," Francie said, "I was already a believer in the ways God works, but she was the flower I found growing up from the crack in the sidewalk."

"I'm guessing I was the weed?" Sam interjected.

Francie shushed him with a wave of her hand. "When you bring your lover home to me, I'll tell her as many beautiful things about you."

"Thank you for sharing all this," Carter said in reply.

Francie quietly appraised Josie. "Your new last name will take some getting used to, Josie…what is it again?"

"Waterhill," Nico answered.

"What made you choose it?" Francie asked.

"It's complicated," Josie said. "And honestly something I've never shared with anyone, not even Myra."

Suddenly all eyes were on her, and a wave of vulnerability washed over Josie at the prospect of saying it. Still, she knew there was no better place to start than in this room where her two lives blended together more easily than she'd have dreamed.

She wiped her mouth and folded her napkin on her lap. "When Sam dropped Zoe into my arms and told me to run and not look back, that's what I did. He didn't mean forever, but I knew I needed to get away until things cooled down. And then—" An unexpected wave of loss washed over her at the memory of losing Sam. How much more was still buried inside? "When I found out I'd lost him, I assumed everyone else in this world was lost to me as well. So, I kept running. I'd been on the road with Zoe for six days, just wandering, sleeping in women's shelters and bus stations and train stations and relying on the kindness of strangers for food and diapers for Zoe. I was exhausted and afraid, and I knew I couldn't go on indefinitely with her."

Josie cleared her throat and took a swallow of water. Aside from the sounds of Sofia's kids, who'd gone into the living room and were playing with toys, it was quiet enough to hear the bubbles of carbonation escaping the can of soda Nico had opened. "But she kept looking up at me with Sam's eyes, and I—I just couldn't part from her. I was sitting in a bus station in Spokane, and I don't know, I started praying. Really praying, harder than I'd ever prayed in my life. Maybe it's because I was so completely out of options that I took it as a sign, or maybe it really was an answer to my prayer, I'm not sure. But this older man was looking through a rack of travel brochures, and he knocked one out. It skimmed across the floor, practically landing at my feet."

"Was it for Galena?" Sam asked. "Is that why you went there?"

"It wasn't just for Galena. It was for a restaurant there, a mom-and-pop diner known for its waffles. How it ended up a thousand miles away at a bus station in Spokane, I wish I knew. My guess was that someone dropped it off. I still have it in a drawer back home." She shrugged sheepishly. "It said something about being just the place to lose yourself in history and enjoy a meal the way grandma used to make. The big thing about it; it was called Josie's."

She shrugged her shoulders at the murmurs of appreciation that circled the table. "Since I had nothing to lose, and I didn't want to stay on the West coast, I decided to go. As soon as I did, things started falling into place. That very man ended up giving me the bus money after we struck up a conversation. I hate it, but I forgot his name, I was so sleep deprived that day. A woman noticed I couldn't pay for a meal and gave me a hundred dollars to tide me over until I found better times, telling me to pay it forward when I did. Which I've done several times over. There were a dozen other things too. The trip took three days and a lot of bus changes, but Zoe and I made it. So, I finally got to the restaurant only to find it had gone out of business several months earlier."

Carter squeezed her hand. "It was on the corner of Water and Hill streets, right?"

Josie looked at him in surprise. "As far as I know, you're the only one who's made the connection. How did you figure it out?"

"It came up in an old Galena newspaper article when I Googled you."

"Then what happened?" Sam asked. "How'd you hook up with Myra?"

Josie could only shrug. "That was the easy part. I was sitting on a bench wondering what next when she walked by. There was something about her that reminded me of home the very same way you did when I first saw you, Francie. I remembered how Sam and I had helped carry your groceries when I saw Myra struggling with the same thing. Only she had a lot more steps to carry them up. When we got to the top, she invited me to her house for tea. And Zoe and I never left."

"Damn," Nico said.

Francie poked him with the tip of her fork. "I told you, talk to God earnestly enough, and he'll answer you. You just have to listen."

When Nico looked at Josie in disbelief, she raised an eyebrow. "All I can say to that is Galena is exactly what I would have painted had someone asked me to paint the perfect place to lose myself—or find myself, I guess. I'm not the accountant I planned to be, but I run a tea garden, and I love it a lot more than I ever would have enjoyed helping people keep their finances straight. And years later, when I was finally ready for more, even if I didn't know it at first, the perfect guy to fit into that world came knocking on my door.

"So, the thing is," Josie added, flattening her hands on her lap, "at the risk of sounding like my name-changing mother—I'm pretty certain Josie Waterhill is who I was meant to become when I entered this world."

"And Mr. Writer over there fits the bill for her," Nico answered, looking from Carter to Josie, a teasing look in his eyes. "You don't see me objecting. So long as he knows that if he ever hurts you, I'll lose myself in history long enough to kick his ass."

"You'd have to get in line, because I'd kick it first," Sam interjected, tossing a partially eaten bread roll at him.

"Boy, you're gonna have to put on some weight first because, right now, you're skinny enough a strong wind will blow you over."

Josie squeezed Carter's hand under the table. "Since you've been around Sam a month already, you'll believe my saying that they've had a tendency to be overprotective forever. And they rev each other up."

Carter winked. "Good thing I'm head over heels in love with you and have no intentions of doing anything to hurt you, because I'm way less inclined to get an ass-kicking by Nico than I would be by Sam."

Nico raised his glass to Carter. "Sounds like your boy has good sense, Josie Waterhill."

Francie raised her glass as well. "If we're going to toast, it should be to new beginnings, and to a homecoming that was long overdue. Life is complicated and not always fair, but let's make of it the best we can and pray God will guide us along the way."

"Amen to that," Carter and Sam said in unison. As everyone raised their glasses, Josie promised herself that no one at the table would ever slip out of her life again.

Chapter 39

THERE WAS A PERFECT view of the backyard from Myra's room where Josie was finishing getting ready. A foot of accumulated snow had been cleared off the walkways and patios. It was a sunny and bright Saturday afternoon and the day after Valentine's Day. White lights surrounded the bases of the largest trees, giving the yard a fairy-tale feel. Swaths of evergreens dotted with red roses and red berries were draped and tied throughout the veranda, which was being warmed by several tall stainless-steel heaters that were already on and burning.

An elegant but simple wedding. The second one here in six months.

Several fire pits reflected on an ice sculpture—a large claddagh ring in memory of Myron O'Brien, who'd helped bring Carter and Josie together eighty years after his passing.

Downstairs, close to forty guests filled the rooms, waiting to head outside when the ceremony began. Carter's parents were here, as were a few of his friends from New York. Nico had first politely declined Josie's invitation, but Francie had somehow changed his mind. They'd come with Enzo and Nico's girlfriend, with Nico claiming he'd promised to bring Enzo before the last of the winter snow melted. They were downstairs, mingling with what Nico had labeled a bunch of rural Midwesterners who weren't fazed by a foot of snow.

Returning from downstairs, Myra came up behind her as Josie retouched her lipstick. The gown Josie had chosen from a shop in town was long and winter white and had a simple elegance that Myra said suited her perfectly as soon as she'd tried it on.

"You're as beautiful as they come, dear." Myra closed a hand over her shoulder.

"She looks like my mother," Sam scoffed from his spot on Myra's bed where he was teaching Zoe how to shoot spitballs using leftover pieces of the baby's breath woven into Zoe's hair. "Especially with makeup on. I keep waiting for her to throw back a shot and start yelling at me."

Zoe giggled. "What's a shot?"

Josie pointed a finger at her brother. "I do not, but if you shoot any more pieces of that baby's breath at me, I *am* going to start yelling. Besides, don't you think you should get back to your date?"

Last week, Sam came home announcing he'd met someone— at Galena's oldest and smallest hole-in-the-hill Episcopal church of all places, a picturesque stone chapel nestled in the Galena hillside. He'd been out walking and had heard an organ. On an impulse, he'd headed in for a bit of soul searching. Never in a million years would Josie have guessed that the young woman he met inside was Kristin Richards, Zoe's teacher. Since then, they'd gone out a few different times and, considering her connection to the flower girl, Sam invited her to attend today.

Sam pushed himself up from Myra's soft mattress and slipped back into the coat of his rented tux. "Straighten this ridiculous tie for me, will you?" he asked, walking over.

Josie tugged at Sam's collar and tie until they were straight and even. Looking into his clear hazel eyes, she could still see the boy who'd stacked crates in their bedroom and stole Ramen Noodles out of her bowl when she wasn't looking. "Your being here to walk me down the aisle makes everything perfect, you know?"

"Yeah, whatever," he said, "only why do you have to look so much like mom?"

"I hate to break it to you, but you didn't land so far from that tree either." She kissed him heavily enough on the cheek that she left behind a smear of lipstick.

"Come on, Zo," Sam said, waving her over, "let's go find Kristin."

"You mean Ms. Richards," Zoe said. "We're supposed to call her Ms. Richards."

"Yeah, well, you can. I'm exempt since I'm out of elementary school, kid."

Sam opened the door to reveal Carter on the other side, about to knock. Buttercup, who'd soon be carrying Josie's ring in a satchel tied to his collar in the ceremony, pushed inside and began his rounds, giving everyone a thorough sniff before hopping onto the bed.

"It's bad luck to see the bride before the wedding," Myra said.

"It doesn't have to be, Myra," Josie said. "A very wise woman once told me luck is nothing more than what we make it."

Zoe wrapped herself around Carter's leg as Sam opened the door wide. "I waited for this my whole life," she said, grinning as she pulled away.

"You don't have to wait till the ceremony is over, if you don't want to, Zo," Carter said, squeezing her shoulder.

"Nuh uh. You have to marry my mom to become my real dad."

"Is that so?" Carter laughed, bending over to plant a kiss on her forehead. "Then I can wait a little longer too."

With Sam's DNA sample—and his blessing—Josie and Carter had seen a lawyer to begin the process of making Zoe's adoption official. Josie was also doing it right and legally changing her name from Pictures to Waterhill. The whole thing would be a complicated process, but thankfully she'd tucked away a bit of money to cover the expenses.

"Anyone mind if I have a minute alone with my bride?" Carter asked.

"We were headed out anyway." Sam led Zoe out of the room along with him. "See you downstairs."

"I need to check the kitchen." Myra paused to smooth out the top of Carter's tux. "I don't think even that grandfather of yours could have made a more handsome groom."

"Well, I don't know about that, but he couldn't have made a more devoted one."

Once they were alone, Carter shut the door and joined Josie at the dresser by the window. Just as she suspected, he looked phenomenal in his black tux.

She nodded toward the backyard. "It turned out beautiful, didn't it? For a bit of a rush."

But Carter had eyes only for her. "You look—" he stopped and shook his head. "I'm speechless."

"Like my mother, according to Sam."

"If that's true, then I can't believe she never made it in pictures."

"No pun intended, huh?" Josie laughed.

"Yeah, none intended."

"What made you come up? We're getting married in ten minutes. And please stop looking like you want to kiss me. I don't have time to redo my makeup."

"I thought of something when I was downstairs."

"What was that?"

"The very first time I saw you. Do you remember what you asked me when you opened the door?"

"Ah, no, because seconds later I practically fainted."

"You asked if I was here for the wedding."

Josie laughed. "That's right; I'd forgotten."

"Yeah, well, I want to revise my answer."

"If I remember correctly you made one of your very Carter-like comments, but you didn't say no."

"True, but I should have said emphatically yes."

She made a face. "Yeah, I think that would have come across as creepy."

He grinned and pulled her close. "Well, is it creepy now if I tell you this is absolutely the best day of my life?"

"No, not at all. It's the best day of mine too. So far, anyway. God willing, we have a lot more to look forward to."

When his lips closed over hers in response, she didn't object, even though she knew they wouldn't stop in time for her to redo her lipstick.

Acknowledgments

From the loosely woven strands of an idea after my first visit to Galena years ago to the well-scrubbed revisions of *Summer by the River*, this story has come together with the help and encouragement of many. In writing this book, I chose my favorite Midwestern small town as the setting, and the plot and fictional characters sprang to life as a result. Like kids going off to college, these characters have become companions in my daily life that I will miss as this book goes to print.

While the writing process can be solitary and occasionally stressful, receiving encouragement as I wade through "all the things" from my writer besties Amanda Heger and Angela Evans makes all the difference. Here's to those dinners when we can get together and Zoom calls and writing dates when we can't. Thank you to Angela, Pam Trader, Kathi O'Neal, Theresa Schmidt, and my go-to beta reader, Sandy Thal, for their feedback on this story in the various stages in which they read it. Thanks also to my mastermind sisters Bree Liddell and Ciara Brewer for helping to keep me accountable in so many ways and to Ciara for being my tea aficionado.

Thank you to my brilliant editor, Deb Werksman, for her insight and guidance in revisions and for helping me see both the inscrutable and the glaringly obvious that I'd gotten too close to spot. A heartfelt thanks to my publisher for taking this story to publication, and for the entire team at Sourcebooks who all do so much to enable books like this one to find a way into readers' hands. Thank you to my loyal agent Jessica Watterson of the Sandra Dijkstra Literary Agency for her constant support and for her guidance with the LA flashbacks in this story.

Thank you to my parents for all their encouragement over the years and for being my biggest cheerleaders along this journey. Thank you to my ex-husband, who first journeyed with me to Galena, and for all the support in the early years of my writing career. Finally, thank you to my teens, Ryan and Emily, who've grown up with a mom who writes and who think nothing of my diverse Google search history or of trekking along on my research forays. None of this would be the same without you.

About the Author

Debbie Burns is a 2019 National Readers' Choice Award finalist and 2019 HOLT Medallion Award of Merit recipient. Her highly praised Rescue Me romance series features happily-ever-afters of the two- and four-legged kind. She lives in Saint Louis in a gingerbread house that's almost cute enough to eat. In her free time, you can find her enjoying time with her two teens, two phenomenal rescue dogs, and a somewhat tetchy Maine coon cat who everyone loves anyway.

For her latest release info, you can sign up for her newsletter or read more about her at authordebbieburns.com. You can also find her on Twitter and Instagram (@_debbieburns), on Facebook (@authordebbieburns), and on BookBub (@AuthorDebbieBurns).

LEAN ON ME

First in the powerful new Family Is Forever series from award-winning and national bestselling author Pat Simmons.

Tabitha Knicely is overwhelmed with sorrow and exhaustion caring for her beloved great-aunt, whose dementia is getting worse. When her neighbor Marcus Whittington accuses Tabitha of elder neglect, he doesn't realize how his threats to have Aunt Tweet taken away add to Tabitha's pain.

Then Marcus gets to know the exuberant elderly lady and sees up close how hard Tabitha is fighting to keep everything together. Tabitha finds herself leaning on Marcus more and more. And he's becoming more than happy to share her burdens…

**"Heartwarming bonds of family and friendship…
sure to tug at readers' heartstrings."**

—*Publishers Weekly*

For more info about Sourcebooks's books and authors, visit:

sourcebooks.com

THE SHOP ON MAIN STREET

New York Times bestseller Carolyn Brown brings her trademark Texas twang to this hilarious novel of love and revenge.

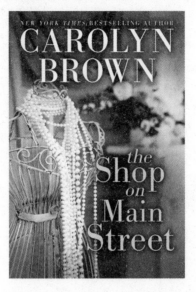

Carlene Lovelle, owner of Bless My Bloomers lingerie shop, has everything she's ever wanted: a loving husband, a successful small town business, and great friends who never disappoint. But that all changes when Carlene finds a pair of sexy red panties in her husband's briefcase. She knows exactly who those panties belong to—they were purchased from her very own shop.

Carlene is humiliated. But, even with her life is in a tailspin, Carlene finds she has all she needs as the ladies of this small town rally around and teach her that revenge is a dish best served red-hot.

**"Will have you howling with laughter...
I guarantee you will enjoy the ride."**

—*Book Junkiez*, 5 STARS for *A Heap of Texas Trouble*

THE SISTERS CAFÉ

New York Times bestseller Carolyn Brown brings her unique voice to this poignant and hilarious novel.

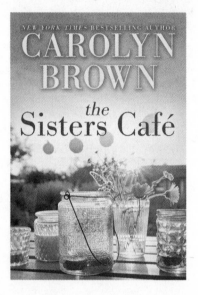

Cathy Andrew's biological clock has passed the ticking stage and is dangerously close to "blown plumb up." Cathy wants it all: the husband, the baby, and a little house right there in Cadillac, Texas. She's taken step one and gotten engaged to a reliable man, but she's beginning to question their relationship. Going through with the wedding or breaking off her engagement looks like a nightmare either way. She knows her friends will back her up, but she's the one who has to make a decision that's going to tear her apart.

"Amazing dialog and storytelling...you need to get your hands on *What Happens in Texas*."

—*Fresh Fiction*

IT STARTED WITH A SECRET

Their happy-ever-after is within reach...but
only if they're willing to tell the truth.

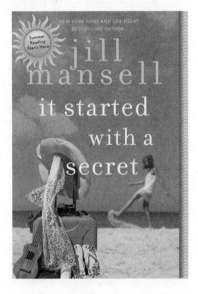

Lainey and Kit arrive at their new jobs in blissful, summery Cornwall
only to find themselves in the midst of a lovable but chaotic family—
where every member is having an identity crisis at the same time.
Widowed mom Majella has done her best for years, but can't quite
grasp why things are falling apart. It's what she doesn't know that's causing the chaos, because everyone is keeping secrets.

In classic Jill Mansell style, our heroine and her friends are drawn
through a hilarious multi-generational soap opera in which, by the end,
happily-ever-afters are available to anyone willing to tell the truth about
their heart's desire.

**"Jill Mansell captures your heart and keeps you
turning pages...Laugh out loud entertainment."**

—*Fresh Fiction* for *Kiss*

MOOSE SPRINGS, ALASKA

Welcome to Moose Springs, Alaska, a small town
with a big heart, and the only world-class resort
where black bears hang out to look at *you*.

Sarah Morgenthaler

The Tourist Attraction

There's a line carved into the dirt between the tiny
town of Moose Springs, Alaska, and the luxury resort
up the mountain. Until tourist Zoey Caldwell came
to town, Graham Barnett knew better than to cross
it. But when Graham and Zoey's worlds collide, not
even the neighborhood moose can hold them back...

Mistletoe and Mr. Right

She's Rick Harding's dream girl. Unfortunately, social-
ite Lana Montgomery has angered locals with her
good intentions. When a rare (and spiteful) white
moose starts destroying the holiday decorations every
night, Lana, Rick, and all of Moose Springs must work
together to save Christmas, the town...and each other.

Enjoy the View

Hollywood starlet River Lane is struggling to
remake herself as a documentary filmmaker. When
mountaineer and staunch Moose Springs local
Easton Lockett takes River and her film crew into
the wild...what could possibly go wrong?